F

CONFESSIONS OF A
GRAMMAR QUEEN

"I absolutely adored Eliza Knight's *Confessions of a Grammar Queen*, a deeply feel-good story of a female copy editor at a 1960s New York publishing house who summons the courage to fight for what she deserves in a *Mad Men*–esque, male-dominated workplace designed to keep her down. I cheered as Bernadette stopped shrinking from her coarse, chauvinistic boss; delighted in her decision to form a book club of like-minded women; blinked back tears as she worried about losing her brother in Vietnam; and rooted hard for one of the most satisfying love stories I've read in ages. The icing on the cake is that some of the chapters are from the viewpoint of Bernadette's dog—an enormous Harlequin Great Dane named Frank—whose dedication to 'his girl' and tender insights about her life will touch your heart. An inspiring story of friendship, determination, and finding the courage to stand up for oneself, woven through with a deep love of books, *Confessions of a Grammar Queen* is one of my favorite novels of the year."

—Kristin Harmel, *New York Times* bestselling author of *The Book of Lost Names* and *The Stolen Life of Colette Marceau*

"Eliza Knight's latest is *Lessons in Chemistry* meets *Mad Men*—plus an adorable dog! Whip-smart Bernadette Swift has brains, style, and ambition to burn, determined to work her way up from first female copy editor in her office to first female CEO of a publishing house. On her side, she's got an army of friends in her feminist book club, a handsome senior editor paying court, and a devoted Great Dane named Frank—but with a spiteful boss and an army of snickering coworkers determined to see a woman fail at any cost, will Bernadette ever be able to crack that glass ceiling? *Confessions of a Grammar Queen* is just a delight from start to finish!"

—Kate Quinn, *New York Times* bestselling author of *The Briar Club* and *The Diamond Eye*

"Bernadette Swift is the friend and mentor we all wish we had. Quirky, heartwarming, and full of wit, *Confessions of a Grammar Queen* is a story of breaking glass ceilings, one book at a time. Sometimes, all it takes is one fearless woman to turn the page on an entire industry. Eliza Knight's latest is utterly charming!"

—Sarah Penner, *New York Times* bestselling author of *The Lost Apothecary* and *The London Séance Society*

"*Confessions of a Grammar Queen* is the ultimate women-supporting-other-women book. Bernadette Swift is a spirited heroine you want to root for and the point of view from her dog, Frank's, perspective was adorable and fun. Knight is the ultimate queen bee Grammarian as she brings the struggles of women in the '60s to life with her incredible research and perfect prose. If you've ever silently (or not silently) corrected someone's grammar, this book is for you!"

—Madeline Martin, *New York Times* bestselling author of *The Booklover's Library*

"In *Confessions of a Grammar Queen*, Knight masterfully immerses the reader in a *Mad Men*–esque world of fun book talk and female worker camaraderie. When the adorable and ambitious Bernadette Swift sets her sights on becoming the first female CEO of a major publishing house, she finds herself fending off all manner of workplace harassment and starting a revolution (even including a march in the Manhattan streets!) with her band of lively coworkers and book club friends. With secondary narration on occasion by Frank, Bernadette's protective and task-hungry dog, Knight has crafted a tale full of heart, pluck, and determination with a heroine as engaging and likable as they come."

—Natalie Jenner, international bestselling author of *The Jane Austen Society*, *Bloomsbury Girls*, and *Every Time We Say Goodbye*

"A compelling story of breaking down walls, the power of words, strength in determination, the primacy of friendship, and, last but not least, the love and devotion of a Great Dane who will steal your heart—and perhaps your dinner. I highly recommend this absolute delight!"

—Katherine Reay, bestselling author of *The London House* and *The English Masterpiece*

"*Confessions of a Grammar Queen* is for everyone who loved *Lessons in Chemistry*—but it's even better because instead of chemistry, it's about books! I adored main character Bernadette, whose pluck and charm have you rooting for her throughout the story as she navigates love, the sexist 1960s publishing industry, and a boss who just wants to keep her in her place. This is going to be THE book of the summer, so make sure you get your hands on a copy!"

—Natasha Lester, *New York Times*
bestselling author of *The Paris Orphan*

ALSO BY ELIZA KNIGHT

My Lady Viper
Prisoner of the Queen
The Mayfair Bookshop
Starring Adele Astaire
Can't We Be Friends
The Queen's Faithful Companion
A Day of Fire
A Year of Ravens

Confessions *of a* Grammar Queen

Confessions *of a* Grammar Queen

— A Novel —

Eliza Knight

sourcebooks
landmark

Published by Sourcebooks Landmark, an imprint of Sourcebooks
P.O. Box 4410, Naperville, Illinois 60567-4410
(630) 961-3900
sourcebooks.com .

Cataloging-in-Publication Data is on file with the Library of Congress.

Printed and bound in the United States of America.
VP 10 9 8 7 6 5 4 3 2 1

*For my fellow logophiles. The ones who grew up
reading the dictionary for fun and still get a kick
out of exploring the meaning of words.*

Chapter One

IF IMPELLED TO IDENTIFY SOME of the skills she had mastered since graduating summa cum laude from Barnard College and coming to work at Lenox & Park Publishing a few years ago, Bernadette Swift would declare she was an eliminator of subject-verb disagreements, a clarifier of pronoun antecedents, a proponent for perfect comma placement, and a liberator of clichés and ambiguities from the page.

At the moment, however, her boss seemed to have missed the nameplate on her tidy desk that read: BERNADETTE SWIFT, COPY EDITOR.

Instead of holding out a manuscript for review, he had a wrinkled, white oxford button-down shirt in his hand—with a coffee stain on it.

For over a millennium, women have been in charge of cleaning the stains off men's clothes. Coffee in particular is epically difficult to remove from starched white fabric. But Bernadette wasn't Mr.

Wall's wife, or even his secretary. Neither of those facts could be stated aloud at this moment, however; not if she wanted to keep her job.

So, she kept silent as she watched his mouth moving. Watched his eyes scanning—and not just her face either. And she thought about how for the last biennium, she'd been charged with getting his coffee, then for what felt like longer than just a few years, taking his shirts to be laundered when he inevitably spilled his dark roast down the front because he was a cloven-hoofed artiodactyl of the *Suidae* family. In other words, an utter swine.

She'd learned from her veterinarian father all the correct biological genera, and she enjoyed tacking them onto human behavior.

Although, that wasn't really fair to pigs, now was it? The ones she'd grown up with on her family farm had been adorable, even when covered in muck. Especially Amaranth, who'd been her pet named after her favorite color—though obviously a pig could never be quite as pink, but she'd always been a lover of big words, squeezing them in wherever she could, even if on a beloved swine.

To be clear, Mr. Wall was never adorable.

Meaty fingers snapped in her direction, yanking her back to reality. "Miss Swift? Did you hear me?"

Unfortunately.

Bernadette glanced around the bustling copyediting room at the typewriters clacking, men sporting Beach Boys floppy hair-styles bent over stacks of galley pages with their red pencils in hand, pages of *Webster's Third New International Dictionary* being flipped, everyone busy and not looking in her direction.

Maybe they were blissfully unaware of what was transpiring. They dedicated a lot of time to pretending she—the sole female junior copy editor—didn't exist. Her male colleagues were never asked to perform such menial tasks for their boss. Tasks that were not part of the job description of a copy editor. Which she was. A fact that Mr. Wall often disregarded. One day, he would not dismiss her so easily, when it was her name on the placard outside the CEO's office and her desk pristine on the inside.

Bernadette met her superior's eyes, watery blue like a child who'd been overzealous in dowsing their watercolor paints in an attempt to bring the pigment back to life. She wanted nothing more than to grab on to each end of his waxed, dark handlebar mustache and yank the smirk off his face. Instead, she sat on her hands, with their neatly trimmed and pink-painted nails, and said, "Yes, Mr. Wall."

Generally, Bernadette had a nearly infinite amount of patience. Working in an office surrounded by men who treated the copy-editing department like a boys' club meant she needed it. But there was something about her boss that had the power to bring up what her female friends called her "nicey-nice shield." That deactivated a part of her that wanted to rebel against being asked to perform tasks her male colleagues were never subjected to simply because of their gender.

So far, she'd tamped that urge down and allowed herself to be a doormat. Once a precedent was set, it was hard to change.

Besides, she could push back against injustice, or she could keep her job. And she liked her job, except when she was dealing with Mr. Wall or others of his ilk. So, she rose from her chair, the creaking sound drowned out by the work carrying on around them. Her fingers brushed Mr. Wall's as she reached for the shirt, and it was hard to keep a shudder at bay.

"I need it back by lunch. I've got a meeting." Mr. Wall's gaze traveled toward her lips, and she pressed them inward as if to ward him off.

"Try smiling a little more." He gave her a lascivious grin. "Women are prettier when they smile."

What a cliché. She'd have drawn a fat red line through that quip in a manuscript and written, "Try to be more original."

Wall turned away without so much as a thank-you. "And get me your pages by four o'clock," he said over his shoulder as he headed to the door and the corridor beyond.

Bernadette frowned as she held the sullied garment out in front of her. Any outsider seeing her bustle off to handle the coffee stain would assume she was Mr. Wall's personal assistant. Although even secretaries weren't in charge of laundering garments. At least according to their written job descriptions. All these tasks seemed to be excused by one little line that someone, undoubtedly a man, seemed to have added to every description: "and other duties as assigned."

The line would be more accurate if it said, "and other duties as assigned, provided the employee in question is a woman."

Granted, before she was hired that wouldn't have been necessary in the publishing house's description of the work of a junior copy editor. Bernadette was the first and only female copy editor at prestigious Lenox & Park. She'd been hired just as they merged from separate entities into one with an ampersand, shortly after she'd graduated from college. *Number one in my class with an English degree, not a laundry degree or an MRS.*

She'd only made it halfway through the stack of proof pages on her desk, with her red pencil lying beside them, and they begged her not to leave, but what choice did she have?

The sound of her sigh was drowned out by the sound of typewriter keys clacking and the swish as sheets of paper were removed from a working pile and placed on the completed pile. Ten people worked under Mr. Wall in this copyediting department: six copy editors of varying junior levels and four senior copy editors. Bernadette was somewhere in the middle. She'd been at this job for the last several years, and the majority of the books she'd worked on had hit bestseller lists.

Words were life, and working at a publishing house had been her dream ever since she'd picked up Lewis Carroll's *Alice's Adventures in Wonderland* and its sequel *Through the Looking-Glass* at the store when she was seven and paid for the books with her birthday money. It's where she became enamored with words, especially the frabjous ones like *burble*, *mimsy*, and *galumph*—all words coined by the author himself. When she wasn't ensconced in reading fiction, she'd taken to studying the dictionary, a hobby her brother, Benjamin, had often ridiculed. But his laughter was always cut short by her linguistic skills and retorts that stung mostly because he didn't comprehend their meaning. Her affinity for perusing the dictionary had paid off in more ways than one.

And what she wouldn't give to have her brother with her right now, rather than him being overseas training South Vietnamese soldiers. At least for now, he swore he was safe.

Growing up, her friends had called her Queen B, and not because she was the bossy type but because she won every spelling bee she'd ever entered. Bernadette quite literally was the

Queen of Spelling Bees in Maryland and possessed a ribbon to prove it.

Now her dream was a reality. And at home in the tiny apartment that she shared with her Great Dane, Frank, whom her brother had given her as protection, she had an entire bookshelf devoted to the books she'd worked on. Like literary trophies.

Taking shirts to be laundered, however, was not part of her dream. Seeing no other choice, because tossing his soiled shirt in the trash wasn't an option, Bernadette stepped around her desk, her legs feeling like slimy, sluggish gastropods.

Mr. Wall… She knew precisely why he asked her to do the demeaning things that he did. From the moment she'd been offered her copyediting position, it had been obvious he didn't feel she had the right to be there. Mr. Wall was from a class of men who believed women were only good for one thing. Well, maybe two. And it wasn't working in what he deemed to be a male profession. It didn't matter to him that just last month the Women's Equal Pay Act had been passed; there'd been no raise for her, nor did one appear to be coming. Of that, she was sure.

If Mr. Wall had been in his position when she applied, she'd never be a copy editor. Even with the recommendation of Mr. Bass, a legend in the world of publishing and chairman of the executive board. She'd met Bass when he'd come to Barnard to speak to English majors about working in publishing. And Bernadette had marched right up to Mr. Bass afterward and asked if they were hiring. The bright eyes of her youth had yet to bear witness to the blinding truths of reality—that her boss and colleagues would think aspirations of one day being the first female CEO of a major publishing house were unrealistic.

As she exited the copyediting department, Bernadette glanced at Sarah Yeager, the department secretary. Petite and with a penchant for beige clothing, ballerina-tight hair buns, and a lack of accessories, Sarah blended into her desk most days. Mr. Wall's office was inside the copyediting department, at the back. It would have taken him only another dozen steps to find Sarah, but he seemed to see Bernadette's skirt and stop every time. Maybe it was because Sarah did such a good job of not standing out.

Bernadette's mother had told her from a young age that colors were made to be worn and symbolized an expression of one's inner spirit. It was a lesson she took to heart.

Sarah smirked and tapped the silent receiver of the phone on her desk with the tip of a pink pencil she'd clearly pilfered from Bernadette's desk. "I'd offer to take the shirt to the dry cleaner's, but I'm really busy answering the phone."

The day's crossword puzzle lay in front of Sarah. None of the boxes had been filled out, but plenty had been marked and erased.

Ignoring Sarah's jibe about being "busy," Bernadette read the first clue on the puzzle. The irony of the answer was uncanny. "Six down is lackadaisical."

Sarah rolled her eyes. "Like I'm going to fall for that."

Bernadette shrugged.

She marched down the hall to the elevator, stabbing the button with her index finger and noting the smudge of black ink, and counted the ticker as it showed the levels the elevator had to climb until it arrived at her floor. Her image reflected back at her in the gold mirror surface of the elevator doors: blond hair and pink headband à la Brigitte Bardot, pink lipstick in the same shade, a black pencil skirt and matching jacket, and a pink and white polka-dot silk blouse.

Bernadette believed that one could convey professional and fashionable simultaneously. Plus, she didn't shy away from makeup. Not since she'd come to New York and experienced her first makeover at Elizabeth Arden's salon.

"Taking one for the team again, I see?" Graham Reynolds, executive editor, took up the space beside her, the messenger bag he used as a briefcase slung casually over his broad shoulder. Looking at his reflection beside her own in the elevator doors, Bernadette took note that his short brown hair was fastidiously styled and his face cleanly shaven, which only made him, and his perfect bone structure, stand out more.

He had a cavalier attitude and an irritating sense of style to go with his Paul Newman jaw. Most men in the office wore the same professional outfits their fathers and grandfathers wore. But instead of a skinny tie, Graham had donned a thick and often colorful one. And she couldn't ignore how his socks often matched his tie.

If she didn't have to work with him, she'd be impressed.

Bernadette redirected her gaze firmly to the elevator ticker. She'd gotten mixed up and heartbroken by a handsome face before, and she wasn't going to replicate that mistake. "Skipping out early, I see?"

"If only." He held out his hand. "Let me take the shirt."

"What?" Bernadette gaped, her gaze swiveling toward him. "I'm not in the mood for games, Mr. Reynolds. Didn't your mother teach you it isn't nice to tease?"

"We've known each other for years, Miss Swift, and it's still Mr. Reynolds?"

"It will always be Mr. Reynolds." She clutched the shirt closer, realized what she was doing when the distinct, unpleasant combination of coffee and sweat infiltrated her nostrils, and then pushed it back out again.

Graham shrugged. "Just trying to save you a few steps. The dry cleaner is on the way to my meeting."

This time Bernadette turned her whole body to face him, acutely aware that even in heels she had to look up. "Your offer was in earnest?"

There was nothing on his face to indicate it wasn't. In fact, he appeared completely genuine. "Earnestly, yes. I've seen the stack on your desk. You don't have time to run errands. I think Wall gives you more work than the rest."

Bernadette had suspected the same thing on numerous occasions.

Graham nodded, then leaned forward like he was going to tell her a secret. "And I'll even tell them to rush it."

"Why?" She pursed her lips, the shirt hanging heavy between them.

Graham righted his stance and eyed her, not in the usual way men seemed to devour her, but more like he was studying her, trying to understand the nuances of her being. That was also uncomfortable because she didn't want to share. "I think the question is, why not, Miss Swift?"

Bernadette flicked her gaze to the elevator ticker. Any moment, the gaping maw of the transportable box was going to open, just like it had in the novel she'd been copyediting the day before.

"Because you have better things to do. Like edit books. Or go wherever it is you're going."

In the hierarchy of the editorial department, he was just below the chief. Why would he want to help her?

"And so do you, and as we just discussed, your pile is taking over your desk."

Bernadette gave him the serious look she'd perfected over the years that said, *Now listen carefully.* "Okay, take the shirt." She held it out. "But I'm not going to dinner with you."

Graham's face fell in mock disappointment, and he pressed a hand to his heart as if she'd shot him. "I wasn't going to ask. But I guess that also means you won't go home with me either, huh?"

Bernadette's tongue stuck to the roof of her mouth, leaving her unable to form the proper retort his insolence deserved.

"I kid, I kid." He held up his hands, laughing. "I meant to meet my mother, but I can see how it might have come out... differently. Listen, Miss Swift, I'm not in the business of seducing coworkers. Just trying to help. Besides, several manuscripts in your stack are on my list."

"Fine." She jutted her chin and held out the shirt with both hands, glad to be rid of the insulting task just as the elevator dinged. "Thank you for your help, then."

"My pleasure. Professionally." He chuckled and took the shirt, stepping onto the elevator with a crooked grin that Bernadette couldn't quite decipher.

Several words came to mind—provocative, beguiling, charismatic...all the things she didn't want to think about him. Graham Reynolds, who could have any woman in this entire building. But she wasn't looking for a man. Especially not inside the walls of Lenox & Park. She'd made that mistake when she was an intern. Late hours with a fellow intern had led to an inappropriate kissing session on top of galleys. She'd ended up with ink on her rear, a broken heart, and the fear her mother would somehow hear what had happened and arrive in New York City to drag her back to Maryland "where she belonged."

Ugh.

She whirled away as the doors to the elevator closed, taking Graham and the shirt with it, and marched back toward her office.

"Making friends?" The sarcasm in Sarah's tone was unmistakable.

Unlike you. Bernadette longed to say the words aloud to Sarah, who happened to be the biggest apple polisher in the office. But she didn't because a woman like Sarah wasn't likely to listen. Even if she should.

Bernadette had come across so many Sarahs in her life that it was hard to keep track. So instead, she said, "Keep that up and I won't help with your crossword anymore."

Sarah scoffed, not having a comeback, and turned back to her silent phone.

Bernadette settled at her desk and slid the pile of printed papers, the latest book she was copyediting, toward her. It was a mystery novel by John Dickson Carr. She plucked a new red pencil from a stash in her pink glass holder and got down to grammar business. She'd read Mr. Carr's *The Hollow Man* in college, and as with the other authors she'd worked with during her internship and permanent position at Lenox & Park—including Patricia Highsmith and the late Eleanor Roosevelt—she felt electrified as she turned to making copyedits. There was just something so satisfying about making the words flow properly.

What are you trying to say here? she wrote in the margin after circling a particularly clunky sentence.

Balls are round, no need to overexplain. She struck through a redundant word.

Onward she went: improving readability, correcting grammar. She flipped through *Fowler's Dictionary of Modern Usage*, *Webster's Third*, and *The Elements of Style* interchangeably. And she made note of things that required fact-checking. Glancing at the clock, she realized it was already eleven thirty.

She'd only made it halfway through the manuscript. If she was going to complete it by four o'clock as demanded, retrieving Mr. Wall's shirt was going to be a stretch. It also meant she'd probably be working late and would once more miss out on the feminist book club she'd been thinking of joining. The books the club was reading promised to be quite a bit different than the ones she worked on during the day, and the notion was quite intriguing.

Wall ought to keep an extra shirt in his office anyway since he spilled so much.

Problem-solving was not apparently his forte.

Well, shirt or no shirt, she wasn't skipping lunch. That was her personal form of protest in this unjust moment. Slinging her purse over her shoulder, Bernadette decided she'd eat her packed vegetable sandwich on a bench outside to get some fresh air. She could practically taste the chopped peppers, carrots, and cucumbers mixed with mayonnaise and spread on the fresh bread she'd baked over the weekend. With a snap, crackle, pop of her knuckles, Bernadette once again made her way to the elevator, pressing the down button. As she waited, men in suits passed a woman with a stack of stuffed folders so tall it blocked her face as she tried to maneuver down the hall. They were completely oblivious.

"Need help?" Bernadette asked.

Sarah peered over the top of the stack and Bernadette immediately regretted asking. But maybe the offer would help the sour secretary warm up to her a little—though that seemed a long shot since several years of attempts had thus far failed.

"No." Sarah wavered on her feet. The top two folders slipped and slid to the floor, papers scattering across the polished tiles of the elevator lobby like snowflakes on Christmas morning.

Though helping the killjoy was the last thing Bernadette wanted to do, especially at the risk of losing her quiet bench for lunch, she did so anyway.

"Thank you," Sarah said begrudgingly. "And you were right. It was 'lackadaisical.'"

Bernadette smiled, though she didn't show teeth. She surrendered the recovered folders to Sarah. Getting on the next elevator, she looked at her watch. Eleven thirty-seven. She gave a sigh. Seemed she was not going to get that sandwich in the sun after all and would have to go straight to the dry cleaner.

The elevator doors slid open on the ground floor to reveal Graham Reynolds, again.

Inside, Bernadette groaned until she saw that he held Mr. Wall's shirt, neatly bagged on a hanger.

"You picked it up." She didn't hide the shock in her voice. "What are you after, Mr. Reynolds?" She switched to a joking tone, even though she meant what she was about to add. "I'll not be inveigled."

"Inveigled?" He chuckled as he stepped into the elevator and passed her the shirt. Surely an executive editor knew what *inveigled* meant.

Before she could step off, the elevator started to move up again and Graham quickly pressed the button to their floor.

"You're an executive editor. You have a secretary. Why are you running errands?" Bernadette peeked through the top part of the paper encasing the shirt, noting the stain was completely gone. *Until tomorrow.* She glanced toward the copyediting office, hoping Mr. Wall hadn't just witnessed the exchange, but the only one staring at her was Sarah.

"Elise is out on maternity leave for the next five weeks." He glanced toward Sarah. "And well, Miss Yeager doesn't like me much."

It was surprising, given Bernadette's issues with Wall, that women in the office received any maternity leave at all when there were no laws that required employers to offer it.

"Why's that?" As much as she tried to ignore Graham's charm, he really had an abundance of it.

"She thinks Elise should have been let go and that we should hire someone new. And that the someone new ought to have been her."

"Most men would have let Elise go."

Graham chuckled and looked right at her. "I'm not most men, Miss Swift."

Before she had a chance to reply, he walked off toward his office, a much too happy whistle on his lips.

Chapter Two

FRANK

THERE IS A GRASSY SQUARE in the middle of the sidewalk where I'm walking myself. In the center of it is a tree with a trunk that seems to have stopped thickening, unlike the trees in Central Park that grow so wide whole bunches of kids can hide behind them. It is one of the hundreds, probably thousands in New York. Each minuscule prairie with a stunted tree at its center.

I don't know why these street trees stopped growing—maybe because they only have such small patches. What I do know is that the odors emanating from their two-by-two-foot squares could span miles. As if every dog within a one-hundred-block radius has marked each patch, as well as the old man who sleeps on the corner that we give the occasional breakfast muffins to.

I'm Frank, by the way.

Bernadette is my girl—and she has no idea I'm out for this walk alone. I do it every day: patrol the neighborhood, make sure everything is all right. Mostly it is, but sometimes it isn't and I have to save a cat, thwart a thief from stealing a purse, or alert a mother her child is dangling from the fire escape.

My girl taught me the word *minuscule*. And she also told me the story of the tiny prairies while we were running through the park. I wonder if I dig and dig and dig hard enough at the patch, can I make a new prairie? My own addition to the collection?

Whenever I try, Bernadette stops me. I'm pretty sure it's because she doesn't want me to leave her, though she swears it's because giving me a bath in her tiny tub is laborious.

I guess she doesn't realize that if I was going to go anywhere permanently, I'd take her with me. Just like I try to bring her into the tub. That's my mission—keeping Bernadette safe—which also means keeping our neighborhood safe. I used to have a different mission when I was with her brother, Ben, but he said he couldn't take me with him. That I had new orders. No more search and rescue.

"Hey, Frank!"

I'm distracted by the boy who rides his bike with the bag full of papers. I'm also aware of how he wobbles slightly on the bike as he tosses me a treat. I'm aware of everyone and everything.

I leap into the air and snatch the piece of bacon. It's a distraction from what I really want. And I'll allow it, because bacon is heaven.

The thing is, I love paper. The smell, the taste, the crinkly sound.

Bernadette always takes one piece of paper from the boy and then lets me shred the rest when she gives the simple command: *Wall.* I don't know why that's the command, but when I hear it, I know I can rip into the paper like I used to rip into the barriers during practice rescues.

But I'm not allowed to touch the papers on her shelves—the ones that are bound together. I tried once, and she didn't make me any pumpkin cookies for a week. Lesson learned.

Wall and Wall only.

I hop up onto the crate beside the dumpster. The dumpster is closed, and the perfect height to jump onto the first fire escape. Up above, the window is open as I left it, but by the time my girl gets home, I'll have it closed again.

No sense in worrying her with my daily patrol—a dog's gotta do what a dog's gotta do.

Chapter Three

"THAT WAS A NEW RECORD for you, Frank. You only stopped to mark twenty-seven of the forty-eight trees we passed." Bernadette removed the leash from Frank's collar and gave him a good scratch behind his white-and-black ears, then checked his paws for dirt, wiping them clean.

Her mother had always said cleanliness was next to godliness, and Bernadette didn't exactly adhere to that particular line, especially because she didn't feel at all like a deity, but she did truly prefer not to vacuum every day.

Frank's Harlequin Dane body was huge. His back fell at her hip height, and he weighed more than she did now that he was full grown. Standing next to Frank was like standing next to one of those oversized chairs at the Coney Island Boardwalk.

Returning his leash to its hook beside the door, she flipped on her transistor radio, removed her walking headband that said, *Who's walking who?*, and waved her arms in the monkey dance to "Mickey's Monkey."

"What do you think of the Miracles, Frank?" She danced her way over to her basket of house headbands on the coffee table by the mustard-colored couch that used to sit in the living room at her parents' house and plucked out one that was a subdued pink with French baguettes embroidered across the rim.

Frank whirled in a circle, then flicked his gaze toward his tin water bowl, which she'd refreshed right before they left.

"Ice?"

He opened his mouth, panting, his version of "yes." She'd named him Frank because since he was a puppy, he'd let her know, without artifice, exactly what he needed and wanted at all times. *I want ice. I want a treat. I want paper.* He'd not changed. She loved that about him. Too bad few people were as authentic.

Before he was hers, Frank had been slated to be a search-and-rescue dog with her brother Ben's unit. However, missions changed, and Frank—formerly Private Swift—had been let go. Bernadette had been hesitant at first with the gangly six-month-old puppy, but the moment she'd looked into his eyes, her heart had melted.

Bernadette moved to the tiny kitchen of her one-bedroom apartment, ignoring the newspapers and magazines stacked neatly on her counter and organized by both date and alphabetical order. During the newspaper strike that had finally ended earlier that year, she'd had slim pickings. She'd had to turn to the *Village Voice* and the *Wall Street Journal,* rather than the *Times* and the *Daily News,* which had been her go-to papers.

She kept her newspaper reading to Fridays, because then at least she had the weekend to process any harsh news regarding the situation in Vietnam. Once she'd read them, she set the newspapers aside as daily treats for Frank. She opened the Frigidaire to chip off a few chunks of ice from the block for Frank's water bowl while he licked his chops in anticipation.

The morning was relatively cool for August. Bernadette hoped that meant they'd soon be leaving the heat of summer behind for autumn, which was her favorite season. Watching the chlorophyll slowly break down in leaves, draining them of the green masks of spring and summer and restoring them to their natural yellow or orange pigments, was fascinating. A slow and colorful reveal.

Walking Frank in the warmer months was always tough. The heat slowed him down, and she knew from the longing looks he gave their apartment door on particularly hot days when they left that he'd much rather remain indoors. But even if he urinated at the first available tree to tempt him, exercise was important. For both of them. Without her morning walk, Bernadette lost a bit of her edge and felt a little sluggish. Exercise invigorated her and gave her brain the acuity boost she needed.

Dumping the chunks of ice into Frank's water bowl, she put the special dog breakfast muffin she made him in the bowl next to it, then got herself ready for work.

"Now, you be a good boy and protect our realm," Bernadette said from the door, grabbing her purse and her lunch bag—an old shoe bag. "Mrs. Morris will be by around lunchtime for a visit."

Frank gave a mighty bark, then hurried over to where he'd discarded the newspaper she'd gifted him that morning.

"Oh, I almost forgot. Thank you for the reminder." She pulled out the crossword page and handed Frank the rest back. "Now, what do we do to the Walls of the world?"

Frank growled, shook his head, and proceeded to shred the

paper. He wouldn't stop until it was nearly dust. When Mrs. Morris, her landlady, came by in the early afternoon, she would collect the dusty shreds of newspaper. Mrs. Morris had a cat and she loved to use Frank's discards for her litter box. Her husband had died a few years ago, so she loved to spend a little time with Frank, who absolutely needed a midday break from the monotony of window watching.

Dressed in her typical pencil skirt, today in charcoal gray with a bolder geometrically patterned pink-and-blue blouse, identical headband, and matching gray blazer, she slipped on her walking shoes and put her heels in her bag. Hand on the door, she said goodbye to Frank, and just as he did each day when she left for work, he abandoned his paper project temporarily and loped over to the window to watch her as she disappeared down the street.

Bernadette locked the apartment—a task her mother inexplicably worried about and perennially assumed her daughter never did—and made her way down the three flights of stairs.

Construction near the bus stop narrowed the sidewalk and made the streets feel more crowded. She picked up a few sentences here and there about the Cold War with the Soviet Union, and the increasing tension in Vietnam, but hurried past. Words on the street were heresy, and she didn't want other people's opinions to twist her up.

Settling into her usual seat on the bus, she pulled out the crossword and a pink pen. She was only a few stops from work. Just enough time to fill in a few words before hopping off and hurrying toward the building. She was nearly at the door when a bicyclist whizzed by. Whizzed by on his Schwinn so fast that her hair blew into her face, threatening the careful flip she'd styled. Whizzed by so fast a spoke on his bike snagged on her pantyhose, giving her a mighty wrench and nearly toppling her to the ground. While she avoided the pavement, her lunch did not. It went flying.

As the man disappeared, she stared down at the tear in her pantyhose, which would be completely obvious to anyone who saw her. It looked like she'd been attacked by a werewolf with a hunger for nylon.

She couldn't go into work like this! Sweat started on her brow, and she sucked in a hard breath through her nose.

"Not even a sorry from that crazy rider."

Bernadette glanced up to see Melanie Woods, the building receptionist, and her friend, standing before her, holding out her dropped lunch with one hand while she stubbed out her cigarette beneath the heel of her white leather knee-high boot. Dressed in a white-collared, teal floral-patterned dress, with white sleeves and white pockets, and a matching white belt cinched at the waist, Melanie was the calming balm necessary on such a rocky start to the day.

Melanie had always been sweet. A few years older than Bernadette, she had kind eyes and a warm soul. Her red hair was styled like First Lady Jacqueline Kennedy's, and she wore a teal pillbox hat with a sparkling flower brooch in rainbow colors.

"I don't have an extra pair of pantyhose in my bag." Bernadette groaned. She couldn't go to work in this state, but the nearest department store was at least a few blocks away. "I normally do, but I used them last week when I got snagged on a filing cabinet."

Melanie smiled and rummaged around in her purse. "I have some in my purse you can have." She pulled out a pair of rolled-up light pink tights. "Sorry, I like them in color."

Far from being put off, Bernadette was elated. She'd not had the guts to buy a pair of colored tights yet, even though they were all the fashion rage. "They're perfect, thank you. I'll replace them this afternoon on my lunch break, I promise. A girl can never be without an extra pair of pantyhose, as I've just proved."

Note to self: Buy two emergency pairs.

"I couldn't agree more."

They walked into the building together, and an idea came to Bernadette. Maybe she should invite Melanie to the book club. They'd spent a number of hours at Sunday brunch discussing books and bolstering each other up before the new workweek started. But as she was about to ask, Melanie hurried behind the reception desk where the phone was already jangling and waved goodbye. Bernadette slipped into the elevator, which was miraculously already there, with a plan to ask Melanie later.

Before going into the copyediting office, she hurried to the bathroom to change her pantyhose, tossing the destroyed pair into the trash. Men who pretended not to notice she existed whenever their boss was disparaging her always noticed if a woman had a run in her stockings. They liked to point it out and say things like, "You're in such a hurry that your hose are running away from you," and other such baloney that generally made no sense.

"You're late." Sarah stepped out of a stall, a new shade of pink on her normally bland lips—a shade that looked very much like Elizabeth Arden's Paradise Pink, which Bernadette had worn the previous week. Perhaps she was rubbing off on Sarah. Though her usual beige dress, which she must have in every style, blended into the background.

"Waylaid by a bicyclist with a sharp spoke." Bernadette hid her smile as she washed her hands, counting the requisite thirty seconds to destroy all germs. Bacilli loved to hide under people's fingernails. "That's inappropriate." Sarah gave her a look that said Bernadette had a dirty mind that needed washing.

Bernadette laughed, but judging by the pinched and pretentious expression on her face, Sarah wasn't making a joke. *Killjoy.*

"Waylaid—it means I was intercepted or accosted."

Sarah looked horrified. "By a bicyclist with a sharp spoke. Save your lewd excuses for your cyclist boyfriend." She dried her hands on a towel and rushed out of the bathroom, leaving Bernadette to shake her head.

If ever there was someone who had perfected the concept of a wet blanket…

Pantyhose refreshed—in all their pink glory—she made her way to her desk. She sat down behind a pile of manuscripts that nearly blocked her view of the room and started to organize them according to the publishing schedule. The title on top made her grimace: *From the Front: A Paratrooper's Memoir.* As if she needed more reminders of war.

"You're late," Mr. Wall accused, tugging at the collar of his already stained oxford shirt.

Bernadette was, in fact, never late. A glance at the clock showed she was actually seven minutes early. Technically, she didn't need to be here until nine o'clock. But people were used to her habit of showing up early, which she only did because of the extra tasks Mr. Wall often gave her. Well, and her fondness for timeliness.

He tapped an empty mug he was holding and pointed at the Chemex brewer. *Me Tarzan, you Jane.* Wall would be just the type of ape to misquote the book too.

Bernadette opened her mouth to remind Mr. Wall that (a) she wasn't his secretary and (b) he could make his own coffee if he put two brain cells together.

"Oh, dear, the coffee's not yet been made?" Sarah pushed into the copyediting office, her voice surprised and a disappointed glance cast in Bernadette's direction. "I didn't realize. I'll make it straight away." She looked at the glass brewer—which reminded Bernadette of a science experiment—confused, touching the glass carafe, the wooden collar. Beside were the electric kettle and the bean grinder. Within a few minutes, she'd figured out the kettle was already full of water Bernadette had measured the day before. She ground the beans and then poured them into the filter she'd placed in the top cone of the brewer. At first, she was a little fast with the water, splashing it onto her hands.

"A slow circle," Bernadette offered. "Helps with the grounds soaking up the water."

Sarah didn't offer a word of thanks but followed Bernadette's instructions.

When the coffee was brewing, Sarah flashed Bernadette a triumphant glance and said, "Just like riding a bicycle."

Bernadette gaped, heat flooding her face.

"Yeah, a bicycle," Wall said.

Bernadette flashed her boss a look, but he was smiling at Sarah as if she were a bright and shiny new toy found buried and forgotten in the back of a closet.

Bernadette supposed the realization that he had two wenches to brew for him was enough to tickle his tiny little heart and his big ego.

"You're so good at that," Bernadette said with a smile she hoped looked authentic. "I think it best you do it each morning."

Turnabout was fair play. If Sarah thought she'd stick her with the sharp spoke, she didn't realize Bernadette was about to stick her with the coffee chores.

Sarah's eyes brimmed with animosity, but her smile was that of a well-trained secretary—unfaltering. She nodded, because it *was* in her job description after all, right there where it said *and other duties as assigned.*

"That stack needs to be done by four o'clock, Miss Swift." Wall loomed in front of her, breaking her thought stream.

"Impossible." Bernadette hadn't meant for the word to slip out. But it was absolutely inconceivable for even the most talented copy editor to properly annotate, tighten, recalibrate, and red pencil a manuscript in a single day, let alone what looked like eight.

Mr. Wall's handlebar mustache twitched. "Impossible? Make it possible. Evans, Marshall, and Greene are out for the rest of the week. Stomach bug."

She glanced around the room at the other copy editors, who didn't have a stack even half as high as hers. Maybe she'd need to go home with a "stomach bug" too. But that only reminded her of her brother, who'd been locked in the camp latrine the first week he'd landed in Vietnam after drinking contaminated water. She might prefer that to facing off with Wall.

However, her mouth didn't seem to agree. "What about the other copy editors in this room?"

There was a notable electricity in the air. Bosses were meant to be respected, their orders executed. They weren't to be countered, and especially not by a woman. But Bernadette didn't want to follow the rules. She wanted to be the one counterbalancing.

Wall eyed her, as if trying to decipher her mental state. "They have their own assignments, *Swift*." He said her name with a hiss like it hurt his throat to push it out.

Bernadette kept the bristle from her tone. "So, while they have a workload of one, I now have the workload of four?"

Wall looked ready to square off in a boxing match. "Can't do it?"

Having watched her brother face schoolyard bullies, Bernadette understood an intimidation tactic when she saw one. Not that her boss would hit her—not with his fists anyway. But the workload? The workload was an intimidation punch in the gut. And while normally she wasn't one for confrontation, and in fact believed rules were in place for a reason, this seemed like one of those moments where she should oppose an inequality. "I'm more than happy to do it, given a proper amount of time."

"Saying you're too slow?"

Bernadette kept her hands at her sides when she wanted to raise them. This was getting out of hand. "Mr. Wall, with all due respect."

He held up his hand mere inches from her face and her blood heated to boiling. "I knew you couldn't cut it in this business. Mr. Bass had no business hiring you."

That wasn't fair. And it wasn't true. Bernadette fisted her hands at her sides to keep from lifting the stack of galleys and page proofs and tossing them violently in his face. Attempting to keep her voice steady, she said, "I believe that Lenox & Park's reputation would be compromised if I rushed through copyedits on any man-uscript. Let alone four in one day."

Mr. Wall narrowed his eyes and then flicked them behind her. She turned to see Graham Reynolds push through the glass door and then lean casually against it, hands over his chest as if he were watching a ball game on a high-perched television at a bar.

"Came to let you know that we can push those copyedits on Evans, Marshall, and Greene out a week or so. We have enough lead time."

"Ah." Mr. Wall glanced at Bernadette. "You see, Miss Swift, there's no need for you to compromise Lenox & Park's good reputation with your shoddily rushed copyedits."

Her mouth fell open. Even Sarah, who was still filling mugs, looked shocked.

It took a feat of immeasurable willpower to keep her voice and outsides calm seas, when inside she was a raging tempest. "I assure you, compromising my work or the reputation of this publishing house has never crossed my mind."

The comment had been meant for Mr. Wall, but it was Graham who answered.

"I know," he said with a smile in her direction and then a more serious stare at her boss.

Was it possible he heard the conversation before he opened the door? Mr. Wall seemed bound and determined to see her either fired or, better yet, quit. The realization was a powerful jolt. And to turn her words around on her was downright diabolical.

"Coffee?" Sarah asked, holding out the cup to Mr. Wall and then one to Graham, who said, "I'm all set. Thank you, Miss Yeager."

Graham watched as Wall gave him a last, uncertain look, then ambled back to his office. Then he too ducked out.

Still shaken at having to defend herself over nothing, Bernadette sat at her desk and spent a minute organizing her pencils and straightening her knickknacks, which gave her a sense of order and calm. She moved aside the manuscripts newly assigned to her due to the absence of her coworkers. She doubted they were sick. Evans, Marshall, and Greene were known to frequent the Writer's Block bar across the street after work. Her guess was they'd likely imbibed too many old-fashioneds and were all home nursing hangovers.

Bernadette couldn't imagine doing that on a work night. It was hard enough for her to get any respect around here. If she called in sick after a night of drinking and anyone even suspected it, she'd be fired. Not that she ever got so boozed as to be sick. But Mr. Wall, who also knew of the trio's after-hours bingeing, didn't seem to care. Boys will be boys.

Well, she could ruminate on how their bad behavior was constantly overlooked because they weren't women, or she could get down to grammar business. Already enough of her morning had been wasted on utter ridiculousness. Red pencil in hand, she set to revising something she could change—words in a book, rather than a world that seemed unwilling to revise its composition.

Word echo on purpose in opening line?

What's the antecedent?

No such word, but nice try. Use "facetious" instead?

Sociopath not in use until 1914, and your story takes place in 1903. Maybe lunatic? Maniac? Insane?

The hours raced by. At noon, she pulled out her lunch bag, determined that today she'd get to eat beneath the cerulean sky. She glanced toward Mr. Wall's office. He was yelling into the phone, so it was the perfect time to slip out without him noticing.

As she was headed outside, she smiled and waved to Melanie,

who was chatting with Gary, the lobby guard, leaning against the desk. Melanie had a natural rosy tint to her cheeks, not a hair of her Aqua-Netted bouffant out of place. When Gary noticed Bernadette, he backed away from the desk with a shy wave at Melanie and disappeared outside.

"He was awfully chummy." Bernadette eyed a bouquet of flowers left behind by Gary. "And are these violaceous flowers from Gary?"

Melanie sighed. "Yes. Violaceous. I like that."

"It's a fun word for purple."

"Purple is my color. Gary's a doll. And he also brought me this." She held up a steaming disposable cup. "Hot cocoa."

Bernadette smiled. "Never thought to have hot cocoa in summer."

"It's my favorite."

"I'm off to have lunch and get your stockings. I didn't forget."

"You don't have to do that. I've got dozens." Melanie sipped her hot cocoa and let out another sigh.

Bernadette tapped a pink nail on Melanie's reception desk. "I'm thinking about joining a new book club. It's just for women, reading female empowering books." Bernadette leaned over the desk, whispering, "Interested?"

"You bet I am! Will we be reading the *Kinsey Reports*?" Melanie gave a feigned look of shock.

Bernadette, however, was genuinely shocked, and she struggled to keep her face from showing it. She'd never heard anyone speak about the *Kinsey Reports* before and knew of them herself only after seeing a brief article about them in the newspaper. Was reading one of them an option for a book club?

"*Sexual Behavior in the Human Female,*" Melanie whispered behind her hand as she glanced toward the door, which opened for another round of employees. "I've been wanting to read it, but I've been too nervous to get it from the bookstore."

Bernadette waited for the elevator to close behind those who'd just arrived, then asked, "Did you read the first report: *Sexual Behavior in the Human Male?*"

Melanie rolled her eyes. "Who needs to read that? We get a daily sample just walking down the street."

Bernadette couldn't help the snort that escaped her. "To be honest, I haven't read either of them. Maybe we should suggest them to the club. I'll let you know the day and time."

Bernadette hurried outside to the small park beside the building. As she sat on the bench, the heat of summer was whisked away by a zephyr that rustled the leaves in the park. She opened her waxed-paper-wrapped sandwich. Today was simple fare: aged cheddar and tomato, with a leaf of lettuce to separate the soggy tomato from the bread.

As she chewed, she contemplated what had happened that morning.

Even with the Equal Pay Act passed earlier in the year, she'd heard rumors that some of her male colleagues were making two-thirds more than she was. If she asked for a raise, Wall wasn't likely to give it—even though he was quick to give her more work. He'd think she was demanding and ungrateful. She wouldn't put it past him to pay her less just to spite her. New York was expensive, and as it was, she had a hard time living on her salary. In fact, she was supplementing it by tutoring some of the children in her building and editing papers for university students.

And she didn't live lavishly. Her small apartment was more of a couple of boxes taped together. When her parents had come to visit for the first time, they'd been horrified she'd be willing to live in such cramped quarters when they had a perfectly good farmhouse in Maryland.

They'd spent the whole trip reminding her she was always welcome to come back home. Her mother had assured her she'd soon find a husband if she just moved back. That her veterinarian father knew plenty of young animal doctors looking for wives. And that was the path some of her fellow graduates had taken, while others decided to pursue careers like Bernadette.

But Bernadette wasn't going to succeed by getting married even if being unmarried complicated things. In fact, marriage itself was orthogonal to her career aspirations of becoming a CEO. At least in her own mind.

With a few extra minutes and her sandwich scarfed down, Bernadette purchased three pairs of stockings—all pink, two for herself and one for Melanie—then walked past the New York Public Library on Fifth Avenue.

It was her favorite place in the city. From the majestic stone lions standing sentry at the bottom of the front steps to the endless shelves full of books inside. Books had always brought her solace, so the library was her metaphorical comfortable chair at the heart of Manhattan.

Comfort: from Latin *confortare*, also meaning to strengthen. So essentially, the library made her stronger. Who could argue with that?

"Bernadette?"

Penelope Grynd, her roommate in college, came hurrying

down the library steps with a stack of books in her arms. Her hair was neatly coiffed, and she wore a brightly colored plaid shift dress of yellow and green with large daisies artfully arranged on the fabric.

Bernadette brightened immediately, giving her longtime friend an awkward hug around the books. "What are you doing here?"

"Lunch break and books. Doesn't get any better than that."

"How's it going at Doubleday? It's been ages since I saw you last." Penelope had been hired as a secretary at the same time Bernadette had started at Lenox & Park. When they'd marched across the stage at Barnard, they both had the same aspirations to become publishing executives one day. Thus far, Penelope had not been able to break away from her secretarial duties.

She shrugged, a flash of disappointment crossing her face. "I spend a lot of time doing things that aren't in my job description. But I'm learning a lot, and one day I'll be an editor, instead of the errand girl."

Bernadette grinned. "I didn't have to make coffee this morning."

"Progress." The two of them laughed and Penelope leaned closer. "So, have you given any more thought to the book club I mentioned? I know the gals would be happy to have you with us. Next meeting is in two weeks."

"Yes! And my friend Melanie would love to come too. I was just chatting with her about it this afternoon."

"Perfect. I should warn you, since our books have a feminist angle and the head librarian isn't too keen on having a bunch of feminists meeting at the library, we keep it hush-hush and pretend we're reading classics."

"Clandestine reading. Reminds me of when I was a teenager and trying to hide from my mother that I was reading *Lolita.*"

Penelope laughed. "I remember those days. My dad couldn't figure out why our flashlight was always out of batteries."

"I blamed it on my brother until one Christmas morning he made quite a big deal out of getting me my own Eveready flashlight."

"Big Ben always trying to outmaneuver."

"I might be good with words, but Ben has always been good at tactical warfare." Bernadette bit her lip. "A blessing and a curse."

What her brother didn't know was that the gift he'd taunted her with in their teens still sat on her bedside table for late-night reading—and the occasional Frank walk in the dark.

Chapter Four

DESPITE GRAHAM TELLING WALL IN front of everyone that he wouldn't need those extra manuscripts Bernadette had been assigned until the following week, that didn't stop Wall from hounding her until her ears buzzed from his constant droning.

Exiting the elevator in the lobby of Lenox & Park after hours for the second night in a row, Bernadette was glad it was Friday. A whole weekend of no Mr. Wall, and only the newspapers and magazines she'd been avoiding reading to contend with. The lobby was quiet, most employees having left hours ago. The lights were dimmed, and the telephone was silent. Bernadette's heels clicked on the polished floor. She'd been too tired to change into her Keds sneakers.

A loud bang to her right startled her enough that she spun on a wobbly heel, prepared to see Wall crashing through the lobby like Godzilla, but it was only the janitor emptying the trash.

He gave a short wave and an apologetic smile. "Sorry, miss."

"Have a great weekend."

Poor Frank was probably worried out of his mind that she was coming home so late. Thank goodness her landlady, who she'd called hours ago, had agreed to take him out, feed him, and keep him company. She would need to bake something special for Mrs. Morris this weekend as a thank-you.

Maybe she'd make oatmeal cookies. Mrs. Morris liked them, and Frank did too. He was due a special treat for being so patient with her. And an extra-long walk in the morning if it was cool enough outside. Or maybe she'd take him to Central Park instead. Frank loved to chase his ball in the park, and she loved the arboreal tranquility.

Heading for the front glass doors and the darkened street beyond, Bernadette thought that the idea of her riding the bus at this hour would give her mother heart palpitations. Bernadette wasn't worried. She'd yet to be accosted, despite riding the bus this late on numerous prior occasions. And if she was, Benjamin had shown her a few tricks to protect herself. Though, performing a heel stomp, elbow jab, and head butt to your brother in good fun was quite a bit different than doing so to a stranger.

She pushed through one of the doors, the balmy evening air hitting her in a *whoosh*. The streets were far more alive than the building she'd come out of. They were filled with honking cabs, buses, trucks, automobiles, and the occasional motorcycle. The scents of slightly burned roasted nuts and boiled hot dogs permeated her brain.

"Don't normally see you here this late." For the second time this evening, she was startled. Glancing to her right, she spotted Graham Reynolds, adjusting his Converse laces in the ring of light from a streetlamp. He wore a pair of green shorts with white stripes down the side and a white T-shirt that said *Central Park Scrum* and showed off muscles in his arms that his normal button-down clearly hid from view.

Bernadette straightened her purse, though it wasn't slipping even an inch off her shoulder. But the act of doing something normal seemed to bolster her. "I'm not usually. What are you doing here so late?"

Graham stood up, his messenger bag slung over his body cross-ways, looking way too casual and somehow managing to steal the oxygen from the air. "Deadlines. Production schedules."

Part of her wanted to open her mouth and let the week's torments gush out, but another part of her wasn't sure she could completely trust Graham with her expostulations on Wall's management style. Yet another part of her wanted to ask him why he was dressed—or rather so *un*dressed. "Same."

"I'm off to rugby. The battle usually eases some of the work tension."

Rugby? Graham Reynolds played rugby? Now the T-shirt made sense. She knew nothing of the sport, except that scrum was a play on the field. For just a moment, because she could see the corded muscles of his forearms, she imagined him in shorts, muscular legs braced against a body barreling toward him. A flush heated its way from her chest to her face, and she was grateful for the dim streetlights so he couldn't see her thoughts. "I suppose my commute is a bit like that." She'd certainly had to elbow her way onto the bus last night.

"Walking or subway?"

"Bus for me. But I am thinking I need a bike." She started walking, not wanting to linger. Not wanting to imagine Graham in shorts for one more second.

"Gonna steal one from a rack?" he teased.

Bernadette turned back. "Got any wire cutters?"

Graham smiled and patted his briefcase. "Always. Want me to walk you to the bus station?"

No one was left at work, and if they were, they weren't going to waste time staring out the window. She could let him walk her, but she didn't want him to read too much into it. Plus, she wanted to establish that she wasn't at all afraid of walking in the city at night or being a woman on her own. "I'll be fine."

"I wouldn't mind."

"I appreciate the offer, Mr. Reynolds, but I'm perfectly capable. And I'm sure your teammates don't want you to be late." She turned away.

"Wait."

She paused, turning slightly.

"I have something for you." He fished in his bag and pulled out a folded piece of paper. "Think about it."

Bernadette reached for the paper, pinching the corner as far away from his hand as possible. "Think about what?"

"You'll see." Before she could respond and ask him what he was talking about, Graham sauntered off in the opposite direction from the bus station.

Then she saw him unlock one of the bikes and climb onto the seat.

"You had a key this whole time," she called.

He grinned. "I'd have cut my own lock just to make good on a promise though. Read the job opening." He pointed at the paper she still clutched in her hand. "See you Monday."

Job opening? Bernadette unfolded the paper and squinted in the streetlight as he rode away.

For a brief moment, she thought it was going to be a notice for a secretarial position. Thought he was playing a cruel joke. But it wasn't.

Vacancy: Senior Copy Editor, Lenox & Park.

Her jaw unhinged slightly in surprise. The advertisement was one she'd seen on the bulletin board by the break room. A zillion times she'd reached for it, but never tore it down. One of those times she recalled Graham stopping to eye what she'd been looking at.

What had stopped her wasn't the job title or the description but that she would need to apply to none other than Mr. Tom Wall.

Senior Copy Editor.

Wall hadn't announced the position was open to anyone in their office. The flyer had just appeared, printed on plain stock and pinned to the board like a notice he hoped no one would notice. Had one of the trio—Evans, Marshall, and Greene—decided he didn't want to come back from his alcohol-induced binge? Had one been fired? Or was the position simply opened because the publishing house needed more than the three senior copy editors they had already?

So many questions and zero answers. Answers she wasn't likely to get from her boss either. In fact, if Wall saw her standing there reading the job description with a hint of want in her eyes, he'd laugh her all the way down Fifth Avenue.

Bernadette shook her head. Yeah, this wasn't happening.

She lifted her gaze toward the bike rack, but Graham was already riding his Schwinn down the street. When he reached an intersection, he glanced back, his hair blowing in the wind like a Vitalis hair tonic advertisement she'd seen printed in *Glamour* magazine and gave a little salute before turning the corner.

What the hell was he up to?

Why would he have given her this job advertisement unless he thought she was up for the job?

Bernadette allowed her gaze to travel once more over the advertisement. She was more than qualified for the position. And she was damn good at copyediting. But would Mr. Wall ever even consider a woman for a senior copy editor?

He seemed to enjoy making her current job a living hell.

If she was to become a senior copy editor, he would have to acknowledge that she was more than a glorified personal assistant. That she had a real talent, that her skills were important to the publisher. That a woman was just as good at the book business as a man.

Mr. Wall—and the other copy editors in her department— would have to respect her.

Bernadette shoved the paper into her purse and hurried toward the bus station, praying she hadn't missed the bus. Fortunately, the doors were just closing when she ran up, and the driver reopened them for her. The entire trip home, her brain rocked back and forth with the stop-and-go traffic. Did she actually have the guts to ask for the promotion?

She scooted off the bus at her stop and hurried down the sidewalk, weaving around other commuters and past a few kids out late playing jacks. Lit up by streetlamps, the buildings here were shorter than in the publishing district, only four to six stories tall. The merchants who tugged out their carts of vegetables and other goods in the morning had already hauled their items back inside, leaving a wider berth for her to hurry home. Half a block from her apartment, despite the soft violin music of a street player, she heard Frank's howl, as if he sensed she was nearing home. Mrs. Morris must have left the window open to give him some fresh air.

Bernadette smiled, slipped off her heels, and ran the rest of the way, weaving around trash cans brought out for the night and ignoring a rat who was making off with a half-eaten bagel.

Mr. Jacobi, whose apartment was on the fifth floor, tipped his hat as he held the door open for her. "Your boy is excited to have you home," he teased.

"I hope he's not too loud."

"We love him. Keeps the neighborhood safe. Always be grateful to him for that warning from my wife's baking incident. And to you for the lessons."

Mrs. Jacobi wasn't exactly the best cook. At least once a week when Bernadette had first moved in, there was smoke coming out of the Jacobi windows as Mrs. Jacobi attempted a new recipe. And one time in particular, she'd set her oven on fire when she forgot she was making a cake and went out on an errand. Frank had alerted the building at the smell of smoke, and Bernadette and Mrs. Morris had been able to put the fire out before it did any real damage. Bernadette had offered Mrs. Jacobi a few cooking lessons, and ever since then, there hadn't been any more fires.

Bernadette grinned. "That's what neighbors are for." She waved and took the stairs two at a time until she reached her apartment door, where Mrs. Morris, draped in a worn peach dressing gown and slippers, was struggling with a key.

"Oh, dear, you're back. Thank goodness! I thought poor Frank was going to have a heart attack."

"I think he heard me coming." Bernadette smiled, hearing the thump of Frank jumping down from his perch and coming to the door. "Thank you so much for taking such good care of my boy. I couldn't do this without you."

Mrs. Miller smiled warmly, her hand touching Bernadette's arm. "To be perfectly honest with you, dear, it is I who should thank you. I've been so lonely. Without Frank and Mr. Crumbs to care for, I'm just not even sure what I'd do."

The woman's loss had hit her hard. Her entire adult life had been devoted to taking care of her husband and this building.

"I have an idea." Bernadette stuffed her heels under one arm and pulled out her own key, since seeing her seemed to have kept Mrs. Morris from the task of unlocking. "Do you read?"

Mrs. Morris chuckled. "Not since I was in grade school."

"I have a wonderful book for you." Bernadette slipped her key in and turned the lock.

Mrs. Morris looked skeptical. "I suppose I'm willing to try."

As Bernadette opened her door, Frank leaped on her, nearly knocking her backward. Her shoes went flying. Mrs. Morris caught one and Frank caught the other. "Oh, you silly boy. I missed you too."

Shoes retrieved, Bernadette urged him inside, then knelt to give him a good belly rub, cooing at him while Mrs. Morris beamed at them both.

"One second, I've got to get something for Mrs. Morris." Bernadette hopped up and ran over to one of the many bookshelves—categorized by genre and author name—lining her baroque-papered wall just behind her small couch.

She ran her finger over the titles until she found it: *Jane Eyre* by Charlotte Brontë. In fact, she had seven copies of the novel, all different editions. She sighed as she withdrew the latest printed edition with a creamy background and Jane front and center on the cover in a dark gown, watching as Mr. Rochester rode his horse away from Thornfield Hall.

"This is my favorite book." Bernadette handed the volume to her landlady. "Have you read it?"

With a shake of her head, Mrs. Morris turned the book over to read the back. "I'm afraid not."

"Well then, you're about to enter the fascinating world of a young girl who is orphaned and abused. A plain Jane, an underdog really, who is… Well, I don't want to spoil it."

"Your enthusiasm is contagious. I'll start tonight. Did you edit this one?"

Bernadette let out a short laugh. "I wish. Miss Brontë actually penned this novel over a hundred years ago."

"Ah, so it's a classic."

"It is."

Mrs. Morris bent low and gave Frank a scratch before scooting off.

With just the two of them remaining in the tiny space, Bernadette asked, "Ready for supper?"

Frank barked once and went to the kitchen. His prepared meals were in the fridge, separated into Tupperware that her mother had given her. Mother had meant for her to use it for her own meals. Well, what she didn't know couldn't hurt her.

Weekends were for meal prep, baking, and the odd jobs Bernadette did for extra cash. Her mother had looked distastefully at the impossibly tiny kitchen and remarked that she didn't know how Bernadette got a glass of water, let alone cooked, and Bernadette had teased back that she didn't even need to get out of bed to whip up a batch of Julia Child's French onion soup. Of course, her mother didn't find that funny at all, although she did approve of Bernadette's favorite television show: *The French Chef* hosted by Julia Child herself.

Bernadette pulled out the Tupperware marked F for Frank and scooped a portion into his bowl. Chicken, carrots, and rice were on the menu for tonight.

Her own prepared dinner was Julia's Poulet Sauté aux Herbes de Provence and potato pancakes, which she reheated in the Hotpoint oven. While she waited, she poured a glass of Chablis and set her tiny table for one. Melanie liked to go home and make a vodka gimlet, but Bernadette had never acquired a taste for hard liquor.

As she ate her chicken in a garlic-herb butter sauce, she mulled over the senior copy editor position. "What do you think about me asking for a promotion?"

Frank lifted his head from his bowl to stare at her. He cocked his head to the side, ascertaining she wasn't going to share a piece of her chicken, and then went back to eating.

"Not sure if I should take that as a good sign or a bad, Frank. Bark once for yes, and twice for no."

Frank glanced up, chewed his food, then barked once.

"I was afraid you were going to say that. And if anyone was here with me, they'd wonder if I'd gone mad talking to my dog." She sipped her wine, then cut into her potato pancake, smearing it into some of the delicious sauce.

They finished their food, and she took Frank down for a walk, lighting their way with her Eveready. Frank sniffed all the spots until he found the perfect one by his favorite tree. She thought it was funny that he sniffed everywhere as if he might change his mind one day, when they both knew he was only ever going to do his business in one place. As fastidious as she was.

"Evening, Miss Swift."

Bernadette nodded to her neighbor, Joon, who lived in the apartment beside her with his sister, Hana. If her mother thought her apartment was small, what would she think to know that two people lived in the same-size box right next door?

"Tell Hana I said hello."

Joon grinned and tipped his hat as he entered the building.

Bernadette loved living on this block. She'd been there since she graduated from Barnard and had the contract from Lenox & Park to prove she could pay her rent, not to mention her brother had been with her to meet with Mrs. Morris's husband and cosign on the lease, assuring if she fell behind, he'd pay the difference, and then privately threatened to call their parents, who would cart her back to Maryland.

It was odd that as a single woman with a job, she had a hard time convincing the landlord to rent her the apartment. As if because she was a woman she'd fail to pay. What sense did that make? A man could rent his own apartment without question. Did Hana ever get upset about that? She was a pharmacist and spent her days filling prescriptions. So, she could help save lives, but not rent her own place?

As hard as it was to get the apartment, Bernadette prayed every night that Mrs. Jacobi on the fifth floor didn't burn the place down with her calamitous cooking. She'd even offered to teach her to cook a few things. After all, because she'd grown up on a farm, cooking had been a major part of Bernadette's life. That and books. But Mrs. Jacobi swore she just hadn't found the right recipe yet. Although if one couldn't toast a slice of bread without setting fire to it, Bernadette was fairly certain it wasn't the recipes that needed fixing.

Back in her apartment, Bernadette changed for bed and pulled out another copy of *Jane Eyre*. If there was one thing she'd learned from reading that book at least a hundred times, it was resilience. Jane was not afraid to go after what she wanted. To tell people when they weren't treating her right.

Bernadette reached for the journal she kept beside her bed, always with a pen, and flipped it open.

Lessons I've learned from Jane Eyre: "I am no bird; and no net ensnares me; I am a free human being with an independent will."

Not even Mr. Wall could hold her back, though she knew he would try.

"I'm going to do it, Frank. First thing Monday morning."

Frank made a sound of acquiescence, his head heavy on her hip from where he lay beside her. Bernadette rolled toward the window, the curtains partially open so she could stare up past the building across the alley to the night sky. That was perhaps the one thing she missed about the farm in Maryland: the ability to always see the sky and the endless possibilities that lay within its sparkling landscape.

Change was intimidating. But since when had she ever backed down from a challenge?

Chapter Five

FRANK

I TAKE THE STAIRS TO the first floor and give a little scratch on Mrs. Morris's door.

She opens and I sniff, taking in the scents of toast and tea. At first, her gaze is over the top of me, and her brows wrinkle in confusion until she looks down. Behind her I can hear the jangle from the bell of her cat, Mr. Crumbs.

"Oh, you are a dear, aren't you?" Her voice is scratchy, the pitch higher than Bernadette's.

I hold the bounty clenched between my teeth. A small paper bag and, inside of it, the oatmeal cookies Bernadette made for her.

She gives me a good scratch behind my ear, then takes the bag and invites me in. I can't stay long, but I'm willing to sit with her a spell since she's so lonely. Mr. Crumbs hisses at me and then darts to hide beneath Mrs. Morris's bed.

"Your girl is so thoughtful," she's saying as she bites into a cookie and sits on the couch. I lay at her feet, hoping for a few crumbs to drop. She pats my head and gives me a bite. "My daughter is coming for a visit soon."

I've met Mrs. Morris's daughter exactly one time, but it wasn't for very long. She'd come by to pick up a few boxes on her way out to California, where she lived by the beach. I love the beach. Sometimes when we go home to the farm, we get lucky and take a drive to the ocean. I chase the seagulls and stomp through the waves. I gobble up every french fry Bernadette tosses me and then lick the empty box when she's done.

"Might be staying longer than a few days this time," Mrs. Morris says. "Seems her husband has taken a liking to some floozy. My Wallace would have never dallied with a floozy."

I wish I could ask her what *floozy* means. It sounds like a bird at the park, but judging by the sadness in her eyes, the bird might have died.

I bark and she smiles down at me. "I quite agree. Her husband needs a good bite. I heard you used to chase the foxes off. Maybe I should take you with me to California?"

I bark again. If her daughter is married to a slinky fox, I'd be happy to chase him off. Soon, it's time for me to say goodbye, and I return to our apartment on the fourth floor, ready for the next delivery.

Bernadette took me through the building to meet our neighbors when we first moved in. I'm good at listening to commands. Probably because before I was hers, I trained with Ben in search and rescue. If I can find a man trapped under a burned-out building or climb a ladder into a window, delivering oatmeal cookies to our neighbors is a breeze.

But missions change, and a few years ago, I found myself in

a car, riding away from the familiar scents of the military base I'd spent my first six months at.

Before long, we were nearing a city. This city. I could smell it as we crossed over a bridge—car exhaust, human waste, food, and rats. I've caught a few of those nasty things. Before we'd gotten off the bridge, I could hear the city. And just like the base, the city is never quiet.

But even still, I've found peace here with Bernadette. And for every bag of cookies I deliver, I get a bite myself. Some of those bites I squirrel away for my daytime escapades. Even dogs have their secrets, and because of my training, I've never met a window I couldn't open.

When I return to the kitchen after delivering to the Lee siblings next door, Bernadette is staring into the place where water comes out. The faucet is off, and her hands rest on the edge. She doesn't see me or hear me at first, and I wonder if she's asleep standing up with her eyes open.

I nudge her leg, and she looks down. For the briefest second, I sense worry in her, before she shakes her head and gives me a kiss between the eyes.

She doesn't talk about it much, but I wonder if she misses her brother, Ben. I miss him too. I haven't seen him on my daily jaunts. Haven't smelled him either. I wish I could ask when he is coming back.

Chapter Six

BERNADETTE HAD ALMOST NOT ANSWERED the phone when Penelope called, mired in worry for her brother. But the shrill *bdring, bddrrringgg, bddrrrinnnnngggg* could only be stopped if she picked up the receiver, as if the phone grew louder on purpose, taunting, mocking her with its need to be answered.

Today was his twenty-seventh birthday, and he should be home, blowing out the candles on a cake their mother had baked. Instead he'd be spending it in Nho Trong possibly blowing out the flames of their enemies. But she preferred to think of him as safe there as he'd been in Saigon. She'd sent him a card and twenty-seven chocolate bars, hoping the delivery made it in time, and that right about now, he was opening the box and biting into the candy with his platoon.

But Penelope's invitation was the perfect distraction—one Bernadette had also extended to Melanie. A Mary Shelley birthday celebration, complete with costumes and readings from *Frankenstein*, promised to be frighteningly delightful. Bernadette had originally declined, but Penelope had called one more time to ask her to come.

In his last letter, Bennie had made her promise: *Keep living your life, little sis. That's why I'm here, helping freedom reign.*

It was a direct order from Sergeant First Class Benjamin Swift. Tonight was time for her to comply.

Outside of the Caffe Shakespeare literary coffee shop, a line of people as long as the Hudson waited to get inside. Some wore ghoulish Frankenstein costumes, and like Bernadette, at least a dozen others were dressed as Mary Shelley, down to the ringlets at their ears. There were a few Lord Byrons or Percy Shelleys, Victor Frankensteins—the monster's creator, and sickly-looking Elizabeth Lavenzas.

Bernadette was glad for the literary-themed parties at Barnard, or else she wouldn't have had the perfect dress—made by her mother—for this occasion. A high-waisted, light-pink muslin gown in the style of the Regency era with mauve roses embroidered and buttoned up the back and a matching mauve sash at the waist. She'd had to ask Mrs. Morris to come over to button her up since she couldn't reach. An invite to the older woman had been declined, though she had asked to sit with Frank instead.

"Bernadette!"

Bernadette whirled to the call of her name from somewhere down the street. Rushing toward her, heels clacking on the pavement, was a woman, face as white as death, lips as black as night—and her once-red hair streaked with black and flying behind her as if she'd been electrocuted. She wore a simple, long and flowing white cape dress, which fluttered with every step, and a smile that assured good times.

"Melanie, my goodness. You're the bride of Frankenstein."

"Ha! Yes!" Melanie laughed, causing several heads to turn. *Frankenstein* is one of my all-time favorite books—and movies. And you, looking so adorable as a Regency writer. Let me see your haunted expression of a writer with such ghostly demons battling in your mind."

"Oh, I don't think she was as haunted as all that, but she was clever. How is this?" Bernadette made a face that she hoped to convey both haunted and clever, but Melanie only laughed.

"That is the very face you make whenever you talk about Mr. Wall."

That had Bernadette in stitches. She wiped at the tears forming from laughing so hard. "I'm glad you could join me."

They found Penelope inside, instructing tonight's readers and looking generally harried. The Chiffons' "One Fine Day" played on the jukebox. The place was jammed, but luckily they found a small unoccupied round table and ordered chai teas.

Melanie picked up a tented menu. "Interesting. They have a Mary Shelley cocktail. Champagne and blackberries."

"That sounds good! We should try it after our tea."

"I'm in. Now, give me another Shelley impression."

Bernadette cocked her shoulder and affected what she hoped was Mary Shelley's voice but probably came out more like she was trying to imitate Mary Poppins. "'It was on a dreary night of November that I beheld the accomplishment of my toils.' One of my favorite lines."

"Oh, Bernadette, are you auditioning to read?" Penelope bent to give her a hug. She too was dressed as Shelley, but in a more somber getup of black.

"Most definitely not." Bernadette crossed herself in mock horror.

"I can read if you want," Melanie volunteered. She cleared her throat before saying, "'Beware; I am fearless, and therefore powerful.'"

"You're a regular thespian," Bernadette said, complimenting her.

"I may or may not have tried my hand on Broadway before humbling myself to the desk and telephone. Though I must say, having a stable income beats living with my parents."

"Amen," Bernadette and Penelope said at the same time.

"I have the perfect part for you, dear bride of Frankenstein." Penelope wiggled her brows and Melanie clapped.

"I'm so sorry, I forgot to introduce the two of you. Penelope, this is Melanie, my friend from work I was telling you about."

"Ah, yes," Penelope said, leaning close. "I heard you are interested in our book club."

Melanie glanced at Bernadette, both of them nodding. "Oh, you bet I am."

Penelope grinned. "Our next discussion is on Betty Friedan's *The Feminine Mystique.*" She glanced around as if people might be listening in and then leaned in a little closer. "A week from now, Tuesday night, seven o'clock at the library."

"After hours." Bernadette pressed her fingers to her lips in pretend shock.

"We have connections," Penelope said with a conspiratorial smile. "Connections that will get us in. Connections that will get us out. Connections that will ensure we remain the elusive and secretive women's book club."

"This is going to be so much fun," Melanie said.

"You know Mary Shelley was a feminist, too," Bernadette said. "A lot of men prefer to just think about the monster she penned, but she was the daughter of Mary Wollstonecraft, and her *Vindication of the Rights of Women* was a trailblazing treatise for the feminist movement back in the day."

"And probably still today," Melanie added.

"Absolutely. I'll see you both in a few. My Victor Frankenstein just showed up." Penelope hurried toward her husband, whose name was also Victor and who also happened to be a doctor.

Bernadette and Melanie both sighed at the same time as they watched the two of them embrace.

"How's it going with Gary?" Bernadette asked, blowing on her hot tea.

Beneath the white paint on her face, a faint blush appeared on Melanie's cheeks. "He asked me out to dinner."

"Did you go?"

"For next weekend. But I'm not sure I want to."

"Why not?"

Melanie did a little shake of her head. Her hair, which somehow was still standing on end, trembled. "I don't know if I'm ready for a relationship."

"Dinner doesn't mean you have to get married."

"True. But it might. First, it's dinner. Then it's dinner and a show—and you know I love a good show. Then it's 'Hey, why don't I come over and make you a steak?' and 'My mom wants to meet you.' Then our families get together, and the next thing you know, he's down on one knee in the middle of Times Square, holding up a diamond that he spent most of his savings on asking if he can be tethered to me for the rest of his life. Because let's face it, it's not the rest of mine. The man always dies first, and when he does die, I'll just be crying over having less laundry to fold and fewer dishes to wash." Melanie sucked in a lungful of air, as if she'd been underwater during her entire monologue.

"Well, how about when you go to dinner, you put in a request to do it differently than that?"

"A request?" Melanie frowned.

Bernadette nodded, her face serious. "Just say no to Times Square. And how about you share the laundry and dishes."

Melanie looked horrified. "What man in his right mind would share chores?"

"The man who wanted to spend the rest of *his* life with you. And if he's single right now, the man who's already doing just that."

"Good point. And if wants to sweeten the deal, no meeting his mother."

Bernadette laughed at that. "A no mother-in-law rule?"

"One can dream."

The laughter faded from Bernadette as in that moment all the joy was sucked from the room like a bird sucking a mollusk from its shell, when a familiar pouty face appeared in the crowd behind Penelope and her husband.

"Sarah?" Bernadette frowned in the direction of her secretary, who was also dressed like Mary Shelley, though her gown was a creamy beige in color. She was walking arm in arm with another Mary Shelley, and they were giggling. It was a side of Sarah Bernadette had never seen before—her countenance happy and not full of bitterness—and she found it to be quite jarring.

"*The* Sarah?" Melanie's head swiveled in Sarah and her friend's direction.

"The one and only. I should say hello."

"Why?" Melanie wrinkled her nose.

"Because if I don't, she's sure to turn it around on me somehow."

Bernadette moved toward Sarah. She didn't know what she thought Sarah did on the weekends, perhaps plotting out how else to torment Bernadette or toiling over a black cauldron. But dressing up and coming to a book reading? She never would have guessed.

Bernadette reached the small booth where Sarah sat whispering with her companion in equal beige tones as if they both wanted to blend in. However, in the maroon booth, they only stood out. "Sarah."

Sarah glanced over, eyes popping enough to bounce off the ceiling, along with the jolt of her body. "Bernadette." She picked up a glass of champagne sans blackberries, the same beige as her dress, sipping as she watched Bernadette over the rim with a not-you-again expression.

"What are you doing here? I've not seen you at Caffe Shakespeare before."

Sarah's lips twisted and a short laugh escaped her. "You think you're the only one who enjoys books? Think I'm only good enough for answering the phone? That my 'simple mind'"—at this, she made quotes with her fingers, shocking considering Bernadette had never once said she was simple, in fact the opposite—"can't appreciate the literary nuances of Mary Shelley's penmanship?" Twin splotches of red marked Sarah's cheeks.

Bernadette bit the tip of her tongue, instant guilt making her skin itch. When Bernadette had spotted Sarah in the crowd of Shelley wannabes, all she'd seen were the mocking, disdainful, hurtful glances that Sarah had chucked toward her for years. "I'm sorry. I just…" Bernadette cleared her throat as if that would help shoot the words out better. "I didn't expect to see you."

Sarah didn't reply, but the pinched expression said quite a lot more than any words could: *You're dismissed, go away, don't come back another day.* The literary secretary really was good at nonverbal communication.

"Enjoy the reading." Bernadette glanced at Sarah's friend, who avoided eye contact and pretended she didn't exist, while flicking a fly toward Bernadette that was hovering over what looked like hot cocoa. Another cue to get lost.

Bernadette supposed she deserved that.

"As if we'd be here if we weren't planning to do just that," Sarah snapped back, but there was a hint of hurt in her eyes as she set a glare so heated on Bernadette that it might have lit a fire.

Bernadette nodded, not trusting herself to reply.

She turned around, not catching whatever snarky comment Sarah made above the tap on the microphone and Penelope's voice telling everyone they were going to start soon.

Cheers made the air inside the small coffee shop vibrate against Bernadette's already buzzing ears. She hurried back to the safety of her seat on feet that felt numb, grinning just as numbly at her friend.

Melanie bumped Bernadette's shoulder with her own and whispered, "You okay?"

Bernadette gave her a small smile. "Yeah. Just put my foot in my mouth and paid for it."

Melanie glanced toward Sarah. "Hard not to with that one. At least you were wearing stylish shoes when you did it."

Bernadette stifled a laugh as two chocolate cake slices were delivered by Pearl, their favorite baker at the café. She was older, streaks of gray in her dark hair, but the only lines on her smooth brown skin were around her eyes, which crinkled when she smiled.

"Thank you, Pearl. Not sure what we're going to do when you retire next year," Melanie said.

"I'm teaching my granddaughter Gladys all of my recipes. You'll be in good hands."

"Now, stuff your mouth with this cake instead of her foot, Queen B. It will taste better," Melanie said.

Stuffing her face was indeed a much better option. The chocolate cake melted on her tongue, enough to take the sting out of her embarrassment.

"Don't worry about Sarah. It seems like some women really shine when they denigrate other women. It's not always just the men trying to put us in our place." Melanie scooped up some chocolate icing and licked it off her fork. "Sarah strikes me as one of those."

"I can't help but wonder why," Bernadette mused.

"Who knows." Melanie shrugged. "Probably her parents and mostly her mother. We all get it from somewhere, don't we?"

Chapter Seven

IN ALL THINGS, BALANCE WAS important. Formed from the Latin *bilanx*, which literally means "two pans," and weighing and measuring each—a feat Bernadette currently found herself undertaking. The balance of a personal life and work. Physical balance so one didn't fall over when walking or riding a bike or off a ladder when changing a light bulb. Balance between what mattered and what could be brushed aside.

But sometimes it was much simpler and smaller. Currently, Bernadette was focused on balancing dozens of wrapped cookies in her hands, while holding her purse and lunch sack and opening a door.

Clearly, this weekend's baking had been over the top. Bernadette tried for the third time to grasp the door handle to Lenox & Park. And as with prior attempts, as she did, one of the items in her possession started to slip.

At last, the door magically opened, swung wide by Melanie, who grinned at her, eyes shining through purple cat's-eye glasses that were the perfect shade to match her knee-length sheath dress.

"Those smell delicious." Melanie held the door as Bernadette came in and then began restacking some of the falling cookie packages on the edge of the reception desk. "I'll get the elevator button for you."

"Thank you so much. I might have splatted on the concrete if not for you. Take a pack. I brought some for you."

Melanie took one of the waxed-paper-wrapped bundles. "Yum. How did you have time to bake all these?"

Bernadette let out a small laugh. "I bake when I'm stressed."

"Stressed?" Melanie frowned. "Are you all right?"

"Nothing a little baking couldn't solve." Bernadette grinned and rushed into the full elevator, ignoring the muttered annoyances from the men who'd stacked themselves in like a deck of cards and now had to give her ample space so as not to touch her, though something did brush her hip and she hoped it was just a briefcase.

After putting away her purse and lunch, some balance restored, Bernadette delivered a package of cookies to Sarah's desk, though she wasn't there, and then took one down to Graham as a thank-you for nudging her about the job listing.

She knocked on his door, and he glanced up, dark circles under his eyes as if he'd turned around on his bike Friday evening, come back to the office, and worked straight through from then until now. But his hair was combed, his face cleanly shaven, and his brown and white polka-dot shirt was wrinkle-free beneath a brown vest, so he'd clearly been home at some point.

"A little token of my thanks." She held out the package of cookies, admiring his polka dots.

Graham took the offering, and she noticed he had a small cut healing on the right side of his forehead. "What did I do?" he asked, drawing her eyes back to his.

"I'm guessing a rugby injury?" she answered.

Graham chuckled and touched the faint line. "You're correct. But I meant to deserve cookies."

"Oh, right." Bernadette let out a soft laugh, trying to hide her embarrassment at having been studying him. "You helped me remember something."

She started to turn to go, but then he asked, "What's that?"

Bernadette contemplated giving him a vague answer, something impersonal and noncommittal. After all, they weren't really friends, were they? But he'd given her the job announcement. He'd taken Wall's shirt to the cleaners. So, she was ready to give a piece of herself—even if it was a small one—back. Balance. "That I am no caged bird."

He smiled, peeling back a corner of the wax paper and pulling out a crumb of one cookie. "No net ensnares you?"

"You've read *Jane Eyre*."

"What respectable editor hasn't?" He popped the crumb into his mouth, brows rising. "These are good."

"You may be surprised at what editors haven't."

"Why's that?"

Bernadette shrugged. "Many a male counterpart has deemed Brontë unworthy."

"I make it a point to avoid the ignoramuses of the world." Graham pulled out a whole cookie this time and took a massive bite.

"As do I." Her stomach did a little flutter that unnerved her. *Ignoramus*... He had no idea how much that word meant to her.

"Mmm. Oatmeal raisin."

"With walnuts."

"Even better. Thank you, Bernadette. And good luck. Hope you get the position."

So, he had figured out what her *Jane Eyre* reference meant in this case. She smiled and backed out of his office. In her own office, she delivered the other copy editors cookies, before walking slowly up to Mr. Wall's office—sans coffee. Which, she noted, he had a steaming cup of on his desk. A look back saw the Chemex brewer carafe filled and Sarah returned to her desk, examining the package of cookies.

Sarah glanced around, her expression confused. Then her eyes fell on Bernadette, and she frowned. Frowned like she'd just found out the cookies were made with sawdust and rat turds rather than sugar and raisins. Eyes on Bernadette, she dumped the cookies in the trash can beside her desk, then lifted her chin as if to say her loyalty could not be bought.

What a scurrilous move. Bernadette let out a sigh. Warming Sarah up to her was clearly going to take an eon.

Bernadette knocked on Mr. Wall's office door, where he was shouting into the phone and snapping his fingers at her to enter. Hadn't his mother ever taught him snapping at people was rude?

She opened the glass door, shutting it quietly behind her so as not to disturb whoever it was he was shouting at, although they probably would have been grateful for infringement. His office smelled like coffee and sweat, a sour combination that she wasn't sure the cookies could sweeten. She placed the package on his desk and waited, not wanting to sit unless he asked her to, and also because she'd rather be able to run out of his office quickly than to have to battle a chair that might prove a cumbersome adversary.

Holding the receiver between his chin and his shoulder, he peeked into the cookie package and pulled one out, shoving the whole thing into his mouth without even bothering to take a bite. Crumbs flew from his gluttonous lips as he kept shouting. Then, he waved her away with a dismissive hand, not even a thank-you or an inquiry as to why she was there.

Given he was still on the phone, she couldn't tell him she'd come in about more than cookies.

Fine. Let him get doped up on her delicious treat, and then she'd come back when he was happy from the sudden rush of sweet endorphins.

Back at her desk, Bernadette had a hard time focusing on her work. That was rare for her. She generally had laser focus. But she could feel the advertisement for the job opening burning in her purse even though it was tucked away in her desk. For the next hour she stood up at least twenty times, preparing to return to Mr. Wall's office, the words on the tip of her tongue that she wanted to apply for the position of senior copy editor. But each time, he picked up the telephone before she could cross the threshold.

At lunchtime, he stormed out for a meeting, and rather than wait at her desk for his return, with her nerves for company, Bernadette went to the park and sat on her favorite bench in the sun. She closed her eyes for a second, breathing in the balmy air, feeling the gentle breeze on her skin. Letting the luminous sky warm her skin and assuage her worries.

"So, Miss Swift, have you applied?"

Bernadette didn't turn at the sound of Graham's voice, but she did open her eyes. "Are you now the voice of my conscience?"

Graham chuckled and came around the bench to face her. He had a hot dog from a nearby stand, all loaded up with pile of mustard.

"I'll have you know I will not take your shirt to the dry cleaner when you spill that chemical-laden yellow paint." She pulled out her carefully wrapped apple-and-cheese sandwich on fresh sourdough and took a satisfying bite.

Graham considered her sandwich, then took a large bite of his hot dog, no spillage, offering an obviously false frown. "And here I thought I'd racked up plenty of points by helping you with Mr. Wall's shirts."

"You have a point. But alas, I have not received any cookies from you." She took a bite of her sandwich.

He grinned around a swallow. "Is that a challenge?"

"Definitely not."

For a few moments they just ate. Her sitting. Him standing. As Bernadette took her last bite, she crumpled up the wax paper from her sandwich and rose, tossing it into a nearby bin.

Graham followed behind her, adding his yellow-stained napkin to the trash. "You ready?"

"For what?" Bernadette knew exactly what he was asking, but just thinking about it made the sandwich she'd just eaten feel like she'd stacked a pallet of books in her stomach.

"To fight for your future at Lenox & Park."

"Is it in jeopardy?" she teased, trying to lighten her own sense of doom. Besides, she didn't need Graham Reynolds's help. Pursuing a promotion was her responsibility.

Graham shrugged. "I suppose not. But you don't strike me as a woman who is satisfied staying in her lane."

"An interesting turn of phrase. I'm not a weaver, Mr. Reynolds. I stay the course."

"And sometimes, to stay the course, Miss Swift, you must rise over a hill. Or mountain."

Wall Mountain.

Lenox & Park Mountain.

Woman Mountain.

Bernadette suppressed the urge to huff, because he was right. "True. But I came out here to enjoy my sandwich and contemplate my life. Not have you contemplate it for me."

"Touché. Shall we contemplate mine then to make it even?" He held his arms out to the side as if offering for her to take a stab in this witty game of banter.

"No. Badinage is not my forte." She glanced up at the building, and the clay in her belly turned to bricks.

"Badinage?" He chuckled. "Haven't heard it called that outside a book. You're not even a little bit interested?"

"No." A lie. She very much wanted to turn this conversation around to be about him, but if they did that, she'd never make it into Mr. Wall's office.

"Ouch. A near-fatal wound." He pressed his hands to his heart.

Bernadette rolled her eyes. "Hyperbole." Graham Reynolds's charm was disarming. If she wasn't careful, she'd end up in the same spot she'd been during her internship here at Lenox & Park— and that wasn't going to get her anywhere.

"I live a hyperbolic life," he said.

That made Bernadette laugh, because the way he worked was antithetical to his statement. Although his interest in playing such a rough sport as rugby put a spin on things. "Have a good afternoon, Mr. Reynolds."

She hurried ahead, so they wouldn't enter the building together. It was bad enough that if anyone looked out their window and saw them talking, they'd chalk up her entire career to sleeping with an executive editor. She wanted to make it to the top without that sort of wholly fictional blemish on her reputation.

Before she could lose her nerve, Bernadette marched right past her desk, gave two swift knocks on the glass, and entered Mr. Wall's office without waiting for permission. He wasn't on the phone, and before he could open his maw and tell her to beat it, she said, "I want to apply for the senior copy editor position."

A flicker of unease—*dare she think panic?*—passed over Wall's countenance before he quickly shuttered his expression. "No." His tone was clipped and curt. Without waiting for a response, he looked back at the folder on his desk.

"Let me rephrase. Mr. Wall, I am applying for the senior copy editor position. I have been with Lenox & Park for several years now and have shown exemplary performance. I—"

"You're still here?" He frowned up at her, completely denying the very existence of anything she might have just been saying.

Bernadette would not be discouraged. *First female CEO. First female CEO.* There were stepping stones to get to where she wanted to be, and this was one of them. "Sir, I am applying. Please consider my experience—"

"I said no." This time he slapped his folder closed and glared up at her as if she were a teenager asking for a later curfew. No consideration. No deliberation. No discussion. Cut off as if she were insignificant. Dismissible.

Bernadette gaped at him. Then she noticed the empty packet from the cookies she'd given him that morning—still on his desk, crumbs spilling out of it onto the pages of a galley proof, adding insult to injury.

"Was there something else, Miss Swift?" He looked at her as if she'd just dumped her trash on his desk.

A lump formed in Bernadette's throat, but it wasn't one that had her wanting to cry. Instead, she burned hot with anger. Like she could swipe everything from his desk and just roar in his face. Completely animalistic and feral.

The man was dismissing her. Acting as if she were a bad clause in a poorly constructed sentence. Why was she still working here? She could probably get a job at Harper or Doubleday in a flash. And maybe she should.

Except wasn't that what he wanted? For her to flee from Lenox & Park. To be rid of her. To fill his copy room with men, men, and more men. She was the only woman in the copyediting department who wasn't a secretary. And she needed to hold fast to that. To make room for more women coming up behind her. The only way to do that was to push back. To be the albatross in his male-dominated dominion.

And she knew exactly how to do that.

Bernadette left the office and went straight to the elevator. With irritation she punched the button and crossed her arms, her foot tapping impatiently.

"Everything all right?" It was Graham again. He looked at her, and then back toward the copyediting room, where several of her male counterparts were leaning into Mr. Wall's office, their laughter echoing. They'd either overheard her attempt or Wall was telling them all about it.

She glanced at him standing there, a manuscript in hand, and while she wanted desperately to gripe at the injustice she'd been served, she clammed up, offering him a curt, "Copacetic."

"You don't seem copacetic," he pushed.

"I will be."

"Anything I can help with?"

Bernadette let out an exaggerated "No."

"I'm here if you need me, Miss Swift."

She looked back at him, taking in the earnestness in his gaze. How was it that every other man in this building was on the other side of the fence? "Just taking a trip to the archives."

"Sounds enchanting."

The archives were enchanting, but she didn't want to give away what her plans were. So, she changed the subject. "What are you reading?"

"A few submissions. This one is about an alternate universe."

"That's where I feel I've been living lately."

He chuckled. "With Wall as your boss, no doubt."

Bernadette's foot stopped tapping, and she was about to ask Graham why he was being so supportive of her, but the elevator door opened.

"Happy hunting," he said, giving her a salute with the manuscript in his hand.

"Thanks." She stepped into the elevator, her heart pounding as she made her way down to the basement of their building.

It'd been ages since she'd gone to the archives, which was one of her favorite areas of the building. There was something so magical about a windowless room filled with books that held views of the world and universes beyond.

The elevator doors opened to the yellow flickering ethereal light of the fluorescents on the ceiling. She was met with a peculiar silence that always had gooseflesh rising on her skin—but not in a scary way, more like she was excited. As if the basement offered up secrets she was about to discover.

Bernadette stepped off the elevator. Straight ahead was a wrought iron gate and beside it the only person she'd ever seen at the archives. A man dressed in his Lenox & Park guard uniform, so old he might have been sitting there since the building was erected. To the left was the mail room, where she could hear the clerks chatting as they sorted. And to the right, a wall of plaques.

"Good afternoon, Mr. Towne," Bernadette said.

He blinked open his eyes, caught in a nap. "Morning, Miss Swift."

The archive gatekeeper might have been old, but he had an impeccable memory.

"What can I do for you?" he asked, straightening his cap, which had been conveniently pulled down over his eyes to ward off the lights.

She should have brought him cookies and made a mental note to bring him some tomorrow. Hopefully, Frank hadn't gotten into the batch she'd stashed on the counter. But if he had, she'd just make a new one.

"I'm looking for a book. An older title."

"Which one?"

"Out a couple of decades. *Lions of New York*."

"Ah, yes." Mr. Towne stood, opened the gate and made his rickety steps down the center of dozens of darkened shelved books, reminding her of the stacks at Barnard's library. "It'll be on these shelves."

"Thank you."

Mr. Towne made his slow way back to the gate, and Bernadette shifted into the stack of shelved books and boxes. She scanned every book as she went, hoping the title would stick out at her, but it took a good twenty minutes before she found it—shelved out of order, which made her think that Wall probably came down here to stroke his ego.

Lions of New York was the first book Wall had copyedited. It had hit the bestseller list out of the gate, which of course he took credit for even though he hadn't written it or developmentally edited it. Not that a copy editor's job wasn't just as important. They were the polishers, the correctors of grammar and heinous word choices. But they didn't shape the narrative. That was the author's job, with help from their developmental editor.

Bernadette went to the back of the archives, finding a seat at a table stacked with papers, books, and boxes as if someone had left their job and not come back to clean it up. Grabbing several pieces of paper and her red pencil, which she'd tucked behind her ear, she flipped the book open to the first page and started to read. Halfway through the first paragraph she found the first mistake. She wrote it in red on the paper, cut off the strip, and tucked it into the book.

Ordinarily, she would have marked up the pages and created a style sheet. But she didn't want to ruin this copy of a printed book, and if she only wrote down the errors and page references on paper, Wall wouldn't be as affected as she needed him to be.

She wasn't really sure how much time went by. There was no clock and no windows to judge the passing of the hour. She could have been reviewing the book for thirty minutes or much, much longer. But by the time she'd done enough to make a point, there were dozens of strips of paper with red on them tucked into the book.

Bernadette took the book to the gate where Mr. Towne dozed.

"I'll bring this back to you tomorrow." She wiggled the book in his direction.

"Thank you, Miss Swift."

"Have a good night, Mr. Towne."

He glanced at his watch. "It is getting to be that time. Good thing you called it quits. Wouldn't want you to walk home in the dark."

From any other man she might have bristled, but Mr. Towne had a genuine grandfatherly concern in his tone.

Bernadette smiled and nodded. "Thank you, Mr. Towne."

As she made her way down the hall to the elevator, she could hear a ruckus coming from the mail room, and then peals of laughter that made her smile. If only her department could have such a sense of camaraderie and fun. The mail clerks always delivered the mail with a smile as if they had the best job at Lenox & Park. Maybe they did.

As she rode back to the eleventh floor, her palms clammy, fingers trembling, she gave herself a pep talk. She could not walk into Mr. Wall's office with her nerves showing. Not unlike a wolf out for blood, he'd smell weakness in an instant and pounce.

They called your edits Swift-proof in college for a reason. Get it together.

By the time the elevator opened, she felt more confident than when she'd left it. She marched toward the copyediting department, ignoring Sarah's judgment-filled glances. Bernadette knew the secretary wanted to ask her where she'd been in a neglecting-your-work sort of way. As if her dumping on Bernadette would somehow make a difference in her own advancement or placement at the company. Why did women do that?

If she didn't have this one singular thing she needed to get done before she lost her nerve, she'd ask Sarah why. But as it was, the pep talk in the elevator was starting to wear off, especially at the sight of her boss behind the glass walls.

Straightening her shoulders, Bernadette marched past Sarah, past her male colleagues, who glanced up at her with stares that said, *Where have you been*, and *You're in trouble*. She ignored them all.

There was only one person she was focused on right now, and that was Mr. Tom Wall.

Bernadette gave his door two swift knocks and then entered. He was about to speak, but before he could, she moved forward, holding out the copy of *Lions of New York*, with hundreds of white and red tabs fluttering out from between its pages.

"*Lions of New York*," she said. "Arguably the book you're most proud of."

Wall looked horrified. "What have you done to it?"

"Gave it a Swift-proof copyedit."

"You what?" he growled, standing up behind his desk, meaty hands planted on the surface as if that would intimidate her, make her scamper off like a child threatened with a ruler by the headmaster. She got the distinct impression that his bluster was a carefully constructed ruse to hide his insecurity. How curious.

Bernadette did the opposite of what her boss most likely intended for her. Rather than scampering, she closed the distance between herself and his desk and slapped the book in the center of it, their eyes nearly leveled as they faced off. She was not going to back down. Either he would reject her, or he would accept her, or somehow manage to do both.

"I want the senior copy editor job. And I've just proven I'm more than qualified, Mr. Wall. Look at the book. Look at the copyedits."

"I should fire you." There was a low rumbling in his throat.

Bernadette didn't flinch. "Why?"

He visibly ground his teeth, "You're being disrespectful and wasting your time."

"I don't agree. I didn't mark up your book to embarrass you. Only to prove a point: that I am qualified for a position you're denying me the chance to apply for. Take a look. Please."

She hated having to plead, but if he didn't even look at her work, she'd wasted a day. And worse than that, it meant she had no path forward at the publishing house. Her options were plead for a minute to secure her future or bow out to face uncertainty.

Muttering something unintelligible and likely insulting under his breath, Wall picked up the book and started to sift through the pages. His silence was not encouraging. For a man who spent 90 percent of his day on level loud, his silence was a thunderous thud. A blaring boom. She watched the knot of his thick neck bobbing up and down as he swallowed, his cheeks growing redder, a bead of sweat and then another forming on his brow. Was he…nervous?

But after what felt like the length of time it took for tectonic plates to shift, he gave a great sigh, slammed the book down, white and red strips spilling onto the surface of the desk, and grimaced.

Wall's expression was resigned, resentful, bordering on rage.

"Throw out the slips and put the book back into archives." The underlying message was not to share with anyone that she'd bested him.

"And the job?" she pushed.

The outer crust of Wall's emotional layers cracked, revealing molten rock beneath.

Bernadette braced for the eruption, praying she didn't get burned.

Chapter Eight

"YOU'RE A STUBBORN WOMAN, SWIFT." Mr. Wall's mustache wobbled violently as he barked out his contempt. Perhaps he'd circle the desk next to mark his territory.

Bernadette knew he meant it as an insult, but she was honored. Stubborn also meant persistent, steadfast, tenacious. Those were all qualities she was proud to possess.

She didn't acknowledge his words in any event, waiting for his denial of her promotion. Mentally preparing her inevitable resignation. A resignation she couldn't financially afford to give. But neither could she afford to remain in a place where she had no upward mobility. Settling was equivalent to accepting a stagnant life. And there was no way she was ready to pack up her red B pencils.

"I've assessed the other applicants already and…" He visibly gritted his teeth as if what he was going to say was literally causing him pain. "The senior copy editor position is yours."

Bernadette bit the inside of her cheek to keep her mouth from falling open. Had she heard correctly?

"Temporarily, Miss Swift. I'm not convinced you're up to the task."

Temporarily. But still. *Hers.*

"Thank you—"

"I'm not paying you what I pay Marshall, Evans, and Greene. You'll get a ten-cent raise and not a penny more."

"But, sir, that is hardly fair."

"You'll take it, or you'll leave it."

The ink was barely dry on the Equal Pay Act, and Mr. Wall was ostensibly tearing it up in front of her face.

"You've yet to prove yourself capable of the position, and I'm not paying you for it until you do. You can either take the job or find another publisher to work for," he pontificated.

Exactly what she'd been preparing to do moments ago.

Wall might be reluctant to admit it, but he knew for a fact she was more than qualified for this position, and that she worked harder than Evans, Greene, and Marshall put together. And from his strange reactions, she rather thought he might be intimidated by her abilities.

A fire lit inside her. Working harder than the trio of bozos made her worthy. Her immaculate grammar advice made her worthy. Hell, even that she got the job in the first place made her worthy.

They faced off across the desk. Bernadette contemplating whether to dig her heels in or accept his offer as is. She was going to take it no matter what. After all, she'd gone to the trouble of editing *Lions of New York* merely to demand she be given the opportunity to apply. She'd gotten that and more. Whatever he said about it being temporary, she'd gotten the actual job.

A larger victory—making that job permanent and getting paid what the male senior copy editors did—had to be approached in steps. Half of her saw the logic in this; walls, whether stone or Mr. Wall, didn't fall at a single blow.

But the other half of her was still gritting her teeth. That half found it demeaning that if one of the other copy editors had decided to apply for the job—Bob, for example—there would have been no half steps. No "temporary," no waiting on a raise. He would have been offered what Evans, Green, and Marshall were getting, and Wall would have poured him a bourbon to toast his new position. Then again, perhaps Bob had applied and been denied.

Bristling, she decided she'd take her extra eighty cents a day and put it into her rainy-day fund.

And when she proved to Wall she was indispensable, she'd make him eat the wax paper she'd brought him cookies in.

And she wouldn't be bringing him any more cookies. The man didn't deserve anything from her other than what her actual job was.

"I'll consider the offer," she said. Even though she knew she should say yes, she couldn't quite bring herself to do it on the spot.

"You'll consider it?"

Bernadette nodded. "Yes, sir. Happy to consider it. Appreciate the offer."

Wall was fairly sputtering now. "You walk in here, marking up my book, and when I finally offer, you just say you'll consider it?"

His face had gone red, even to the tips of his ears.

"Yes. I'll give you my answer tomorrow morning."

Bernadette turned her back on him and headed for her desk,

straightening her pink polka-dot headband as she went. She took her purse out of her desk, tidied the surface of her work area, and walked out of the copyediting room. The men who'd all stayed behind—no doubt to watch the exchange—stared after her. She let out a breath and registered that whatever ladder she was trying to climb, she'd just risen a rung.

Elation bubbled in her veins.

She'd done it. The first chip in the brick bastille that Wall had erected around her.

"Did you get fired?" Sarah asked with a hopeful smirk. "Guess you shouldn't have played hooky like that."

Bernadette paused in her steps, meeting Sarah's hostile gaze. "Actually, I was offered a promotion."

Sarah's smile twitched, then fell, her eyes widening in surprise when she realized Bernadette wasn't prevaricating.

Bernadette's chin jutted forward. "Enjoy the cookies."

Sarah's gaze went to the unopened package she'd pulled out of the trash at some point but was probably too afraid to eat since Mr. Wall liked his secretaries thin and often remarked on that.

Bernadette half expected to see Graham by the elevator or climbing onto his bike outside, but their paths didn't cross. As she made her way toward the bus stop, she realized how disappointed she was that they didn't. She wanted to share her news with someone, and Melanie had already gone for the day.

But that was fine. She'd share her news with Frank, who always seemed to appreciate her stories, especially if they were accompanied by a treat. And maybe Mrs. Morris would be up for a chat about *Jane Eyre* over a glass of chilled white.

When Bernadette got off the bus, she ran down the street,

jumping over a runaway kickball, and took her apartment stairs two at a time, catching Frank as he leaped up, large paws landing on her shoulders.

"I did it, boy." Leashing him, she took him down to the street— meandering over the sidewalk, passing the brick apartment buildings and shops—to the small neighborhood park where children played and mothers mingled. As she watched them, she didn't have a feeling of want, but rather a sensation of nostalgia. A longing for days when kids played on the playground together. Innocence before boys realized they needed to be tougher and girls let them.

Frank barked and tugged at the leash.

"Ready to go home already?" she asked.

But Frank wasn't tugging in the direction of home. Ears perked, his body stiff and on alert, she tried to see what he saw, but whatever had spiked his radar wasn't readily apparent. On instinct, she let go of his leash. The moment the restraint was loosened, Frank darted off. Bernadette chased after him as he headed toward a thick oak, howling a warning at the nebulous sky.

Then Bernadette caught sight of a small pair of children's shoes poking out from around the back of the tree, and just beneath Frank's howls, she heard the audible sobs of a child.

"Are you all right, sweetheart?" Bernadette asked the little boy, no more than seven, who held his arm close to his chest.

"Hurts." Fat tears dripped down his dirt-smudged cheeks.

"Did you fall out of the tree?"

He nodded between sniffles. "My brother said I couldn't climb it. But I did."

"Brothers can be vexing, can't they?" Bernadette glanced around the park, through the throngs of Frisbee throwers, dog walkers, and children playing tag, hoping to find a parent frantically searching for a child. Finally, she spotted a woman in sky-blue skinny capri pants and a soft-as-cashmere short-sleeved sweater in the same shade calling out a name she couldn't hear over the wind and running this way and that as if searching for something or someone lost.

"Frank, watch the boy." Bernadette dashed toward the mother, waving her arms. "Over here!"

Panic covered the woman's face, and then relief when she saw it was her child, followed by panic again that he was injured. She lost one of her shoes as she rushed forward, stopping to pick up the white ballet flat, but not putting it back on.

"Oh, Dougie, what happened?" The mother crouched, examining the obviously broken arm.

"I fell," the boy wailed.

Lifting her child into her arms, the mother nodded to Bernadette. "Thank you for finding him."

"It was all Frank." Bernadette rubbed Frank's head and gave him a good pat. "He's got quite a sense for these things."

Bernadette couldn't count the number of times Frank had come to the rescue for those in their community.

On the way back to her apartment, she stopped by Mrs. Morris's apartment. But her knock went unanswered. Perhaps her neighbor had gone out to play bridge with friends. Bernadette cleaned off Frank's paws, put away his leash, changed her headband, and then finally picked up the pink telephone receiver and dialed her parents. Her mother answered on the third ring, a little breathless.

"Mom, are you all right?" Immediately Bernadette's mind went to her brother.

"Oh, perfectly. Just caught me in the middle of tidying." The relaxed tone of her mother's voice was a welcome relief to Bernadette's worries.

"Still? Have you had dinner?"

"Of course. Meat loaf and mashed potatoes."

"And you're still cleaning?" This was what Bernadette didn't want. To clean all day long, prepare dinner, which she would likely eat cold as she tended to everyone else—which would be a shame since she took cooking so seriously—and then when it was over, still keep on cleaning until it was bedtime, and then do it all over again with only a few hours' sleep.

"Have you ever thought about not doing that?" Bernadette asked.

"Not doing what, dear?"

"Cleaning nonstop. Maybe after dinner, you could just relax?"

Her mother laughed. "And who would do the dishes?"

"This might sound crazy, but Dad?"

That got her mother really going, laughing loud enough that Bernadette had to hold the phone away from her ear.

"Living in the city is having a silly effect on you, Bernie. Your father spends all day working both with his animal patients and on the farm. Why on earth would I make him work when he's done?"

"You spend all day working too, Mom. But in the evening after supper, he relaxes. When do you relax?"

"I relaxed when I was younger. The spoils of youth are spent by the time you reach my age."

Bernadette frowned. That didn't make any sense. "I didn't realize there was a limit."

"There is. And I spent mine in a city, much like you. You'll learn it isn't all it's cracked up to be."

Bernadette sank into her chair. Her mother, a city? "When?"

"I used to write for a magazine."

"What? No." Bernadette frowned, racking her brain for any previous mention by her mother about working for a magazine. There was no doubt her mother loved magazines; there were piles of them on the table in the living room at home. There was no doubt her mother loved fashion, as evidenced by a closet full of unworn dresses, and even the little designs she embroidered on her apron. There was no doubt that her mother knew the names and tactile feeling of every textile. But write for a fashion magazine? Why had she never told her? Not only had she kept it secret, but she'd balked at Bernadette doing anything writing-related, as if a woman working was a nascent idea.

"I had a fashion beat. Rode the train into New York twice a week to submit articles."

"Why have you never told me this?"

"Didn't I?" Her mother sounded genuinely confused.

"No, you most certainly did not. And when I wanted to go to New York City for college, you told me I was crazy. When I wanted to work for a publisher, you asked why I'd want to do a silly thing like that."

"I did. It's true." There was a long pause. "I suppose I didn't want you to suffer the disappointment of losing what you gained."

"Why would I lose it?"

"Oh, dear, all women do in the end."

Bernadette frowned. "I don't want to be all women."

"That's what we all say."

"I got promoted today, temporarily." Adding that on made it sound like she was giving credence to her mother's prediction. That any promotion she had wasn't going to last.

"What sort of promotion?" Her mother had the class not to say *temporarily*, and Bernadette was grateful for that.

"Senior copy editor." She refrained from telling her there was a minuscule raise, knowing that would only add context to her mother's argument.

"Oh, Bernie, that is wonderful. I'm so proud of you."

"Thanks, Mom."

"Now, tell me, any handsome suitors at Lenox & Park?"

Graham Reynolds flashed before her eyes and she was as swift to slide him aside. "Only if you count old Mr. Towne in the basement archives."

Her mother laughed. "What a sweet old man he must be to guard the dusty stacks."

"I think it gives him purpose. Something we all need."

"Hmm."

"Have you ever thought about going back to writing about fashion?"

"Fashion for farm wives?" Her mother laughed again. "Look at the way the mud speckles across my boots, high fashion indeed. Or the originality of my apron—made one of a kind by each bold yet innocuous stain."

"Perhaps you could submit that to *Good Housekeeping*."

Her mother laughed, but the pause at the end told Bernadette she'd struck a chord.

"You are a wonderful mother and a wonderful farm veterinarian's wife, but that is not all you are."

"I'm also a herder of the pigs and a milker of the cows."

Bernadette chuckled. "You know what I mean."

"I do, Bernie, I do. Now you go out and copyedit until the cows come home, snuffling around and asking not just for their oats, but the sweetness of hay."

"I will. And seriously. Think about a farmers' wives' fashion piece."

"Oh, stop. Would you like me to read the latest letter we've had from Bennie?"

"Of course." She adored her mother for reading those letters. The tradition had started when he'd gone to Fort Bragg in North Carolina. Few and far between now that more than one ocean separated them. It meant so much to hear how her brother was doing.

When he'd first gone to Saigon, Bernadette had sent him a package of cookies. By the time they arrived weeks later, they had to have disintegrated into moldy dust, but Ben told her how wonderful they were anyway. His letters were full of false promise and hope, like the commercials showing women in heels working wonders with mechanized exercise. Bernadette wished he'd be honest. She worried about him more rather than less because she knew he wasn't telling the hard truths like she read in the papers or saw on the news.

"Give Frank a good head rub for me," her mother said as they said their goodbyes.

"I will." Bernadette glanced at Frank, who appeared to be listening to their conversation intently.

Her mother rang off, something about a scrubbed pot not scrubbing itself.

Bernadette took a seat on the couch and patted the spot beside her. Frank lumbered over, lifting his large body to join her and then laying his heavy head in her lap. "My mother was a fashion writer. Rode the train into the city two days a week, and never thought to tell me."

Frank let out a sigh that sounded very much like the one she too pushed out. How was it possible that in all this time, her mother hadn't mentioned it and simply encouraged her to come home or to find a husband. As if Bernadette's true purpose in life was to start a family, and that she was just wasting time and putting off the inevitable. As much as Bernadette liked the idea of being born, and she didn't want to change that, she hated that in order for that to have happened her mother had to give up her dreams.

Now that she thought about it, her mother had some truly amazing dresses in her closet that she never wore, and every once in a while as a child, Bernadette caught her putting them on and twirling in front of the mirror. Her mother could laugh as much as she wanted at the suggestion of returning to her dream, but the truth was right there in the quiet moments when she thought no one was looking. In the twirling in the mirror and the fashion magazines under the latest *Farmer's Almanac*.

Bernadette had another reason to keep climbing. She had to do it for her mother. To show her that she could be both a wife and whatever her dream was. Fashion writing, copyediting, singing, practicing medicine. It didn't matter.

And she was going to prove that.

One copyedit at a time. And to whatever woman would listen. There were plenty of trailblazers ahead of her who had taken up the reins, and she was going to be right there behind them.

Eleanor Gould Packard, a copy editor at the *New Yorker*

magazine, was one of those women who had inspired Bernadette when she was in college. She came to speak during a seminar with the English department. A woman unafraid of working in a man's world. A woman determined to show off her wordsmithing skills.

During World War II, women filled jobs in warehouses, factories, businesses. Jobs needed filling, and women were willing and able to do the work. But when the war ended, so did their place in the field. Men took back their jobs and pushed women back into the kitchen. They'd been working for nearly the last two decades to get their jobs back.

Bernadette wandered into the kitchen and pulled out a cookie, munching on it as she made a little package up for Mr. Towne. She could worry forever about whether or not any progress she made would be taken from her.

Yet, there was something inside her that burned to take up the lighted flame for women in the workplace. And all the Tom Walls in the world weren't going to be able to stop her.

Chapter Nine

FRANK

THE APARTMENT IS A MENAGERIE of scents. The sweetness of baking, the sadness of sorrow, the static of unspent frenetic energy.

I learned about a menagerie last week when I wandered into the Central Park Zoo, which smelled like animals and popcorn and sticky kiddie fingers. One of the kind zoologists said if I didn't want to become a part of the menagerie, I'd best run along home.

My girl is on the couch, a piece of paper in her hand, which she'd removed from another paper she called an envelope. It shakes, not with an invitation for me to take it and shred it, but with something else. A mixture of fear and melancholy that comes from inside Bernadette and ends in the trembling, crinkling paper.

Say it, say Wall. *Please.*

I'd snatch the paper and give it hell. Rip to shreds the very thing that made my girl feel anything but bliss. But she doesn't say *Wall.*

Instead, she says, "Why does Bennie have to be so good at what he does?"

I want to answer her. To tell her it is the very same reason she also achieves what she sets out to. That some people can't *not* succeed. They work and work and work until they are their work.

I've seen it on the people we pass in the streets. I see it in her. I saw it before in Ben and his unit.

In moments like these, I ponder what to do. I could sneak up onto the couch and cuddle her. Or I could shred her woe with a rambunctious romp.

I decide on the latter—especially because it is going to make us both feel better.

Energy escalates in me, and I leap from my sitting position to stand. The sudden movement startles my girl, and she peeks over at me, eyes cloudy, then registering.

"What is it, boy?" Bernadette leans forward, making eye contact.

I've got her now. I whirl in a circle, bend my body nearly in half as I twirl and twirl and twirl, then stop, feet braced, tongue out, staring at her. *Are you ready, B?* I ask in my head, hoping the question makes it from my brain to hers.

And then I let go. I zoom around the room, jumping onto the couch, over the coffee table, in tight tiny circles, then wider and wider, leaping from one place to the next as fast as I can. *Zoom, zoom, zoom.* I am a ball bursting through the air. I am a Frisbee soaring. I am the whirling, turning, spinning contraption at the children's playground. Faster and faster. Spinning and spinner. I am…getting dizzy.

The small space can't accommodate the largeness of me, and I crash into the wall with a loud bang. *Woof.* I shake off the dizziness.

Bernadette laughs as she jumps up from the couch to come rub my shoulder where it hit the wall, the paper that made her sad lying on the couch, forgotten.

"Everything peachy keen, you big oaf?" she asks. "I might need to call you Frolicking Frank from now on."

A knock sounds at the door, and I sniff. I can already smell it's the female Lee from next door. She smells oddly like peanut butter and pickles. But she's nice enough so I don't judge her flavor combinations.

"Don't you zoom out of here." Bernadette wags a finger at me, and then she opens the door.

"Is everything all right?" the neighbor asks, peering at me from over my girl's shoulder.

"Perfectly. Frolicking Frank was just having a fit of the FRAPs. Silly boy." She says this latter part to me with a grin and a wink.

Frenetic random activity periods—FRAPs. That's what she calls it whenever I feel the need to zoom about like I belong on the Roosevelt Raceway.

Hana Lee looks relieved and smiles. "I heard a crash. I'm glad he's all right. Thought maybe you were hurt."

I venture over and let her pet me so she is reassured that we are well. *Peachy keen.*

"Thanks for checking." Bernadette shuts the door and looks down at me. "I think we'd better take this tear outside. What about you?"

I bark in agreement. While she's putting on her shoes, I sneak over to the couch and sniff the paper. It smells like Ben, and now I understand. This is one paper I don't want to shred.

We rush down the street, weaving in and out of people, and I keep an eye on my girl. I sense the same need in her to run. To burst. To let the energy flow. I pick up the pace, tugging on the leash, and she glances down at me, her sadness replaced by a beam of delight.

"Are we going to race?" she asks.

Now I smile, lips peeled back, my teeth showing, eyes squinted. Oh yes, I smile as hard as I can. I love to race. I stretch my legs out before me, energy and speed bursting through me with the speed a squirrel would be jealous of.

Bernadette laughs as she too lets her legs push out, the soles of her sneakers thwacking over and over and over. All the way to the park.

But then she stops in front of a cart that smells like meat and bread and spice.

I cock my head, sniffing. Delicious enough to roll in.

"One hot dog, please." Bernadette shoves a hand in her pocket, producing green paper.

Hot dog? What?

The man hands her a meaty link wrapped in bread, and she tops it with something spicy-yellow.

"Want a bite?" she asks me, holding the decadent treat aloft. "According to someone I know, there's nothing like a New York hot dog."

I don't like that it's called a dog, but the smell makes me drool and I lift my tongue from where it's curled all the way to the sidewalk to lick my chops.

"I thought so." Bernadette breaks off a piece and holds it out to me. "Gentle."

As gentle as my watering mouth will allow, I take the hot dog from her offering fingers, and…I think I've gone to heaven.

I watch her take a bite. *Drop it drop it drop it.*

She wrinkles her nose. "Nope. Still don't see it. You can have the rest."

Jackpot.

Chapter Ten

WITH A PACKET OF COOKIES tucked into her bag for Mr. Towne, her favorite headband tucked into her hair—the one that sparkled with pink and silver sequins—and wearing a freshly pressed black pencil skirt and matching jacket with her favorite pink blouse that had a little bow at the throat, Bernadette stepped off the bus and walked with purpose toward the Lenox & Park building.

Today was the first day of the rest of her life. The first day in a new chapter she was embarking on not just for herself, but for other women.

There was no hesitation as she gripped the cool metal handle and yanked open the door to the building. No hesitation as she marched over the threshold.

Melanie glanced up from behind her reception desk and offered her a smile. "I love that blouse." Melanie touched her throat. "The bow is très chic."

"Thank you," Bernadette said with an extra bounce in her step. "It's my lucky blouse."

"What are you getting lucky with today?" Melanie wiggled her brows and popped the end of her pencil between her teeth.

"I hope the rest of my life."

At this, Melanie dropped the pencil and clapped. "Oh, does that mean you're going to finally agree to a date with Mr. Reynolds?"

Bernadette's smile faltered. "What?"

Melanie grimaced. "Did I read that situation all wrong?"

She wasn't wrong. But Bernadette wished she were.

"Yes and no. He'd like that, but I was speaking of professional luck." Bernadette drew closer to the desk so their conversation wouldn't be overhead. "I'm going to accept the promotion I was offered."

"Oh, that's even better," Melanie replied with delight.

"It is, isn't it?"

Melanie pursed her lips, resting her chin on her hand, almost wistful. "I would love a promotion."

"Ask for one."

Melanie laughed. "Once a receptionist always a receptionist. You know what they say—a mail clerk starts at the bottom and works his way to the top, but we receptionists, we just work."

"What's the harm in asking? That's what I did. Can you type?"

"Of course. I went to secretarial school."

"Then the next stop for you is a position as someone's secretary."

"What if they say no?" She bit her lip pensively.

"They might." Bernadette leaned her elbows on the desk. "Then try harder. Don't give up. We have to advocate for ourselves. There won't always be someone else who cares as much as we do."

Melanie looked thoughtful as she sat back in her chair. "I'll think about it."

Bernadette glanced at her watch. It was a quarter to nine, and if she didn't get upstairs now, she'd be later than her usual early time. Not an auspicious start for accepting her new position.

But when she arrived at the copyediting department, Mr. Wall was absent. His office door shut, lights out. Half the other copy editors weren't in either. Their desks were littered with yesterday's work, as if they'd walked out in a coup.

Mystifying. Wall was always in by eight to make sure he had all the assignments ready for everyone by nine.

Bernadette walked out to Sarah's desk, surprised to see she wore a red silk scarf at her neck, offsetting the rest of her typical beige. "Has Mr. Wall been in yet?"

Sarah didn't look up from the fingernail she was filing. Readying her talons to scratch. "Called out sick." Her smirk was a sharp swipe.

Bernadette felt the blood rush from her face and pool in her knees, which she pressed together to keep from wobbling.

"Odd. He's never called out in all the time I've worked here."

Sarah let out a long-suffering sigh and glanced up. If eyelids could be defiant, hers would. "Bunch of the others called out too. Heard they had a good time at Writer's Block bar last night."

Bernadette had a sudden, unpleasant thought. She'd told him she would give her answer this morning. He'd been offended that she'd dared to make him wait, so now he was punishing her by making *her* do the same.

Did he tell anyone about the offer? If not, his truancy might mean more than delay.

With Wall AWOL, there was nothing for Bernadette to do but go about her day as if nothing had happened. As if she wasn't about to be a senior copy editor. Glancing up from her pages at one point, she noticed several of her male counterparts smirking. They must have been in on the scheme but decided not showing up at the office would only put them behind.

By lunchtime, Bernadette was so frustrated that she considered going home sick for the rest of the day. Pushing away from her desk, she tossed her red pencil into the pencil holder. Then straightened the pencil because her irritation was not its fault. This was not how the first day of her new and improved life in publishing was supposed to go.

She was sick of being thwarted by Mr. Wall over and over again. But if she went home, he won.

So instead, she took her packed lunch to her usual spot in the park. A newsstand directly across from her had a spread of papers with big, bold words splashed across the fronts.

200,000 MARCH FOR CIVIL RIGHTS IN ORDERLY WASHINGTON RALLY

Bernadette had heard Martin Luther King's inspiring speech on the radio. The radio hosts remarked about the massive crowd. There'd been a number of authors and musicians and actors there. An interesting note that stuck with Bernadette was that some Black women were excluded from officially speaking, including Lena Horne, who was escorted away from the podium with Rosa Parks and Gloria Richardson.

Josephine Baker spoke briefly before performing, and Mahalia Jackson sang onstage along with Bob Dylan and Joan Baez. It was an incredible show of support for jobs and freedom, advocating for the civil rights of Black Americans. Especially after what she'd read this summer about the Black students who'd attempted to enter the University of Alabama and were blocked by the Alabama governor, forcing President Kennedy to call in the National Guard. Segregation didn't make sense to Bernadette, just as the barring of equal rights was ludicrous. Civil rights, women's rights… They were human rights. She hoped that this march and its success worked.

Bernadette's gaze slid back to the other headline she'd been trying to avoid.

KENNEDY CRITICIZES DIEM'S GOVERNMENT: ASKS UNITED FRONT IN SOUTH VIETNAM

Diem was the current prime minister of South Vietnam and, from what she'd read over the weekend, was apparently corrupt. Not the words a concerned sister wanted to hear when her brother was training an army that answered to Diem. Ben's last letter had not remarked on any sort of conflict, however. Instead he talked about the lush green countryside and the mosquitoes that could rival a summer by the lake.

Squinting to read the headline was only giving her a headache and making her stomach sour. She bit into the Julia Child-type sandwich and tasted crisp, tangy apple; salty, buttery cheese; doughy, fresh baguette; and stringy, sour stress.

She shouldn't be reading the news. It wasn't Friday. She was breaking her own rule.

"I don't think I've ever seen you frown so much before. Well, unless you were looking at me, which you weren't, so who am I competing with?"

Bernadette glanced up at Graham Reynolds, another hot dog in hand as he stared down at her. He'd removed his vest and rolled up his sleeves, relaxing on his lunch break.

"You really ought to have better taste in lunch."

Graham held out his hot dog and examined it, his expression overly exaggerated as if he were trying to find the meaning in the meat-packed casing and flimsy bread. "Ah, so it is my poor culinary choice that has you frowning."

"No." The word came out a lengthy sigh.

"What then?" Graham took a rather large bite of his hot dog.

Should she confide in him? Political upheaval was definitely off the table. But work? Bernadette decided the way this day was going, she had nothing to lose, and he had, after all, been the one who'd given her the job announcement to begin with.

"Mr. Wall offered me the job yesterday. Albeit temporarily."

Graham wiped mustard from the corners of his mouth. "Isn't that a reason to smile rather than looking dour?"

"It should be. But I told him I needed to think about it and would give him my answer today." She wrapped up the rest of her sandwich, thinking that Frank might appreciate the snack later. Unfortunately, her own appetite seemed to have absconded along with Wall.

Understanding dawned on Graham's face, and he looked as disappointed as she felt. "And he's not in."

"Bingo." She made a clicking sound with her tongue as she winked and pointed at Graham. "First time since I've worked for Lenox & Park. If that isn't a clear message, then I don't know what is."

"For what it's worth, Wall did put your name in through personnel."

Bernadette looked up sharply. "How do you know?"

Reynolds shrugged. "I may or may not have asked to be notified when the position was filled. There was a note on my desk this morning. Congratulations."

"Thank you." She didn't even try to hide her smile. She might not be interested in him as a man, but Graham was a good colleague.

He smiled and took another massive bite of his hot dog, causing a significant blot of mustard to tumble toward the ground. He hopped backward just in the nick of time, and the mustard mess landed a mere half inch from the toe of his polished leather shoe, where it was immediately pounced on by three pigeons.

"I won't say I told you so," she teased.

"Perks of being a rugby player. I'm an expert at avoiding mustard bombs."

"Let's hope my brother is too." She'd said the words without meaning to, and now that they were out there, she couldn't pull them back. Clearly, she'd grown more comfortable with Graham over the time she'd worked at Lenox & Park than she realized.

Her gaze settled back on the newspapers about the Vietnam situation, and Graham's gaze followed.

"How is your brother?" Graham asked.

"I believe he's well. We don't hear from him that often, but we *do* hear from him. And that's better than a lot of families can say." *Dead men can't write letters.*

Graham nodded. "There will come a day when we have more than just our special forces over there."

"I hope not."

"Like yours, my brother is special forces. He just returned from his six-month tour."

"Ben is due back stateside in two months." She really hoped he wouldn't have to go back, but currently the boys were on six-month rotations from Fort Bragg. She just wanted her brother home and safe and the war to be over. "Did you ever think about joining the military?"

"I was in the navy when I was eighteen. Feels like a lifetime ago. Served for four years, then went to college. Decided I was better suited to publishing."

"Why's that?"

Graham gave an embarrassed grin. "I get seasick."

Bernadette couldn't help laughing.

"I think they were glad when I didn't re-up. Mops got a lot of use when we were deployed."

"That had to have been awful. I'm sorry for laughing."

Graham chuckled and shrugged. "I think I blew past a few records for vomiting onboard thirty-eight times in a twenty-four-hour period."

"Nothing wrong with doing your best at whatever it is you excel at—even if that's returning your lunch."

That had Graham snorting. He popped the rest of the hot dog into his mouth, chewing thoughtfully as he balled up his napkin and tossed it in the trash.

"Let me buy you a hot dog sometime, Miss Swift."

"I'll pass."

"Not a hot dog fan? Or not a Graham fan?"

Bernadette smiled. "I'm not a hot dog fan—and I'll have you know I've tried. I know that makes me very un-American. And as for Mr. Reynolds, he's all right in my book for now."

"I'll take that as a compliment. Do you like burgers? Pizza?"

"I do love a good margherita pizza, even better with mushrooms."

"So, I'll buy you a slice of that sometime instead of a hot dog."

Graham really was persistent. And it wasn't as if she didn't enjoy their conversations. In fact, he was starting to grow on her. "I'll consider your offer."

Graham's eyes twinkled as if he'd unlocked a difficult achievement. "Fair enough."

Bernadette sat quietly, unable to believe she'd really agreed to a future lunch with Graham. Mixing work and pleasure—bad idea. She'd have to find a way to avoid that actually happening.

"Want me to go with you to personnel?"

"Why would I go there?" Bernadette stood, smoothing her skirt.

"To accept your position."

"Don't I need to tell Mr. Wall first?"

Graham shook his head. "He's out sick, and personnel has been notified you have the offer."

"But I wanted to accept to his face."

"I bet you did. But arriving at work tomorrow to find you are already a senior copy editor will have a similar effect, I think." Graham chuckled.

"Good point." Bernadette picked up her lunch bag.

They walked back toward the lobby of the building, and she

glanced up at the glass windows, wondering who was watching them. The sun reflected off the glass, mirroring the sky rather than revealing every face and every pointing finger and every judging eye. All of which was probably in her head anyway.

It wasn't. As soon as Bernadette and Graham stepped off the elevator on the eleventh floor, Sarah gave Bernadette a pointed look, as if to say, *I see you, and you're getting too close.*

She might not like Sarah, but it was a fair warning. Unfortunately, if a woman appeared to have a good relationship with a male in the workplace, people quickly jumped to the idea something inappropriate was going on.

Although she had agreed to pizza, but on the condition that they discussed work. Not a date. Still, she couldn't keep the guilty expression momentarily from her face, certain Sarah saw right through her and had devised all sorts of nefarious scenes in her mind for what had happened at lunch, and maybe even in the elevator.

Bernadette cleared her throat, paused her stride, and nodded to Graham. "Have a good day, Mr. Reynolds." As if that was going to deter Sarah from spreading rumors about them.

"Miss Swift." He looked at her oddly, understanding she was dismissing him, but not sure why.

Without another word or glance for either Graham or Sarah, she headed in the direction of personnel.

The human resources secretary smiled pleasantly and placed a call to the personal manager. A second later, Bernadette was ushered into the quiet office that smelled like an odd mix of sandalwood and mothballs. The manager, comfortable in his tweed jacket, sat with hands folded on top of his desk. She imagined between dealing with conflicts and new hires he would sit back and strum a ukulele.

"I am here to accept a promotion to senior copy editor," she said.

The manager, a middle-aged man with light-colored hair that reached the collar of his shirt—too long for the office—smiled warmly. "Ah, yes." He glanced down, frowned slightly, and then said, "I believe you mean temporary senior copy editor."

Bernadette clenched her teeth through a smile and nodded.

"I have the paperwork here. Have you notified your supervisor?"

"Mr. Wall is out sick."

The manager tapped the folder with his index finger and pursed his lips. "Well, perhaps you ought to notify him first that you are accepting the offer."

Bernadette's skin prickled with embarrassment. Graham had told her this would be a fine course of action, and yet it seemed he'd gotten it wrong. "Should I ring him at home?"

"Do you have his home number?" The manager looked horrified.

"I do not. But I assume this office is in possession of it." Bernadette tried to look confident. Hadn't she just told Melanie that morning that the only way to move forward was to ask for the things you wanted?

"I do not think we ought to call Mr. Wall while he is ill."

"Well, what do you suggest then?"

What if Wall decided to stay out of the office longer? A week? A month? Could he do that? She might never formally begin her position, and then her situation would be worse than temporary.

"You can fill out the paperwork accepting the offer. And, I suppose, move to your new desk. No harm in that."

Bernadette pictured the copyediting office and the empty desk in a group of four where the senior copy editors sat.

"But, as only your supervisor can give you assignments, until Mr. Wall returns, you'll continue to work on your existing projects."

"Thank you, sir."

He nodded, brows still pinched, clearly not liking that she'd come down here to expedite the process rather than waiting like a good girl for Mr. Wall to return whenever he decided to stop punishing her for asking for a promotion.

There was no other way to describe it. This was clearly Wall's way of trying to put her in her place. But if he hadn't learned from her copyediting *Lions of New York*, then he hadn't learned at all. Bernadette wasn't going to sit back and let the world and men of the office pass her by. She wasn't satisfied with a steady line. She wanted to rise. Upward mobility. Why should she remain stagnant while the rest of her colleagues did not?

Bernadette filled out and signed the paperwork showing the measly raise and bearing the word TEMPORARY in bold. Then handed it back, her heart thudding against her ribs. She'd done it. One rung higher, and she wasn't going to stop climbing now, or stop encouraging other women to climb too.

Not even Sarah's glowering could keep Bernadette from grinning as she returned to the copyediting department and began gathering up her pencil holder, nameplate, papers, and a picture of Frank in a bow tie from her desk.

One of her male coworkers swiveled in his chair, ankle crossed casually over his knee, elbows resting on the arms of his chair, fingers steepled. "Canned, huh?"

Bernadette looked him right in the eye. "No. Promoted."

"How?" Greene shot forward on his chair so hard he nearly tumbled. "Wall's not here."

"He offered yesterday."

Greene frowned. "And you just now decided to let us know?"

Bernadette hated the fact that instead of being congratulated, she was being censured, as if accepting the position was wrong. "I didn't realize you were my keeper."

"I'm the most senior of senior copy editors."

"And?"

He bristled, and she decided to ignore him. Greene was not happy she'd been promoted, that much was obvious, and now it would appear she'd have more than one naysayer to deal with.

"Listen, Greene, I'm not stepping on your toes by being promoted. You're still the most *senior* senior copy editor. Whether it had been me or someone else, the desk was going to be filled."

Greene grumbled something under his breath that sounded like *damn woman*. Bernadette chose to pretend she hadn't heard. She was not giving him the power to put a damper on this monumental moment.

She carried her bundle to her new desk and began setting up. Next, she transferred the contents of her drawers until she'd cleared out her old desk and the new one looked thoroughly "Bernadette."

She sat down, admiring her handiwork and then the view from her new desk. The whole office lay in front of her, and she could see through the glass walls into the space Sarah occupied. It wasn't that different a view than her last, but it felt different.

For the first time that day, Bernadette smiled with genuine glee.

Chapter Eleven

BERNADETTE ARRIVED FOR HER SECOND morning as temporary senior copy editor thirty minutes early, raring to go. Raring to go and praying that Wall would be at his desk.

He was. And he scowled at her through the glass of his office door the moment her black pumps crossed the threshold into the copyediting department. She imagined that beneath his desk, one foot pawed the ground with aggressive force. His bull eyes narrowed on the red tones of her blouse, but rather than jump out of the way, she was going to face his charge head on.

"I accepted the position yesterday, at personnel. The personnel manager told me I could go ahead and move."

"*I'm*"—he stabbed his chest for emphasis—"your manager."

Bernadette drew in a long breath, trying not to let him see that he was ruffling her feathers.

"My apologies, sir. I was under the impression that since the position had been offered and you were out sick, I could accept via the manager in human resources."

"And who gave you that impression?" His hands were on his hips. He was trying to intimidate her. Making his arms bigger like animals in the wild. Or a teacher she'd had in primary school who'd like to stand big and lean over students when reprimanding them.

"Personnel, sir." She wasn't about to throw Graham under the proverbial bus.

Wall grimaced as if he realized that it was his own fault for having informed them to begin with, and that his plan to make her feel small wasn't working. He'd have to try harder to rattle her cage.

"Well, get to it, then. You've got a lot to prove."

She wasn't going to let his attempts at making her feel unworthy triumph. Wall was clearly intimidated by her initiative, and especially after how she'd corrected his own prized project. And she couldn't blame him. There was a measure of risk in having marked up the book, but it had paid off. Now it was time for her to be prudent.

"Yes, sir." She kept her voice even. Then before he had a chance to yell at her some more, she turned away from him and went to her desk where there was a fresh stack of manuscripts.

Looking at the massive pile, she guessed there'd probably be no lunch in the park today. And she bet by the time the clock ticked five, she was going to be cross-eyed.

"Challenge accepted," she whispered to herself.

Arranging the stacks of manuscripts in order, she took up her red pencil, threaded a piece of paper into the typewriter so she could create a style sheet, and then started marking up the pages. Every return of the carriage to start a new line of type was a victory.

The office slowly filled as she put circles on commas, drew a caret like an upside-down V when she needed to indicate an insertion for a missed word. She was aware of her male coworkers leaning against each other's desks and watching her as she marked a paragraph symbol for a new line.

She was also keenly aware of their lack of work, but she couldn't dwell on their shortcomings or the fact that they were quite possibly rooting against her. The stack on her desk wasn't going to edit itself.

Even when Mr. Wall came over, circling her desk like a shark biting and bumping in an attempt to weaken her, she kept going. Marking paragraph symbols where needed, correcting spelling. Eventually he got bored and went back to his office.

As she suspected, at lunch she didn't have time to stop working. Or eat.

Someone put on the radio, listening to the news. And for once she was thankful to hear Mr. Wall bark: "Turn that crap off. I'm tired of hearing about the Cold War."

A cup of coffee appeared on her desk around one o'clock, and she wasn't sure who put it there. But she appreciated how it took the edge off the gnawing hunger she felt thanks to missing her daily sandwich. By three o'clock, she couldn't sit any longer. The coffee meant she needed a restroom break or her bladder would burst. Leaping from her chair, she rushed to the bathroom.

Sarah entered the bathroom as Bernadette washed her hands. The secretary approached the sink, leaning close to the mirror and putting on lipstick—the pink one Bernadette had suggested.

"Sick?" Sarah's tone scratched along Bernadette's nerves like an irritating particle stuck between her teeth. "Woman troubles?"

"Nope." Bernadette stared, daring Sarah to say what she really wanted to.

"Oh. The way you rushed in here, I thought you might have found yourself in trouble…" Sarah's voice trailed off, her scratch not having the reach she'd intended.

"Needed to use the toilet." Bernadette grabbed a towel, wiping away the water and Sarah's questions. How dare she insinuate that Bernadette was knocked up?

Sarah looked disappointed, as if she'd wanted Bernadette to be in a position that would ruin not only her career efforts but also her reputation. While she would have liked to stay and find out exactly what was going on in the secretary's mind, Bernadette needed to get back to work.

Greene, Evans, and Marshall were standing over her desk, their backs to her. Shoulders shaking as they laughed over something they were looking at.

"Can I help you?" Her voice held the same bite as her elementary school principal's.

The men jumped back but had the audacity not to look guilty when they met her gaze.

"Did you need something?" Bernadette marched over to her chair and pulled it out. Putting space between herself and the nosy cretins.

"Just admiring your style sheet," Greene said with a smirk.

Bernadette narrowed her eyes and looked down. The page was full of her notes on character names, dates, places, the usual style-sheet verbiage, but at the bottom, something had been added.

Queen B has big juicy balls.

Bernadette frowned. They were trying to embarrass her. Hurt her. Make more work for her. As if that was going to make her toss her red pencil and run out of the building. But she'd grown up with a brother, so she was largely immune to such juvenile hijinks. Plus, it wasn't the first time she'd heard of the word *balls*. In fact, Ben had written *balls* all over her diary once. Even drew a graphic and disturbing picture.

A few days ago, Bernadette would have just sat down, tossed the style sheet aside, and started over. She would have allowed their asinine games to eat away at her, but she'd not do or say anything about it.

Not today. Bernadette was about to break another rule. The rule that said women weren't supposed to talk back. Were supposed to keep calm and quiet.

"Gentlemen," she said coolly. "It appears that one of you must have followed me into the bathroom to catch a glimpse of my big juicy balls. Do I need to let personnel know about that?"

Their mouths fell open, and Bernadette couldn't help feeling a little smug about that. Deep down, they knew their behavior was not only childish but also against company policy. They might be able to get away with it with someone else, and over the years there were several things she'd looked the other way at, but this? No. She'd have to retype the entire style sheet. And if she was going to keep her job here, they needed to understand they couldn't intimidate her.

"What seems to be the problem?"

Bernadette smiled at Mr. Wall, who was looming out of his office door.

"Oh, Greene here just volunteered to retype my style sheet since he got a stain on it." She looked at Greene, daring him to say otherwise, and watched as Greene's face waffled back and forth about whether he should bet on his friendship with Wall in that moment or just suck it up.

Greene grumbled something, took the paper out of the type-writer, and stomped back to his desk.

"Get back to work. Books don't copyedit themselves," Wall grumbled.

The other two stared for a moment at Bernadette. Then clearly decided it was better to keep their mouths shut and simply whirled on their polished shoes.

The rest of the day didn't go much better. Every time she walked past someone's desk the men would "shh" each other loudly, and then cough out "Grammarian," as if it were a bad word and they didn't want her to hear that they'd said it.

But at least no one had the "juicy balls" to touch her style sheets—or anything on her desk, for that matter.

And Grammarian wasn't an insult. After all, Eleanor Gould Packard at the *New Yorker* magazine was the Grammarian because of her genius with words and her understanding of language and writing.

Bernadette decided to own the moniker. And to show her pride in it, she sewed the word in silver sequins onto a new pink headband, wearing it to work like a crown. Greene, Marshall, and Evans stopped coughing it out after that, especially when she looked them right in the eyes, daring them to keep going.

There was power in this newfound confidence, even if she still sometimes had to rush to the bathroom just to breathe.

Of course, Wall didn't make her job any easier. But she never expected that he would. Every morning when she came in, there was another, higher stack of manuscripts on her desk. Piles so tall it looked like paper trees had been planted.

But instead of being daunted or surrendering to Wall's obvious desire for her to complain or, worse still, fail, Bernadette pulled out her new chair, stuck a new piece of paper in her typewriter, plucked out a fresh red pencil, and started marking pages. She was not giving up. Not allowing herself to fail.

But they didn't stop trying.

On Wednesday morning, her chair was missing and she walked around the office trying not to stomp her feet until a janitor walked through the door scratching his head and looking puzzled.

"Is there a Miss Swift present?"

"Here, sir," she said.

"I believe I've found something in the janitor's closet that belongs to you, ma'am."

"Let me guess, a chair?" Her voice sounded tired even to her own ears.

He cocked his head, eyebrows shooting up a little in surprise. "How did you know?"

"Lucky guess." Bernadette offered him a smile, reminding herself that it hadn't been he who had taken it.

As she exited the room to retrieve the chair the janitor so kindly brought out to her, a sputter of laughter trailed behind her. *Immature lickspittles.*

But it appeared the jokes weren't done yet. When she returned from lunch and tucked her paper into her typewriter, she started to press the keys, glancing at her notes as she typed, only to look up and see that the paper was blank despite her having written at least several lines.

"What now…" she muttered under her breath.

Bernadette peered closer. Punched a key. A depression of a B appeared on the paper but no ink to go with it.

Gritting her teeth, she opened the top compartment of her typewriter to a noticeably missing ink ribbon. Of all the juvenile…

"Has anyone seen my ink ribbon?" Evans asked.

Bernadette started, spinning around in her chair to see that the entire office was missing their ink cartridges. The murmur of irritation and accusations rose. But she remained noticeably silent. Uncertain if this was a prank on her or someone else.

"What's all the racket?" Wall barged from his interior office, glowering at them.

"All our ink's gone missing." Marshall leaned back in his chair looking a bit too pleased with himself. "I say, Miss Swift, what's that in your drawer?"

"What?" Bernadette glanced down to see that her bottom desk drawer was partially ajar. She hadn't noticed that when she came in.

Before she could open it, Wall bulldozed his way forward and yanked it open to reveal a dozen ink cartridges.

"Really, Miss Swift? A prank? I expected better of you."

Her eyes bulged, anger and embarrassment fighting for a place to be first in line. "I didn't take them."

Over Wall's shoulder, Marshall grinned just like the Cheshire cat in *Alice's Adventures in Wonderland*.

"Our timeline doesn't have room for games, Miss Swift. You, of all our copy editors, should know that." Wall dismissed her by turning around to head back to his office.

"Yeah, Miss Swift." Evans's voice was full of sarcasm as he snatched one of the ink ribbons, as if she were the mastermind behind such an elaborate scheme.

On instinct she gathered the guts to spew an insulting retort.

To call him every name in the book. Wanting to blast him with her grasp of language and his inferior intellect. But, lowering herself to his level, to all their levels, wasn't the way to get back.

So, instead she stood and faced her crowd of tormentors and resorted to a more mature parlance. "Gentlemen, I must apologize. I had no idea that I was so intimidating, and that you are all so timorous in my presence that you must antagonize me with such bellicose behavior. I'll step out a minute to allow you to regain your bearings."

The silence that followed was a sweet gift indeed—and continued for the remainder of the day.

Bernadette arrived at work thirty minutes early on Thursday, a new start time that she'd set for herself, if only to thwart any pranks. This was of course dismaying to Frank, so she'd promised him a long meander through Central Park this weekend. If she was the last to leave and the first to arrive, how much could they really do?

As she approached her desk, it was immediately obvious someone had been messing with her things. Her pink pencil holder with a "B" stenciled on the front was completely devoid of red pencils, of which she kept a large stash.

She glanced around the still-empty office.

After yesterday, she supposed she should have expected retaliation. But there'd been a significant part of her that hoped it was all over.

Every desk but hers had a full supply of editing pencils. She couldn't help picturing someone taking her pencils and redistributing them among the other copy editors. One for you, and one for you... But a look at a few of the pencil holders found none that she could identify as her own. And she would have known them, had she seen them because each of her pencils had "B" carved in the top. It was a brand of pencil she'd always loved to use because she'd been known as Queen B for so many years. Everyone else used what they were supplied, but she was partial to the B pencils, as they had a softer lead that seemed to stick better to the paper and not smear.

She stared out the window of the office toward Sarah's desk. The secretary wasn't in the office yet either. Bernadette had a sneaking suspicion Sarah was in on this. That wasn't a very charitable thought, but at the same time, Sarah had proven many times over that she was most definitely not on Bernadette's side.

Before she could change her mind, Bernadette marched over to Sarah's desk. No red pencils. But Sarah would be smart enough not to leave them in plain view.

Bernadette opened the first drawer on the left. No pencils. But the drawer to the right held all twenty. Bernadette stood staring at the pile, feeling devastated in a way she hadn't initially when she'd realized they were missing. Actually, seeing her belongings there, maliciously taken, was crushing.

As she contemplated what to do, letting out the breath she'd been holding, Bernadette decided to take back her pencils. To dare Sarah to come find her and accuse her of going through her desk. That would be rich.

Not wanting to be caught staring in the secretary's drawer, she extracted her pencils, closed the drawer, and went back to her desk to get started on her first book.

Sarah arrived. Bernadette shot a few glances her way, but Sarah avoided looking in her direction. As guilty as a child who'd emptied the cookie jar and still had chocolate smeared on their face.

Bernadette decided to force the issue—another rule broken.

She had retreated from her paper mountains to face the woman head on. "Good morning, Sarah."

Still, Sarah wouldn't make eye contact. Instead, she kept busy shuffling the papers on her desk. "Morning."

"I was missing a few things from my desk this morning."

Sarah's hands froze as she set a file folder down. Then she whipped her gaze upward, glaring defiantly.

"Are you accusing me of something?" Her tone was shrill, defensive.

Bernadette remained cool, casual. Even folded her manicured hands in front of her. "I'm just wondering if you saw anyone poking around."

Sarah stared at her, right in the eyes. It appeared that Sarah felt a need to pile on with the others in the office. "I'm not a guard. Ask Mr. Towne to come watch your desk."

Bernadette smiled. "Maybe I will. He's very good at his job." She chose that moment to take the red pencil behind her ear and twirl it between her fingers.

Bernadette watched, a sadness creeping over her as Sarah's eyes grew as large as dinner plates. The secretary pressed her lips together and yanked open her drawer, saw the pencils were missing, and slammed it shut again. She didn't return her gaze to Bernadette, instead stared straight ahead.

"Is there anything else, Miss Swift?" Sarah asked coldly.

"I certainly hope not."

By lunch, Bernadette needed a breath of fresh air, and she was starving. She'd been skipping lunch all week, and her stomach was finally rebelling. Besides, no lunch is not a good long-term strategy. If she starved to death, the boneheads would win.

Too bad she hadn't packed anything. Then she reminded herself living and working in the city meant there was always food to be had. Just not one of the hot dogs Graham liked to eat. Bernadette grabbed her purse, making sure to tuck pencils inside, and hurried to the elevator.

In the lobby downstairs Melanie waved. "How is it going?"

"Could be better."

"I'm sorry. If it makes you feel better, someone walked through the lobby today with dog poo on their shoe and told me as an afterthought."

"What?" Bernadette glanced around the polished marble floor half expecting to see brown smudges.

"You'd think they'd have noticed they smelled like shit outside and tried to clean it off." Melanie rolled her eyes and gave an annoyed flip of her lustrous hair, which bounced right back into place.

"At least they didn't ask you to clean their shoes," Bernadette offered.

"A blessing. You wouldn't believe the things I see. No one notices a receptionist, but I see it all." She pointed at her eyes and then outward. "Sorry, not you, sir."

Bernadette looked over her shoulder. An executive was shaking his head and tightening his tie as if the action would make him stand taller. Then he moved past her and out of the building.

"Your stories are always good for a laugh." Bernadette grinned.

Melanie wiggled her brows. "I aim to please."

"I'm going in search of a sandwich. Can I get you anything?"

"No, thank you. I packed." She tapped a tin lunch box on her desk.

Half a block away, Bernadette popped into a deli. As she read the menu, she felt eyes on her. Glancing up, she spotted Graham at the register paying for a sandwich.

Well, it appeared the world was against her today.

Chapter Twelve

"YOU FOLLOWING ME, SWIFT?" GRAHAM'S voice parted the crowd of lunchtime talking heads until it reached her.

Of all the places. "I thought you were a hot dog fan, Mr. Reynolds."

"Someone told me I need to try new things." He held up a carryout bag, evidence of his culinary change of heart.

She smiled as he approached, the air in the too-small deli growing tomato bisque thick. "What did you get?"

"The club."

"Hmm." She glanced back toward the menu, already knowing what she wanted but needing the momentary break from eye contact.

"Not a club fan?"

Bernadette returned her gaze to his, her pulse quick and jagged enough to chop up a head of lettuce. "Not a ham fan."

"Who doesn't like ham?" Graham had the cheek to look shocked.

"I had a pet pig growing up. Amaranth, and I swore to him I'd never eat him or any of his kin. I'm thinking the chicken salad. With a pickle."

"No pet chickens?"

"Not since she tried to peck out Amaranth's eyes. My sworn enemies."

Graham's smile was a slice of layered chocolate cake, devious, decadent, and definitely bad for her.

Bernadette turned away from him to order her lunch, hoping he'd take the hint and leave, but there he was, hovering by the door.

"Eating in your usual spot?" Graham held the door open for her and they walked out together onto the busy sidewalk, jostling for space on the concrete.

"I should eat at my desk." She glanced at the Lenox & Park building down the block, stress from the number of pages she still needed to copyedit gnawing at her.

"You might get your pages dirty. And nobody does their best work on an empty stomach. Might as well feed the brain."

"True." She headed to one of the benches outside their building. They might be friendly, but she didn't want him to get used to eating at her favorite bench. Mostly because she was afraid she might think about him when she was there, and that was supposed to be her meditating bench.

"Mind if I join you?"

"Suit yourself." They settled on a random bench. Bernadette made sure to put some distance between them, not wanting to have people talking.

"Want to talk about it?" Graham unwrapped his sandwich and bit down, crunching on the toasted bread.

"Is it that obvious?" She plucked a chunk of chicken that was in danger of falling out from between her two slices of whole wheat and popped it into her mouth.

"Even if it wasn't. I've got an idea what the old-boys network at Lenox & Park is capable of."

"That's been made very clear to me as well, thanks to this promotion. Yesterday, after I went to the restroom, I came back to find the ink ribbon missing from my typewriter. At the start of the week, someone wrote something vulgar on my style sheet, then my chair disappeared. And this morning, all my B pencils were missing."

"Wow. Taking it back to grammar school."

"I must have been luckier in grade school than I am now. I missed that foul phase. Maybe now is my time to make up for it. Except this job was only offered on a temporary basis. If they can make me screw it up…"

"They can't, Swift. Don't let them break your bal…spirit."

"Thanks." She took a bite of pickle to hide her smirk.

"Want me to warn Wall to get his people's act together?"

Bernadette shook her head so hard her headband nearly flew off. The last thing she needed was Graham stepping in to save the day. "No. No. He'd probably take them all out for drinks, and I'm hoping when they see I'm not ruffled, they just give up."

"It's true that bullies thrive on reaction. But they also just thrive on the power trip. If it doesn't stop, let me know. I want to help."

Bernadette considered informing Graham that the word *bully* originally stemmed from the 1530 Middle Dutch word for *boele*, which actually meant "lover," and was translated into English to mean "sweetheart." Fascinating how a few hundred years changed things.

They parted ways outside the building doors, with Graham needing to meet an author and Bernadette trying hard not to drag her feet as she walked inside. An effort helped by the wave she got from Melanie as she headed for the packed elevator.

The copyediting department was empty. Presumably everyone else was still at lunch.

Bernadette breathed a sigh of relief. At least she'd get some time to herself to work without feeling like a curiosity on display. But as she got closer to her desk, her relief faded and then evaporated.

Someone had spilled coffee all over the pages she'd worked on this morning. Brown seeped into the paper, warping it in waves, and smearing the typed ink into an unreadable mess. The only thing not smeared was the red pencil markings.

Insert an apostrophe.

Direct to you

'ly

Check dates here. Encyclopedia says...

Tears stung Bernadette's eyes. Until this moment, when her red pencil shone out through the brown liquid and smeared typed ink, Bernadette had been determined to keep her cool. But this was the last straw. Hours of work ruined.

Thank goodness no one was here to witness her unraveling. That would have been the rancid icing on a rotten cake. The very thing they wanted to relish.

"Oh, you're back."

Bernadette whipped around to face Sarah. Never show

emotion in the workplace. She was breaking her own rules left and right. She angrily wiped tears from her face, taking in the startled expression of her secretary, a wad of towels in her hand.

Guilt pinched the corners of Sarah's eyes, and she nervously fingered the red scarf at her neck.

"You did this?" Bernadette's voice came out a rasp, and the ache of being stabbed in the back by the only other female in the department was overwhelming.

Sarah grimaced and offered a small shrug. "It was an accident. I was putting...something back."

"Oh, something else missing from my desk?" Bernadette's hands fisted at her sides. She'd been so busy with her copyedits that she hadn't noticed what else was missing. "Let me guess... You found whatever it was exactly where you put them in *your* desk."

Sarah swallowed, her mouth a thin line, but at least she didn't have the audacity to lie this time.

"You know, I get enough flak from the men in this office. It would be nice to have some support from the only other woman in our department. But instead, you're part of the problem. Why? What do you get out of it?"

"You—"

Bernadette held up her hand. "No. Not me. *You.* What do *you* get out of it?"

Sarah didn't have an answer.

"We don't have the same job. I'm not taking anything from you by getting a promotion. I earned that spot. Why would you want me gone?"

Sarah flicked her gaze toward Greene's desk.

"Oh, I see. Boyfriend put you up to it." Bernadette narrowed her eyes, and pointedly regarded Sarah's empty ring finger. "You know he's married right?"

Sarah thrust the towels at her, chin up obstinately. "I was going to clean it up."

"Be my guest." Bernadette swept her hand toward the mess, then stood back, arms crossed over her chest. No way was she going to take those towels and capitulate to Sarah's mulishness.

"I'm going to get another copy of this book, since you ruined this one." Thank God there was one. The only thing that was going to save her here was that they had copies of the manuscript held in archives just in case. "When I get back, I expect my desk to be the way I left it before you started doing your boyfriend's dirty work. And by the way, if he's asking you to do that stuff, you realize he's a bad guy, right? He's not going to leave his wife for you. Even if he does, who's to say he won't do the same to you? Respect yourself more."

Bernadette stormed toward the elevator, fuming all the way down to the basement and muttering to the walls as she went.

"Miss Swift." Mr. Towne sat up a little straighter when he saw her, a grin on his wrinkled face. "Glad to see you back here. Loved the cookies, and my wife, Mabel, said thank you."

Some of the anger ebbed at seeing his face and at his words. "My pleasure. I'll bring more next time I make a batch."

"You're a doll."

More like a rag doll today. Bernadette moved past him into the archives and located the copy of the damaged manuscript. Then she made her way to the mail room, which also doubled as the copy machine room, using the Xerox to copy the pages that Sarah had ruined, and trying hard not to curse as the machine felt the need to throw a tantrum in that moment. Fortunately, she was able to slap it back into submission. She returned the original to the archives and then was back at her desk, which looked neat and tidy, the way she liked.

The rest of the day went suspiciously smoothly.

Sarah avoided her. That, Bernadette had expected. But surprisingly, so did the rest of her coworkers.

Their snubs didn't bother her. They were less potentially destructive to her career and besides, Eleanor Roosevelt, whom Bernadette met on an internship during her time at Barnard, once said in an interview that "A snub is the effort of a person who feels superior to make someone else feel inferior. To do so, he has to find someone who can be made to feel inferior." Later, the quote was paraphrased to: "No one can make you feel inferior without your consent."

Bernadette had always found the quote to be inspiring—and wrote it in her quote notebook. To think that a person could only be brought down if they allowed themselves to be was a notion to live by. Except that in reality, it was easier said than done. She realized that she'd let all the nonsense this week from her superior-feeling coworkers bring her down. That had to end. Now.

Drawing in a deep breath, she let it out slowly as she flipped the pages of the new copied pages and rewrote her notes. She wasn't going to let them get to her anymore. Because Eleanor was right.

Queen B, the Grammarian, wasn't about to just sit back and take their crap. She was going to do something about it.

Melanie shouldn't have to deal with everyone's shitty messes. Sarah shouldn't feel she had to sleep with someone in a superior position just to get by. Her mother should be able to write fashion articles and not work herself to the bone from sunup to sundown. And Bernadette shouldn't have to worry about the stupid pranks so she could just do her damn job.

After she made the necessary copyedits on the page, her brain started to grow a little sluggish. Already this had been a long day. Normally, she would have gotten a coffee for a pick-me-up. But, Bernadette decided, she was going to be boycotting coffee from now on. No better time than the present to become a tea drinker.

Using the electric kettle, she heated some water and placed an Earl Grey into her mug. As it steeped, she wondered if the strength of it would help her get through the rest of the day. Back at her desk, she slipped the notebook from her purse that she kept her favorite quotes in. Sometimes the literary love bombs helped her in moments like this. She flipped the pages until she came across a quote from Eleanor Roosevelt that made her smile. "A woman is like a tea bag; you never know how strong it is until it's in hot water."

If only she could write the former first lady a letter now and let her know how much inspiration she was leaving behind for women. Perhaps the best way to honor her would be to spread her message.

In the meantime, she added a teaspoon of honey to her tea, the same as she planned to do with each smile dispensed to her coworkers. After all, kill them with kindness was an adage to which she adhered.

Chapter Thirteen

FRANK

I'M RACING OVER A FIELD. A flash of red-gold fur fleeing in front of me. The frantic warbling of chickens behind me. Nobody messes with my chickens—unless it's me. That fox isn't going to make an Old Yeller out of me—

"Frank?"

I jolt out of the dream to see Mrs. Morris in the doorway. "Are you quite all right, dear?"

I stretch and shake the cobwebs of sleep from my head. She asks me that every time I nap. I'm aces, just exhausted from my early-morning rounds of the neighborhood. I cock my head to the side as she enters. She sinks to the floor, smelling of peppermint and toast, and strokes a hand over my head. "My Wallace had a dog when we were first married. Her name was Amy. Probably as big as your head. She used to dream like you. Running, whimpering. I wish I knew what it was you were chasing."

I wish I could tell her about the foxes. The chickens. I wonder if Mrs. Morris has ever ventured beyond this building and the block she walks me up and down. As soon as we get to the corner she stops, whirls around, and marches back. Like there's an invisible fence there she can't cross. My girl told me Mrs. Morris has agoraphobia—that being outside on the streets mostly is terrifying for her, and that our landlady is grateful to me for forcing her out into the city air.

"Want to come have lunch with me?" *Scratch, scratch* behind the ears.

I glance toward the window. It's midday. My girl won't be home for hours, and I'd much rather spend the time with Mrs. Morris than alone. My patrol this morning was fruitful and draining—some fools messing with the paperboy. They called the boy a chicken-livered skunk, which he didn't understand because his English isn't that great. But when I assessed, he was most certainly human, so maybe his English didn't have anything to do with it.

Besides, I need to have another parlay with her cat. Mrs. Morris and I have a deal that suits us both. I stand up, and she uses my back to haul herself up off the floor. She's slim and brittle, so I stand firm to let her. She doesn't bother with my leash, no need. I protect Mrs. Morris just like I do my girl.

We walk down the stairs to her apartment, and she takes out her key with hands that are veiny and spotted. As soon as the door creaks open, I catch the scent of her cat—Mr. Crumbs. He lets out a retched noise that is half meow, half screech. The brown and gold of his splotchy fur is puffed out.

"Oh, Crumbly, do be polite to our guest."

He hisses at me. I grin as best I can. He hisses again.

I worry he may have forgotten our pact.

Mrs. Morris pats my head and goes into her tiny kitchen. I stalk forward, as slow as possible to Mr. Crumbs where he perches like a king on the back of an upholstered chair. Scratches on the wooden legs and tears in the fabric prove he has no manners.

I sit, big enough that our eyes are at level. I stare into two wide green eyes with black slits in the center that remind me briefly of a snake I encountered once stealing eggs from my chickens. Those eyes send a message: *Get out and stay away from my housekeeper, drooling peasant.*

Don't you remember me? I mean you no harm. I have come for a cookie. The ones she doesn't let you have.

Hiss.

I put a paw up on the arm of the chair, a peace offering. *We can share the cookie. Cookie, cookie, cookie.*

Mr. Crumbs stares at me a long while, the slits of his feline eyes widening and shrinking as he contemplates. Then he smacks me in the face—a vicious love tap. With this message, I know he has remembered our delicious deal.

"Oh, Crumbly, that's not very nice." Mrs. Morris rushes from the kitchen, a delicious cookie in hand. Not a dog cookie. But a human one. Gingersnaps with caramel icing that she picks up from the corner store once a week. "Here you go, dear."

Mrs. Morris gives me a cookie in apology. I chomp, decadent flavors bursting on my tongue, and deliberately drop a crumb on the floor in payment. Mr. Crumbs lets out another screeching *mrowww* and leaps onto my back, then to the ginger and icing gift on the floor.

Mission complete.

Chapter Fourteen

EXHAUSTION WORMED ITS WAY THROUGH every limb as Bernadette climbed into bed, the old springs creaking—a relic of her grandparents. The mattress bounced as Frank leaped up to join her. There was a great effort in lifting her hand to rub his overlarge head, and even more of a labor to lift *The Feminine Mystique*, which sat waiting for her on the polished walnut night table.

As she had every evening this week, she looked forward to the dormancy of night, when the neighborhood quieted. With nostalgia, she pulled up the patchwork quilt her mother had made her from all of her favorite childhood dresses. The only sounds were an occasional taxi honking, followed by the hiss of a bus's breaks or the faint blow of the train's horn on the distant rail as it pulled into Penn Station, and Frank's steady breathing.

"Don't go all torpor on me, boy." Bernadette nudged Frank from his instant hibernation and cracked open the book, having read aloud the past couple of nights in hopes that would keep her awake.

Frank popped his head up, tongue rolling out as he panted a *yes*.

"All right, then, let's see… Where were we?" She pulled the bookmark from its spot and started to read about the roles and expectations of women in society. How the image of a housewife, of what a woman should want to be was a fabrication, exacerbated by the end of World War II, when women who'd gone out to work in factories and other typically male jobs were sent back home to the kitchen.

Bernadette had been so young during the war, but she did remember there being a time when her father was gone. He'd served in the Veterinarian Corps, and her childhood dog, Beau, had been retired from the trenches with honors, coming to live with them at the end of his service.

But how had her father's return affected her mother? Bernadette racked her brain but determined she'd just been too young to remember much.

A few seconds later—*or was it hours?*—she woke to being smothered. Glimpses of light peeking through the barrier. Something stuffed against her mouth.

Bernadette gasped for air, her breaths fluttering the pages of the book that had fallen on her face as she read. Not smothered after all. With a tired groan, she marked her spot and placed the book on her night table, pulling the chain on the porcelain hurricane lamp that had belonged to her mother before she was married.

She'd be lucky if she finished reading by the end of the month, but certainly not before the book club meeting. Flopping over on her side, she was rewarded with a slobbery lick on her cheek.

"Night, night, Frank."

In the daylight, walking over the New York Public Library's beaux arts marble floors—between palatial walls and columns, beneath ceilings that were works of art—was transformative. But the library's Astor Hall was lit only by four marble and gold-filigreed lamps so tall a ladder was necessary to change the light bulbs, so at night her pink ballet flats tapping on the wide majestic stairs were transcendental.

Inside the library was cold, so she was glad she'd opted for her black Audrey Hepburn cropped pants, a sleeveless pink turtleneck with matching cardigan, and a pink-and-white polka-dot silk scarf at her neck, with a matching headband holding back her bouffant, which hadn't wanted to bouff today.

Melanie had pulled up to Bernadette's apartment on her scooter—wearing a dress and heels—and tapped the rear seat for Bernadette to hop on. She'd clung to her friend as they zipped through city traffic, Melanie shaking her fist at more than one driver before they'd parked and entered the library through the side entrance reserved for the janitor.

They made their way to the room Penelope had commandeered for the evening, which was unsurprisingly filled with relics of Mary Shelley and her contemporaries.

"You made it." Penelope rushed forward, tugging Bernadette into an Estée Lauder Youth-Dew hug. "With how busy you've been at work, I didn't think you'd be able to come. And Melanie, I'm so glad to see you again. Let me introduce you both to the rest of the gals."

Beyond the three of them, about half a dozen other women were present, ranging from Bernadette's age to her mother's.

"Hi, I'm Ruth." Dressed in a simple royal-blue dress, her hair pulled back, she had a kind smile.

"Ruth is a law professor at Rutgers."

"About to be," Ruth said. "We start classes next month. And this is my friend Julie. We were at Columbia together."

Julie's grip was strong, her fingers stained with ink, which Bernadette could commiserate with. Before she could ask what it was Julie did, she was introduced to Georgie, a nurse, and Jenny, who worked with Penelope at Doubleday Publishing. Patty was the last to introduce herself. She glanced shyly around the group as she said hello. According to what Penelope had told Bernadette earlier, she'd actually spotted Patty at her neighborhood grocery store a few days ago, staring at the dime romance novels. Her husband had chastised her for reading "rubbish." When he wasn't looking, Penelope invited her to the book club.

"Who has finished the book?" Penelope asked as they all sat in upholstered chairs that had been gathered into a circle.

Four hands shot up right away, including Melanie's.

"And the rest, halfway?"

Everyone nodded. Bernadette had planned on finishing it, but work had been especially insane lately, and several nights when she'd intended to read, she'd ended up falling asleep before she'd even been able to crack the book open.

Penelope stroked the cover of the book on her lap as if it contained precious secrets. "I propose that we discuss the first half of the book tonight and save the second half for our next meeting in two weeks. It's that important."

No one objected. Everyone was eager and energized to dive in.

"Our previous feminist book was one of fiction. This time

around, we've chosen one of nonfiction. But if I'd be so bold as to make the claim that it is extremely important for us to be reading such a groundbreaking book. It's stirring up a lot of conversations, a lot of which are controversial, on the mystique of the ideal woman. Who we should want to be—and making us ask, 'Is this all?'"

Bernadette thought of her mother, waking every morning before dawn. Gathering eggs. Milking cows. Hanging laundry. Was that all? Was that really how she would begin every morning until her spine curved, and her fingers refused to cooperate, and each step was a labor in itself?

Patty raised her hand, and Penelope called on her to speak. "Has anyone else had to disguise the book? I took the paper cover off one of my cookbooks and put it over. My husband hates what he calls 'feminist rubbish.' I think the fact is he feels quite threatened by female intelligence."

There were more than a few nods, which shocked Bernadette. The only time she could remember hiding a book was when she'd snuck one of her mother's romance novels as a teenager.

"I took the cover off a child-rearing book so I could read it on my morning commute on the subway and on my lunch break." Georgie rolled her eyes. "Heaven forbid a bunch of people who've studied science see me reading a well-researched book on social reform and raising teenagers."

"Obstetricians might be out of a job," Penelope said, laughing.

"And me too, considering I'm a labor and delivery nurse." Georgie laughed. "Must have been self-preservation that made me do it."

"What about you?" Penelope asked Bernadette.

She shook her head, still mystified by other people feeling the need to censure one's reading material. "Frank doesn't care what I read as long as I give him treats."

"Oh, just like a man." Patty made the comment loudly as she smoothed a skirt that reminded Bernadette of one she'd worn to a sock hop in grammar school.

Bernadette laughed. "Frank is my dog, though he is a male dog."

That gave all of them a round of laughs.

Jenny cleared her throat. "My husband saw me reading it in the tub."

Everyone grew quiet. Quiet enough that Bernadette could make out the ticking of her watch. So quiet, as if everyone was holding their breath, waiting to hear what happened, and quiet in their concern for what that answer might be. "He asked me to read a passage aloud. I think he thought it might have been a sexy book by the title. I am an avid Harlequin novel reader."

"What did you read him?" Bernadette asked, the rest of them leaning closer for the answer.

"The line that reads: 'If the secret of feminine fulfillment is having children, never have so many women, with the freedom to choose, had so many children in so few years, so willingly. If the answer is love, never have women searched for love with such determination. And yet there is a growing suspicion that the problem may not be sexual, though it must somehow be related to sex. I have heard from many doctors evidence of new sexual problems between man and wife—sexual hunger in wives so great their husbands cannot satisfy it.'"

Mouths dropped, and if there'd been flies, they certainly

would have found a home. That quote was from a section of the book that Bernadette had yet to reach.

"What did he say?" Patty asked, near breathless, her hand at her throat.

"He asked if I was having my appetite satisfied." Jenny shrugged. "And then asked me questions about the book. He seemed genuinely concerned about the mystique of feminine ideals."

Bernadette glanced at Melanie, who had her head cocked as she eyed Jenny with curiosity.

"You're a lucky woman," Penelope said.

"Oh, Penelope, we all know your Victor probably would have said the same thing," Ruth chimed in.

Penelope smiled in answer.

"And what about the two of you? Are you married? Seeing anyone?" This question from Georgie was directed at both Bernadette and Melanie.

"I've had dinner with a man who wants to be my other half," Melanie said. "But I'm going to have to give him a few test questions, I think. And also, I'm not really sure I want to get married."

"What questions?" Bernadette asked. A latent curiosity unfurled, curling its finger, beckoning the hush-hush questions in her mind to be answered. What could be asked of a man to ascertain whether he was open and receptive to her choice of reading materials and a woman's place in society?

Melanie tapped her lip. "Hmm. Perhaps I'd start with his opinion on whether he would find it acceptable for his wife to work. I like to work and find it fulfilling."

"That's a good place to start," Patty said. "My husband says it wouldn't look good to his peers if I were working, so I quit my job. Well, more like I was let go after I got pregnant with our first. I used to work at an art gallery owned by Jane Bass, and I dabbled in a little painting myself. To be frank, I think my talent intimidated him. He always likes to be the most interesting person in the room, which doesn't leave space for anyone else."

Jane Bass! That was Mr. Bass's wife. Bernadette was about to mention it when Georgie leaned forward to Melanie. "Let's say you are working, and you both get home around the same time. Ask him which nights of the week he'd want to be in charge of dinner."

"And how many kids he wants." Patty wagged her finger. "I wanted two. Ended up with five. Don't get me wrong, I love them all. But that's managing a small business when you get to those numbers."

"And," Bernadette, thinking of her mother, added, "ask him how you will split the household chores."

That suggestion received several gasps. "That might be going a step too far," said Patty, her mouth turned down in disappointment. "My husband is entirely too busy for that."

"But isn't that exactly it?" Bernadette asked. "The book says itself that a woman feels the need to do everything. That in today's society, she can't seem to find satisfaction until she's made home-made bread, cleaned the entire house, raised eight children to be perfect human beings, ironed the shirts, kept her body in shape, is always presentable and smiling, and has dinner on the table at six o'clock sharp. And if she wants to work, she has to do all of that and maintain her job. It's impossible unless her husband shoulders half the burden."

Patty took that moment to toss out a jibe, "Wow, Penelope, you didn't tell me you invited Betty Friedan herself to the meeting."

The group grew silent, and Bernadette felt the sharp sting of the comment as if Patty had taken extra-sharp scissors to her normally thick skin. She wasn't sure how to respond in a way that wouldn't exacerbate the situation. But fortunately, she didn't have to, as Penelope took that moment to clap her hands down on her knees before she spoke.

"If I had, would you be turning your nose up at her like you are now? Other women are part of the problem. Expecting each other to excel and achieve this feminine mystique that Mrs. Friedan is trying to uncover for us all. Bernadette was just bold enough to say it."

"She's not married. She couldn't possibly understand." Apparently, Patty was digging her Miss Wonderful kitten heels—and her boorish comments—into the wooden floor.

"I think because she's not married yet is exactly the reason we need to be having this discussion," Georgie said. "We need to have the opinions of women no matter their age or marital status. We are all affected. Besides, Mrs. Friedan said that no woman gets an O from mopping the floor, and we might as well start spreading that message to women before they get married, right?"

There was a murmur of agreement from the other ladies present.

Bernadette shifted in her chair, crossing one leg and then the other. But it wasn't physically that she was uncomfortable, rather emotionally—and a little embarrassed. She'd never heard women speak so openly about sex before. And it wasn't as if she didn't know what sex was. There had been the heated relationship during her internship. And she'd had a scare when her period was late, fortunately only by a few days.

The room was charged with energy, and when she looked at Penelope, Bernadette saw she was grinning wide, while Melanie was staring at Patty like she'd like to toss her into a mixing bowl and whip her up into a meringue.

"This is exactly the kind of lively discussion I was hoping this book would produce." Penelope's voice was as giddy as Frank on muffin-making day. "We should all feel free to share our opinions, no matter how contrary. It's conversations like these that get things done."

Patty half smiled and touched her hair. But beneath her smile, Bernadette could sense a subtle shift. If only they could get that shift moving across every female in the city, the state—the world. A ripple churning into a wave.

"I didn't mean to offend," Bernadette said. "And it's true I'm not married. But I have observed my mother and father's relationship. And she is the epitome of just what Mrs. Friedan is talking about. Working from sunup to sundown and never asking for help. And it's not just at home. I get asked to make coffee all the time at work, and that's not my job. I'm a copy editor. If a woman isn't satisfied in her life outside the bedroom, what guarantee is there that she will be when she does get between the sheets?"

"Me too—well with the coffee, that is," Penelope said in chorus with the other ladies, who also agreed that they were constantly asked to do things that didn't fall within the scope of their positions.

Patty eyed Bernadette with an intensely curious stare. "A copy editor?"

Bernadette nodded. "At Lenox & Park."

Patty's mouth fell open slightly, her cheeks turning a shade of pink that could have matched Bernadette's headband. "I didn't realize they had female copy editors."

"I'm the only one."

Patty's mouth thinned, but she didn't say anything else, and Bernadette continued the previous track of the conversation, not wanting to veer too much off the topic at hand.

"Even with the Equal Pay Act that was passed, we're not being compensated at the rate of our male counterparts, but we're being asked to do the same amount of work, and more often more, just to prove we belong there. At home we're asked to do more. More, more, *more*. It's exhausting, and probably why half of us haven't been able to finish reading this book." Bernadette sucked in a deep breath, having pushed all the words out while barely breathing.

"What should we do about it?" Melanie asked.

Bernadette shook her head. "Our disquisition is a start."

At Melanie's questioning look, Bernadette said, "These sorts of discussions and examinations can only bring light to the subject. Look how much we've learned already."

"Reading these books certainly helps," Ruth offered. "And I for one am glad to have my eyes open. You know when I went to law school, one of my professors actually asked me why I was there taking the place of a man. As if a woman didn't have a place in making the laws that would govern her life and those of her children. I'm grateful to have married a man who believed the opposite."

"Maybe there are more men out there who want their wives and daughters to shed the feminine mystique than we give them credit for. Right here in this small group alone, several of you have pointed out your husband's support of your pursuits." Bernadette thought of Graham, something that was happening with increasing frequency. He too was a man who supported a woman's choices.

Patty snorted. Her arms were crossed. Her ankles were crossed. Even her perturbed facial features seemed crossed. "And maybe there aren't."

"But maybe there are," Jenny said. "My husband, Penelope's husband, they aren't the only ones. We need to have more of an open mind. Maybe they can help us."

Bernadette uncrossed her legs and pressed her shoulder blades into the chair. The wooden slats against her spine seemed to pat her on the back, encouraging her to ask the question. She met the eyes of each woman present. "What are some things you've always wanted to do but couldn't?"

"I'm a runner," Georgie said. "I want to be able to go for a nice long run without men thinking my uterus is going to fall out from the exertion of it. I've had three kids. If pushing them out kept my uterus in place, no amount of jogging is going to do the trick."

Ruth chuckled. "Those vibrating exercise belts are more likely to have our uteruses falling out."

"I wanted to go to Yale, where my father went," Julie said. "Can you imagine if I'd been able to join the Skull and Bones order? Columbia wasn't half bad, but Yale… I would have loved that."

"I want to serve on a jury," Jenny said. "But rarely are women called up. Seems like a jury of one's peers is always male dominated."

"I don't want to be the default parent—you know, the one who is always responsible for the child," Ruth said. "I'll never become a Supreme Court justice if I am. Yet every time Jane needs something at school, they call me first. And, when I went to Sweden to do research for a project, I took her with me. No questions asked—and I loved every minute of it, don't get me wrong, but I was there working. Guaranteed if it had been my husband, sweet Jane would have been at home with me. And on that note, a judge at a trial I saw there was seven months pregnant and not in the least worried about the security of her job. That needs to change here."

"Seven months?" Georgie's eyes dilated the way her patients likely did when they were in labor. "I think as soon as I started to show they were trying to kick me out of the hospital. Afraid I'd spread the disease of pregnancy to the other nurses."

Ruth chuckled. "You'd think doctors would have a better understanding of how that works."

"Don't get me started," Georgie said with a laugh.

"I don't want to make dinner every night. For once, I want to be served and serviced with a smile. My husband is such a bull, just riding over me." Patty let out a frustrated huff. "I'd like to walk in the door, kick off my shoes, and pour an old-fashioned with no other worries for the night."

"I wish there was a birth control pill readily available," Melanie burst out as if she'd been holding the words in and couldn't stand it any longer. "Let's be realistic. If I'm going to marry my guy, I want to make sure I'm not stifled in the O department. And I don't want to get pregnant while I'm trying to figure it out. Nor do I want to depend on a condom."

Ruth started to clap, and soon, surprisingly, even Patty begrudgingly lent her applause to the boom.

Then Patty stood up. "I also want to get a divorce on the

grounds of not liking my husband. He's an asshole. And I can't. I have to stick with him for the rest of my life because he's not actually doing anything wrong. He's just a jerk."

Bernadette sat in the same shocked silence as the rest of the room. She hadn't realized how hard it was to get a divorce, but Patty was right. There was always a reason, someone at fault for doing something to the other. Though in Patty's case, it sounded like her husband was mean, and that certainly counted in Bernadette's mind. "And you should be able to. All of you. Have you talked to a lawyer? We have a couple right here." She hooked her thumb toward Ruth and Jenny.

"We'll chat after," Ruth said.

"Absolutely." Jenny nodded. "I think being an asshole is an excellent reason for telling him to hit the road."

Patty took a deep breath, a look of relief on her features. "Thank you."

"What about you, Bernadette?" Melanie asked. "What do you want?"

Penelope knew, but only because they'd shared late-night cocktails at Barnard where they split open their chests and pulled out their deepest, most secret wants. "I want to be the first female CEO of a major publishing house. And I want all of the things you guys want too. Why shouldn't we have that?"

A coded knock—*tappety tap-tap-tap*—sounded at the door.

Everyone stood, gathering their purses, books, and jackets to leave, while Bernadette and Melanie glanced at Penelope. Who was knocking?

"Ugh, that's Dave," Penelope explained. "He's the janitor who lets us in on his cleaning shift. Meeting adjourned."

"Wait." Bernadette held up her hand, hoping to keep everyone for a second longer. "I just want to say one more thing."

The ladies sat back down, watching her intently as if she held the answers to solve the world's problems.

"When union workers are unhappy, they strike. The suffragettes held strikes. We should strike."

"I'm not really the poster and shouting type." Patty made a face that matched the prickly personality she'd shown since Bernadette met her.

"Not an official strike," Bernadette explained, the ideas in her mind taking root and growing into a web, long and winding, and coaxing. "There's just too many things we want to solve to try and do it all at once. But many small rebellions can add up to big changes. One coffee cup *not* made at a time. One dinner not made at a time. One race you run at a time. One time you don't answer the school phone call or tell them to call your husband. Pick one thing you can do to start the change, and then do that thing one minute, hour, day at a time. I'm not making coffee anymore. And I'm not going to listen to my boss, who says I'm not qualified to keep my promotion. I'm fighting for myself one grammatical error at a time."

Melanie grinned, her thoughts melding with Bernadette's. "We're going to start a revolution."

"That's right, ladies." Bernadette suppressed a whoop and stood. She thrust her arm out, wiggling her fingers. "Who's with me?"

Eight hands landed on top of hers.

Chapter Fifteen

BERNADETTE'S SHOULDER SANK WITH THE weight of her purse. Not just the weight of one hundred sheets of pink Xerox paper, but the weight of responsibility every sheet brought with it. Determined to take a lunch break, no matter how short it was given her heavy workload, she carried the unwieldy purse down to the basement where the copy machine was and surreptitiously looked around.

The mail clerks were all at lunch, and the machine loomed before her like a centurion at a gate denying her entry. Battling with the Xerox machine was always a losing conflict, and this time she was going to be loading it with paper that didn't belong.

The longer she dawdled, the more likely she was to be caught. Though she was a stickler for the rules and was pretty sure copying a flyer she'd made to encourage women to join her strike probably went against policy, she was also willing to bend her conscience just this once. Well, in fact, it seemed like bending the rules was becoming sort of a habit for Bernadette. But all for a good cause.

What she was about to do was empowering for the women at Lenox & Park, and certainly in her new leadership position inspiring her colleagues was important, wasn't it?

Bernadette carefully loaded the pink paper into the machine, setting aside the white so there would be no mistake by the cranky device as to which paper to select. She placed her flyer on the glass, closed the lid, ticked the number of copies up to one hundred, then pressed the button.

The Xerox whirred to life, coughing and belching. Bernadette held her breath, ready for the battle that was surely to come. But there was no struggle. Instead, the Xerox started to make copies without balking, spitting one pink flyer out over and over again.

Bernadette's feet tapped the floor in a victory dance, which prompted her to look around and make sure no one had seen it. Easy breezy.

She picked up the first sheet and frowned, flipping it over. There was nothing on it. She checked the next and then next. Blank.

What on earth?

None of the sheets had the printed flyer on it. How? How? *How?*

She opened the lid and saw straight away that she had put the original flyer upside down and inadvertently copied the back of the paper instead.

My goodness, as if she needed more stress in this situation.

Quick as a whistle, Bernadette reloaded her one hundred pink sheets, flipping the flyer over, and pressed the Go button. *Second time's a charm, or at the very least, please let it not be a complete failure.* Her foot tapped. "Come on, come on," she crooned, stroking the Xerox, which made zero sounds.

"Please, work for me," she murmured.

Nothing.

She glanced at the side clock…nearly a quarter after noon. If she didn't hurry, the mail clerks would start funneling back in, and any secretaries who needed to ship something or copy a manuscript would be down here, and she'd be found out, drowning in a sea of pink paper. All efforts to entice her female comrades to rise futile.

Bernadette reset the machine and gave it a slap for good measure. She counted to ten, trying not to let the increased pounding of her heart accelerate with each ticking second. At last, the machine whirred itself to life and started to spit out pink paper complete with her words.

WOMEN IN THE WORKPLACE
Confessions of Office Buffoonery
And Occupational Malapropos
Caffe Shakespeare
Friday, 6:00 p.m.

Bernadette beamed down at the copies in her hands and then neatly tucked them and the original, into her purse. *Grand slam.* Hmm, what was the rugby equivalent of her baseball terminology? And why was she thinking at all of rugby—and, in essence, Graham?

Bernadette straightened her headband and punted Graham from her mind.

12:13.

She still had seventeen minutes.

Seventeen minutes to conquer, not squander. First stop, the break room on this level. She found the coffee filters and folded a pink flyer into the packet. Sadly, a woman would probably be the only one to find it—which was her purpose. It wouldn't do for the men to realize she was calling women to hash out their harassment.

She repeated this on every floor, tucking a folded pink sheet into the coffee filters. Then in the ladies' rooms, she taped the flyers to the back of the stall doors so women would notice as soon as they sat down.

Back at her desk by 12:33.

Three minutes late, and the only one back. She picked up her telephone and dialed Penelope at Doubleday.

"Did you do it?" she asked, keeping watch on the door.

"Yea, and the flyer's up on the bulletin board at the café. Mission accomplished."

Bernadette grinned. "All set here too."

"I can't wait for Friday."

"Me too." A flash of beige hurried across the corridor outside the office. Sarah. And in her hand was one of the pink flyers. "First hurdle incoming. Sarah must have found one of the flyers in the restroom."

"Oh no. Do you think she's going to report you?"

"She'll need to prove it's me first. But I have no doubt she's going to try to do something about it."

"Good luck."

Bernadette hung up the phone, picked up a red pencil, and pretended to work as she spied Sarah through lowered lids like a sentinel for women's rights. She expected to see her nemesis get on the elevator with the flyer and take it straight to personnel, where she would then get permission to start an investigation into who would be so bold and crass as to try to start a revolution.

But Sarah surprised her. Sarah surprised her when she didn't get on the elevator. Surprised her when she didn't even go near the elevator.

Instead, she marched up to her desk, looked around, and then opened the drawer, pulled out her purse, and did the most surprising thing of all: tucked the pink paper inside. Then she shut the drawer, glanced toward the office, and met Bernadette's gaze with an intensity that was incinerating.

Sarah frowned, then turned around, sitting at her desk and pulling out a piece of paper to load it into her typewriter as if nothing had happened. As if she hadn't just found the pink flyer that could possibly get Bernadette fired.

Too simple.

Why wasn't Sarah pushing through the door to accuse Bernadette of making the flyers?

Better yet, what did she intend to do with the flyer in her purse?

The questions burned inside Bernadette. It took an immeasurable amount of restraint to remain at her desk. And even more willpower to work on the manuscript in front of her. Her skin itched with the need to question Sarah, and every time Sarah moved, whether to answer the phone, or carry a file somewhere, Bernadette tensed, waiting for the onslaught.

By two o'clock, Sarah still hadn't said a word, and the men were all back from lunch. Someone asked about coffee, and Sarah made the pot, discreetly tucking the pink flyer from the filter packet into her pocket.

Discreetly.

Antithetical to all things Sarah. She normally pointed out each flaw that stuck in her craw. Discreet had not been a skill in the secretary's repertoire, even when she'd been sabotaging Bernadette.

Every transgression. Yet here she was, protecting the flyers as if she'd made them herself.

Unless she had some other ulterior motive. What if she planned to collect every flyer and destroy them?

Bernadette worried her lower lip until the skin started to peel. She pulled out her lipstick and reapplied.

As Sarah passed, she looked right at Bernadette, her features tense and strong, as if to say, *I know what you did, and I won't let you get away with it.*

Bernadette pasted a smile on her face, trying to impart friendship, but pretty sure she probably came off looking more like she'd eaten a rotten egg.

Sarah sniffed, her chin tilted in the air as she returned to her desk.

She knows it's me. There was no way she didn't.

For the rest of the day, Bernadette felt like she was waiting for the floor to drop out from underneath her. She'd had too much coffee and not enough food, and the jitters of so much caffeine made their way through her body, causing her to squirm and wriggle like a toddler who'd eaten too much birthday cake. What she needed was a good long walk with Frank and a delicious hot meal.

What she got was a moment with her notebook, pulling it open and reading a Jane Eyre quote, her breathing steadying. "I remembered that the real world was wide, and that a varied field of hopes and fears, of sensations and excitements, awaited those who had the courage to go forth into its expanse, to seek real knowledge of life amidst its perils."

That was exactly what Bernadette was doing. She was audacious, dauntless, a woman with a red-pencil sledgehammer about to break down syntax Walls.

The clock on the wall ticked sluglike toward five o'clock. Finally, only half a minute. *Thirty, twenty-nine, twenty-eight, twenty-seven…* The second hand inched toward twelve and her freedom.

Ding ding ding.

She jumped from her desk faster than Evans, Marshall, and Greene, grabbed her purse and lunch bag, and marched out the door. Unfortunately, right on the heels of Sarah. They stepped onto the elevator together, both of them staring straight ahead, doing their best to ignore the existence of the other. As the doors started to close, a familiar hand stuck through the gap—Graham.

Her stomach did a little flip as he joined them. Bernadette had never been so relieved to see the man in her life. But then she was immediately filled with unease, hoping she didn't let on in front of Sarah that she and Graham had become friendly. She didn't need the woman to have any more ammunition against her.

"Evening, ladies." His grin had the power to melt the ice on Sarah's personality.

Sarah smiled and touched her hair, although she didn't have a single strand out of place in her tight ballet bun.

"Evening," Bernadette said, glancing sideways at Sarah and wondering just how many pink flyers she had in her thick purse.

"Glad to have made it halfway through the week already." Graham loosened the tie at his throat.

"Mm-hmm."

"Have you ever been to Caffe Shakespeare?" Sarah asked him, and Bernadette stiffened. What was she up to?

"Can't say that I have. Though I heard there was an excellent Mary Shelley reading the other night."

"There was. Usually, some interesting things are happening there every weekend," Sarah said. "You should check it out if you're free."

"Not every weekend," Bernadette felt the need to interject, though her nervous laugh didn't do her any favors.

"Oh, that's right, you're there all the time." Sarah slid her a sly look. A look that promised now that she'd interjected that bit, Graham was sure to crash her Friday night confessional.

"I do go sometimes with friends, but not all the time. Probably not this weekend."

Graham looked between the two, picking up on the tension, but politely turned back to the elevator doors, ignoring it.

Bernadette's neck flashed with heat that she was sure was climbing toward her face like the red ivy in autumn on Anne Boleyn's Hever Castle.

At last, the elevator dinged and she practically shoved both Graham and Sarah aside in her haste to get out. To avoid them both outside the office, she made a beeline for Melanie's desk. She actually did need to talk to her and let her know about the flyers and Sarah.

Melanie took one look at her face, eyes wide, and then stood up. "Everything okay?" she whispered, eyeing Sarah and Graham.

"Have a good evening, ladies!" Graham gave a casual salute, a maddening dimple showing in his cheek when he smiled.

Why did he have to be so handsome?

Sarah was watching her with those beady spider eyes, but when Graham held the door for her, she was forced out of the building. Thank goodness.

As soon as the coast was clear, Bernadette blurted it all out. "Sarah found one of the flyers, two actually that I know of, and put them in her purse."

Melanie nodded, unfazed. "That was a risk we knew would happen."

"True, but she kept giving me looks like she knew it was me who made and distributed them." Bernadette straightened her headband as if that might help straighten out her current situation. "I'm doomed."

"I'm assuming she would know. You said as much yourself." Melanie started to tidy up her desk, putting away stray paper clips, slips of paper, and pens. Why didn't she seem as worried? Bernadette's job was on the line here.

"Again true. But she practically invited Graham to the café."

Melanie stilled and looked up from her tidying. "Oh… Now that I hadn't thought of."

"Exactly." Bernadette grabbed a stray paper clip hidden behind a desk plant and handed it to Melanie like one soldier handing another his weapon. "This could be an epic disaster."

"Although, didn't you say yourself that it was Graham who has been pretty supportive of your promotion?" Melanie cocked her head to the side, thinking. "This might not be as terrible as you think."

Bernadette winced as her teeth once more found anchor in her bottom lip. She really needed to stop doing that. "Maybe not."

"So, what are you worried about?"

"I really don't know." She tapped her fingers on top of the desk. "I think it's just Sarah working my nerves up all day."

"Then let it go. If he shows up, he's not going to shut us down. And I doubt he'd want to."

"You're right."

Melanie fluffed up her hair and winked. "I know. Now get home to Frank. I need to shut this desk down."

"Thank you for calming me down." Bernadette laughed. "I'll see you tomorrow."

"You bet."

Feeling marginally better, Bernadette exited the building to the slowly cooling air. They were a couple weeks away from it being officially autumn, and she was very much looking forward to the cooler days.

As Bernadette headed toward the bus station, heels clicked the pavement behind her at a clipped pace. She turned to see Sarah hurrying toward her, lips thin, eyes pinched, arms pumping like she was punching the air in front of her. She half expected Sarah to leap onto a broomstick and start chanting, "Double, double, toil and trouble." Bernadette braced herself—and her tongue—for the incoming attack.

"Did you make those flyers?"

The woman didn't even try to be subtle.

"What flyers?" Bernadette didn't owe her anything, especially not a confession. Confessions were going to be saved for Friday night, and not with Sarah present.

"You know what flyers I'm talking about."

Bernadette just cocked her head, waiting for both sound and reason and expecting neither. Perhaps that made her foolish.

"The pink ones about women in the workplace."

Bernadette just stared at her, trying not to give anything away, like when she was a child and she and Bennie had gotten into their mom's hidden stash of chocolate but didn't want to confess to being the one who'd depleted her supply.

Sarah huffed. "Buffoonery, malapropos."

Bernadette smiled. "Oh, I did see those."

"Right. Well, I don't care if you don't want to admit it. I just wanted you to know that you're going to stir up a lot of trouble."

"Don't you mean you're going to stir up trouble?" Bernadette crossed her arms. If Sarah was going to chase after her and start a confrontation, then Bernadette wasn't going to just take it.

Sarah narrowed her eyes but didn't confess to any nefarious plans. "Men don't like it when women step on their toes."

"Then they'd best not put their toes in the way of our shoes."

Sarah wrinkled her nose. "Does that even make sense?"

Bernadette shrugged. "Either you're with the pink or you're against it, Sarah. The choice is yours."

Sarah puckered her lips, tightening her purse at her shoulder. "You're going to make it worse for the rest of us."

"I'm not the problem, Sarah." Those simple words were loaded with implication. How many times had Sarah actively tried to sabotage Bernadette when she'd only ever tried to befriend her?

Sarah looked ready to say something but then thought better of it and spun on her heels. Over Sarah's head, Bernadette could see Graham looking her way as he climbed onto his bike. It'd been a few days since they'd been able to talk, and she found she missed it. But at the same time, she didn't want to give him the impression that she was ready or interested in a relationship.

Even if she was starting to feel like she was.

He raised his hand, a subtle wave. And she was unable to not return the gesture. Her hand hung there suspended for a second too long, like her breath, until the hiss of the brakes of her bus prompted her to finally move.

Would it be so bad if he showed up to their meeting?

She'd prefer him to any of the bulls at work—especially Wall. She could imagine him barging into the Caffe Shakespeare and picking up teacups and coffee mugs and just chucking them around in a rage, glass and porcelain shattering.

The man really needed to do something about his anger. Not that it was her place. She felt bad for any woman he was married to. She'd never met his wife, as he'd never brought her around, not even to the annual holiday parties, and he had no pictures of her in his office. For all Bernadette knew, the woman could be a ghost.

At her apartment door, Mrs. Morris was just leaving.

"He's such a dear, good boy," Mrs. Morris said.

"Frank adores you."

"And really, dear, you should keep that window closed. He could escape."

The window was open? She distinctly remembered closing it. Bernadette smiled gratefully. "Of course, I'll make sure to latch it. I must have forgotten. Thank you."

Mrs. Morris started to walk away, her shoulders slumped more than usual.

"What are you doing for dinner? Would you care to stay? I'm

making Julia Child's Chicken Waterzooi, and with a name like that I can't eat it alone."

Mrs. Morris smiled. "I would love to. Can I help cook?"

"Of course."

"I'll just need to get Mr. Crumbs his dinner."

"No problem. Frank and I need to get in our walk. I'll knock when we're back."

An hour later, Mrs. Morris and she each had a glass of pinot grigio and were prepping vegetables, chicken, and creamy sauce. Bernadette ladled servings into two bowls and set them on the table.

Frank watched them. Not to be forgotten, he also had a chicken and vegetable dinner.

"Mrs. Morris, how do you feel about being a landlady?"

Her neighbor paused to reflect on the question. "I don't quite recall what's it like not to be. Though I do remember it being a bit more fun when Roger was here with me. And less expensive. He used to do all the repairs himself. Now I either hire someone or give a rent discount to one of the lads. Mr. Lee next door to you is really good about helping."

"I'm glad you have some people in the building to help." Bernadette wished there was something she could do to help, but when it came to handiwork, she'd done a lot more damage than good whenever she tried.

"Why do you ask?"

"Mostly out of curiosity. I've been talking to friends a lot lately about women working."

"Good for character. No one should sit idle. Even mothers at home are working themselves to the bones."

"They are."

"My daughter Harriet worked herself silly trying to please, please, please that imbecile she's married to."

"Imbecile?"

"Indeed. It's a rather delicate situation."

Frank barked, and Mrs. Morris turned to him. "You've been quite supportive in listening to me babble, you sweet thing."

"He's kept your secrets well."

Mrs. Morris laughed. "He's a good listener. Seems Harriet's husband has turned his eye to another. She's going to try to divorce him, but since she's spent the entirety of their marriage taking care of the household and watching the children, she's not got any money to her name, and he's threatening to leave her with nothing and take the children if she files."

Bernadette let out a heavy sigh, her heart twitching with sympathy. "So, she has two choices: stay with the man who is stepping out on her, or lose everything including her children?"

Mrs. Morris nodded, her mouth turned down in disappointment. "Not a good situation."

"Not at all. She needs a good lawyer. I may be able to get her a recommendation."

"Oh?" Mrs. Morris's face lit up with hope.

"I met a couple of lawyers—women—earlier this week. And maybe they have a friend or two in California."

"Oh, that would be so wonderful. Thank you, Bernie."

Bernadette smiled. "We women need to stick together."

Chapter Sixteen

BY TEN IN THE MORNING on Thursday, Bernadette had a lot of regrets.

She regretted coming in to work.

She regretted taking the position as senior copy editor.

And she regretted most of all her inability to just Hulk out on Mr. Wall.

Sitting in his office, her knees pressed firmly together, heels digging into the carpet as if her posture might somehow anchor her in place, she listened as he raged against the manuscript for which she'd come into work extra early to meet the deadline. She watched as spittle flew, and he wrinkled the pages while shaking them toward the sky as though both she and her red markings were the blight of his existence.

"This is an embarrassment to the department," he scoffed. "You, Miss Swift, are an embarrassment. To think I gave you, a *woman*, the opportunity to prove yourself…"

Wall's logorrhea went on endlessly, but she stopped listening, letting it drone into a dull and muffled echo, like being underwater and playing mermaid. *Wahh, wahh, wahh...*

She'd done a good job on the copyedit, despite it being one of the most poorly written books that she'd had to work on to date. A celebrity memoir by an actor who decided one morning to pick up a pen and become an author. Except he couldn't write, and his editor had likely thrown up his hands in defeat, given the state of the manuscript when it landed on Bernadette's desk.

But as these things went, celebrity memoirs were all the rage. People loved to dive into the life of a celebrity. To see behind the closed doors. Voyeurs with the perfect vantage point to snap a picture.

They'd never appealed to her, and neither did the rag mags. Bernadette was much more interested in losing herself in a novel with characters she could root for, not the latest gossip about who was wearing what, and who threw up on So-and-So's shoes.

"Are you even listening to me?" Wall plopped down on the chair beside her, his cheeks red, face purple. For a moment she thought he'd collapsed.

The scent of his morning coffee breath mixed with cigarettes wafted in the air, and she tried not to gag on the noxious smell and his proximity.

Wall placed the manuscript on his desk, patting the paper like it was a good boy. His temper morphed before her eyes, brows unfurrowing, lips turning into a congenial smile—though there was something predatory about it that made her skin crawl. The sudden change set off a five-alarm bell in her head.

"Now, listen, Miss Swift." The fringe of his pale lashes dipped as he scanned her from head to toe and back. The anger and bluster from seconds before shifted.

She stiffened in her chair, not liking where this appeared to be headed. Or how easily his mood could change. Like Jekyll and Hyde, and she couldn't figure out who she was dealing with at any given moment.

"I'm *listening*." She emphasized the word, hoping it would pull his attention back to the moment at hand and not wherever else he'd gone.

"I know you had your heart set on being a senior copy editor. Probably on rising up the ranks of Lenox & Park too." He walked his fingers up imaginary stairs in the space before her.

She nodded, not trusting her voice to push out of her sandpaper throat and not sound garbled or high-pitched with apprehension.

"I want to help you do that."

Her back stiffened. "Sir, begging your pardon, but you just spent the last quarter hour telling me that my work was…subpar."

Wall glanced toward the windows in his office, and she did too, seeing that all the boys were head down, busy, busy, busy bees, not paying a lick of attention at first glance, but she knew them better. They all had their ears trained toward this room, hoping to catch even just the slightest sound that they could inflate into all sorts of erroneous gossip.

"It's true, I did, and you know I'm not a liar."

Bernadette gritted her teeth. That was a lie right there. Her work was impeccable, and the only thing she could discern from his hyperbolic ranting was that perhaps she'd done so good a job he had to take her down a peg just to keep her guessing.

"I'm trying to be fair here to everyone," he said. "Including you."

What was he talking about? She felt like she'd turned the page in a book only to find she'd missed the last three chapters.

As she studied his face—the waxy look of his handlebar mustache, the flick of his tongue over the cracked skin of his lips, the blatant lecherous look in his eyes—she felt it. The subtle slide of his clammy hand on her thigh, a coarse callus catching on her pantyhose. Time froze, and she sat the way a deer in the fields of the farm hesitated when faced with the grunting engines of a tractor. What felt like unending seconds passed as she tried to decipher whether what was happening was real or imagined. But the threat was evident. Creepy, crawling spider fingers inching upward in search of a victim to grab, subdue, and then suck out its insides. The curve of his lewd smile when she didn't instantly move.

Call it shock. Call it a blip on her brain monitor. Call it a momentary out-of-body experience.

Call Mr. Wall lucky she didn't punch him right in the fucking nose.

Bernadette snapped out of her momentary catatonic state, slapped his hand away, and said, "How dare you!"

"Miss Swift, we can work this out. You want to keep this job, and I want something from you too." His hand returned, only this time he squeezed her knee as if doing so would keep her in place, would convince her that she wanted this too.

But no amount of convincing on earth would ever make her do whatever it was he was asking for. "Mr. Wall, this is highly inappropriate." She stood up, the move hiding the shiver that coursed through her entire body, the kind of whole-body visceral racking that was an involuntary response to complete and total disgust.

Wall stood too, his eyes level with hers. "If you want to keep your job, Miss Swift, there are certain things that are required of you."

"Yes, fixing dangling modifiers and misspelled words and altering paragraph starts, not whatever it is you were just implying I should give you."

He snorted, his eyes somehow beadier than before, twitching and shifting like a hawk who has a field mouse in his line of sight.

"You'll learn to play the game one day, Miss Swift. Perhaps today your sensibilities are too delicate, but soon you'll understand what it takes to get ahead. And you'll do it. Because you're a go-getter, a real *ball*buster." The last of his words were said with a sneer she felt all the way through her body.

Still, by some miracle, she kept herself composed. "I will get ahead on the merit of my work, sir, and nothing more."

"We'll see." He stabbed a finger into the manuscript pages. "But not with work like this."

Bernadette pressed her finger into the pages too, as she met his gaze. A duel of the minds. "I did a damned good job on this manuscript, and you know it. Don't insult us both by denying it."

There was a flash of knowing in his eyes, a subtle acknowledgment, which was all she really needed. He could lie all he wanted, but the truth was, she had done a good job, and he was just playing with her, trying to get her to bend to his will, trying to get her to give him sexual favors to keep her job. Disgusting.

"If we're done here, sir, I have more manuscripts to work on."

"We may be done for the moment, Miss Swift, but we're not *done*. And don't even think of running to personnel about this. They won't believe you anyway. It's just your word against mine, and everyone knows a woman is never to be believed over a man."

The audacity. The outright, flagrant narcissism.

"Do not touch me again." Bernadette's voice trembled with rage, her fists clamped tight at her sides. It was a miracle she didn't haul off and deck the scumbag. But that would be assault, and as he said, no one would believe her anyway. What she wouldn't give for just a smidge of leeway in time where she could scratch his watery eyes out.

She turned her back on him, risking a pinched bottom as she marched out of his office, and slammed the door a little too hard on the way out. Something fell of the wall inside, banging against the floor, and Wall cursed her name through the glass. But she didn't turn around. And she didn't sit at her desk.

No, she needed air before she clawed at her neck until the skin was shredded and there was nothing left of her to breathe.

She rushed to the elevator, hitting the button, but the ticker barely moved, stuck on level eight. The stairs. Yes, she would take the stairs.

Chapter Seventeen

BERNADETTE FLUNG OPEN THE EMERGENCY door, not caring who saw. They all thought her a bit batty anyway. With a clammy hand clinging to the cool metal of the stair rail, she hurried down the stairs at a pace that was likely to trip her and then she'd be tumbling over herself down, down, down until she smacked onto the bottom floor in a puddle of rage and disappointment.

In the lobby, Melanie took one look at her face and leaped up from her desk, hurrying around the side and to Bernadette.

"Gary, watch the phone," she ordered the guard, and then grabbed hold of Bernadette's arm and led her outside. "What happened?"

Bernadette's throat had collapsed, and it was either gasp for air or try to speak, and she opted to breathe.

Melanie steered her around the corner of the building, away from the prying eyes of walkers, and leaned her against a wall.

"In and out, that's it. Just breathe."

"He… Wall… He touched my leg. Told me I needed to do things. To let him do things to me, if I wanted to keep my job."

Melanie's mouth fell open. "What? You need to report him. No way should he be getting away with being handsy."

"He said no one would believe me."

The look on Melanie's face said he was right.

"I can't go back up there."

"Take the rest of the day off."

Bernadette sank down to a crouch, her head in her hands, elbows on her knees as she tried to reconcile with what just happened.

"If I do that, then I'm done for. It will be proof he got to me. I'll have to quit like he's wanted me to since the first day I started. This is all some sort of power play. A game I don't know anything about or how to play."

"Game, shmame, who cares why he's doing it. The fact is, you can't let him get away with it," Melanie said. "Report him. So what if they don't believe you. At least you'll have made the report, and if it happens again, or to someone else, they will have that on record. The man has tried to take you down by diminishing your work, and because you didn't cower at his words, he's moved onto a much more sinister course of degrading you. He's not going to stop unless you make him."

Melanie had a good point. But Bernadette didn't want to put herself in the situation of being a troublemaker either. Women were always thought to be the cause of such things. That they were asking for it. And Wall…he'd make sure to put her in the worst light.

"I'll think about it. But in the meantime, I need to go back to my desk."

"What about Graham? Could you at least tell him?"

The thought of telling Graham was even more mortifying than telling personnel, but he was her friend, and he knew what an asshole Wall was. If any male in the office was going to believe her, it was him.

She nodded. She would confide in Graham. He would know what to do.

Her legs still shaky, she stood, ready to face the monster all over again or, at the very least, to avoid him for the rest of the day. She dusted off her rear, fearing sidewalk grime when she hadn't thought of it before. Melanie gave her a once-over, straightened her headband, and swiped at a smear of makeup at the corner of Bernadette's eye.

The walk across the hall from the elevator to the office loomed long, and her feet felt like she was dragging cement blocks. Sarah was perched on her chair, filing her nails and glaring daggers at Bernadette. There wasn't anything unusual about that, except that there seemed to be more venom behind her stare this time than before.

Wall's voice boomed from down the hallway. Good—he wasn't in his office, so she could get to her desk without having to bump into him.

Except, what he was saying caught her ear.

"Yeah, decided to give this one a whirl myself since Brogan had such a hard time with it."

Brogan was the editor who'd worked on the celebrity memoir.

"Wasn't easy, but I think I caught all the snags. Celebrity memoirs…" He let out a low whistle. "This one's going to sell."

Bernadette could not believe her ears. As if his earlier aggression and encroachment on her person weren't enough of an insult, he was claiming her work as his own.

Bernadette's mouth fell open. Fists clenched, she turned on her heel, prepared to launch herself down the hallway. To throw all of her rules out the gosh-darn window just like Wall. That conniving, no good, lecherous motherfu—

"Miss Swift."

Bernadette whirled to see Graham. His voice a soft reach in the torrential monsoon of her mind.

"I was wondering if you had a moment to discuss a manuscript with me?" The lift of his mouth in an imploring grin was a flickering light in the endless dark.

And yet part of her wanted him to go away. To not have had such good timing, stopping her before she did something she would enjoy in the moment and regret later.

Numbly she nodded, her steps brittle as she followed him to his office. If he'd not arrived when he did…There was no telling what state she, and Wall, would be in right now. Her mind went straight to a feral cat fight she'd seen outside the barn once on her family farm. Vicious and intransigent. Neither willing to yield.

"Would you care to take a seat?" He indicated a chair as he took his seat opposite, sliding into it so casually it took the edge right off her.

She shook her head, feeling like if she sat down, she might actually break. "I'd rather stand."

Graham stood from his chair. "We'll both stand, then." He eyed her for a minute, assessing in a way that felt like concern more than anything else. "I overheard you talking to Melanie."

Bernadette's cheeks flamed. How? She hadn't seen him walk

past. Though she wasn't really paying attention either. She opened her mouth but really didn't have anything to say. Only mortified blah, blah, blahs. For a woman who obsessed over words and their origins, Greek or Latin, being at a loss for them was unnerving.

"Were you spying on me, Mr. Reynolds?"

He quirked a brow at her formal use of his name. "No. Just passing by and heard you in distress. I didn't want to interrupt…" He looked a little embarrassed now, sheepishly smiling. "I supposed in a way you might say I accidentally eavesdropped, but I certainly didn't spy. Do you want to talk about it?"

Bernadette sighed and shook her head. "If you overheard, then you know." Then she thought better of it. "And now, because I've refused his…advances, he's claiming credit on my work."

"The celebrity memoir?"

She nodded. "You heard that too."

"I did."

Tears stung her eyes, angry hot tears. *Tearian*, Old English, meaning *to weep*. Good, she was coming back a little to herself. "Maybe I should just quit."

"What?" Graham's shocked expression surprised her. "Why would you do that?"

"Maybe I'm not cut out for this business. I'm certainly not going to…do what he wants me to. And if that's the way things are done. I just can't." She shook her head so violently her headband slipped. All of the bestsellers on her shelves at home, the ones she proudly displayed for having been a part of, said otherwise. And it only made her angrier that Wall had the ability to shake her foundation. "And if he's going to constantly find ways to degrade me and diminish my work, I'll never get ahead here."

Graham opened his desk drawer and pulled out a bottle of Canadian Club rye whiskey. "I don't normally drink at work," he said. "And I'm assuming you don't." There was a smile in his voice as he said that. "But, this moment seems to call for a stiff one—and not the kind offered by Wall."

She let out a little moan.

"Too soon?"

"Way too soon. But I will take that drink."

"The man is clearly insecure. Extremely so. Why else would he take credit for your work and try to thwart you from a promotion when he has no basis for doing so? You're getting closer to his job and he doesn't like it."

"I think you're right."

Graham took out two glasses and poured a finger in each, and then handed her one. He clinked his glass to hers. "To Bernadette Swift, long may she reign as Grammarian of Lenox & Park, the destroyer of misogynist bosses and comma misuse."

Bernadette let the whiskey fall down her throat, burning a path as it removed the bad taste of Wall's advances from her mind.

Since she wasn't an imbiber of spirits, the whiskey almost instantly made her feel warmer, lighter.

"Do you want me to escort you to your desk?"

Bernadette's heart melted a little at the offer. It was encouraging to know that not all the men in the office were as awful as the ones she dealt with on the daily. "No, but thank you for the offer."

"I'm going to report him," he said, taking her glass.

"Please don't." She sighed, her request not completely full of conviction.

Graham set the glasses down, returning his gaze to her. "I have a responsibility to do so. He can't treat you that way."

"He won't be fired, and it will only make my life harder."

"He deserves a reprimand, and you deserve better."

Bernadette nodded. "You're right. I'll report it myself."

"Want me to go with you?"

She smiled, wishing she could hug him. "No, I don't need a fixer, Graham. Just a friend. But thank you for the whiskey."

"Take a mint." Graham chuckled. "If you show up with whiskey breath, they won't even bother taking notes."

"Good point. Thank you again." She popped one of the red-and-white mints on his desk into her mouth and then made her way to personnel.

The same incense-burning, tweed-jacket-wearing manager was in his office. He seemed mildly annoyed to see her but indicated she should take a seat.

"I'm here to make a report."

He took out a pad of paper, clicked open a pen, and stared at her. "Go ahead."

Bernadette drew in a breath, trying to center herself away from his judging eyes. The way he was looking at her made her wonder if her boss had already come by. Warned him, old-boys style. "Mr. Wall touched my leg. He insinuated I should…provide him with favors to keep my job."

The manager sighed, unclicked his pen, and set down with pinched fingers. The only mark on the page was a black dot of ink. The finality of that black dot made her head pound.

"What is it that you want to report?" he asked.

Was he actually asking? Had he not heard her? But his annoyed expression answered both those questions. "The inappropriate-ness of that exchange. The discomfort at being told I needed to... perform."

Tweedledee sat back in his chair, and she half expected Tweedledum, a.k.a. Mr. Wall, to come waltzing around the corner. "Did he touch anything other than your leg?"

"No."

"And did he...show you any parts of himself?"

"No." The horror of imagining such a thing was enough.

"Then you have nothing to report." The way he rubbed his hands was like he was dusting her and her report off.

Bernadette's mouth fell open. "But, sir, he—"

"Miss Swift, you've been on the job here for a few years. To be frank, I'm surprised this hasn't happened before. And by hap-pened, I mean someone flirted with you. Someone showed you preference. But nothing happened, correct?"

She swallowed. Something *had* happened. Hadn't it?

"He touched my leg."

"But it's just a leg."

Just a leg...?

"Do you ride public transportation, Miss Swift?"

"Yes."

"And you sit beside other people on said transportation?"

"Yes."

"Then I'm sure you're touching legs with other people all the time."

"I didn't say our legs touch. He touched my leg with his hand. He squeezed my knee. He basically told me to sleep with him."

"But he didn't force you."

Her nails dug into the arms of the chair, and when she spoke, her voice was strained and so distant it barely registered as her own. "What you're saying to me is that he can touch me, squeeze me, but as long as it's not my breast, my—"

He raised his hand to stop her. "Please do not say such inappropriate things."

Bernadette burst from her chair. "You are no better than Mr. Wall."

"I will have to report you for your insolence."

It took everything within her not to say, "Report this," and show him the finger Mother had told her never to flash at anyone.

"I hope your report includes the fact that I came here to tell you my boss propositioned me. If not, then your report means nothing." And she stormed out.

Wall was going down. And so was personnel.

Chapter Eighteen

FRANK

MY GIRL IS CHOPPING AT the same speed I've seen chipmunks dig in the dirt. The same speed the shoplifter from Pop's around the corner tried to make off with a case of soda pop. Fast, furious, and frenzied. There's a tension to her that isn't normally there, and she keeps muttering things under her breath that sound like *son-of-a*, *mother-fudge*, and *no-good-no-brained*, but no actual words that make sense in the combination with which she's saying them. Flinging vowels and consonants and anger together the way she tosses the ingredients to a salad. A little of this, a whole lotta that, and a pinch of other.

What did the carrots do?

I lift up to the counter, pressing my paws into the surface to get a better look. They look the same as always.

Bernadette turns sideways, her eyes at my eye level. I lick her chin.

She laughs and wipes her chin on her shirt. "What are you doing, boy?"

I bark at her. *Are you okay?*

She drops the knife in the pile of overchopped vegetables and grabs my face with both hands, her fingers behind my ears massaging while her palms press to my jowls.

"I love you, Frank. You're reliable. And you really get me."

I bark, *Yes, I love you too.*

I have a feeling she's about to say something, the way her lips curve in the corners when she's about to form words, but the phone rings, interrupting.

She lets go of my face, gives me a pat on the head, and picks up the receiver. I hop down off the counter and sit, watching.

"Bennie?" she shrieks.

Ben? Our Ben?

I bark. I want to hear.

"You're coming home? When?"

Ben is coming home? I turn in a circle, my tail nub wiggling as fast as Bernadette's been chopping.

"Oh my God, I can't believe it."

She sinks to the floor, tears streaming down her face, but she's laughing. All the things she's doing are a contradiction to one another.

I lie on the floor beside her, my head in her lap, and her hand on my back trembles. Through the receiver that she holds to her face I can hear Ben's low rumbling voice. Vibrating through my girl are a relief and happiness I haven't felt from her in so long. The pent-up energy that felt like it was an eruption waiting to happen has disappeared.

"Does Mom know? Of course, she knows. I can't wait to see you. Be safe. I love you."

The other side of the line goes quiet.

I look up at Bernadette, who is smiling through her tears. "Ben's coming home," she says. "He's got leave in two weeks for a little while."

I pant and smile. I love Ben, but I love more when my girl is happy.

"We'll visit the farm."

I jump up, whirl in another circle. The farm is my favorite place. The wild viridescent—that means *green like grass*, my girl told me—prairies, the cows, the pigs, the abundance of squirrels. No leash. Just me and the wind in my face, the earth beneath my paws, and rodent tail just inches from my biting grasp.

Bernadette's mom tossing me hunks of whatever roast she's got in the oven because she says I'm a great taste tester. Her dad giving me sips of whatever is in his cup. I don't like the taste, but I love the attention.

I feel that frenetic energy kicking in, and I bark a warning. Bernadette's going to want to move before I start zoom, zoom, *zooming*.

Chapter Nineteen

ON FRIDAY EVENING, BERNADETTE STOOD outside Caffe Shakespeare, staring through the window at people sipping and casually chatting. Dion's "Runaround Sue" filtered through the open door from the jukebox. Others sat alone, reading a book, titles she recognized like Sylvia Plath's *The Bell Jar* and *The Man in High Castle* by Philip K. Dick. None of her friends were there yet, and no one inside looked like they were waiting for someone.

The sun had already started to set, the streetlamps humming to life, and traffic behind her was its usual honking and cursing glory. Music streamed from car radios, Dion's "Runaround Sue" and Elvis's signature vocals crooned "Can't Help Falling in Love" somewhere behind her in a strange duet.

Admittedly, she was thirty minutes early to the meeting, but she wanted to be there when everyone showed up. Whoever everyone was.

"I thought you might be here." Sarah's cantankerous voice

broke through Bernadette's contemplations, her reflection showing up in the window beside Bernadette's, still wearing that splash
of red across her throat.

The very last person Bernadette wanted or expected to see.
Sarah just wouldn't go away, like a pimple on prom night.

"Sarah, lovely evening." Bernadette's sarcastic tone belied her
words. "I did mention to you I come here often."

"And tonight, of all nights?" Sarah crossed her arms over her
chest, staring at Bernadette with eyes that she probably wished
were X-rays into people's souls.

"No better night to be here." Bernadette shrugged, even if she
didn't feel at all as casual as that gesture was.

"Hmph." Sarah's chin jutted, and she squinted into the café,
her eyes meeting Bernadette's in the reflection. "I know why you're
here."

Bernadette didn't flinch. They'd been doing this dance since
Sarah was hired. Tonight of all nights wasn't going to be the
moment she tripped. "For a cup of tea?"

"No. Because of the flyers you made." Sarah's finger stabbed
forward, into Bernadette's reflection.

Ironically, "Big Girls Don't Cry" by the Four Seasons filtered
through the café door as someone exited.

Bernadette let out a long-suffering sigh. Sarah was exhausting,
and even if she wanted to hold up this pretense for eternity, why
bother? Sarah wasn't going to let up, and she wanted to go inside.
Bernadette turned from the window and faced Sarah head on.
"Did your boyfriend send you sniffing about? Or maybe you're
here on an errand for Mr. Wall, hoping to get ahead?"

At the mention of Wall's name, Sarah's attitude shifted from righteous indignation to smug satisfaction and a hint of accusation. "Oh, like you have any right to talk."

"What's that supposed to mean?"

"I saw you letting Wall feel up your leg." Sarah rolled her eyes.

Heat flooded Bernadette's face, and the sick feeling in her stomach that she'd had for the last two days returned with a vengeance that threatened to make itself known in the nearest toilet or flower pot, whichever came first. She swallowed down the bile.

"You don't have any idea what you're talking about," Bernadette seethed.

"Oh, don't I?"

"You don't." Bernadette's voice sounded choked, like she'd inhaled too much smoke coming from the fire of Sarah's vindictiveness.

"You may have had enough skill for Mr. Wall to give you a temporary promotion, Bernadette, but really, offering to sleep with him is so beneath you. I was starting to think you were better than that, but it's women like you who give the rest of us hard workers a bad name."

The words flung from her mouth like bullets firing in rapid succession were too quick to dodge. Even if they weren't accurate, they still grazed.

Bernadette opened her mouth to speak, but her throat was closing, words choked off by frustrated tears.

Sarah sniffed. "I thought so." And then opened the door to the café. She was barely halfway through when she looked over her shoulder. "I'm going to expose you for the fraud that you are."

Bernadette stood stunned, all the things she could have said flooding her as Sarah disappeared inside. The words, the truths, the hypocrisy of Sarah accusing her of doing the exact thing she'd been doing herself a few weeks ago when she'd stolen pencils and spilled coffee. Of all the fabulous words she'd gathered in her vocabulary vault, the only one she could think of right now was *bitch*.

"You're here early. Like minds." Penelope pulled off the paisley scarf she had wrapped around her hair, her smile fading as she took in Bernadette's expression. "What's wrong?"

"Seems like someone at work witnessed Wall's advances and took it the wrong way. She's here to expose me as a fraud."

Penelope frowned. "But you aren't. It's easily explained."

"She didn't believe me. All it takes is one seed of doubt."

Penelope put a hand on each of Bernadette's shoulders. "Anyone who knows you knows you'd never seek out that kind of attention. Don't let her get to you. There will be easily a dozen or more women at this meeting tonight that will shut her down, and I'm happy to do it before this meeting even starts. Who is this anyway?"

"Sarah."

"*The* Sarah?"

Bernadette couldn't help a tiny, miserable laugh. Penelope said it with the same shock that Melanie had the night of the Mary Shelley party. "The one and only."

Penelope rolled her eyes. "My God, the woman is such a cranky square."

"I don't know why she hates me so much."

"Most women hate other women because they are jealous."

Bernadette recalled the first time she'd scrolled through the dictionary after a particular girl had been mean to her in the sixth grade and her mom had said she was jealous. *Jealous* stemmed from the Latin *zelus* meaning "zeal," which meant "eagerness, ardent interest," leading her toward the word *fervor,* which was "an intense feeling or expression." Her mom had also said that the girl would grow out of it. But, some girls grew into women who still harbored those intense feelings. That almost made her feel bad for Sarah.

Through the window, Bernadette watched Sarah order a drink and then find a place to sit in the corner. She pulled out a notebook and was scribbling in it…with fervor. "Probably writing down all of the nasty things she wants to say about me."

"I'm talking to her." Penelope opened the café door just as Melanie arrived, and filled her in as they entered in a few simple words. "Sarah's causing problems."

"Ugh." Melanie rolled her eyes. "Why?"

"We're about to find out."

Bernadette was gathered in the tide of her friends' protectiveness, their arms sliding through hers as they marched in a line toward her archnemesis. Together the three of them stood in front of Sarah's table. Sarah must have been pretending that the long shadows of their presence weren't darkening the pages of her notebook. Penelope cleared her throat, and Sarah sighed, glancing up in typical annoyed fashion.

"I'm not going to change my mind," she said before Bernadette's friends even had a chance to speak.

"That's fine," Penelope said. "'Ignorance is bliss,' they say. They also say ignorant bitches are miserable."

Sarah's mouth fell open, and she glanced at Bernadette. "This isn't helping you."

Bernadette wanted to high-five Penelope, but had to play it cool.

"Listen, Sarah," Bernadette said, her voice finally returning. "I didn't invite Wall's touch. I didn't want his touch. In fact, I told him to not touch me ever again, and do you know what happened? He threatened my job. I went to personnel and told them how he'd violated me, and do you know what the manager said? He basically told me to suck it up, and that it was a woman's lot."

Sarah's expression was blank as she took it in, but there was something in her eyes that registered. The skin of her neck turned nearly the same shade as her scarf. She'd been in this position before. She knew what it looked like. So why was she accusing Bernadette?

"You're right. I did make those flyers. I did invite women here tonight to talk about the issues they've been facing to see what we can do about it. Why would I do all of that and then try to sleep with my boss? My *married* boss? That would make me a home-wrecker and a hypocrite."

At the mention of home-wrecker, twin circles of vermilion showed in Sarah's cheeks. After all, she had been sleeping with either Evans, Marshall, or Greene, and look where that had gotten her. Exactly nowhere.

"You're either part of the problem, or part of the solution," Melanie said. "What side do you want to be on, Sarah?"

"If it's not the solution, then I suggest you leave," Penelope added. "Before the women who believe in Bernadette and this cause come in and hear what you're saying."

Sarah closed her notebook, tapping a short, unpainted nail against the tan leather cover. "I don't want to be a part of the problem," she said at last. "But I'm also not part of the solution."

"Then we're at an impasse," Melanie said.

Sarah nodded, swallowing, but said nothing.

"Let her stay," Bernadette said. "Maybe she needs to hear what everyone has to say."

Penelope rolled her eyes. "Fine, but if she tries to say one wrong thing about you…"

"I'm sorry," Sarah said. "I misunderstood what I saw. And I wrongly assumed you invited his advances."

Bernadette was too shocked not to stare, open-mouthed, feeling a little like a fish on a pier flopping aimlessly in search of the sea. "Thank you."

"Penelope, hi," Ruth and Julie arrived, hugging each of the women. A moment later the rest of the book club arrived.

"Mrs. Wall," Sarah said, standing abruptly from the table, her gaze on Patty.

Mrs. *Wall?* Bernadette shook her head, certain she'd heard wrong, but Melanie and Penelope were gaping exactly the same way at Patty. And Patty was saying, "Sarah. Lovely to see you again."

Bernadette breathed in quickly through her nose, feeling like her world had careened a little on its axis. There were only two reasons why Patty wouldn't have told them who she was, especially when Bernadette confided she worked at Lenox & Park and that she was a copy editor. One: She'd been sent to spy on them and was reporting everything they said to Wall. Two: She was embarrassed that Wall was her husband and didn't want them to know.

Recalling nearly every word that Patty had said at their meetings, she hoped it was the second one. Patty had claimed to want a divorce. If Bernadette was married to Mr. Wall, she'd find grounds to divorce him too. But still, she needed to clear this up, and fast.

"You're married to…Mr. Tom Wall? As in the copy chief at Lenox & Park?" Bernadette asked.

Patty nodded grimly. "The very one." Patty peeled off her cardigan and tucked it neatly on the back of a chair. "I'm sorry… I should have shared that. But I didn't want you to…" Patty blinked, her cheeks turning from pink to red. "I didn't want you to think less of me because of Tom. He wasn't always so… *Tom*."

Bernadette shook her head, though she appreciated how his name became an action verb. "I wouldn't judge you, Patty. You're not your husband. But I'm not sure…" She wasn't sure Patty should stay. This had bad idea written all over it.

"Oh, don't worry, dear. I won't be telling Tom anything. He despises me going to any sort of meetings, so he thinks I'm at evening services at our church." She leaned in, lowering her voice to a whisper. "I need this… I…" Her voice trailed off.

Bernadette nodded and squeezed Patty's hand, offering her comfort. How could she deny her ability to attend? Bernadette only had to work with Wall. She couldn't imagine having her personal life tethered to him. Patty was right. She did need this. "I'm glad you're here."

She hoped that Patty had indeed had that conversation with Ruth and Jenny about filing for a divorce.

About a dozen other women filed in, and when they had all settled at tables, Bernadette stood and walked to the stool that had been placed where live musicians normally played music and poets regaled with the rhythms and rhymes of their stanzas.

"Hello, everyone. I'm Bernadette Swift, and I wanted to welcome you all tonight to a confessional of sorts. Not the kind where you tell me your sins, but instead, the transgressions against you in the workplace or at home. What made you want to come out tonight. I'll start."

Bernadette drew in a deep breath, her eyes meeting Patty's. "Recently, at work, I was given a temporary promotion. Not because I'm not qualified for a permanent promotion, but because I'm a woman."

Heads shook and mouths turned down. A few grumbled how they'd had the same experience. Patty met her eyes, not with anger, which Bernadette had been worried about, but understanding.

However, what she had to say next, she couldn't say was about Mr. Wall, not with his wife sitting there, listening to how he'd touched her. And yet, this was a confessional, and she was here to share her experience. Still, she didn't want to break the woman's heart either.

"This week, however, feels like I've experienced the darkest of days of working yet. A man in authority propositioned me. I turned him down, but was threatened that if I tried to say anything, no one would believe me. I wanted to stay quiet. Because which of us really wants to make an uncomfortable situation more uncomfortable?"

Nods, murmurs of understanding.

"But a friend pointed out that if I remained silent, then the same person would be able to do what he did to me to someone else. So, I spoke up. And was promptly shut up. But I'm not here to shut up any more. And neither are you. So, who's going to share next?"

Penelope marched up to the stool, and Bernadette took her chair. "I applied to be an assistant editor. They hired me as a secretary. I was hit on within thirty seconds of sitting at my desk. I started to keep a paper clip collection. One clip for every inappropriate gesture and word. Let's just say, what started as a tiny glass used to store sugar has turned into a five-gallon jug that is close to tipping over."

Melanie was next, and Penelope settled back down next to Bernadette. "If I had a nickel for every time a man asked if I was wearing pantyhose or skin, I'd not need to work. Maybe that's what we should do? Start charging for the insinuations and alleged compliments? Who's next?"

A dozen hands shot up.

Georgie sprinted to the front, grinning at everyone. "I'm a labor and delivery nurse. Every day I'm subjected to men talking about women's vaginas—" She made a wincing face and stared toward the baristas. "Sorry for saying 'vagina'… Anyway, they don't talk in the way you'd think. Nothing clinical. They compare, they insult, they praise. As if we're not worried enough about what we look like downstairs, let alone the fact that in labor that thing morphs into alien territory. Whenever I can, I bite back, saying something like a woman can give life, but she can also take it away."

Bernadette laughed. "Does it work? Do they get scared?"

"Sometimes," Georgie said. "But when they stay all cocky, I ask if their wife has had a baby. Normally they have, so then I pretend to be surprised and I ask if it's theirs. That riles them up. They ask me why I'd say that, and then I reply, 'Oh, any man who's that ignorant about vaginas probably doesn't know how to use one.' I'm surprised I still have a job sometimes, but my boss is a woman, so I'm lucky, I guess."

Patty rose slowly, walking up to the microphone and clearing her throat. She opened her mouth, then closed it. Hands folded in front of her, she looked prim and small. She took a step away as if she'd changed her mind about speaking. But then her eyes met those of Bernadette, who was nodding encouragingly.

"I've not had much experience in the workplace. But I did go to art school, and the number of times I was asked if I needed a male to pose nude for me was astonishingly more than I was asked to strip down. I took every opportunity, of course, because practice makes perfect. But what those arrogant males didn't realize was that I was also creating a portfolio of their…" Patty paused to clear her throat. "Parts, shall we say, and I passed them to my friends before they went out on dates to make sure they were really invested in the whole…package."

That was not what Bernadette expected. She couldn't help the snort of a laugh that erupted, joining the other women in resounding applause.

"Women should know what they're getting into, right? Wish a friend had done the same for me." Patty grinned, then took her seat. She glanced at Bernadette, placed her hand over hers, and squeezed, adding, "That was fun and freeing."

"It is. Thank you for sharing with us." Bernadette grinned, glad that Patty had stayed after all.

"Oh, me next!" Ruth leaped out of her chair, smiling as she approached the stool. She faced the crowd like she was facing a jury, except this was a group of her peers she wouldn't have to do any convincing with.

For the next thirty minutes, women stood and confessed to the sins of the men at work. The flirtations, the double entendres, the overwork, the lack of work, the belittling. Until there was no one left but Sarah.

Slowly, she stood, clearing her throat, and approached the stool. She gave a tiny wave, unsure of herself in a way Bernadette had not witnessed before.

"Hello. I'm Sarah. I agreed to sabotage a female coworker because a man promised me attention and a promotion."

The room sat silent, riveted. Bernadette could barely breathe.

"I did not get a promotion. And I lost the attention. Worse, I sabotaged a good woman. And I'm sorry." At the last word, her gaze locked on Bernadette. As shocking as her confession was, the actual sincerity in her tone and her expression overwhelmed Bernadette.

Without thinking, she stood and marched to the front. Sarah took a step back, perhaps afraid that Bernadette might go catty and scratch her eyes out. Instead, she decided to shock Sarah too. With her arms outstretched, Sarah winced, and Bernadette pulled her in for a tight hug. For a breath, Sarah's body was stiff as the polished floor beneath them. But finally, she hugged her back.

"Thank you," Bernadette whispered.

Sarah nodded, pulling a handkerchief from her pocket to wipe her tears and nose.

"Now, ladies, what are we going to do about it?" Bernadette said to the crowd.

"Sarah Grimké—mother of the suffrage movement, said, 'I ask no favor for my sex. All I ask of our brethren is that they take their feet off our necks,'" Ruth said. "And that is all we want, right? To stand, to breathe, to walk into work without a comment about our skirts, or a look that makes us feel we might be assaulted, or to be assaulted and touched inappropriately."

"It's time to take this strike a step further," Bernadette said. "It's time to stop being quiet. It's time to say no, to take action."

"We could do a march," Georgie suggested. "Martin Luther King's March on Washington worked to bring attention to civil rights. Maybe a march for women's rights could work for us."

"Dr. King's speech was inspiring," Ruth said.

"Incredibly," Bernadette said, the other women murmuring their agreement.

"We could also do a walkout," Sarah added.

Bernadette nodded, feeling for the first time in a long time like they might just get somewhere. "I like both of those ideas. A week from today, we'll walk on Park Avenue," Bernadette said. "No posters. No flyers. Just women walking down the street, all of us dressed in pink. A week should give us plenty of time to spread the word."

"I'm in!"

"Me too!"

"And when do you think we should do the walkout?" Jenny asked. "The march is a great idea to get notice, but we won't have as much of an impact on a weekend."

Bernadette nodded. "True. How about Monday a week from tomorrow at three o'clock. We will all stand up and walk out of our offices. Whatever impact we start next Sunday with our march will be followed up on Monday, our message ringing loud and clear."

"Where should we meet?" Penelope rubbed her hands together with excitement.

"What about the library? The center for knowledge."

"Yes! And we'll make more flyers to pass around in secret."

With their plans in place, Bernadette left Caffe Shakespeare feeling lighter than when she'd come in. That was in large part because of her confession, and hearing the confessions of others, knowing she wasn't alone. But an even bigger chunk of the relief pie was what happened with Sarah.

Given the venom she'd been on the receiving end of, to say it surprised her would be an understatement. Sarah held the world record for minutes of glaring. But it had taken guts to stand up there tonight in front of everyone and admit to being a bully. To admit that she'd wanted the attention and the promised elevation and was willing to hurt someone else to get it. To admit she was sorry, and that she wanted to make a change.

Bernadette respected her a whole lot more after hearing that. And she knew what a good group she had, because no one had stood up and shouted at Sarah. No one had called her names or tried to make her feel any worse than she already did. Instead, they'd embraced her just like Bernadette.

This was what holding each other up meant—actually doing that, in good times and bad.

Chapter Twenty

TALL, SMALL, AND IN BETWEEN, women of every age, race, and background, dressed in an undulating wave of pink fashion, strolled up Fifth Avenue in Manhattan with one thing in common: their desire for equality. Or even just a little acknowledgment that being a woman didn't make them inferior.

Body parts shouldn't make a difference when it came to equal pay or respect.

Bernadette couldn't stop smiling at the stunning turnout. Proud of the women she'd gathered around her. Proud of the cause, and proud that she was a part of something bigger than herself. A cause that could really change things for women not only in this city but possibly across the nation if they got loud enough.

She straightened her Queen B headband, wearing her comfortable Keds, a pair of pink capri pants and a pink T-shirt that said *Grammarian*. She walked between Melanie and Penelope, clad in similar outfits. In a floral pattern, Melanie's shirt said *Girl Power*. Penelope's T-shirt, however, stole the show. In a lighter shade of pink, there was a delicious-looking cinnamon bun in the center, surrounded by the words *Synonym Rolls the Way Grammar Used to Make.*

There were about two dozen women in all, not an especially large crowd, but they still drew attention. Heads poked out of doors, windows, and cars.

Watching a female sea of pink skirts, blouses, hats, and scarves, smiling and chatting with each other. The sparkles of their pink earrings, necklaces, bracelets, and headbands caught the sun, creating mystical rainbow prisms.

"What's going on here? A parade?" someone asked from the sidewalk.

"Is it a holiday? Did we miss something?" another shouted from a car.

Bernadette proudly announced, "We're walking for women's equality in the workplace." Frank barked in agreement, her ever-present, trusty sidekick.

She'd put on his pink collar, which she'd embroidered in black with his name so people wouldn't call him Francine. Besides, there was nothing wrong with a male wearing pink. In fact, she thought they ought to wear it more often. Call it *salmon* if it made them feel better.

An old man waved his hand at them in that *ba-shoo* kind of way, meant to make her feel like her actions were nonsense. But his Scrooge-like manner was erased by a woman who rushed out of a shop.

"All this pink! Does my paisley count?" She plucked at her dress, which looked very much like an Emilio Pucci that Bernadette had seen in *Vogue.*

"Of course!" Bernadette beamed.

The woman jumped into the crowd, welcomed into the fold with open arms and introductions. The funny thing was, for Bernadette, New York had always been a kind of fend-for-yourself place, and today was proving that maybe it wasn't as much of a lonely city as she thought.

As they reached the Lenox & Park building, a familiar figure stood by the bike rack. She'd recognize the shape of his shoulders, the flip of his hair anywhere. Did Graham never stop working? Catching sight of the pink horde, he paused and glanced up, a grin forming on his face when he recognized her leading the pack. He was dressed more casually than during the week in jeans and a plaid button-down oxford in light shades of blue and was that *pink*?

"A lovely splash of pink on an otherwise overcast day." He tossed his head, swinging his hair out of his eyes. "Good afternoon, ladies." His charm immediately won over every woman present, including Bernadette.

"Good afternoon, Mr. Reynolds." She tried to keep her face neutral, but she feared by the way his smile widened that he could see she was happy to see him.

Women nodded as they passed on both sides of them, and closed ranks again, leaving Bernadette and Graham hidden within a wall of moving rose, blush, and coral.

Frank idled closer to Graham, sniffing his shoe, his pants, his outstretched hand. He cocked his head then, looking between the two of them as if he sensed something she didn't.

"This must be Frank." Graham crouched so they were at eye level and, at Frank's insistence, gave him a good scratch behind the ears.

"The very one." Frank had a discerning sense for people and

their character, and his easy acceptance of Graham had her heart melting a little.

"Such a friendly boy." Graham grinned up at her, genuine and jovial. The kind of smile that said this moment was making his day. "And gigantic."

Bernadette chuckled. "He is that. Like a miniature horse."

"What are you up to?" Graham stood, watching the ladies pass.

Frank sat, leaning against Bernadette's hip. "We're marching for women's equality in the workplace."

"I dig it." Graham nodded. "May I join you?"

She frowned, not in a mad kind of way, but more like baffled. A few of the passing women paused who'd heard him ask. In fact, the murmurs echoed through the crowd, knocking into each woman like dominoes until they all stopped walking and turned to face them.

"Don't you have rugby or something?"

"Saturdays are for scrumming."

Bernadette chewed her lip, still unsure of how to respond. "But you're a man," Pointing out the obvious was perhaps not the most genius response, but he was. Why would he want to join a women's march?

Graham shrugged, casual, not in the least bothered by nearly three dozen women staring at him. "Men can want women's equality in the workplace, too, can't they?"

He had a point. A damned fine one at that.

"Yes." There was no hesitation when she said it because it was absolutely true. And the more men who believed in it, the better off everyone would be.

It started as one clap from somewhere in the back of the crowd and ramped up to a thunder of applause. A few of Bernadette's friends pushed through from the end of the line, appearing before her and Graham like reinforcements on a battlefield.

"No, no. No clapping." Graham laughed and waved for them to stop; then his tone turned more serious. "You all deserve the applause, not me."

Why was he so...*charming?* There had been a distinct moment in time where she'd looked at him, felt all the things a woman would feel when gazing at an attractive man—tingles in her limbs, whirls in her belly, a fluttering in her chest—and had soundly slapped that heightened awareness out of her way. But here, now, this, she was fully conscious of the man standing in front of her—and how very much she wanted him to be right where he was.

Breaking the staring spell, she smiled at her friends. "Ladies, this is Graham Reynolds. He's an executive editor at Lenox & Park." *And my...friend?*

"Working on a Sunday?" Patty asked, nervously glancing at the building as if she expected to be caught standing there by Mr. Wall, though she'd already told them all he definitely wasn't in the office.

"I work every day that ends with Y." Graham chuckled, his response gaining several titters from women captivated by him.

Bernadette pressed her lips together to keep from laughing at the quiet sighs and fluttering lashes of a few who were absolutely falling for him.

"That seems unfair," Ruth said. "Everyone deserves a break."

Graham grinned. "Some men's vices are worse. I'm just a workaholic."

"That's true, it could be a lot worse." A few of the women confirmed, mentioning their own bosses' vices of booze and women. Graham made apologies on behalf of all the brainless idiots, which only made them step closer to him.

"Shall we?" Bernadette attempted to redirect the crowd. They were losing sight of their purpose, and if they didn't hop back on the equality train soon, it was going to completely derail.

"Yes." Graham abandoned his bike on the rack, his briefcase still slung over his shoulder. He rolled up his sleeves to his forearms and she tried not to look at the exposed skin there. The cord of muscle, the vein that cut like a river over his arm. A flash of him standing in the glow of a streetlamp dressed in shorts and a tight T-shirt assailed her. She blinked and then did the only thing she could think of: she marched.

They continued to turn heads as they meandered down Fifth Avenue, and Graham was just as vocal as the ladies in informing people what they were marching for. Bernadette couldn't help but notice that people seemed more receptive when he made the announcement.

At one of the kiosks, they were treated to free coffees and waters—including a cup for Frank, who lapped it up, leaving long strings of water dripping from his jowls.

"How far are we marching?" Graham asked, blowing into his steaming cup. "Who's got the map?"

Bernadette bit her lip thinking about many times her mother had grumbled about her father not looking at the map and getting lost every time. Now here they were, and a man was asking about it as if he were actually interested in their projected path.

"That wasn't something we'd discussed." She pursed her lips, gazing at the crowd and thinking she could march all day as long as it meant she could spend time chatting with Graham.

Enthusiasm was still showing on everyone's face, and no one yet seemed tired, but they had been walking for about an hour so far.

Penelope wrinkled her brow. "Washington Square Park is just ahead. We can make a loop and head back to the library going up Sixth Avenue. A few of the ladies left their bicycles there."

The marble arch entrance to the park loomed ahead, and behind it the beautiful golds, reds, and oranges of the leaves changing color. Frank tugged on the leash, sensing a park in his future and, with it, a million places to mark and twice that many squirrels to chase. "That works for me. Everyone?"

"Yes!" Cheers went up, which drew the attention of passersby—a few giving a rollicking whoop in return.

They made their way around the park to Hangman's Elm, where apparently traitors were hung during the American Revolution, and then out to the intersection of Waverly Place and MacDougal Street.

"Eleanor Roosevelt's old house." Graham nodded toward an older building just across Washington Square West. "She lived here when I was at New York University."

Bernadette stared at the English cross-style brown brickwork, the iron door beneath an ornately designed iron awning flanked by limestone columns, and arched tracery stonework around the windows. She imagined what Graham might have been like in college, her mind creating an image of him that looked much like he did now, only with a stack of books in his hands, and it made her smile.

"Did you ever meet her?" Bernadette glanced up at Graham, watching the way his eyes scanned the building with interest even as his mind scanned his memories to answer.

"I did." He turned his attention to Bernadette. Why hadn't she noticed before just how blue his eyes were? "She was quite a figure around here. How about you?"

Bernadette tore her gaze from Graham and watched Frank snatch a fallen leaf off the ground. "I admired her very much and felt very lucky to work with her during my internship at Lenox & Park."

"Funny, I had the chance to work with her too when I first interned," Graham chuckled, which caused Frank to bark like he'd been left out of a joke.

"Small world." Bernadette tugged a small piece of a cookie from her skirt pocket that she'd packed for Frank and tossed it to him. He caught it midair with a smack of his jaws and jowls.

"Sometimes, yeah."

The group headed down Waverly, then up Sixth, gathering a few more people along the way. When they reached the library a short time later, they'd grown from a couple dozen people to nearly sixty. Even in her wildest dreams about today, Bernadette had never guessed they'd get these kinds of numbers, or make the impact it appeared they had.

"Thank you all for joining us." Each of Bernadette's words was punctuated by Frank. "This has been so fun. And Frank adores you all."

The women agreed, hugging, high-fiving, and then started to disperse, but Graham lingered. Melanie wiggled her brows at Bernadette while shoulder bumping Penelope, who gave her a thumbs-up. Frank lay down, accurately assuming Bernadette was in no hurry to leave.

"I'll see you tomorrow." Graham waved at the departing ladies but didn't make a move toward his bike. Instead, he tucked his hands in his pockets and rocked back on his heels.

"I should warn you," Bernadette ventured. "We're walking out of the office tomorrow at three o'clock."

Graham raised a brow, though he didn't appear as shocked as she expected. "Who?"

"The ladies and I. It's a walkout to gain attention to our cause, but also to show how much we're needed. No one there to make coffee, copies, or conversation."

Graham nodded slowly, as if thinking about every possible outcome. "As an executive, I can't make a formal comment, but as a friend, I think you're on to something."

Bernadette kept her smile small, though on the inside she beamed. And she didn't realize how much the word *friend* would rankle when she was starting to want to be more than that. "Thank you."

"Now I have a question for you."

Melanie and Penelope had sidestepped away, whispering, and Bernadette was certain they were talking about her.

"What's that?" She folded and unfolded her hands in front of her, suddenly not sure at all what people did with their hands, their arms, when in conversation. They were hanging there awkward and useless. At least the cement of the sidewalk was holding steady and keeping her from sinking into the depths of the earth.

"How about that slice?"

Bernadette flicked her gaze toward her friends, who nodded,

not even trying to hide that they were listening in on the conversation. Their encouragement notwithstanding, the truth was, she *did* want to go with him for a slice of pizza. If he wasn't interested in her, and what was important to her, then he wouldn't have come on the walk. And he certainly wouldn't be asking her out for pizza.

"Do they allow dogs?"

Frank popped his head up, observing Graham as if to say, *I like pizza too, buddy.*

"In fact, they do. They have outdoor seating and I've seen dogs there before."

Bernadette's stomach did a pirouette that made her momentarily feel off balance. They were doing this.

"Then I accept."

Behind Graham, Melanie and Penelope waved and sauntered off in the opposite direction.

Eating in Graham's proximity wasn't new, because they'd met by accident at her bench and shown up at the deli at the same time, but this, this was definitely different.

It was a turning point between them that made her so nervous, her lips felt as tingly as her toes. Frank looked up at her, his eyes squinting as he must have felt her nerves through the end of the leash.

"Ready, boy?" she asked. He hopped to his feet, leaning his thick ribs against her leg.

"Just a couple blocks this way." Graham offered his elbow, and she stared at it a moment. "You can take it. Promise not to bite."

Bernadette laughed and, with her free hand, took hold of his offered elbow, marveling at the heat beneath his shirt and the solidness of his arm.

They headed past the library toward Bryant Park, Frank stopping to sniff every tree they passed.

"Sorry," she said.

"Oh, don't be sorry. Sniffing is how dogs see the world. And man, it must be fascinating."

Bernadette flashed him a smile. It was kind of unfair that Graham seemed to improve and grow on her with every passing minute.

Ray's Pizza was on a corner a few blocks away, and outside there were several café tables set up, a few of them free.

Graham pulled out a chair for her and, when she was settled, went inside to grab a couple of menus.

"What do you think?" Bernadette asked Frank.

He sniffed the iron pedestal of the table and then sat, staring at a pizza on another table. Drool gathering, he licked his chops.

"Yeah, me too, bud. But I meant about Graham."

Just then, Graham returned with the menus and sat opposite her, and Frank nudged his hand for a pet, giving her the answer she'd sought.

"Want to split a margherita pizza with mushrooms?" Graham asked.

"You remembered." If he didn't stop being so charming right this instant, her heartbeat was certainly going to pop the clasp in her bra from pounding so hard.

He grinned as if to say he remembered everything she said, which had her toes curling in her shoes.

"And you like mushrooms." She couldn't help the mesmerized lilt in her tone.

"Surprising given my hot dog tendency?" He wiggled his

brows and Frank's brow furrowed as he leaned forward and bumped Graham's arm with his nose. "You like hot dogs, Frank?"

"He does."

"What about mushrooms?"

"Those he will spit out. But I will treat him to my crust."

Graham looked at her, shocked. "You don't eat the crust?"

She shrugged. "If it's not smothered in cheese, why waste the space?"

"Good point."

There was a moment's pause, their eyes locked, and both time and the beat of her heart stilled.

Bernadette tapped her fingers nervously on the table, searching for something interesting to say. It wasn't as if she didn't talk to Graham all the time. Or that she hadn't seen him spill mustard all over the sidewalk from his hot dog. They'd just shared a whiskey in his office.

So why was sitting here across from him in a restaurant making her mind go all fuzzy? Graham was busy making faces and oohing and aahing over Frank, not seeming in the least bit nervous.

A waiter arrived, saving her from having to think about conversing. A pizza order and a glass of wine later, she came up with the perfect question.

"Do you have a dog?"

Graham turned toward her, smiling. "We had several growing up, but I haven't had the chance to get one on my own, though I'd love to. The hours wouldn't make it really fair though."

"I'm lucky to have a neighbor who is sort of like a nanny to Frank. Otherwise, he'd be a very unhappy boy."

"Lucky dog."

"He's a bit spoiled, but with a face like that, how could he not be?"

Graham gave Frank a healthy scratch behind the ears that got his rear foot thumping and shaking their table.

Bernadette's wine started to tip over, but she saved it at the same time Graham saved his. They laughed, and Frank rubbed his head on her arm for some love.

"You're a good boy, Frank."

"I'm really glad I ran into you today," Graham said.

"More like I walked into you."

"True. All the same, I'm glad." His eyes were sincere, and again that fluttering in her belly made it hard to swallow.

She had it *bad*. And she'd been trying to hide it from herself for a while. "Me too." The words were soft but sincere.

There were so many things she wanted to say. That she wished they'd gone out together sooner. That she was so impressed by him and his ability to see past all the male chauvinistic tendencies in the workplace. That she wanted to do this again.

Graham wasn't a man who was scared by women. Nor was he one to think that a woman getting ahead somehow took something from him, or made him less male. He made it a point to empower women. And that only made him more attractive.

She opened her mouth to see what came out first, when their pizza arrived, set on a pedestal in the middle of the table, the cheese steaming.

"That smells delicious," she said.

"You're going to love it."

The waiter handed them each a plate, and Graham motioned for her to hold hers up so he could serve her a gooey, scrumptious slice.

The first bite was even better than she imagined—transcendent. The second bite went to Frank. She tore him off a piece of her crust with a little cheese melted to golden brown. He swallowed it whole.

Graham grabbed another slice. "So, the walkout tomorrow."

"You think we shouldn't do it?" She picked a mushroom off the slice and popped it in her mouth.

"No, no, I was wondering if I could join you. I know as an executive I shouldn't, but honestly, I think it's important enough that someone in my position does."

Bernadette's throat warmed with emotion, and she found it hard to swallow what was in her mouth. She took a sip of wine to bolster herself. On the one hand, she was appreciative of his desire to help, and on the other, she didn't want him doing this for her, for the other women. They needed to be able to stand on their feet.

Graham held up his hands. "I can see your hesitation. I don't want to make you or the other women uncomfortable. I just want to support your cause." He met her eyes, his filled with sincerity. "To support you, Bernadette."

Filled with pizza and the prospect of this march being a success, made more so by the presence of supportive men, Bernadette changed her mind. "Of course you can. I think that would be a great message to send."

"I bet Bass would like to come too."

"Mr. Bass?" Her stomach plummeted. Bass had stuck out his neck for her in getting this job. Was what she was doing now going to disappoint him?

"The one. He and his wife do a lot of work for women's rights."

She set down her pizza, wiping her oleaginous fingers on her napkin. "I had no idea."

"He doesn't talk about it too much at work, but I've been to a few of the charity events he was speaking at. I think he'd be proud of what you're doing. And I know for a fact he'd be extremely disappointed in the way Wall has treated you."

Frank, who was always ready for the *Wall* command, snatched her greasy napkin and shredded it.

Bernadette laughed as she picked up the shredded pieces of napkin.

Graham chuckled and tossed Frank a hunk of his pizza crust.

Bernadette sighed, picking up the conversation about Wall again. "My boss has set up a boys' club in the copyediting office that I can't seem to break through, that's for sure."

"But you're on your way. Every manuscript with your initials on it, every day you keep showing up, takes the boys' club down a notch. And now this? Someone's going to have to start paying attention. And if we can get Bass in on it, then you'll have a supporter on the executive board."

She nodded, nervous about how she would go about doing that. Mr. Bass was… Well, he was Mr. Bass. If she saw him in the office, she was more likely to melt into a stumbling puddle, all vowel sounds and no consonants. "How should we go about it?"

"I may be able to put a bug in his ear."

"That sounds more like it will irritate him." In fact, her own ears started to tickle at the thought, but she chuckled at her joke.

Graham laughed and pointed at her. "You're right. That's an idiom that sounds awful."

"Agree." Bernadette giggled, tossed her crust to Frank, and

then grabbed another slice. Frank caught the crust midair and chomped it once before swallowing. "You're going to choke, boy. Chew a little more."

"How about I just give Mr. Bass a call with a heads-up? Won't hurt to have the exec board on your side when all the other Walls in the office start going nuts."

At the name Wall, Frank did his due diligence again and snatched Graham's napkin, shredding it. Graham chuckled and snatched up the pieces. "He sure likes napkins."

"I should have warned you. W-A-L-L is a trigger for him."

Graham laughed harder. "That's hilarious."

"So, you don't think Bass will try to stop us?"

"I don't." Graham's tone was full of confidence.

"If you think it will help, then I trust you."

Graham smiled. "I never thought I'd hear you say the words."

Heat flushed her cheeks, and she smiled. "Not words I utter often." And it was true. Somehow Graham had snuck his way behind her defensive wall and picked up a shield to fend off everyone else.

"I'm honored to have gained your trust."

"You earned it, Graham." He didn't say it, but they were both thinking it… That was the first time she'd not called him Mr. Reynolds.

Chapter Twenty-One

MONDAY ROLLED AROUND AND BROUGHT with it rain. Not just a sprinkle for an hour with the sun then popping out, but the dark, angry clouds and fat, cold drops of autumn. The relentless kind of rain that lasts for hours, days, even a week.

Bernadette didn't begrudge rain. After all, she'd grown up on a farm, where any type of precipitation was cause for celebration.

But today, the day she was going to officially toss her own rule book out the window, the rain felt ominous. A warning from the universe, underscoring the doubts she'd battled since hopping on the revolution train.

Still, every thirty minutes, Bernadette stood from her desk and quietly shuffled to the windows in the copyediting department, staring at the slick pavement and somber city, hoping that by some miracle, the clouds would part and the sun would dry up all the cement. Today was not a good day for rain.

At least the clouds had gone from dark gray to light, an indication that soon the rain would let up. She just hoped it was by three o'clock. The walkout was happening whether they'd be shielded by umbrellas or not.

After lunch, Mr. Wall seemed agitated behind his office door. Pacing, snarling, so twitchy she expected to see him lose it like Hitchcock's Norman Bates and open the door to call for "Mother."

Truthfully, the man could probably use a session with a shrink. As much as she despised him, she didn't want him to drop dead of a heart attack.

As she watched him, Wall suddenly froze and dropped into a chair. Her eyes widened, wondering if she'd just jinxed him into a cardiac emergency. Then he blinked and snapped up his telephone, and she breathed a sigh of relief.

One time on the farm, when she'd been about seven, she picked up a chicken and it just went limp in her arms. She'd thought it was dead until her mother said it was something chickens did. "Chicken fear," she'd said. Later Bernadette had looked it up and found out it was basically a catatonic state the chicken put itself in out of fear of dying.

Bernadette pressed her lips together to keep from smiling. It really was fitting that she was comparing her boss to the farm bird, because he was rather a yellow-bellied chickenshit.

She'd mostly avoided Wall today, asking Greene to carry in a manuscript she'd turned in when he was headed in that direction. Of course, Greene had given her a look that said she should go eat rocks, but Bernadette didn't let that deter her. The less time she could spend with Wall—alone—the better. Especially since it had only been a few days since he'd propositioned her, and she'd been shut down by personnel on handling it.

A buzz of activity outside the copyediting office snagged

Bernadette's attention. She'd missed who had been walking by, and from the look Sarah was giving her, and nodding her head down the hall as if she should come and look, Bernadette's heart was doing a little skip in her chest.

Ever since the confessions at the café, Sarah had been much more amiable toward Bernadette, but despite her geniality, there were brittle edges and an entire subterranean level of Sarah that had yet to be smoothed and excavated. Bernadette didn't one hundred percent trust her, not after all she'd done to hurt her, but she was getting close, and that gave her hope.

A glance at the clock showed it wasn't three o'clock yet. They had two hours to go before the walkout.

The answer to her question came into view before she'd reached the entrance to the department—Mr. Bass.

He was dressed in an impeccable pin-striped suit, and his silver hair shone without a strand out of place. He was as impressive today as he'd been the first time she'd seen him when she was a college student. But not in an overbearing way. There'd always been something kind in his stance, and in the way he really paid attention when people spoke, that drew in her and others.

On the other side of the glass wall, he greeted Sarah, both of their expressions pleasant, but Bernadette couldn't hear what was being said—and she was dying to know. Was he here because Graham had called him and he approved of the walkout? Or was he here to put a stop to the walkout before they even had a chance to do it?

Mr. Bass was on the executive board of the publishing company, but that didn't mean he was in the office every day. They were graced with his presence perhaps only once a month when they had their meetings. And the last one had been only two weeks ago. There could be no coincidence that he was here today.

Or could there? Was his presence the reason Wall seemed especially off his rocker today?

Nerves prickled her skin until Bernadette felt like she had a bunch of ants climbing up and down her hair follicles. This was ridiculous. Mr. Bass was a man she admired, and he'd always been nice to her and supported her work at Lenox & Park. Bernadette stood, smoothing her clammy hands down her skirt, and was stepping around her desk to go and greet him when Wall burst from his office, glared at her, and then marched toward Mr. Bass.

Bernadette sat back down at her desk. She'd have to wait her turn, for she certainly wasn't going to interrupt Wall and risk humiliation.

She remained a spectator behind the glass, observing Wall shake Mr. Bass's hand, pretending that her boss was an upstanding citizen rather than a philandering, woman-hating cad.

Wall pinched a handle on his mustache, giving it a little twist. Perhaps a sign he was nervous that Mr. Bass was here. As if to give credence to those words, Wall glanced toward her, and the watery blue of his eyes turned glacial.

He had to have known she'd gone to personnel. Even though the manager had refused to take notes, he most certainly would have warned Wall of her complaint. But he wouldn't have known that Graham was going to call Bass, so he was likely having a bit of a meltdown moment inside his moldy head.

Good.

She shouldn't be the only one filled with nerves. In fact, she shouldn't be nervous at all. Offended, disgusted, ready to tear his mustache off—yes. Wall was a parasite, and he deserved to be uneasy, exposed, tossed out with the garbage.

A moment later Mr. Bass sidestepped Wall, in an awkward shuffle where from all outward appearances it looked like Wall was trying to get in his way. But he lost the battle, and Mr. Bass entered the copyediting department. Dusting off his jacket sleeves as if dusting off Wall's idiocy.

Bernadette pretended not to have noticed, but she didn't hide her pleased smile.

"Miss Swift." His smile was genuine as he approached her, and she was quick to stand and hold out her hand to shake his.

"Mr. Bass. It's always so lovely to see you."

"Likewise. I've been hearing good things about your work, and I'm pleased you were promoted to senior copy editor."

A rush of thoughts each battled to be the first one she dissected. One, he was hearing good things about her work. And two, he didn't say *temporary*. Had he forgotten the word?

"Lenox & Park is lucky to have you on board," he continued.

Did that mean *permanently*? Bernadette pinched her fingers together. Inside, her brain was shouting questions, but on the outside, she was just nodding along and smiling, murmuring her thanks and expressing her affinity for her job as a copy editor.

"I know you were instrumental in the celebrity memoir fiasco."

Bernadette's tongue went dry. How did he know? Her face must have asked the question because he continued by saying, "I recognized your notes in the margins. A Swift-proof copy." Mr. Bass winked, and she nearly fell off her chair.

Wall appeared behind Mr. Bass, and she glanced at him over

the man's shoulder, watching his cheeks go from their usual typical gray to a ruddy red.

"Thank you," she said. "It was a challenge, but one I fully embraced."

Wall grimaced, turning a shade close to purple.

Bass looked over his shoulder at Wall, and from his profile, it was obvious he didn't bother hiding his disdain for the man. "Is there something you need, Wall?"

Wall sputtered, his tongue finally gaining traction. "No, nothing, sir. Good to see you, sir." And then he walked slowly back to his office, dismissed by Mr. Bass. There was no slamming of the door that was typical but instead a subtle, quiet *snick* that spoke louder than any crash on a regular day.

"Keep up the good work, Miss Swift. I understand there are a lot of challenges here besides memoirs, but know that you and your work are valued. You're a true leader. And I hope that I'm around long enough to see you continue to rise at Lenox & Park."

Until that moment, Bernadette hadn't realized how much she wanted to hear those words from an upper-level executive. To know one's worth and value in the workplace was to comprehend her place in the company. The worries she'd had about being fired, about having to start over melted away like butter in a pan. "I appreciate your support, Mr. Bass, and I'm honored to hear it." And she wondered what Greene, Marshall, and Evans, who were all practically falling out of their chairs to listen, were thinking to hear him speak with her in such a respectful way.

Fishermen loved to cast their nets in hopes of catching the biggest fish, and it was no different with an office apple polisher. Maybe they'd shift some of their biases and take note. Was it too much to hope that she could one day walk into this office and not feel ostracized? Ogled? Other?

Mr. Bass nodded, then leaned forward a little. In a whisper so no one else could hear, he said, "I'll see you this afternoon." Then he winked and wandered around the room, giving each of the other copy editors a moment of his attention.

He'd see her this afternoon…

He was going to go on the walkout too?

That was…both stellar and crazy.

Mr. Bass was likely not sitting at an executive table full of men willing to give women equal opportunity, despite the federal act having been passed. But walking out with the rest of the women in the company, with Graham, would show firmly where his shiny shoes were settled.

Bernadette floated back to her desk, picked up her pencil, and thumbed through *Webster's Third*. Concentrating was hard, but she did her damnedest lest one of the proofers on the other end wonder what had gotten into her in making mistakes or missing things. Bernadette triple-checked her work, not only running through each of her own marks but also verifying the words on the page one more time just in case.

The clock ticked interminably. And all the while she shifted in her chair and scribbled on paper, trying to make time go faster, trying to distract herself, to no avail. Blood buzzed in her veins, her ears ringing and skin tingling with anticipation. Then finally it was quarter to three. Bernadette stood from her desk, her legs trembling slightly with excitement. She went to use the ladies' room, partly because she needed to use the toilet, and partly because she needed some privacy to do some deep breathing.

Wall was not going to be pleased with the walkout—though she did wonder with only her and Sarah in the department how long he would take to notice they were gone. And really, what could he do about it with Mr. Bass on her side?

Sarah walked into the restroom a moment later. Instead of a beige shirt, she wore one in light pink that brought out the gold flecks in her brown eyes. "I'm so nervous." She shook her hands as if that was going to make some of the feeling disappear, as if she could fling nervous energy down the drain with excess water.

"We have support from at least one person on the executive board." Bernadette's voice practically trembled with the thrill of what they were about to do.

Sarah's eyes widened. "Really?"

"Yes."

"So I'll still have a job after today. That's good to know."

Bernadette laughed. "I was a little worried about that too."

"Wall is so volatile."

"Like a caged fox ready to just scratch and bite his way through metal."

Sarah chuckled. "He's rabid all right." Then her expression turned serious. "And I'm so sorry I ever thought you could…that you would…"

Bernadette did the only thing necessary, the one thing she'd learned as a child that she could do. "I forgive you."

Tears wet Sarah's eyes, but she blinked them away, blowing out a breath. "I'm so glad."

They left the bathroom together, both of them carrying their purses. They got a few curious glances, but no one stopped to ask what they were doing. In the elevator, they both slipped out of their pumps and into their Keds as women joined them on each floor down.

By the time they got to the lobby, they popped out of the elevator in a mass of giggles and excited chatter. The energy flowing through the women was enough to make Bernadette feel light on her feet, and she practically floated toward Melanie's desk, where she too was slipping on her sneakers.

"This is incredible, Bernadette." She grinned and wiggled her eyebrows. "And was that Mr. Bass I saw go up earlier?"

"Yes. Has he come back down?"

"A few minutes ago with Graham. They went outside. I assumed to a meeting."

Bernadette licked her lips nervously, wondering if the two men had changed their minds. Why make an uproar with their male colleagues if they could take a step back? She wouldn't blame them if they decided to do that, though it would be pretty disappointing.

But the second she stepped out into the gray—no longer raining—afternoon, those thoughts disappeared. Graham and Mr. Bass were both waiting with a few other men and dozens of women—most of whom were dressed in pink.

"You made it," Bernadette said in a rush of air that sounded almost like an overexcited whisper.

Graham nodded, his lip hitching at one corner, a hint of his dimple showing. "Wouldn't miss it for the world."

"Miss Swift, you remember my wife, Jane." Mr. Bass looked down on his wife with an expression of admiration that Bernadette found inspiring.

"Fancy meeting you here," Bernadette said with a delighted smile.

"Fancy indeed." Jane's expression was teasing and conspiratorial.

The sounds of New York City traffic lightened almost to a pause, and Bernadette looked up, the silence in the city a shock. That's when she saw women spilling out of the doors of the various buildings. Women she hadn't spoken to before or met or even recognized. Women who'd somehow gotten the message through the power of word of mouth that today they would walk out, that they would commiserate together and join their collective forces.

"This is incredible," she murmured, squeezing her hands together. "Gosh, I hope it makes a difference."

"You already have, in every one of these women's lives." Melanie bumped her shoulder as she pointed at the crowd. "None of them would be out here without you."

"Let's hope it works." Bernadette's words were a fervent wish, a prayer to the universe.

"Something's gotta change," Melanie said.

The honking resumed, and was it just Bernadette's imagination, or did the traffic get louder?

"Shall we?" Bernadette lifted up on her tiptoes and gave an enthusiastic clap. "Caffe Shakespeare is about to serve the most patrons they've ever had."

They headed down Fifth Avenue, a bigger wave of women today than yesterday, and they were definitely making a splash.

There were shouts from some of the cabs telling them to get back inside. A few men rushed out of buildings warning women of being fired. But what could they do? The only way anything was going to change was for them to make a splash.

By the time they'd ordered their coffees, Penelope and the other ladies from their book club had arrived too.

"Patty," Jane Bass said, pulling her in for a hug, and then the two of them wandered off to get a table.

Flanked by Penelope and Melanie, Bernadette watched them walk off, surprised to see Patty here, but also extremely glad.

Graham stood by the door with Mr. Bass, talking casually, but with his eyes on Bernadette the whole time. She kept sneaking him smiles, thinking about their pizza date and how he'd walked her home. How on the doorstep to her apartment she hadn't known whether to hug him or shake his hand and had instead given him an awkward wave.

How she'd gone inside and flipped on the radio, dancing to "He's So Fine" by the Chiffons with Frank wiggling circles around her. Even now as she stared at him, she could hear the music and lyrics beating a rhythm in her mind.

"You've got it bad," Melanie whispered, then nodded at their friends. "Doesn't she?"

"What have I got?"

"The look," Penelope commented. "I used to look at Victor like that."

Bernadette wished she could run to the nearest mirror and see just what that looked like. But they were next in line and she was itching for a latte.

"How was pizza last night? We didn't get a chance to talk about it," Melanie said.

"You've got to give us all the juicy details." Penelope wiggled her brows.

"The cheesy details," Bernadette said, laughing. "It was delicious, and he was a perfect gentleman."

"Boring," Melanie teased and rolled her eyes.

Bernadette grinned. "He walked me home."

"And?" Melanie made a rolling motion with her hand.

"I was awkward, as usual."

Penelope laughed. "Tell me you didn't wave like you did when that sweet boy Colin dropped you back at our dorm."

Bernadette let out a long sigh and hung her head. "I did the wave."

Penelope groaned and clutched her chest like she might keel over. "Poor Graham."

"Well, he didn't seem to mind too much.," Melanie flicked her eyes in Graham's direction. "He hasn't taken his eyes off you this whole time."

"True. Perhaps you've met your waving match," Penelope added, laughing at her own joke.

"He loves dogs. And Frank loved him." In Bernadette's world, that made him the perfect boyfriend material.

"A match made in heaven." Penelope and Melanie leaned into each other with the kind of sigh people make when rehashing meet-cute scenes in books.

"I do really like him." Bernadette felt her face heat when her eyes connected with his. She quickly glanced away. "A lot."

"Go talk to him." Penelope nudged her, handing Bernadette her order and another cup from the counter. "Now's your chance to make up for the wave. Give him a latte."

Bernadette smiled and sipped at her latte, meeting Graham's eyes over the edge. He really was watching her. And she couldn't look away. And then she couldn't stop walking toward him either.

When she arrived, she found her throat didn't want to work and her tongue weighed a thousand pounds.

"Good work, Miss Swift," Mr. Bass said, interrupting her rediscovery of speech.

"Thank you, sir."

He nodded and then glanced toward his wife. "Ah, my lovely wife has gotten me a tea."

He walked off, and then it was just Bernadette and Graham. Staring at each other.

"Thank you." Without spilling a drop despite the sudden numbness in her fingers, she passed him the latte.

"You're welcome—and thank you." He tapped his latte against hers. "But for the record, you don't have to thank me. I wanted to help you out. And I support your cause."

Bernadette nodded, wondering if that meant he would also be interested in anything beyond supporting the cause and helping. If maybe the wave had been entirely appropriate on her part because he wouldn't have gone in for a hug or kiss anyway. Maybe it wasn't even a date.

Her mind started to spiral.

"How's Frank?"

"Pizza hangover."

Graham chuckled. "I hope we can treat him to another pizza soon."

So maybe it was a date… "He'd like that. I'll be taking him for an extra-long walk today in the park to make up for it."

"Want company?"

Bernadette's mouth went dry, the spiraling questions she'd had before turning in reverse and rewinding back into the recesses of her mind. Whatever answer she gave now was going to change the course of their relationship. She could say no, and he'd probably never ask her again. Except that Graham was persistent. She could put an end to whatever it was they were starting. And she could be miserable for it.

Or she could say yes. And they could give whatever it was between them a chance.

Of course, he could also just love dogs and want to be around Frank.

"Frank would love the extra company."

Graham raised a brow, his lip twitching in a half smile. "And you?"

So, it wasn't just for Frank. She squeezed her mug so tightly that her fingers went numb.

"I would love the company too."

Graham's smile widened, that dimple in his cheek on full display now. "You fascinate me, Bernadette."

Somewhere in the background, the Crystals' "Then He Kissed Me" started to play, setting Bernadette's imagination on fire. It seemed like all the music these days was playing the themes of her life. She sucked in a breath at the same time she lifted her latte to her lips and ended up breathing in a lungful of coffee and milk. Bernadette coughed so hard it shook her cup, and she ended up spilling it down the front of Graham's shirt.

But rather than be upset, he laughed, took the cup away while calling it a weapon, and then patted her on the back. "Are you all right?"

She coughed a little more, tears spilling on her cheeks, and then she started to laugh. "I'm a mess."

"Hey, so am I." He grinned and pointed toward his shirt.

"I will get that cleaned for you. I happen to know a great dry-cleaning company."

Graham laughed at that and shook his head, hair spilling across his forehead. "And here we are full circle. I would never let you."

"A true gentleman, but seriously. I messed up your shirt. I should get it cleaned."

"I don't think it's your fault."

"Of course, it is. I spit coffee all over you."

"I made you choke."

His words came back to her then: *You fascinate me.*

No one had ever said that to her before, and her face heated anew. Only this time the warmth spread through her like she'd sunk into a steamy bath.

"I don't think it was so much that I choked as that you took my breath away."

This time it was Graham's turn to snort coffee into his lungs.

Chapter Twenty-Two

ONE MOMENT'S ACCOMPLISHMENT DOES NOT always filter over to the next. The world spins on its axis, giving light from the sun and darkness on the other side. That was kind of how the publishing world felt. Yesterday's walkout, the march before, Mr. Bass's support, Graham's, all of it had left Bernadette twirling.

Apparently, she'd twirled too much and woke up on the wrong side of a loop.

Getting ready in the morning had been easy.

Riding the bus had been easy.

Even stepping off the bus onto the busy city sidewalk had been easy.

But trying to get from the bus stop to the Lenox & Park building was nearly impossible.

Outside the publishing offices men marched, dressed in all black like they were in mourning. They carried posters that read *Revoke Women's Equal Pay* and *Go Home* and *Stop Inequity, Save the Men.* They shouted the same things, and they shouted some things worse.

Bernadette paused on the outer rim of the male cluster, trying to process what exactly was happening. Maybe she was still asleep and this was a nightmare. But the chill of the fall morning, the shouts that made her ears ring, was all very real. This was an anti-women's-movement protest. And considering it was outside her place of work meant only one thing: it was in direct opposition to what she'd been able to rally support for.

This attitude of antagonism was the very opposite of what she and her friends had demonstrated. They'd been peaceful. Displaying their ranks, showing that when they left the office things didn't get done. In fact, what they'd come to learn was that the entire industry had needed to shut down for the day. Though women were outranked on every floor, in every department, they were also the backbone of the workforce, the glue that stuck the pages to the spines. Without them, everything fell apart.

The vehemence in some of the men's voices was downright scary. Bernadette searched the crowd for a familiar face in hopes of convincing someone, anyone, to call this charade quits. But unfortunately, she didn't recognize anyone.

Bernadette had two options: she could push through the spiteful horde and into the building, or she could turn around and go home.

Going home meant quitting, and she'd never been a quitter. Though these protesting men were making her nervous, she wasn't going to let that stop her from going to work. She *couldn't* let that stop her.

Pasting on her best I-mean-you-no-harm smile, she passed, nodding, murmuring *good morning*, trying to appear pleasant,

congenial, but it didn't matter. The very thing she was doing—
going to work—went against their cause. Like wolves who smelled
blood, the pack turned on her.

Men jostled her, plucked at her, pushed her. On instinct, she
wanted to use the tactics her brother had taught her. Jab them in
the eyes with her fingers. Stomp on their toes. Kick them in the
balls. But she didn't want this to turn into outright violence.

Another man shouted, "Get out of here. You don't belong!"
so close to her face she felt his breath and the stink of his rotting
breakfast on her cheek.

"Excuse me," she murmured softly at first and then louder,
angrier as she tried to squeeze through. Prickles of sweat broke out
on her spine, cold against the flush of heated anger.

But they took the opportunity to push in, closing ranks until
she was being touched on all sides. Until she wanted to scream
and punch and vomit. God, how she wished Ben were here now
instead of in the middle of a war zone himself.

"Excuse me," she said louder, but that didn't matter. And any
pushing she did only came back at her tenfold.

Their purpose was to not let her in the building, not let her
near the door, and maybe something a little more sinister than
that. She pushed harder, and they pushed back. Someone grabbed
her ass and squeezed hard, a pinch that was definitely going to
bruise. She cried out, stomped her foot, was pleased when there
was a yowl of pain. Screw trying to be polite. With all the leering
faces looming in her purview, it was hard to figure out just who
had pinched her.

"How dare you," she shouted and started to push, needing to
get away. Jabbing, stomping as she went.

That only seemed to fuel their pack-animal frenzy.

"Let her in before I call the cops!" Melanie's booming voice came from somewhere near the building, but with the men closed in around her, Bernadette couldn't see. "Want Gary here to start pounding you with his cudgel?"

"Move." Gary's voice carried over the crowd, the single syllable holding the promise of his exacting punishment for anyone who didn't listen, along with the clang of his cudgel hitting metal in warning.

Though they sneered, they did back off and Bernadette decided she'd take all the sneers in the world just to not be touched. She walked into the building with her head held high, but the moment she crossed the threshold, her knees shook and her hands trembled so violently that she dropped her lunch bag and purse and would have collapsed if Melanie hadn't been there to hold her up.

"Don't let them see you break," Melanie whispered. It wasn't just her words but the familiarity of her friend that was a comfort. "That's what they want."

"Thank you." Bernadette glanced at Gary, dressed in his guard's uniform, fiercely glaring out the glass doors. "Thank you, Gary. I don't know what…"

"Don't think about it," Melanie said. "You're safe. And I've already called the cops. They should help clear this out, or at least provide support to you and anyone else trying to get in or out of the building."

Bernadette nodded, already deciding she wasn't leaving the safe walls of Lenox & Park for lunch, and maybe she could just sleep under her desk. Ask Mrs. Morris to come by and fetch Frank.

"Are you all right?" Melanie asked softly, stroking Bernadette's hair, eyes full of concern.

"I'll be all right." Bernadette spotted her reflection in the bronze of the elevator doors, and noted the lie in her own words. "I'm a mess."

A piece of her blouse had come untucked, her skirt was twisted, there was a button missing from her jacket, and worst of all—her headband, the pink one with a crystal "B" in the center, was gone. She turned back to look outside and saw a man wearing her headband, making an ugly face, and waving his hands at her.

No way did she want it back now, fairly certain that every time she put it on, she would remember this moment.

"Want me to fix your hair?" Melanie moved to her desk, pulled out a drawer, and held up a brush and a comb like she'd come prepared for battle.

Bernadette nodded, unable to speak, afraid that the moment she tried, the numbness would subside into a torrential downpour of blubbering emotion. That had been scary as hell out there. The closest she'd come to a combat situation, and if her brother experienced that with the enemy, gun-wielding soldiers… She shuddered.

"Gary, will you watch the phone for a second?" Melanie called over her shoulder as she steered Bernadette toward the lobby restroom.

"I got ya covered, Melly."

"Melly?" Bernadette asked, a smile in her voice.

Melanie giggled the way she imagined she had as a child when a boy checked the "I like you" box on a note passed in class. "I think we might be dating."

"I want to hear about that."

"Caffe Shakespeare, this weekend."

"Please."

In the restroom, Bernadette put her clothes back in order. Melanie fixed her hair so it framed her face, but there was something noticeably missing without her signature Grammarian headband, and it made her feel vulnerable. She touched up her lipstick and changed her pantyhose, tossing the pair she'd put on this morning into the trash. Even though they were miraculously the one thing not disturbed, she felt cleaner having done it.

In the lobby, Gary had picked up her purse and lunch bag, setting them on Melanie's desk. Through the windows she could see the men still gathered, but also the noticeable uniforms of the police. A few men dispersed, and others held tight to their small cement corner of the world. Proud to be shouting derogatory, sexist remarks.

"Are you going to be okay?" Melanie's lip curled in disgust as she stared out the window.

"I'll be fine. Seriously, thank you." Bernadette hoped her smile conveyed the message in her words, even though inside she still felt violated, unnerved.

"Anytime. I'll keep you posted when they leave. Maybe we'll get lucky by lunch." Melanie shrugged, but the glance she passed Gary said she didn't believe a word she said.

Bernadette hugged her friend and then made what felt like an even longer journey on the empty elevator to the eleventh floor. She rubbed her arms, trying to ward off the chill, but since it wasn't really a temperature issue so much as the problem of having a strange man pinch her hard enough to leave a purple mark, the goose bumps remained.

Sarah narrowed her eyes as she came toward her, some of her usual snark having returned, it appeared. Change took time. Or maybe Sarah felt the need to keep up appearances. Who knew.

"No headband today?"

"How did you get inside unscathed?"

"Oh…" Sarah's animosity melted immediately. "There were only a few of them out there when I arrived, and I happened to come off the subway at the same time as a few others. Safety in numbers."

"I arrived alone. The headband was collateral." Bernadette tucked her purse up on her shoulder, hugging the bag closer with her elbow as if that might give her some measure of comfort.

"Let me get you a coffee." Sarah's tone was soft, congenial even, and the compassion in her eyes, though out of place on her face, was sincere.

Bernadette opened her mouth to protest. She didn't need any favors from Sarah. But Sarah held up her hand. "It's the least I can do."

Bernadette took in a wobbly breath. "Thank you," she managed to say around a throat that felt like her headband had been tied there and invisible hands were squeezing, squeezing.

"No problem."

Bernadette issued her usual good mornings to her copyediting mates, but none of them replied other than a few grunts. That wasn't unusual, as they didn't normally greet her, but there did seem to be some added heat to their typical caveman style of communication. She tucked away her purse, her lunch, and stared at the manuscript piles on her desk. At least she'd be able to lull herself into a fugue state with her work.

From her periphery, she spied Marshall stand up when she sat down—and not move. She ignored him. He cleared his throat. Bernadette guessed he wanted something. Maybe a pencil, a ribbon of typewriter ink, to insult her in some way. He had his hands on his hips and was looking down at her, brows and lips pinched like an accordion file.

The last thing Bernadette possessed was the patience to deal with whatever it was he was about to hand out.

"Those protestors outside are your doing." Resentment wove itself through each syllable, punctuated by his ever-present disdain.

Bernadette returned her attention to the manuscript she needed to start, quipping, "Hardly."

"Do you think they'd be there if you hadn't staged that ridiculous walkout? We have deadlines here."

"It's possible." Bernadette crossed out *wierd* and put in *weird* with the note, *"i" before "e" except after "c" and in weird, rein, deity, seizure. A mnemonic rule of thumb that often thwarts itself.*

"Miss Swift, the question of possibility is not on the table." There was a shift upward in pitch in Marshall's tone that reminded Bernadette of a child's tantrum.

With an annoyed sigh, she put down her pencil and gave Marshall her attention. "Their posters, actions, and words are anti-women's-movement. Whether or not I do anything, the very fact that I'm coming to work is what they are protesting against."

Marshall breathed out hard through his nose. "You drew attention to yourself."

Bernadette glanced up at Marshall, crossed her arms over her chest, and assessed him. The man was an utter imbecile. And she was about to let him have it, her patience gone.

"Who pissed in your porridge?" Sarah set a steaming mug down in front of Bernadette. "Last time I checked, blaming the victim was still on the no-no list."

Marshall seethed, sucking a breath through his teeth, his attention fixed on Sarah. The way his lips twisted, he definitely had a few things he wanted to say, and none of it was going to be office appropriate.

But before he could say a word, Evans shocked them all by saying, "Come on, Marshall. Those idiots outside are assholes. If you don't agree, go stand with them."

"Agree," Greene punctuated with a slide of his typewriter carriage back into place. "We need Miss Swift and Miss Yeager and every other female in this place."

Marshall didn't have a response to that. And good thing, because if he'd tried to say one darn thing against them, Bernadette was definitely going to start flinging her coffee and curse words around.

Fortunately for Marshall's sake, he simply rapped his knuckles on his desk a little harder than was necessary and took a seat.

Bernadette felt it safe to lift her mug then, taking the first glorious sip and thanking Sarah for being the one to brew it. She glanced at Evans and Greene, not really knowing what to say or do, and definitely not having expected their standing up for her. For Sarah. For women's rights.

Just then Wall's obnoxious voice was heard through the glass from the corridor, and disgust seized Bernadette's spine like a high-voltage electric shock. Unpleasant and debilitating. The last person she wanted to see.

She set her coffee down, shoved a piece of paper into her typewriter, and flipped to the next page of the manuscript she was working on, determined not to pay any attention to her boss and to seem deeply enmeshed in her work. If Marshall was ballsy enough to go toe-to-toe with her and blame her for the nonsense outside, Wall was definitely going to go nuts over it.

Bracing for the verbal onslaught, she tapped a little too harshly on the keys.

"Marshall, Evans, Greene, Swift," he shouted. "Meeting in the editorial conference room."

She nodded, not trusting her voice. Bernadette snapped up a pen and pad of paper, choosing to leave her still-hot coffee on her desk in case she couldn't control herself. Marshall sat across from her, glaring, and Evans and Greene sat beside him. A few others joined them, filling up the seats around the conference table.

She was stiff with apprehension, waiting for the accusations to flare, but the meeting was mundane, and there wasn't a single mention of the protestors or the walkout. She didn't know whether to be relieved or more worried.

When it was over, she glanced out the window, down the eleven flights to where she should have seen pavement. Protestors were still outside, so Bernadette ate her lunch with Melanie in the break room. By closing time, most of the group had dispersed, and the cops too. She could get past a few, even if the idea turned her stomach.

Graham stopped by the empty copyediting office on his way out for the day, and just the sight of him took some of the stress off her shoulders.

"Want me to walk you to the bus station?" He was nodding as he said it, a not-so-subtle message she should agree.

"I'm sure I'll be fine." At least she hoped, but she hated to put him out of his way.

"Probably, but I'd like to do it all the same."

Remembering what happened that morning had her shuddering. An escort wasn't a terrible idea. Besides, Graham and she were…what? Certainly, more than friends. "All right."

She was glad she agreed, because the few stragglers who remained behind from the horde looked to be the most vicious, snarling but not going past an invisible line as she left the building. Hungry lions, teeth gnashing, claws swiping.

A cross word from Graham had them quieting, slinking, scowling, but still, the damage was done on the inside. Bernadette squeezed her hands into fists to stop them from trembling.

"I might need to bring Frank with me tomorrow."

"Not a bad idea."

"I'm sure he could sit tight with Gary while I work. I hope. I hope Gary isn't mad about it."

"Or my office—he can guard my door against offensive prose."

She laughed at the image he conjured. "He would probably love that. But, at least with Gary he won't have to go down eleven flights to use a patch of grass—or take you away from your desk."

"True." Graham glanced back at the mercenaries, shaking his head.

Bernadette tightened the belt on her jacket. "I can't believe this happened. It's not what I wanted. I just wanted to draw attention to women's rights. Not the attention of the anti-women's movement."

"Don't let a few angry and dissatisfied people get in the way of your cause. It's not about who pays attention on the outside, but what you've done for the women on the inside. They feel empowered. Ready to take on the world. Ready to ask for what they want. Ready to stand up for themselves. No matter what, you've made changes that can't be taken back."

"I hope so."

"You did. And they *are* talking. And the more they talk and the more they do, the more the world will see them."

"I just don't want anyone to get hurt. They were really…scary this morning."

Graham's arms twitched like he wanted to give her a hug. And Bernadette wanted to feel his arms around her. So why was she holding back?

What was the point? No one was here to see it.

She stepped closer, and taking her cue, Graham opened his arms and allowed her to sink against him. All the weeks she'd spent not letting anyone see them talking outside the office were for naught, and now she was just hugging him in full view of anyone who cared to see. And she didn't care.

His scent surrounded her—peppermint, paper, and ink. The hardness of his body, and the beat of his heart against her cheek. She felt safe in his arms but also *seen*.

"Thank you," she murmured against his buttons.

"For the hug?"

"Yes. And for everything else. I don't know what I did to deserve it."

"You didn't do anything to deserve it, Bernadette. I want to give it because…I—shocker—*like* you."

She let out a mock gasp and pulled her head back enough to look up at him. "You like me?"

"I do." There was a solidness in his words, the same reliability as of a dictionary and the placement of an Oxford comma.

"I like you too."

Graham's smile was so sweet, she nearly got a toothache from it. "Rugby's canceled tonight. Want to have dinner with me?"

"I have to get home to Frank." Her answer was bittersweet. Of course, she wanted to get home to Frank, her beloved companion, but the idea of sitting across from Graham and having his undivided attention for a couple of hours sounded like a luxury she'd been putting off having, and now the opportunity was there to seize it.

"I'll bring Chinese." So casual, so normal. Like they did this all the time.

Bernadette grinned. "Deal."

"What do you like?"

"Anything but duck."

"You got it."

Mrs. Morris was just leaving the apartment when Bernadette arrived, her feet floating on clouds, the protestors and their assault having lost some of their power in light of another date with Graham.

"How is Harriet?" Bernadette had been able to get the names of a few lawyers in California from Ruth and passed them along for Mrs. Morris's daughter.

"Swell, dear. I don't know how I can ever thank you for your help with that matter. She's actually coming for a visit next week with her children."

"That is so wonderful." Bernadette hugged Mrs. Morris, her fragile shoulders warm and soft. "And it was my pleasure. Anything I can do to help, I want to."

"You've already done so much."

"That's what friends are for."

Mrs. Morris smiled, and Frank scratched at the door, having heard Bernadette's voice.

"Oh, before you go. Can I give you my leftover beef bourguignon?" asked Bernadette.

"Julia Child? I couldn't, dear. It's too delicious."

"It is melt-in-your-mouth delicious! And I insist. I was going to eat it tonight, but…I have a date."

"A beau? Is it Graham?" Mrs. Morris's veiny fingers steepled together in delight.

Bernadette had mentioned that she'd gone out for pizza with Graham, and Mrs. Morris had seen him come over for the walk in the park with Frank the next day.

"Yes."

"Oh my. I do hope you have a fabulous time."

"Thank you."

Bernadette rushed into her apartment to an excited Frank, who followed her every move as she tidied and set the table. She changed into a more casual dress, then changed again, afraid the dress was too much. She ended up in a pair of denim pants with a pink sweater and a pink-and-white paisley scarf tied like a headband in her hair.

She pulled out two wineglasses, setting them on the table along with a bottle of cabernet sauvignon, and by the time she'd pulled out the cork to let it breathe, there was a knock at the door.

Frank barked and looked at her expectantly. She drew in a deep breath, marched the seven feet to the door, and opened it to a very handsome and grinning Graham.

He held up a bag of Chinese, the salty and greasy scent making her mouth water. But what made her heart melt was what he held up in the other hand—a small pizza.

"For Frank."

Hearing his name, Frank perked up his ears and cocked his head, his long, pink tongue hanging out.

"That was very sweet of you." Bernadette backed away from the door and ushered him inside.

Her heart thudded in her chest as she watched Graham kneel at eye level with a sitting Frank and present him the pizza like a gift.

Frank barked and then gave Graham a massive lick on the chin.

"He likes you," she said.

Graham glanced at her over his shoulder and winked. "I'm glad to have his approval."

But it wasn't just Frank's approval he had. Bernadette was pretty sure she was all in.

Chapter Twenty-Three

FRANK

EVERY DAY I SIT BY the window and watch my girl walk down
the street, her silhouette growing tinier and tinier until she fades
into the swarm of people and the puffs of exhaust, climbing inside
the big bus, and then, in the squeal and hiss of brakes, she's gone.

For hours.

I wondered where that bus took her. Even tried to follow it
one day, sneaking out through the window, but the bus was hard
to keep up with, and I lost her. Finally, today I got my answer.
Here we are standing in front of a tall, shiny building that she calls
Office. I had no idea what Office was before now. The structure
juts out from a horde of men standing with sticks and paper in
their hands.

The hair on the back of my neck stands on end. I don't like
these men. Something about the way they smell, the air around
them vibrating with the stink of malice.

And they tempt me with *paper*. I practically salivate.

They shake the paper, the edges trembling, beckoning me to taste, to tear, to dominate.

I can't resist, and even though Bernadette hasn't given me the command, I jerk forward, snapping the leash from her hands, and snatch one glorious stick attached to a crinkly sheet—narrowly missing the fingers that held it, this last part on purpose. I shake it with my head until my brain jiggles. My eyes connecting with the man's so he can see I mean business. But the man is shouting, charging, and Bernadette looks scared. Beneath the cacophony of the horde, I sense her heartbeat increasing to a frantic pace.

My mission is to protect Bernadette. I will not fail.

I drop the stick and bare my teeth, lowering into a position I hope the man understands means *back up or else.*

"Good boy, Frank." Bernadette pats my head with wobbly fingers. "It's all right now, boy." Her voice is shaky, her heart racing. "Let's go inside. Just leave it. *Leave it.*"

Inside. I know this word well. It's the same thing she says when we get done with our walks. *Leave it.* What she says when I want to grab the tails of the squirrels.

She's got a hold of my leash, and I can feel her trembling through the long strip of leather.

Dogs have good instincts, but I don't even need those to understand she's afraid of all these snarling men. But I also know I can't fight and protect her at the same time, and I'm outnumbered.

I curl my lip and give a mighty bark. Men part, and I bark again, creating a divide between them and us. I tug my girl toward the doors to Office. I don't like her trembling, and I don't like these men. Maybe I should take a few ankles out while we're on our way? Snatch a few more sticks and crunch until they splinter.

These men remind me of the foxes near the henhouse on the farm, and quite frankly, they could do with a little scare.

But first, my girl.

A man she calls Gary rushes out the door and herds us inside.

"Thanks, Gary," she says. I bark my thanks, too, and start to head toward the door to finish what I started, but Bernadette pulls me back.

"This must be the mighty Frank. My God, he's huge."

Gary pets me. He smells like a garlicky everything bagel. I like him. He's goofy with a toothy grin and happy eyes.

"Frank!" I glance over to see Melanie tiptoe-running toward me in heels that are several inches higher than any Bernadette has ever worn.

I like her too. She smells sweet and always gives me treats. I sniff her hand for one, but it's empty. I lick the palm in case the treat is invisible. It's not.

"Oh, I almost forgot." She tiptoe-runs back to her desk and then brings me a hunk of her bagel with cream cheese. *Delicious.*

"Does Frank want to stay here with us?" Gary asks.

I do. I bob my head, hoping he notices. The closer I am to the enemy, the better to take them out.

"I was thinking maybe. Or I could check with the mail room and see if they need help with deliveries."

"Can you imagine?" Gary laughs.

I cock my head at him because I am very good at deliveries. Why is it funny?

"I can ring down to Mark," Melanie picks up the receiver. "They used to have a delivery dog, and I bet they'd love to have Frank."

"Oh, would you?" Bernadette looks at me. "What do you think? Should you help deliver mail?"

Mail. Paper.

Yes. I let my tongue roll out of my mouth and I sit, hoping she knows that I would love to do that.

"I think that's a yes," she says with a little laugh.

"Mark says go on down," Melanie calls from her desk.

The box we climb into is shaky as it takes us down, and I'm not sure I like it. Stairs are better.

The box opens and I jump out, glancing back and barking at Bernadette to hurry up. Why is she taking so long?

She steps out and greets a sleeping man down the hall who reminds me of Mrs. Morris's Mr. Morris before he went away. Then we go into a room that is every dog's dream. Well, at least it's mine.

Paper everywhere in all shapes and sizes. Sheets, envelopes, boxes, wrapping… It's a veritable treasure trove.

"Maybe this was a bad idea," Bernadette says, seeing the look coming into my eyes.

My tail is wagging, and my blood is zinging. Watch out, world, I'm about to…*zoom*…

Everyone stops and watches as I go. Some laugh, some jump up on chairs. I bump into someone, sending paper flying, and Bernadette is running behind me trying to catch me or at least my leash.

"Frank!" she shouts.

Oops. This isn't exactly the right place to zoom. But what's a dog to do when he's found himself in a dreamland?

I scoot to a stop right in front of a man who has his hands on his hips and his eyes locked on mine.

"Frank, is it?" His voice is stern in a way that means business, but not punishment.

I stare at him, mesmerized.

"If you want to help with the deliveries today, then you can't make a mess."

Noted, I bark.

"Maybe I should take him back up to Gary?" Bernadette's brows are furrowed the way they are when we go to the market and she tries to choose between two ingredients.

"We've got him, Miss Swift." Mark's voice softens. "We've wanted a new mail dog. Frank can have a trial day."

I nudge his hand in a truce and Mark pats me on the head.

"We've got our first round ready to go. You ready, boy?"

I bark, and Mark smiles.

"Let me know if you need anything," Bernadette says. "I'll come back at lunch to take him for a walk. And thank you so much."

"Hey, no worries," Mark says. "I understand not wanting to walk into the building through that throng again. Hopefully they disperse soon. In the meantime, we'll take good care of Frank, and maybe he'll take good care of the mail."

"I think he's going to be in heaven. Just whatever you do, don't say W-A-L-L."

"Wa—"

She cuts him off before he can say the word, and man, am I disappointed. I know how to spell it, but I also know when she spells it out, it doesn't count.

"He'll shred everything in sight. It's a command word," Bernadette explains.

"Interesting choice."

My girl winces. "Well, it seemed okay at the time."

Mark laughs. "We've got this."

Bernadette gives me a big hug, and I lean into her, always feeling comforted by her arms around me. "Be a good boy."

I give her chin a lick. *I promise.*

As soon as Bernadette's gone, Mark pulls out something that looks like a jacket and shakes it.

"Used to belong to Rufus, our old mail dog. He got on real well with everyone. Think you can handle this?"

I bark.

"Good." He straps the jacket around my ribs, and then he starts sticking packages and letters into pockets. "This is how we're going to do this." He starts to explain everything, then shakes his head. "What am I even saying right now? I just need to show you."

If I knew how to laugh, I would. Humans are so weird.

Turns out delivering the mail is exactly the same as delivering cookies. I get to make the rounds of the building, checking to make sure everything is safe. Inside, it is.

I make a lot of friends. Every floor we go on, Mark points me in one direction while he goes in another. I stop at each desk while the workers pull their mail from my jacket. I keep waiting to see my girl, and then at last, there she is, talking to another woman at a desk.

As soon as she spies me, I hurry over. It feels like forever since I last saw her, and I was worried she was lost.

"Frank, you pretty baby," she says.

I'm not a baby, but I sure do love when she coos at me.

"This guy might surpass Rufus," Mark says.

"That's incredible. Are you ready for a full-time job?" she asks me.

Beats sitting at home and staring out the window. Though Mrs. Morris will be lonely. And I may have to sneak out tonight to check on the neighborhood.

Bernadette glances at her wrist. "Time for lunch. You hungry, boy?"

Always.

"I want to show you my favorite bench in the park."

Chapter Twenty-Four

A LOT CAN HAPPEN IN a week.

And for Bernadette, the world she lived in seemed to have changed drastically.

For one thing, she had a new Grammarian headband. This one even brighter pink, and the sequined Grammarian letters were even bigger.

Frank delivered her an interoffice letter that said she'd been hired permanently as a senior copy editor and that she'd gotten a raise significant enough she could easily pay for her expenses. Overwhelmed, she'd had to take a moment in the bathroom just in case she broke down in tears of relief.

Later that afternoon, Sarah took a desk down the hall—no longer a secretary but an editorial assistant. Melanie, too, had risen and was now seated at Sarah's old desk. Every woman in the office was on the rise in just seven short days.

The male protestors against women's equality in the workplace had mostly dispersed. There were a few angry stragglers who either

Frank ran off, or Gary did. Bernadette wasn't scared to walk into work with Frank by her side.

They ate lunch together every day in the park, often joined by Graham.

And when she got home, most days Frank stopped by Mrs. Morris's apartment for a visit. The older woman was in heaven right now with her grandchildren and daughter, who'd flown in from California to spend some time with her. But there was something about the bond Mrs. Morris had with Frank that neither of them wanted to break—and her family just adored him.

"Coffee?" Melanie asked Sarah as she headed toward the Chemex to brew a fresh pot.

"Already made it." Sarah held up her cup. Today she was wearing a light-blue skirt suit. At some point she'd completely shucked beige, just like she'd shucked her mean spirit, it seemed.

"You're too good to me." Melanie's hands fluttered over her heart.

"I'll get the next brew," Bernadette volunteered. When everyone was chiming in to help, it felt good to do something nice for others, rather than being taken advantage of.

"Let me."

All three women turned to stare at Evans, his offer hanging in the air between them like laundry billowing on a line in the yard with the wind kicking up. Should they gather it, take it in, or let it stay out to dry and risk it getting blown away?

"What?" Sarah's eyes narrowed. The history between the two of them had never been discussed.

Bernadette was still not sure which of the boys' club members Sarah had a previous relationship with, but by the way the two of them were looking at each other, she had to wonder if it was Evans.

Evans stood from his desk, shoulders straight, and a determined look on his face. His gaze not wavering. "I said, let me."

"But..." Sarah didn't finish the sentence, but they were all thinking it: *You're not a woman. Why?*

"A man should know how to brew coffee." He shrugged as if this were a totally normal occurrence and conversation at Lenox & Park.

"Why?" Sarah was practically breathless now, her eyes going a little watery.

"Well, to be honest, it's because when I'm at home, I have not the first clue." His laugh was embarrassed, the kind of *he-he* one does when they are trying to hide their feelings, but the sound of it makes it obvious to everyone anyway.

"What about your...wife?" Sarah asked.

Suspicions confirmed. Evans *was* the man she'd been having a fling with.

"Turns out she's more of a baseball fan than I thought."

Bernadette cocked her head, confused. There was a story there that she was going to need to know the ending to—and the beginning and middle.

But Sarah seemed to understand. "Oh, Evans." His name was said like a sympathetic sigh. "Come on—I'll show you."

Bernadette glanced at Melanie, who seemed equally confused, chewing on the end of a pencil.

"We'll have to ask her about that later," Melanie said.

Bernadette noticed how closely the two of them walked toward the break room, their whispers like fast little hisses back and forth.

"Going to book club tonight?" Bernadette hoped that in the quiet of the library all the secrets would be revealed.

"You know I wouldn't miss that for the world."

"Me either. And we can ask her then."

Bernadette nodded but was jolted by a banging on the glass coming from Wall's office. He pointed at her and then at her desk, and she nearly lost her mind at the rudeness of it. The downright authoritarianism of it. Not once had he done that to Evans, Marshall, or Greene. Or anyone else for that matter. Nor was she one to stand around chatting and not get her work done—not that either of those things warranted such a boorish reaction.

And she happened to notice Marshall was smirking about it right now. As soon as he saw her glaring at him, the smirk widened.

"Better get to it before Wall decides to shit his pants," Melanie mumbled under her breath.

Bernadette sputtered a laugh. "I'm so glad you're up here. The comical relief is a balm to the soul."

"Anything for you, doll." Melanie winked and then sauntered back to her desk, smoothing her purple tweed skirt as she sat.

In the last week, Wall had barely spoken to Bernadette, other than the gorilla-type directions he'd just demonstrated. But honestly, that was kind of a blessing. She'd not had to contend with any more of his inappropriate touches, so rather than bang on the glass right back, she rolled her eyes and then went to her desk.

Deep into a lexicography search on the word *iridescent*—coined from the Greek word for "rainbow-colored," which was *iris*—she startled out of her intense focus by the phone ringing on her desk.

Her phone rarely rang. Maybe twice a year. Bernadette picked it up, worried it would be a family emergency. Ben was due home in less than a week, and she'd been bracing herself for news that he wasn't coming ever since she'd found out that it was planned. Call it the pessimist side of her that she rarely let out. No one liked a rainy parade. But it was better to be prepared for the worst and hope for the best than to be heartbroken when the worst happened. Though truth be told, if Ben didn't show up in a week, she'd be heartbroken anyway.

"Hello?"

"Hi." Graham's voice came through on the other end of the phone, and she let the nerves about her brother ride off her shoulders, taken over by a tidal wave of nervous, excited energy.

"You know you work down the hall?" Her voice held a hint of a tease.

"And do you know how hard that is for me? I wish I could move my desk next to yours."

Bernadette laughed, then cut herself off and glanced around to see who was paying attention—which was nearly everyone. Even Wall had come to his glass wall to watch her. Bernadette supposed she rarely laughed in the office, and it had probably shocked them all out of their cranky stupors.

"That would mean we'd both be a drain on the production schedule," she murmured against the mouthpiece, hoping that the heat on her cheeks wasn't as flaming red as her B pencils.

"True. Well, I just wanted to hear your voice."

"Lunch in the park with me and Frank?"

"Wouldn't miss it."

Bernadette hung up the phone, unable to keep from smiling, and so she kept her face pointed toward the manuscript in front of her. They'd been spending a lot of time together. But also trying to keep their relationship private at work. It wouldn't do for people to start spreading rumors about the two of them, or for her to have to deal with any snarky remarks from her male office mates. Graham wasn't in her department, but because he was an executive editor, the rumor mill would be in full working order—grinding, crushing, cutting.

She supposed there were still a few rules in her rulebook she followed.

Lunch couldn't come soon enough. She left the copyediting department, glancing down the hallway to see Graham shrugging into his navy-blue tweed jacket just over the threshold of his office door. His eyes met hers as he sauntered down the hallway dressed in slim navy slacks and a white shirt. From this distance, his tie looked like it was navy with polka dots, but when they reached the elevator at the same time, she realized the dots were actually tiny hotdogs.

"Mr. Reynolds," she said, keeping her eyes straight ahead but meeting his gaze in the bronze reflection of the elevator doors. Her fingers itched to grab his, and it was an effort to keep them at her sides. "Hot dogs?"

"Miss Swift." His slow wink was enough to make her toes curl in her pumps. Why had she waited so long to let him in? "I have a weakness for hot dogs."

Bernadette snorted a laugh. As soon as the doors of the elevator were closed behind them, Graham grabbed her hand and pulled her close. Her eyelids dipped closed and she rose on her tiptoes, pressing a kiss to his mouth, savoring the scent of him, the closeness. Melting into this one stolen moment of bliss. But then the elevator dinged, and they jumped apart as the doors opened up in the basement, where Frank waited patiently on the other side.

"Well, hello, boy." Bernadette tapped her leg, and he sauntered inside, riding it up one level with them to the ground floor and the fresh autumn air.

The new receptionist waved, and Gary held open the doors for them, letting them into the autumn sunshine and the slight breeze that brought with it all the familiar scents of the city.

"Hot dog?" Graham asked.

She was about to answer by holding up her lunch bag but noticed he was looking at Frank, who barked.

"I'll grab him one."

"I'll save our bench." Bernadette wiped a few colorful leaves from the bench and sat down. Funny how a couple months ago she would have died at the idea of Graham sharing the bench with her, and now sitting here in her favorite spot had become something of a tradition.

"One for you and one for me." Graham set the hot dog down on the ground in front of Frank.

"I wish you'd let me bring you lunch." Bernadette opened her lunch sack and pulled out her Tupperware with Julia Child's quiche Lorraine and a spinach side salad.

Graham paused midbite to stare at her lunch, and then he groaned. "I wish I would agree, too. However, not only do I crave this meaty goodness, but letting you bring me lunch just isn't right."

"Why not?"

"I can't agree you shouldn't make me coffee and then expect lunch. I'm a grown man. I can take care of my lunch."

Bernadette stared pointedly at the ketchup and mustard bombs on top of his meat stick. "Eating a hot dog isn't exactly taking care of lunch."

"Says who?" He chuckled and took a massive bite.

"Why don't you come over and help make the lunch, and then you wouldn't feel the same way?"

"Are you offering me cooking lessons, Swift?"

"Of course not. I'm not a chef or a teacher. I just like creating recipes. It's a hobby. Some people paint. Some people put puzzles together. Want a bite to see what you're missing?"

Graham nodded and she held up a forkful. The groan he issued after taking a mouthful of quiche had even her licking her lips. "Your hobby tastes good, B."

She grinned. "Of course, it does. Everything Julia Child puts into a mixing bowl does."

Graham stared a little disappointedly at his hot dog. "And apparently everything you do too. How about this weekend for a cooking lesson—I mean, session?"

"Come early and I'll even show you how to shop at the market." She wiggled her brows as if she'd just offered him something entirely too enticing to pass up.

"Enter a grocery store?" Graham's mouth fell open with mock horror. "Will the homemakers bop me on the head with their heads of lettuce?"

She laughed. "No, just their cucumbers and eggplants."

He chuckled and stared at the last bite of his hot dog. "I'm going to savor this last bite. Who knows when I'll have another."

"There is an appropriate time for hot dogs."

"Oh?" Graham looked surprised. "Do tell."

"At a baseball game or a backyard barbecue."

"Do you go to either?"

Bernadette's smile was nostalgic. "Yes. In fact, my father is a Baltimore Orioles fan, and we spent many a season in the stands. And I'll have you know I've had my share of hot dogs. What about you?"

"Yankees through and through."

She grinned. "We should go to a Yankees versus Orioles game."

"You're on. It'll be a while though. They just played last month, and unfortunately we beat you." The exaggerated, *so sorry* look on his face was anything but apologetic.

Bernadette laughed and held up a finger. "By one point."

"I think you mean 'run.' Did you watch it?" Graham looked surprised.

She shrugged and shook her head. "No, but my father was happy to call and rail on the phone about the injustice of it."

"We'll have to invite him to come along with us."

Bernadette's mouth went dry. She was just getting used to kissing and trusting, and now they were talking about a baseball game with her father next year. She wasn't sure she was ready for that yet. But at the same time, the idea of sitting side by side in opposing jerseys was kind of thrilling.

Frank finished with his hot dog and went about his other lunchtime business. Bernadette put away her Tupperware and cleaned up the Great Dane's mess while Graham chased Frank chasing a squirrel through the park.

She could get used to this.

Funny how time and experience changed things. Or maybe just meeting the right person. Because she'd thought she'd remain single forever. Not for lack of wanting love, but because it didn't seem to fit into the prescription she'd given herself for rising in the ranks. For a career.

But the women she'd met—Ruth, Julie—and the women she knew—Penelope, Melanie—all showed her love and career could work in tandem. It was entirely possible that it would work for her too.

———

Melanie and Sarah waited for Bernadette by the side entrance to the library that evening. Both of them wore long slacks and cardigans, as it had started to grow chilly when the sun went down.

Bernadette always felt a little bit like she was in a spy movie on book club night. Hurrying toward the library in the dark and watching the pedestrians and diners across the street to make sure they didn't see her slip into the shadows at the side of the building and call the police to report a break-in.

"This is all so clandestine." Sarah rubbed her arms from the slowly chilling evening. In just a few months the sidewalks would be dusted in white snow.

"Fun, right?" Melanie said.

They gave the knock—*tappety tap-tap-tap*—and the janitor let them in, glancing out to make sure no one had seen them. The room on the upper level was already filling with women, including Patty. The revelation that Patty was married to Mr. Wall still shocked Bernadette every time she was reminded of it. She didn't want to pry, but she was wondering if Patty had taken any steps in her desire to divorce her husband.

Bernadette stilled, staring at the older woman, still dressed as primly as she had been at the first meeting she'd come to. Patty might have been changing internally, but to the outside world, she was still presenting the same picture. Maybe that was how she coped with the change, or how she avoided having to say anything to her husband about it. It was hard not to see Patty in a different light now that Bernadette knew who she was married to. How did Patty handle the bull at home? Had she felt trapped? Bernadette was aware that many women did feel that way. Leave their husband, lose their family. But now that Patty's kids were grown, did that mean she had more options?

It was inconceivable that Mr. Wall acted like he did at the office and then changed when he walked through the door at home. Though perhaps there was a softness to her boss that he never displayed in the workplace?

But Bernadette didn't think she was wrong in her impression that Patty was unhappy. The things she'd said at the meetings and at Caffe Shakespeare were enough to show that. And she also selfishly hoped this didn't mean Wall was going to find out about the secret book club or Bernadette's part in it. Every time she saw him at work, she felt like they'd built Lenox & Park on Mount Vesuvius and any minute the floor was going to become lava.

"Patty," Bernadette said, hugging the older woman, perhaps with a little bit more compassion than before. Then she turned to Jane. "Mrs. Bass. So lovely to see you again."

"You as well, dear."

Patty blushed and looked away for a second, then leaned closer. "I was hesitant to come tonight. I'll be honest. I've always wanted to read the material, but well, it's a bit scandalous."

This week's book—*Sexual Behavior in the Human Female* by Alfred Kinsey and crew—was scandalous for sure. And if the librarian had any idea they were going to spend the next hour talking about sex, then she would have revoked their library membership, banned them from the premises, and fired the janitor for letting their filthy minds inside. This was a step even above *The Feminine Mystique*, and Bernadette was so here for it.

Melanie's request about the Kinsey Reports had become a reality. Penelope had ordered copies, discreetly delivered in pink wrapping paper to each woman in attendance, and tonight they were going to discuss all the intimate chapters.

Bernadette had devoured the book, tearing off the pink paper as soon as she'd gotten it, cracking the spine, and regretting her lack of respect for her 6:00 a.m. alarm when it buzzed only a few hours after she'd finally passed out. All day long she'd walked around work looking at people and wondering about…that part of their lives. Did they or didn't they? Would they or wouldn't they? She hadn't even been able to look at Graham, since they'd yet to go down a path more serious than a few heated kisses. And since, of course, mostly everything in the book had made her think of him. Naked.

Bernadette was a bit nervous about their discussion. But if she was going to talk about sex and orgasms with anyone, she supposed this was the best group to be open with. A group of her peers whom she admired and respected.

Penelope called the meeting to order and everyone sat down, their copies of *Sexual Behavior in the Human Female* in their laps—Bernadette's pressed firmly against her knees. She wasn't the only one sitting like that. Prim and proper, white-knuckling the pages that had explained more about sex and the way the female body worked than any Harlequin novel she'd ever read. Growing up on a farm—and having an older brother who had no problem sharing his exploits—she thought she knew all there was to know. But no. Oh, there was so much she'd learned. Eyes wide open.

"Who has had a chance to read the book?" Penelope asked, somehow able to maintain a calm tone. Bernadette was pretty sure her voice would have squeaked.

Every hand went up, including her own. No hesitation.

"Finished?" Penelope asked.

Again, all hands shot to the air.

"Well, that's a first," Penelope said with a laugh. At the few book club meetings Bernadette had attended, they'd yet to have everyone finish a book. Some didn't even get a chance to crack the spine. This was either a miracle or a sign that women were seriously curious about their sexuality and that society was lacking in educating them. "Shall we go chapter by chapter, or does someone else want to suggest a topic to discuss?"

"I'd like us to skip all the stuff in the beginning and go straight to nocturnal sex dreams," Jenny said, clearly and at a level she didn't typically use. Every head swiveled toward her. She kept her gaze steady on Penelope. "I... This is going to come off... I'll just go ahead and say it. Has anyone had one?"

Chapter Twenty-Five

"I HAVE AN IDEA," BERNADETTE said the next morning at work.

Melanie bit the end of her pencil, then her eyes widened, and she quickly set it down. After their conversations at book club the previous night, and a lively discussion about oral fixation, Bernadette couldn't help laughing.

"What's the idea?" Melanie hedged.

"What if we do a counterprotest? If these jerks are going to be outside, hounding us to no end, we could make our own posters."

"That sounds fun, but dangerous." Melanie glanced around as if she expected to see the protestors from outside pouring in through the vents. "Also why haven't the few who are left gone home already? This is getting ridiculous. They should follow their comrades."

"Hmm. You're right. It is dangerous. Well, then I have another idea. Have you seen those ads for the coffee vending machines?" Bernadette leaned her hip against Melanie's desk.

"Yes. It's fascinating that you just hit a couple buttons, and —*poof!*—coffee in a cup. I hope one of these days we just have to hit a button and our apartments vacuum themselves."

"Impossible." Bernadette laughed. "But instant coffee? I'm going to ask that we get one. Then no one has to make coffee anymore."

"Do you think they'll go for that?"

"I'm not sure." Bernadette glanced toward Wall's office. "Probably not."

"Maybe ask someone else?"

"Good idea."

As if he heard them discussing him, Wall swung open his office door. "Swift!" he bellowed. "I'm not paying you to chatter on. Get back to work."

Bernadette bristled. She rarely chattered on. And she'd not five minutes ago handed in a manuscript, then gone to use the restroom and stopped by Melanie's desk on her way back.

He jammed his finger through the air toward her desk for emphasis, a habit he'd become particularly fond of. Interestingly, there seemed to be more wrinkles in Wall's clothes than usual. Was it possible that Patty was on an ironing strike?

"Better go before he has a heart attack." Melanie rolled her eyes until only the whites showed. "Or maybe you shouldn't."

Bernadette smirked. "I want no part of him on my hands, including his death."

"In my office," he hissed when she was nearly to her desk.

Bernadette's spine tingled. She'd not been summoned into his office since *the* incident, and to be quite honest, she'd hoped to never go into his office alone again.

She glanced toward Melanie, who was on the phone and made a face at her. At least she knew that her friend would be watching in case something bad happened.

Bernadette approached Wall's office like she might approach a haunted house—with caution, a little bit of dread, and regret that she hadn't brought a whole lot of sage.

She stood by the door, refusing to sit, and he shook his head at her as if she were the one being ridiculous.

"I know you're behind all this nonsense." He waved toward the window, where even from this height the protestors could be seen like miniature furious dolls. "And I'm going to warn you right now, any more shenanigans and you're fired."

Fired? Bernadette swiftly turned her attention from the window to Wall, surprised that he would pin the protestors on her. "What nonsense, sir?"

He whirled his fingers in a circle. "Women's equal rights… I don't need to explain it. You're not an idiot."

That might have been the first compliment he'd ever paid her, however backhanded and out of context.

"I'm serious. I don't care who your friends are. I will fire you, and all of your friends." Now that was an empty threat. He didn't have the power to fire all of her friends.

"Make it stop, right now," he demanded.

Bernadette nodded out of habit when given a direct order, even though every cell in her body was boycotting the very idea of agreeing. Why would she ever agree to *fewer* rights for women? That went against the grain.

Yet, Wall did have the power to fire her.

Unfortunately, even though she was protesting what she

believed in, and what should be common sense, what her tactless boss said was also true. By encouraging the women to walk out on the job, she *had* disrupted the workplace, even if it was to help build them up.

Bernadette was between an equality rock and a keep-her-job hard place.

"Bass won't always be around to save your neck," Wall continued, as if needing to toss in one more jab. Like Mr. Bass was the only reason she was here, and not because her own worth was valued.

There were about thirty-seven dozen things she wanted to say back to him. But poking the bear had never been part of her personality, and she wasn't going to start now. Not with him and not when he held her job status captive and had also threatened her friends' employment.

Bernadette nodded, silent and seething, and left his office, returning to her desk and the pile of galleys she needed to read through.

Across from her, Marshall was sneering in a gloating way that made her want to drop-kick him out the door. She refused to look up at him and give him the satisfaction of knowing she saw his sanctimonious mien.

An hour later, the mail arrived, and Bernadette dropped to her knees to give Frank a hug, needing the warmth of his unconditional love and the comfort she felt when holding his hulking, gangly body.

Her dog looked at her with concern, not-so-little eyebrows quirking up and down as he studied her face.

"Some days are better than others," she said.

Frank nuzzled closer as if he knew she needed a hug.

Wall opened the door, and everything from that moment on seemed to happen in agonizing slow motion.

Frank looked up.

Marshall stood and said, "Mr. Wall, I'll get your mail."

Frank bared his teeth, his loping body charging her boss with a wagging nub tail. Wall's arms were outstretched, his mouth slowly forming the word "Stop" as he retreated.

Then the world went on fast-forward. Frank grabbed Wall's pant leg by the ankle, shaking him like a tambourine, while Wall screeched.

Bernadette shouted, "Frank, leave it," at the same time that Mark from the mail room happened on the fiasco, his expression horrified, and boomed, "Drop it."

Frank immediately let go of Mr. Wall's pants.

Mr. Wall turned to Bernadette and stabbed her through the air with his finger. "Get that damn dog out of here. Last straw. Last straw."

Bernadette swallowed, feeling the blood leach from her face and run down through her body toward her feet. Were she and Frank both about to get fired?

"I'm sorry," she murmured, and took hold of the collar on Frank's mail jacket, leading him out of the office. "It was an accident."

"I know," Mark said, shaking his head. "He was a damn good mail-delivery dog."

"Is it possible he won't be fired?"

Mark shook his head. "Any sign of aggression and it's company policy they have to be dismissed."

"Would you mind holding him for second. I'm just going to grab my things so I can take him home."

"Of course. I'll take him down to the lobby to wait."

"Thank you."

On the verge of tears and with her hands trembling slightly, Bernadette went to her desk to retrieve her purse. She grabbed a stack of manuscripts too.

With her stomach all twisted up, she knocked on Wall's door and opened it when he beckoned. "I need to take Frank home. I'll just take these manuscripts with me to work from there, if that's all right."

"It's not all right," he snarled, teeth as bared as Frank's had been a moment ago.

Mr. Wall's upset was understandable, even if it was an accident. His pants and his ego were destroyed. But still, he needed to be reasonable about her leaving. "What would you have me do?"

"Never bring that menace in here to begin with." He slammed his palm down on the desk for emphasis. "I'm docking the cost of these pants from your pay."

First, she didn't have a time machine, and second, she wasn't sure how docking her pay for pants worked, but she wasn't going to argue. The tear in his pants was absolutely her responsibility. She should never have taught Frank that shredding command, and yet it had been gloriously satisfying to see the terrified look on Wall's face when her dog attacked his pants. For once, Wall had been the victim and not her.

"I've already been told by Mark that Frank will no longer be delivering mail. But I can't leave him outside," she explained, thinking that perhaps he didn't understand her need to leave.

"You take one step out of this building before five o'clock and you're fired."

Why was he making this impossible for her?

Bernadette returned her purse and the manuscripts and then walked down to Graham's office. She had a huge favor to ask of him, and she felt bad for even having to bring it up.

Graham had his back to the door, his feet up on his desk, one ankle crossed over the other, his worn brown oxford shoes tapping each other at the toes. A manuscript rested in his hands while he flipped through the pages.

She knocked on the door, and he turned to see her standing on the other side. Immediately he swung his feet down, a smile on his face, and beckoned in her inside.

"This is a pleasant surprise." He stood from the desk and without thinking came around like he might embrace her, but she held up her hands. "What's wrong?"

"Well, Frank decided to make a chew toy out of Mr. Wall's pant leg."

Graham immediately laughed, then halted and stared at her. "What happened?"

"He's been fired—Frank, not Wall—though it would have been nice had it been the opposite."

Graham frowned, his disappointment as palpable as her own. "Oh no, he was so good at his job."

"I agree. He's going to be devastated when he realizes he can't come to work with me anymore."

Tears stung the backs of her eyes at the thought of telling him, "Stay," when she left the apartment each morning.

"I need to take Frank home, but Wall said if I leave the building

I'm fired. Unfortunately, the incident happened right after he'd threatened me the first time with dismissal because of the protests. Third strike and I'm out."

Graham frowned. "He can't fire you for taking Frank home when he's been dismissed."

She shrugged, unable to pull her spine up the way she normally did. "Maybe not, but he's got other reasons. I'm sure he'd come up with a viable reason, such as being disruptive in the workplace and not completing duties as assigned. It's a risk I knew I'd be taking when I organized the walkout, and I've kind of been waiting for the other book to drop ever since."

Graham ran his hand through his already mussed hair. "What can I do to help?"

"I'm so glad you asked, and please know how much I appreciate you." He really was the best of men.

"Of course. If you'd let me, I'd hug you right now."

"I know." And she wanted him to hug her, desperately.

"So, tell me how I can help?"

"Mark is in the lobby with Frank, and he needs to be taken home. Actually, it would probably be best if he went to Mrs. Morris's." She bit her lip. "I was hoping maybe you could take Frank to Mrs. Morris? I'll call her ahead of time."

Graham's frown deepened. "How about I have a word with Wall? You should be able to leave. And you offered to take your work with you, so it's not like you're just skipping out. Worse case he makes you take a personal day."

"I don't know… Doesn't seem right to have my boyfriend go talk with my boss."

"Boyfriend?" He wiggled his brows.

Bernadette's face flamed. "I know we haven't officially called it, but…yes?"

"I love the sound of that. And I promise, in this case, it's one executive to another. Not a boyfriend." He made an X gesture with his arms.

She wrung her hands together, feeling completely unsettled in her own skin. Today was going all sorts of wrong.

"And if he's insistent, then I will absolutely take care of Frank. But if he says all right, I'll go with you. Either way, Frank's getting my company."

"I don't know how to thank you." The dam was close to breaking.

"You don't have to thank me. Talking sense into Wall is the right thing to do. And I adore both you and Frank. I'd never leave you out to dry."

Bernadette nodded, not trusting her voice.

They exited his office and headed back down to the copyediting department. Melanie stared, practically open-mouthed, likely having guessed what was about to happen.

Sarah, too, popped her head out of her office, heading toward Melanie's desk as if she had something official she needed to discuss with her.

Bernadette stood by Graham's side as he approached Wall's office and tapped on the glass door.

Wall glanced up and rolled his eyes but beckoned them in. "What can I do for you, Mr. Reynolds?"

"I just became aware of what happened with the mail dog."

"Went running to your man, huh?" Wall said with a sneer.

"That is a highly inappropriate suggestion," Graham said, not

looking at Bernadette. His eyes blazed into Wall, and she imagined
that they tunneled back a couple thousand years in time, and the
two of them might have circled each other dressed in deerskin and
holding spears. Though, caveman didn't really suit Graham.

"What do you want?" Wall didn't even bother with niceties.

"I think it only appropriate that Miss Swift escort her dog
home, don't you?"

Wall frowned, because a quarter hour ago it had been exactly
the opposite of what he'd clearly stated.

"We can't let the dog loose in New York. That would be neg-
ligent, especially since he was a great employee."

"Great? You call biting me great?"

"You were charging toward him, to be fair," Bernadette added.
"Perhaps he took your movement as aggression?"

Wall sputtered. "This is ridiculous. I told Miss Swift if she
leaves this building before her time is up, she's fired, and I'm not
going to change my mind."

"I think in this case personnel would agree she should leave to
escort her dog home."

Wall didn't have anything to say to that, because the truth was,
they were likely to side with Graham and Bernadette on that point.

"Fine," Wall growled. "But you're on thin ice, Swift. You'd
better return tomorrow with all of those manuscripts copyedited."

Bernadette nodded, knowing it was a lot to ask—in fact
she was probably going to get zero sleep as well as not be able to
finish—but didn't want to argue, because she had also won here.

"If you wouldn't mind excusing us a minute, Miss Swift?"
Graham asked.

She stared at him wide-eyed, hoping she could convey in

that expression that whatever he was about to do, he shouldn't. Because she didn't want special treatment and she could take care of herself.

But Graham didn't budge, and rather than have a battle of wills play out right before Mr. Wall, who already suspected they were something of an item, she left the office and went to her desk to retrieve her things—including a few of her red pencils. She had a typewriter at home thankfully, so she'd still be able to work on her style sheets.

Melanie approached, her eyes flicking toward Wall's office. Whatever it was Graham was saying, he was doing so at such a low pitch that neither of them could hear a word. She couldn't see Graham's face either, but Wall's cheeks had gone from red to purple.

"What is going on?" Melanie asked under her breath, and then louder for the nosy busybodies, she said, "Miss Swift, can I get you a box for those?" and she pointed to the stack of paper in her hands.

"Yes, please."

"I have one out here." Melanie beckoned her out of the office to her desk just out of earshot.

As they packed the box, Bernadette explained.

"He's giving him what for, I'm sure. Wall needs to be put in his place."

"He threatened my job more than once today. Once before Frank, once with Frank, and once more just now." Bernadette shook her head, staring down at the box now packed neatly with her work. "I wonder if there is even a point to bringing these home. Likely when I walk in tomorrow morning, he's going to fire me for not being able to complete the edits. I'd have to stop time and spend the next three days working round the clock to get it done."

"He'd be crazy to do that. You're an asset here and everyone really loves working with you."

Bernadette nodded in the affirmative, but she wasn't feeling valuable right now. Everything had been going so well and now seemed to be completely falling apart.

Graham finally exited the office, chatted a moment with Evans, and then headed toward the door.

"I'll just grab my coat." He winked at her and then sauntered down the hallway.

"My, he's got it bad," Melanie said.

"What has he got?"

"A crush on you."

Bernadette smiled a little at that, watching him disappear into his office. "I have a bit of a crush on him too."

"He's going home with you?"

"Yes."

"Definitely got it bad." Melanie sighed. "I love love."

"Oh stop." Bernadette laughed.

"What's so funny?" Graham asked, his face cheerful as he returned.

"Oh, I was just telling her about a comedy movie that Gary and I watched the other night."

"Do tell. I love a good comedy."

"*The Thrill of It All.* It's a Doris Day flick."

"Thanks for the recommendation. Shall we?" Graham held out his arm, and Bernadette knew she should not take it, because taking it would mean showing they were an item to everyone watching in the copyediting department, but honestly, what did she care anymore?

Bernadette slid her hand around his elbow and smiled up at him. They stood like that, her leaning against him waiting for the elevator. At her desk, Melanie grinned knowingly. Maybe she was right.

"You know, you're the strongest woman I've ever met," Graham said.

"Funny you should say that when I feel like a mess."

"Even strong people feel like a mess sometimes." They stepped onto the empty elevator, and Graham pulled her against him, finally giving her that hug. "What do you say we go get some ice cream and go see that movie? Take a little break before you dive into your work?"

Bernadette stared up into his eyes, thinking she'd like a kiss too. "I think that sounds perfect."

Chapter Twenty-Six

BERNADETTE WAS CERTAIN THERE WERE moments in time that felt like she and the people she was with were the only ones in the world. Pockets of happiness that she didn't want to end. Laughs, jokes, camaraderie that seemed destined to have happened.

With Graham on her couch, a carton of ice cream between them, Frank shredding paper all over the apartment while they watched episodes of the Marx Brothers and reruns of *I Love Lucy* on her old television, it was one of those never-ending moments. The movies had been sold out, so they'd settled on an evening in instead.

The night ended with a heated kiss.

A kiss that seared her right to the bone.

A kiss that had her taking hold of Graham's hand and leading him to her bed.

A kiss that shed clothes.

A kiss that put them skin to skin, and the very things she'd been wondering about, yearning for, flourished in breaths of pleasure and sparks of bliss.

That night, Bernadette slept better than she had in years, lying in Graham's arms, and was disappointed when he woke before dawn to go back to his apartment to get ready for work.

She sipped her coffee while Frank stared at her, questions in his eyes. Wondering why he'd been replaced on his side of the bed. Why they'd been wrestling all night long.

"It won't be an every-night thing. Not yet," she promised him, at the same time hoping that it would be.

Frank let out a disgruntled sigh as if he sensed the lie in her statement.

"I wish you could come with me to work today."

Her good boy seemed to understand. Frank lay down on the floor and stared at her with sad puppy eyes that made her want to bring him anyway. But the ensuing chaos that would create wasn't worth either of them getting hurt over it.

"I'm going to bring you home a pizza tonight. How does that sound?"

Frank lifted up into a sitting position and barked. Bernadette set down her mug to give him a good belly rub before she got ready for work.

But when she arrived at Lenox & Park, the box of manuscripts she'd brought home untouched—kind of on purpose, kind of not, she had been busy after all—she wished she'd never left her apartment.

Wall was waiting for her by her desk, no telling how long he'd been there, but judging by the dragon fire in his eyes, it had been longer than he wanted. Of course, she wasn't late to work;

she never was. But he always set things up to be disappointed, it seemed. And today was no different.

The office was empty besides the two of them. The Evans, Marshall, and Greene trio never rolling in before nine o'clock, and the rest would be straggling in any moment now.

"Good morning, Mr. Wall," she said, trying to drag out the cheer for him somewhere within her and still sounding as brittle as light-bulb glass.

He nodded toward the box in her hand. "I suspect that's the finished manuscripts?"

And here comes the disaster.

"It is the manuscripts, but they aren't quite finished."

"Then you missed your deadline."

"One is due this afternoon, and two more later this week."

"They were due this morning." There was an edge of glee in his tone.

"I was unaware of the deadline change." Though when he dismissed her last night, she supposed she should have picked up on that. His demands had been a threat. The production windows hadn't changed. This was merely Wall exerting his control over her.

"We can't abide by copy editors missing their deadlines. It puts the entire production of a book in jeopardy and makes every other part of the publishing process fall off the mark."

"I will work on them straight away and have them to you by five o'clock."

Wall snatched the box from her desk. "No, you won't."

"Mr. Wall?" She wrinkled her brow, but her confusion was only partly there. This was like watching invisible ink slowly reveal itself on paper. She knew what was happening about five seconds before it was fully exposed.

"You're fired."

Bernadette's throat went dry, and she lost all sense of words. Fired. Dismissed. Canned. Sacked. In American English, *fired* comes from a combination of two meanings, the verb *discharge*, "to be dismissed from a position," and to *fire a gun*, influenced by the sense of throwing someone out.

But from the way Wall was saying it, Bernadette felt the force of that firing, like Wall had held a pistol right to her chest.

"Don't you have anything to say?" he scoffed.

Oh, there was plenty she wanted to say. None of it was appropriate.

"Don't you want to beg for your job?" he goaded.

Bernadette paused a beat, then said what was on her mind. "Because you want to humiliate me? To have me down on my knees? You'd like that." Bernadette wasn't sure where the words came from, how they exited her mouth, but there they were, floating between them the real issue at stake here.

She wouldn't sleep with him. He was retaliating.

And that was a recipe for an epic disaster that she didn't want to be a part of.

Wall snickered. "I don't need to humiliate you, Miss Swift. You do a good enough job of that on your own." The rake of his eyes down to her knees said more to her than if he'd just come right out and said that's where she belonged.

Bernadette smiled. "You can put me down any way you want, Mr. Wall. But I know my worth, and I know my work. I also know yours, and soon so will everyone else."

She opened her purse, tucked in her tchotchkes from her desk, including all of her red B pencils, while he watched but she pretended he wasn't there. His regard burned through her like a welder's hot iron, but she remained upright, not letting a single part of herself show she was on the brink of a breakdown.

Finished gathering her items and unable to close her purse, the pencil holder poking out of the top, she turned on her heel and marched for the door.

"Don't try anything, Miss Swift," Wall said to her back. "You can't win."

And maybe not. But winning wasn't what she wanted.

What she really wanted was to never see him again. To never breathe the same air. Never feel his eyes raking over her in bold aggression. Never hear another shout. Another slandering line.

Good riddance to Tom Wall, and all the Walls of the world.

Bernadette tapped her foot impatiently, the elevator taking forever to arrive on the eleventh floor, likely because everyone was now arriving at work. As suspected, when the doors opened, Melanie and Sarah stepped off with a few others, their eyes immediately drawn to her overstuffed purse.

Bernadette took their place on the elevator, unable to speak. All the strength she'd had was reserved for facing the bull. But not her friends.

"Where are you going?" Sarah asked, her hand pressed to the elevator door to keep it from closing.

"Home."

"Home?" Melanie asked as if she'd never heard the word before.

Bernadette gave a swift nod. "Wall fired me."

In her shock, Sarah let go of the door, and it closed before she could grab it again. Bernadette sagged against the wall of the elevator. An elevator she'd ridden a thousand times. An elevator she'd flirted and kissed Graham in. An elevator that took her up to where she thought her hopes and dreams would become a reality. And now, it was taking her down, just like Wall had.

In the lobby, she marched toward the door. Gary's smile faltered when he looked at her.

"Miss Swift, is everything all right?"

"Yes, Gary." She flashed him a happy smile that was a hard fake. She was certain he saw right through it. But thankfully he nodded and didn't ask any questions as he held the door open for her.

Graham was at the bike rack, his back to her as he secured his bicycle. She wanted desperately to run to him. To tell him what happened. But she wasn't sure she could handle his sympathy right now. Or how he'd demand to do something about it. Graham wasn't going to just let this go. So, she rushed toward the bus station, hoping he didn't turn around and catch a flash of pink and chase after her.

The moment she put her key in the lock of her apartment, her phone started to ring off the hook. She didn't answer. It was probably Melanie or Graham. Maybe even Penelope, as Melanie was likely to reach out to her to tell her what happened in hopes she could get through.

Bernadette ignored them all, curling up on her couch with Frank and eating leftover ice cream while watching reruns of Julia Child.

A knock sounded at the door, and she ignored that too. Hard

to say she wasn't in with Frank barking and the television playing loudly, but all the same, she just couldn't face anyone.

"Bernadette?" Mrs. Morris's apprehensive voice sounded from the other side.

What could she be doing here? And how did she know Bernadette was home?

Worried now for the older woman, she set the ice cream on the coffee table and Frank took up where she'd left off, licking the inside of the carton.

Bernadette swung open the door. "Mrs. Morris, is everything all right?"

"I could say the same of you, my dear. Your mother has been calling." Her friend was wringing her hands, the worry on her face enough to snap Bernadette out of her funk.

"My mother?"

Mrs. Morris nodded. "She tried to get you at work but they said you'd come home. She said you weren't answering, so she called me hoping I could check on you and tell you to call her back, that it's urgent."

There were very few reasons that her mother would call her at work, and none of them were good.

"Thank you, Mrs. Morris." Her throat felt like she'd swallowed sand.

"Are you all right, my dear?"

Bernadette let out a sigh. "I will be." But that was about as true as Wall calling her to say he'd made a mistake.

She closed the door, promising to come by later with Frank, and then rushed to her phone to call her mother. What emergency could have happened? Something with her father? Her brother?

Her mother picked up on the first ring. "Bernie, where have you been?" Her voice was anguished, and Bernadette had a sense of immediate guilt for sulking all day when her mother needed her.

"What's happened?"

"We went to the airport to pick up your brother, but he wasn't there."

Bernadette's grip on the receiver tightened. "Did you have the time right?"

"Yes, yes. We called his base in North Carolina, and they said he'd not made it back from Vietnam. He's…he's missing."

All the air in Bernadette's lungs came out in a whoosh, and she felt herself sinking to the floor, her butt hitting the carpet, cushioning her physical fall but not the emotional one.

"Where is he?" she asked, knowing that it was an unanswerable question.

"They don't know. He and his unit were on the way to the airfield, and they lost track of them."

Bernadette's mind went blank. As if she couldn't handle even the thoughts that her mother's words brought. As if her brain were suddenly filled with the same foam of the couch.

"Should I come home?" Bernadette managed to ask, fully expecting her mother to say yes.

"No. Not yet. There's a chance all this is…just a mistake." The desperation in her mother's voice was thick as dough, her need for validation rising.

Bernadette hoped it was a mistake, but why would the military say he was missing if he wasn't? If he'd just gotten on another flight?

"Mom, I think I should—"

"No, Bernie." Her mother cut her off, and Bernadette realized the reason she was pushing her away, telling her to stay away, was that if Bernadette came home, then it would be real.

There would be something to be worried about, and right now her mother couldn't think like that.

But Bernadette didn't want to be alone either. She belonged with her family.

"Go back to work, Bernie," her mother said. "Why are you home anyway?"

So, they hadn't told her mother that she was fired. Best for her mother not to worry about that on top of Ben.

"I wasn't feeling well." The lie was as miserable as the ache in her heart.

"Oh dear. Perhaps that nice Mrs. Morris can get you some soup?"

"Yes, soup would be nice." She didn't like lying to her mother, and the truth would have tasted stale on her tongue. "I'll be okay, promise. Keep me posted on Ben, Mom."

"I'm sure he'll turn up." But there was an edge to her mother's voice, one that bordered on hysteria, and Bernadette wished she could hop on the nearest train and go home. But she was afraid her mother would shoo her away. A superstitious woman, she'd say Bernadette had jinxed them when her brother inevitably didn't show up.

And that was not something she wanted to be blamed for. Nor a truth she was willing to acknowledge.

Chapter Twenty-Seven

FRANK

SOMETHING'S WRONG.

The thump of my girl's heart is beating differently today.

I lift the carton of melting ice cream from the table and bring it over to her where she is still sitting on the floor. I nudge the sweetness closer. She smiles, but there is sadness in the gesture.

"You're a good boy, Frank. You can have the rest."

But I don't want the rest.

I want my girl back. I curl up beside her, putting my head in her lap, a position I've been taking up a lot lately. I already decided my rounds of the neighborhood would need to be put on hold. My number one mission is always Bernadette.

Then I remember something.

I hop up and run to her bedside table. I clamp my teeth on the knob, slide open the drawer. I pull out the leather-bound notebook, my tongue touching the tasty paper and resisting the urge to take a bite.

This is the notebook she scribbles in. Making marks and telling me about the things she likes that she's read.

"What are you doing with my quote journal?" she asks, lifting it where I plop it in her lap.

I nudge her hand. *Open it. Read it. Smile.*

She flips through the pages, a little bit of a smile coming back to her face. "You know how to make a girl feel better, Frank. What do you think of this quote from Eleanor Roosevelt? 'Happiness is not a goal, it is a by-product... For what keeps our interest in life and makes us look forward to tomorrow is giving pleasure to other people.' And might I add dogs?"

I nudge her to keep turning the pages. To keep reading. Because it seems like the words scribbled on the page have the power to change her mood, to brighten the dark clouds that float in her eyes. And I like to hear her talk, to tell me what things mean.

"Here is one often attributed to Ralph Waldo Emerson, though no one knows for sure who it really was: 'For every minute you are angry you lose sixty seconds of happiness.' I refuse to give W-A-L-L another sixty seconds of my life. But Bennie..."

Bennie. Our Ben. That was what weighed on her more than anything else.

"I think I need some air. Park?"

I bark. She had me at *air*.

Leash on, we leave the apartment like we do any other day that we've gone on a walk in the park. The leaves are falling, and the squirrels have multiplied in numbers that make me unsure of which way to turn. Right. Left. Up. Down. It's got me twisting in circles, until the leash wraps around Bernadette's legs and she wobbles, laughing, and then crashes to the ground.

"Frank," she gushes.

I lick her face in apology and stand as still as I can, which isn't very, because the furry beasts keep racing past and all I want to do is run and chase.

She unclamps my leash. "Go for it, but you better not stray too far."

I run, barreling down on a squirrel that is headed for a large tree. *No, don't climb it!*

Up it goes, and I'm about to go up too. I jump, press my claws into the bark, but I'm not as limber as a squirrel, and I crash back down to the grass.

I bark up the tree, *Come back. Get down here. Let's do it again!*

The squirrel stares down at me, an acorn between its fingers, and it winks, then runs to the edge of the tree branch, teasing me, back and forth. It leaps, its body airborne, and I think, *Yes, I will catch it*, but it lands on another branch.

Bernadette is watching me, leash dangling limply from her hands. She is so still, so quiet. Like she doesn't know what to do or say. I walk toward her, and she watches me with eyes that don't really seem like they are seeing.

I nudge her knee, her hip, brush my head beneath her hand. *Girl?*

When she stares down at me, there are tears in her eyes. They fall onto her cheeks in big wet drips.

My girl, so full and vibrant. She is lost. And all I want to do is help her find that happiness she read about in her journal. To find herself again.

Chapter Twenty-Eight

BERNADETTE'S MELANCHOLY DID NOT IMPROVE.

Graham suggested on the phone she had the blues, to which she told him the blues etymology dated back to the 1800s when people suffering alcohol withdrawal experienced hallucinations they deemed the *blue devils*, which was later shortened to the *blues* describing a state of depression, and then adopted for the African American music genre in the late nineteenth century.

"More accurately, I've got the *mubble fubbles*, which was a sixteenth-century word for impending doom and feelings of despondency." She lifted her coffeepot and poured, missing the cup by a fraction of an inch and spilling all over the counter. "Dammit."

"I'm coming over." Before she could protest, Graham hung up the phone.

Frank, who'd been staring out the window, trotted over to the kitchen, put his paws up on the counter, and started to lick up her mess.

She didn't know whether to laugh or cry. Laugh because her precious hound was cleaning up after her when it should be the other way around, or cry because Bernadette Swift didn't make silly mistakes or messes, and she never felt this out of sorts.

"You're such a good boy, Frank."

He licked up the last of the coffee and then licked her hand.

Graham knocked on her door shortly after she'd wiped up the slobbered-coffee counter, with the ingredients for double-fudge chocolate chip cookies, a handwritten recipe from his mother, and a lopsided grin.

"I know these aren't oatmeal raisin, but whenever I had a case of the mubble fubbles growing up, my mom baked me these." He set the bag of groceries on her table with the recipe and had barely turned back around before Bernadette tossed herself into his arms.

"Thank you," she whispered, her cheek pressed to his shirt, which was still slightly cool from walking in the autumn air.

"You're welcome." He pressed a kiss to the top of her head. "Let's bake. And if you want to talk, I'm here."

Bernadette leaned back, staring up at Graham, remembering how she used to only stare at him in the reflection of the elevator doors. How she'd sworn to never go on a date with him, and here he was in her house with his arms wrapped around her.

"Let's do this." They measured, poured, mixed, shaped, and baked. But Bernadette wasn't ready to say much. Baking for her was never about voicing, more about thinking. And as she rolled each ball of dough in her hand and placed it on the baking sheet, her thoughts seemed to organize themselves into neatly written-out Rolodex cards.

While the smell of melting chocolate filled her apartment,

they sat on the couch, her curled up with her head on his shoulder, and Frank on the other side of her, his head resting on her tucked legs. She'd always been comfortable in her apartment, but there was something about being surrounded by these two that made her feel even more at ease.

"I'm supposed to go to my book club tonight," she said, her hand resting on Frank's head.

"You should go." Graham entwined his fingers with her free hand.

"I've read the book, but not recently." It'd been assigned in one of her English classes at Barnard and she still had the copy with her notes penciled in the margins.

"What's the book?"

"Virginia Woolf's *To the Lighthouse.*"

"Ah, a classic." Graham lifted her hand to his lips, kissing the back.

"And a look at women's roles in society."

"You should definitely go. Not just for the subject matter, but the company."

The timer dinged for the cookies. Bernadette hopped off the couch, padding the few feet into the kitchen on the pretense of pulling out the chocolate confections but also to avoid answering. With her favorite piglet potholders, she pulled the cookies out of the oven to cool on the counter, their gooey chocolate decadence making her mouth water. Frank looked up at her imploringly, and she pulled an oatmeal cookie out of the jar for him, since she wouldn't let him have chocolate.

"Chocolate isn't good for doggies," she reminded him, but Frank didn't seem to mind as long as he got the other cookie, which he chomped up and swallowed before she even had the lid back on the jar.

"They smell delicious." Hands in his pockets, Graham leaned against the small arched doorframe that separated the tiny kitchen from her living room. He grinned down at the cookies. "Like childhood and happiness."

Bernadette laughed, tugging off her piglet potholders and tossing them onto the counter. "If only we could bottle that scent and smell it often." But her laughter died a second later as she thought about Ben. Her fingers itched to pick up the phone and call her mother, or even the army, and demand answers.

But her mother had said she'd call as soon as they had an update, so Bernadette had to force herself to be patient. Normally, that would be an easy task, but today she felt like a hungry bear on the edge of an empty stream trying to snatch salmon out of thin air.

Graham's hand on her back pulled her out of her head. "They'll find him."

He sounded so sure. She stared up at him, blinked. "I hope so." What worried her most is that they'd find him...but not alive. Planes went missing and were never found. Amelia Earhart's aircraft had never been located, and the rumors regarding her fate ran the gamut from crashing into the ocean to being shot down and then executed. To this day, no one knew what had happened to her.

It wasn't as if her brother had taken a joyride. Or was on vacation. He'd been in hostile territory, and she had a vivid imagination.

Needing a distraction, Bernadette grabbed a spatula, checking if the cookies were ready to be scraped off the baking sheet. One scooped up easily enough. But she started to tremble, her hands shaking the spatula so hard that a cookie fell with a splat to the floor.

Frank zeroed in and darted forward to fetch the forbidden booty. The quickest way for her to block his retrieval was to step on the broken, gooey mess, smooshing the hot cookie into the kitchen floor with her stockinged foot.

The heat of the melted chocolate chips, which had clearly not cooled enough, burned and she yelped at the instant sting.

Frank backed away and sat down just on the other side of the arch, his head cocked, staring at her with confusion and concern.

Graham swooped in, lifting her into the air and sitting her on the counter, then bent to clean up the mess, while her legs dangled over him.

Tears stung her eyes, not so much from the heat of the chocolate on her skin, which barely hurt anymore, but from worry, fear, sadness, and terror over her brother's situation. She felt so unsettled, not fitting into her own skin. Like all of her emotions had swelled and were spilling out of her pores.

"Are you okay?" Graham dumped the broken cookie into the trash, washed his hands, and then picked up her foot to examine the bottom. His eyebrows rose in surprise. "Wow, melted the nylon."

"Really?" Bernadette bent her knee, pulling her foot closer for inspection. Sure enough, there was a hole in the nylon, edges curled and melted, and the pink of the sole of her foot showing through smeared with chocolate. "My pantyhose really ate it, huh?"

Graham laughed, swiping a thumb over the drying chocolate on the bottom of her foot. "A heck of a mess. Probably don't want to put your shoes on with that."

She shook her head and let her foot fall to dangling. "I'm a mess."

"You have every right to be. Today has been a real downer."
Graham placed his hands on the counter on either side of her hips,
as if he were the rope holding her, the unsteady bridge, in place
across a canyon.

"A really shitty day. The worst, shittiest day ever." Bernadette
ran her fingers over his arm, soothed by the steadiness of him.

"There's only one place to go now," Graham said, his expression serious but his eyes dancing.

"To my closet for another pair of hose?" she teased.

"Exactly." His mouth hitched in a grin. "And up. Once you're
at the bottom, you can't go further."

"Frank begs to differ, and the city has his holes to prove it."

Hearing his name, Frank barked and turned in a rapid circle.
Graham chuckled. "No doubt. But you don't dig holes, do you?"

"Depends on who you ask?" She cocked her head the side,
playful, and grinned with nostalgia. "Ben and I used to have to
dig holes all over the farm."

"Okay, farm holes and dog holes aside, I believe the only way
to go from here, Bernadette Swift, is up. You're going to get your
job back, and your brother is going to be found."

She bit her lip, not wanting to burst his bubble. Graham was
working hard to make her feel better, and she completely appreciated that. He was a sweetheart, a gem, and her mood and outlook
had improved with his presence. Without him, she'd still be wal-
lowing on the floor. A sticky, messy puddle.

However, disposition improved or not, she wasn't sure she
wanted her job at Lenox & Park back. The idea of stepping onto
the eleventh floor with Wall huffing and puffing in her direction
seemed tantamount to torture.

Maybe her parents had been right all along, and she should quit this nonsense of trying to be the first female CEO of a publishing house. If she couldn't even keep her job in the copyediting department, then how was she going to run an entire publishing company? She'd barely earned the respect of a few of her male counterparts. And Graham and Mr. Bass didn't count. From her experience thus far, it appeared they were in the minority.

"I can see that brilliant mind of yours churning," Graham said. "Let it keep spinning until you set the needle down, but in the meantime, go get changed. I'll pack up these cookies for you to take to your friends at the book club. You need the distraction."

"You're a good distraction."

"I love being a distraction, sweetheart. But a woman needs her friends too."

Sometimes, she was pretty certain Graham was made just for her. "There's no eating in the library."

Graham chuckled. "There's also no secret book club at the library."

Bernadette waggled her finger at him. "You're playing a dangerous game, Mr. Reynolds." She grabbed the front of his shirt and pulled him close, pressing her lips to his. "I like you," she whispered.

"I like you too."

———

Melanie, Sarah, and Penelope were waiting for Bernadette in the shadows outside of the library. Three huddled figures ballooned out of the darkness against the stony backdrop. If Bernadette hadn't known they'd been there, she might have let her imagination run wild with ideas.

"How are you?" Melanie asked, pulling her in for a hug, her cheek cool against Bernadette's, the scent of her perfume a balm.

"I heard what happened." Penelope hugged her next, still wearing the same floral perfume she'd preferred at Barnard.

"I'll survive. It's not the first time I've hit a rough patch, and it won't be the last. I've nearly got my balance back." Her voice sounded a lot stronger than she felt.

Penelope grinned, both of them likely thinking of the time at Barnard they'd gone skiing at Bear Mountain, taking the train up with a few of their friends. It had been Bernadette's first time, and she'd spent more time sliding on her butt than on her skis. The entire time, Bernadette had said over and over, *Just hitting a rough patch. Nearly got it now!*

"I smell chocolate. Do you have cookies in your purse?" Sarah asked, plucking at the opening of Bernadette's bag.

Bernadette chuckled, patting the full purse. "I do."

"But we can't eat in the library," Sarah said.

"We can't meet in there either." Bernadette turned Graham's cheeky words on her friend and realized in that moment just how much she'd changed from the rule-following woman she'd been just a few months ago.

"You're turning into a real rebel," Penelope said.

"To be fair, if we were actually touching library books, I would not condone sneaking a cookie. But we always bring our own." Bernadette shrugged. "If I get a little chocolate on my personal copy, I'll remember this sweet time with all of you next time I pick it up."

Penelope put her arm through hers as they waited for Dave the janitor to open the door for them. "I heard about Ben." Penelope had a minor crush on Ben when they'd been at school, but Ben had made a pact with Bernadette in their youth never to date each other's friends, after he'd flirted outrageously with one of hers, and she'd returned the favor.

Bernadette sucked in a breath, feeling that aching stab in the center of her chest all over again. "I have to keep hope that they will find him."

"We'll all keep hope." Penelope wrapped her arm around Bernadette's shoulder and gave her a squeeze as they climbed the stairs.

Inside the special meeting room, Patty and Jane, who'd been talking animatedly in hushed whispers, paused their conversation on seeing them enter and rushed forward. But Bernadette was fairly certain she'd heard the word *divorce*...or was that her imagination getting the better of her?

"I'm so sorry about Tom," Patty said at the same time Jane gushed, "Bass is going to get your job back."

Bernadette glanced between the two of them and then reached out, hugging them both close, happy for their friendship. "I'm not sure I want to go back."

"Why not?" Ruth interjected. "You've worked your ass off, pardon my French."

"It's true. And look how much you've inspired all of us," Melanie added. "You can't give up now."

"We won't let you. You need to get back to the grammar business," Sarah said adamantly. "Just like we won't let you eat cookies in the library." This last part she said with a teasing wink.

Bernadette pulled out the little cookie pouches that Graham had put together and distributed them to the group. Melanie took a peek and, when Sarah wasn't looking, popped a piece in her mouth, her eyes rolling in pleasure. She mouthed, "So good."

Bernadette smiled. Being with her friends made her feel like she could finish putting the pieces of her life back together. She'd always had Penelope, but Penelope was married, so they hadn't spent as much time together since they'd both started working full time in the city. And besides Mrs. Morris and Melanie, Bernadette hadn't taken the time to cultivate any relationships. Until recently, she hadn't realized how lonely she actually was.

Feeling overly emotional not just because of Mr. Wall, or Bennie, but because of these women, who had her back. "I really appreciate all of you so much. I didn't realize until I got here how much I needed to see you all tonight."

They moved in, a group hug, surrounding her in warmth and perfume. Bernadette waged an internal battle against the tears that threatened a tsunami.

"No matter what happens with Lenox & Park and my career, I want you all to know that it has been a great honor to belong to this group and to call all of you my friends. And with my brother... Please pray that he's safe."

"Oh, honey, we're praying hard," Patty said, rubbing her back.

"The honor is ours. We're glad to know you," Ruth said. "Good friends are important for women, to remind each other that we're not alone, but also to remind each other of the hard decisions we have to make, and the ones we can hold each other up in. We're here for you, whatever you need."

"I appreciate that so much. I really hope I don't need you.

Please don't take offense at that. I just mean I hope Ben is found safe. And as far as the job, I think this is one thing I'll have to solve on my own, but knowing you all have my back is going to keep me standing on my feet."

"We're here if you need us," Penelope said. "And maybe you can just come work for Doubleday. I've been dying to have you copyediting books over there. I know my authors would be happy."

Bernadette grinned and bumped her shoulder against Penelope's. "We can't both be CEO of the same publishing house one day. I won't encroach on your dream."

"I would never consider you encroaching, but I understand your meaning. If you change your mind, I am more than happy to put in a good word."

"Thank you."

Penelope looked at her seriously. "And Ben… Please let us know when you have news."

Bernadette's throat tightened as she nodded. "I will."

"Before we start," Penelope said, "the votes are in for our next book club read. Zora N. Hurston's *Their Eyes Were Watching God*, about a young Black woman, Janie Crawford, as she searches for independence, self-fulfillment, and love, and navigates gender and race inequality. I've heard it's a great book."

"I've already got my copy," Bernadette said with a grin. "She was a graduate of my alma mater, Barnard."

"One of my favorites," Ruth added.

"Excellent. Now, let's talk about *To the Lighthouse*."

"I could surely use the distraction." Bernadette touched her headband, almost like its sparkle could give her extra strength.

Everyone took their seats, books out on their laps, feet tapping eagerly the way Bernadette remembered in grade school when they'd gather on the carpet for story time.

"First can I just say, wow, Mrs. Ramsey had eight kids?" Melanie started them off.

Patty shuddered. "I only had five. I can't imagine three more."

"Also, did you notice that she is only ever referred to as Mrs. Ramsey? No name of her own. As if she were owned by her husband. I can't imagine only ever being Mrs. Bass. Jane suits me so much better."

"Also, can we acknowledge that Mr. Ramsey is an asshole?" Sarah said. "I mean, he seems to take so much pleasure in making his wife seem silly and insignificant."

"Agree," Bernadette said. "The entire book seemed to be pointing out what a woman's role is and how men expect her to perform in society."

"Now, Lily though," Penelope said, "She is my favorite."

"A woman who doesn't need a man to fulfill her goal. She doesn't aim to be wife, mother, nurturer, but instead to do the unthinkable and chooses freedom and artistic expression," Bernadette said.

"Woolf once said that in order for a female artist to express herself, she had to first 'kill the angel in the house,'" Ruth said. "But I'm not so sure I agree. My angel—me—is still kicking strong with both my passion for the law and for motherhood. I simply have embraced both."

"But," Patty interjected, "you've also got a husband who supports that. My husband never allowed me to choose my art over housekeeping. Like 'the angel' I have sacrificed myself for my family."

But your husband is Tom Wall, Bernadette wanted to say, but instead asked, "What is your art?"

Patty leaned forward, the first genuine show of excitement gleaming in her eyes. "I like to paint, like Lily. I have several pieces around my house. Even a few that people have said I should offer to an art gallery, but Tom would never allow it. He refused to even hang them in his office."

"What if he didn't know?" Melanie suggested.

"Lie?" Patty looked slightly queasy.

"Oh no, I don't think you need to lie. Just don't tell him." Sarah wiggled her brows.

"Lying through omission." Patty cocked her head to the side, thoughtful.

"Not really. Do you tell him when you go to the bathroom?" Bernadette asked, all seriousness with a bit of snark.

"No, of course not."

"It's the same thing. Husbands don't need a rundown of the minute-by-minute activities of our days. So, let's say you just so happen to pop a few paintings into the car on your way to the market, and you just so happen to pass by the art gallery on your way to pick up bread and milk and a chicken, and they just so happen to say they love your paintings and they hang them up? And then you get paid, and more people want your art, and it just becomes another one of your errands on Mondays," Bernadette suggested.

"Your kids are grown," Sarah added. "How much housework could there be with just the two of you?"

Patty frowned, thinking. "A lot more than if it was just me. I sometimes think he's extra messy just to keep me busy. I think he is afraid I'm going to leave him."

"And if you did get paid for your art, you could hire a house-keeper and have more time for your passion, and less time scrubbing," Ruth offered.

"You all paint a pretty picture," Patty said wistfully.

"Not as pretty as the ones you'll sell." Bernadette winked.

"And to be honest, I don't think it's really any of his business, or at least soon it won't be." But Patty didn't expand on that statement, though the future of Patty no longer being Mrs. Wall hung in the air.

"Might I remind you, dear, that you are well acquainted with my art gallery and always welcome," Jane piped in.

Patty blinked, perhaps in shock. Then she nodded. "I'll do it. On one condition."

They waited, eager to hear what it was she'd say.

"Bernadette needs to get her job back. Lenox & Park needs you."

Bernadette bit the tip of her tongue. "My employment should not be what's stopping you from pursuing your dreams, Patty. Women should support each other, not hold one another back."

"All right, you make a good point." Patty leaned forward. "So, let's make it a competition."

Bernadette raised a brow, a slow smile spreading on her face. "And how do you propose we do that?"

"Whoever succeeds first—me selling my art, and you getting your job back—buys the other one the next six book club books."

Bernadette laughed. "Those terms are favorable." And she would be happy to buy Patty those books, because she wanted her to win. To gain some autonomy, and perhaps that would help bolster her in her newfound freedom.

Chapter Twenty-Nine

FRANK

MR. CRUMBS SITS ON HIS usual perch in the worn armchair, giving me the kind of once-over a stingy grocery clerk gave me last week when I was curiously sniffing the apples. *Parsimonious* is what Bernadette would have said.

I'd also recently learned that *va al diavolo* means "get lost" in Italian, although there was some confusion that maybe he told me to go to hell.

To be fair, had he turned his back, I would have absolutely swiped an apple. They're delicious. What can I say? Besides, the little tyke I was walking home after he lost his mother was hungry.

I might be a dog, but even I understand the sounds of a grumbling belly.

You've returned. Mr. Crumbs stretches, his claws poking out from his tiny paws. I might not normally be afraid of something so tiny. After all, my own paws are nearly the size of his head.

But, I've felt the sharp sting of those little daggers more than once.

I have. Mrs. Morris invited me over for company. I relay my message, sitting down to meet him eye to eye.

Around the apartment, I make out the lingering scents of Mrs. Morris's daughter and grandchildren. Faintly like her, and something else. They've gone for now but will be back, so she says.

Mr. Crumbs sneezes and then licks a paw and wipes his face with it. *Do we still have an accord?*

Why are you grooming yourself during our conversation?

He pauses midlick and stares at me as if I've got two mice sitting on my head—hunger and death. *Your presence is answer enough.*

Two could play that game. If he were to find me so foul that he needs to clean himself, then perhaps I am just as offended by his very catness. I lick my paw, and he hisses.

I take it a step further and lick my hind end for good measure.

Foul beast! Mr. Crumbs leaps from his perch on the chair and swipes at me.

I let out a surprised howl, and Mrs. Morris, all tiny, creaky bones, rushes over.

"Oh, Mr. Crumbs, why can't you be a gentleman? You poor pup." She leads me toward her very pink kitchen—the refrigerator, the oven, the sink, the cabinets, even the wallpaper is floral pink— and I turn to look at Mr. Crumbs over my shoulder.

He's back on his perch watching. I hope he doesn't expect me to share this time. Let it be a lesson to him.

Inside her tiny pastel bomb, the scent of chocolate cookies is strong. But as she opens her fridge, I smell something different, something strangely delicious.

"All I have is this ham," she says and pulls off a slice. "I hope you like ham, and I do hope your Bernadette forgives me for feeding it to you. It's not Amaranth, so that should make it easier for her to absolve me."

I have no idea if I like ham, but if it tastes half as good as it smells, I will love it. And Bernadette always forgives me when I do something wrong, so she will surely forgive Mrs. Morris too. Besides, I don't plan to tell her. *Give me the ham, human.*

"Sit, boy."

I do as she says, waiting patiently and taking gently from her brittle fingers. The ham is everything I've wished for. Deliciously meaty, fatty, and also sweet.

From the other room Mr. Crumbs is no longer hissing but making high-pitched wails as he misses out on the treat. His fault.

"Oh, bother. Come here, you grumpy kitty," Mrs. Morris calls. "You can have a piece too."

If a cat could smirk, that would be Mr. Crumbs's expression. Pleased with himself as he comes into the kitchen, his tail wrapping around my leg. He sits perfectly still and stares up at Mrs. Morris.

"Good kitty," she croons and gives him a tiny piece of ham.

The accord is broken. Mr. Crumbs has just learned he can slice me to ribbons and be rewarded for it.

I let out a sigh.

"One more piece, my dear," she says, another delicious slice of ham on her palm.

All right, I decide, I don't mind a little swipe if I get more ham.

"How about another episode of *Lassie*?" she asks.

Oh, yes, please. Lassie is my favorite. Like me, she comes to the rescue when someone is in trouble.

Chapter Thirty

BERNADETTE TURNED THE PAGE IN her journal after writing down a quote from Virginia Woolf, her eyes catching on another passage she'd noted written by Betty Friedan: "It is easier to live through someone else than to complete yourself. The freedom to lead and plan your own life is frightening if you have never faced it before. It is frightening when a woman finally realizes that there is no answer to the question 'who am I' except the voice inside herself."

As the words registered, an idea formed in her mind.

Bernadette flung back the blankets, Frank leaping to stand on the mattress, stunned by her movements. She hurried to her bookshelf, pulling off one, two, then thirteen novels. All of which had been copyedited by her and several had hit bestseller lists and been sold in multiple languages. And she wasn't claiming that the reason they'd done well was her—the authors were all incredibly talented at writing compelling stories—but she had also worked on them. Honed the grammar and word choices.

These were proof she was a good copy editor.

Proof that she shouldn't have been fired. Proof that Wall was holding his own personal feelings of rejection against her. A vendetta.

She put all of the books into a shopping bag and set it by her apartment door. Tomorrow morning, she was going to march into Lenox & Park, and she was going to demand her job back. Working with Mr. Wall was going to be hell on earth, but it beat the alternative, which was letting him shove her into a nonexistent future.

The phone rang just as she settled back under the covers, the yellow glow of her lamp creating a moonlike halo on the ceiling. Bernadette glanced at the clock, the hour hand reaching for ten. Who would be calling her—

She leaped out of bed once more, and this time, Frank barked as he dug his way out of her flung blanket mountain.

Bernadette nearly tumbled in her haste to grab the receiver, slapping her hand against the wall for balance as she rushed to say, "Hello? Hello?"

"Bernie, it's Mom." Those three little words had the power to upend her. The slight quiver in her mom's throat, the hitch at the end of her declaration.

Bernadette's knees started to shake, her spine flat to the wall now, not caring about the pink telephone cord getting tangled on her hips. She wasn't ready for whatever it was her mother wanted to tell her. Not ready at all.

"Mom" was all she could say, and it came out as shaky as her posture.

"It's Ben."

Bernadette's throat closed, her eyes swelled with tears, and she clenched the receiver so tightly that she was pretty certain it was going to shatter in her grip. The plastic shards stabbing into her palm like the news that was about to ram itself deep into her heart.

"They found him."

Images flashed through her mind. Things she'd never seen but could conjure up from thin air. Images of Ben, bleeding and broken. Images of Ben in a casket, his uniform pressed and creased, his face serene. Images that made her tongue numb and bile rise in her throat. "And…is he?"

"He's alive. Injured, but alive."

Bernadette let the air she'd been holding in her lungs out in a whoosh. The monstrous images evaporated. "Alive?"

"Yes." Her mother's voice cracked. "He's alive. There was a crash, their plane shot down, but they hadn't made it too far off the ground. Landed in some trees. Rescued. He's recovering. A broken leg. A few broken ribs. They're going to send him home soon."

Bernadette could hardly believe it. He'd survived the crash. Only a broken leg and ribs. Bones could mend. He was *alive*!

"Oh, Mom, I'm so relieved. I was so worried. I didn't think…" But she couldn't finish the end of that sentence, not if she wanted her mother to ever speak to her again.

"I wish we could see him, but they won't let us over there."

"He's still in Vietnam?"

"Yes. But they said he'd be sent home as soon as he's able to travel. A week or two at most."

"It's a miracle." To survive a plane crash at all was miraculous, but to do so in enemy territory in the middle of another country's war? That seemed like divine intervention.

"That's our Bennie. Always trying to give us a scare." Her mother's laugh was brittle, but Bernadette knew how relieved she must be. The last forty-eight hours had been hell, trying to figure out where Ben was and if they were ever going to see him again. And for her mother to compartmentalize it like she did the time he'd decided hopping from one tree to another was a good idea, or the time he'd decided that he wanted to take up rock climbing and scaled half a cliff without any equipment or shoes… Benjamin was a regular daredevil with not a lick of fear in his body or brain.

"He can scare me any day, just as long as he's still doing it," she said.

"I couldn't agree more."

Until recently, Bernadette had not really been a person who believed in signs. People's declarations of signs changing their lives had always seemed like folderol to her. Nonsense.

But this morning when she'd woken, it had been to the sun and the birds. The bus hadn't been full, and she'd been able to finish her crossword without elbowing the person next to her by accident. And now the sun was gleaming off the glass windows as if the Lenox & Park building itself was inviting her back inside, giving credence to people's declaration, "It's a sign!"

Before Bernadette was even a dozen paces from the office building door, Gary was swinging it open wide and ushering her inside.

"Good to see you back, Miss Swift." His grin was wide, and

she could only hope her reception on the eleventh floor was just as agreeable.

"Miss Swift, shall I let them know to expect you?" The new receptionist, a young Black woman dressed in a saffron minidress with a white collar and cuffs, smiled in welcome.

"No, thank you, that won't be necessary. Melanie's expecting me."

Bernadette shifted the shopping bag of books to her other hand and pressed the button to the elevator. Dressed in her favorite pink power suit, adorned with a black-and-white polka-dot bow tie at her neck, she watched her reflection stare back at her, pensive, with a flicker of determination in her eyes.

It was 9:30 a.m. She'd purposefully chosen to come in after the workday began so that she wouldn't have to wait around for Wall to arrive before she confronted him. That would have left too much time for people to ask questions like *Why are you here?* and *What's in the bag?*

The elevator took its sweet time sliding upward through the walls and floors, the gears crunching and grinding louder than she'd noticed before. Probably more from her nerves than anything else. She could also swear she heard her heart beating in her chest. Finally, the *ding* was so loud as the doors slid open that she flinched.

Bernadette stepped out onto the eleventh floor, her heels clicking on the marble. She straightened her Grammarian headband like a crown. The familiar hum of people working. A phone ringing, the clack of typewriters, the murmur of voices. She didn't realize how much she'd missed it until just now, the cacophony settling over her shoulders like a worn childhood security blanket.

Melanie looked up abruptly from her desk, then leaped to her feet. Doing a silent clap and tap-dancing not so silently, in a vivacious orange A-line dress. Whatever she was mouthing, her lip movements were so exaggerated that Bernadette couldn't make it out.

She hadn't told anyone she was coming, afraid Wall might overhear or in Melanie's case that she might not be able to stop checking the elevator for Bernadette's arrival, thus alerting the department something was up. And the last thing Bernadette wanted was for her nemesis to be prepared for her arrival.

A wobbly smile curved her mouth as she walked past Melanie with a conspiratorial wink. If she stopped to talk to her, she might lose her nerve. The boys' club in the office stopped working in unison, mouths agape as she breezed through the door, their hands poised in midair over their typewriters. Marshall dropped his jaw and his red pencil to his desk. As if time had frozen them all still and only their eyes could move.

She marched over to Wall's office door, noted he was bent over in his chair behind his desk, riffling in a drawer, and that he hadn't noticed her walking in. Probably about to pull a forbidden bottle from the drawer's hidden depths. Without knocking, she opened the door and stepped through.

"You're early," he barked, shuffling papers together and not looking up. If he'd seen her standing there, those would certainly not have been his words.

"I think I'm right on time."

Wall dropped the papers and glanced up sharply, bushy brows narrowing as he gaped at her. "What the hell are you doing here?"

A sick feeling slid into her stomach, the flesh on her arms

prickling with the uneasy sensation. Heaven help her, she'd forgotten how vitriolic he was. How every word dripped with acid and hatred. And the sad thing was, she didn't even pity herself in this moment, but instead his wife. Poor Patty having to deal with his angry self every day for the last several decades. Hopefully she wouldn't have to deal with him for too much longer.

"I want my job back," Bernadette said, her scalp tightening and a shiver threatening to run through her. She straightened her spine.

"Impossible."

Bernadette was not going to be put off by him. Not today. She pulled out the books and started to place them one by one beside each other on the desk. Their covers face up, her literary trophies. Wall stiffened, and the way he placed his hands flat on top of the desk, she had a sudden fear he was going to swipe the books off, sending them flying just before he tossed her out.

"These are just a sample of the bestselling and award-winning books I've copyedited." Her voice remained strong, even though inside her shoes, she was fairly certain her toes had turned to Marshmallow Fluff.

"You think I care about that?" He barked a derisive laugh. "You were a disruptive employee."

"I admit to encouraging the women to participate in a walkout. But we aren't unionized, and strikes are not unusual for those who wish to be heard. And despite that, I don't think one would say my overall performance the last few years was disruptive."

"I beg to differ. Your very presence is a disruption. You had no right to stage a strike." He flung his arm outward, his finger like a limp sword pointing toward the window. "And because of your antics, we had men mulling about outside the building for days. Did you see them out there when you came in?"

She shook her head.

Mr. Wall's lips peeled back into a mean smile, the kind of smile that makes one think of sinister criminals. But instead of being scared of him and that ugly grin, she noted his mustache was tickling his teeth. "That's because when they found out you were fired, they went home."

Bernadette's chest swelled with anger. An angry pitchfork mob, and she had no doubt Mr. Wall would have taken up with them if he'd been allowed.

"I can see you're still upset," she hedged, trying to figure out a plan B. She'd thought that showing up here and presenting the books she'd worked on had been enough. But really, that was her fault, wasn't it? Because with Wall, she was never enough. His wife must have felt the same way.

"Angry?" He started to laugh. "I don't give a shit. There's a difference."

Bernadette had rarely dealt with someone so foul on the inside, and hence she was not as prepared as she would have liked to be in this current situation.

The door opened behind her and Mr. Bass walked in.

"Oh, so you called Daddy?" Wall sneered.

Bernadette didn't even bother to respond. "Mr. Bass, I was just…" *Leaving.*

The angst of dealing with Wall had blood rushing through her veins, and she started to shake. To cover it up, she gathered up the books she'd placed on his desk and tucked them back into her bag.

"Good to see you again, Miss Swift," Mr. Bass said, then he turned his attention on Wall. "What are you still doing here?" Bass's voice was as icy as the mountain caps in Switzerland.

Wall went silent, something she'd never seen before. Bernadette, who'd been prepared to flee from failure and mortification, suddenly found her feet didn't know how to work. She stood immobile, watching, waiting. What did Mr. Bass mean when he asked what Wall was still doing there?

Mr. Bass answered her question in the next breath. "You were supposed to gather your things and leave an hour ago."

Wall must have been taking some time off.

"Do you need me to call security?" Mr. Bass threatened. "Out of respect for your time at Lenox & Park, I wasn't going to do that originally, but I can see you're taking advantage of my generosity."

Security? This wasn't a vacation. What was going on?

Wall cleared his throat, flicked his gaze toward hers, and she swore if he'd had bullets in his brain, he would have fired them at her right then and there. So much hatred aimed her way.

"I'll just be another minute," Wall said tightly.

"Sixty seconds or I'm calling security."

Wall nodded. Bass opened the office door and beckoned for Bernadette to follow. She didn't want to stay in here with the bull, so she followed on numb feet, hoping for an explanation.

"I'm glad you came by today," Mr. Bass said. "I was going to call you and ask you to come in."

The boys at their desks were still frozen in time, eyes rolling like marbles as Mr. Bass led her out of the copyediting department and into the exterior lobby.

She didn't know what to say, so she nodded.

"I'm really sorry about what happened here," he said. "Mind coming to the conference room for a chat?"

"All right," she murmured.

Again, she followed, taking a seat at the conference table. Mr. Bass sat down at the head and steepled his fingers.

"I had no idea that Wall was going to fire you. None of us did."

She nodded, still unsure of what exactly to say.

"When we found out, we were astonished. And then there was a rumor going about that he'd...propositioned you."

She nodded, again her tongue left somewhere in the office behind her.

"And you know how I felt about the walkout."

Bernadette licked her lips nervously, trying to find her voice. "Yes, sir. You've been very supportive of me, and I really do appreciate that."

"I'm happy to invite you back to Lenox & Park. In fact, we're hiring for the chief copy editor position."

Bernadette folded her hands in her lap. She'd never dreamed that she'd be able to come back to Lenox & Park without Mr. Wall. This was amazing. "If I can have my job back, I will be delighted to work for whoever you hire."

Mr. Bass smiled and tapped a finger on the table toward her. "We want to hire you."

"Me?" Bernadette couldn't have heard right.

Mr. Bass smiled. "You. You've more than proven yourself not only as an especially talented copy editor and Grammarian but also as a leader. People respect you."

Ghostly mirages of Evans, Marshall, and Greene floated behind Mr. Bass's head, jeering and taunting.

"I'm not certain some of my colleagues would respect me in that position." She'd voiced the words before being able to tug them back inside.

"I believe they respect you more than you think. I'm not saying it won't be a challenge where some people are concerned, but you are an asset to this publishing house, and we want you to continue to build with us."

Bernadette could barely think, let alone speak.

Chief copy editor?

That was not a position she'd thought to reach for years. Hardly a month had passed with her as senior copy editor. There were three other senior copy editors who had more experience than her. Plus, she was so young…not even thirty.

"Sir, I don't know what to say. Are you sure?" Once again, the words came out before she had a chance to pull them back, to listen to the part of herself that said she'd earned this and had worked twice as hard as Marshall, Evans, and Greene combined to get where she was.

Mr. Bass laughed, his hand slapping against the wood of the table. "You've always been so honest, Miss Swift. It's one of the reasons I admire you. You don't hedge. And your grasp of language is unprecedented. This isn't just me offering either. It's the entire corporate team, the board. We know what you did for the celebrity book, and every other project you've had your hands on. We've seen how you handle the interpersonal struggles within your department, and we see how you've encouraged others to work harder and push themselves up the ranks. You have talent, and as I said, you're a natural leader. You've earned this and we think you'll thrive as chief."

"I want to say yes." Bernadette straightened, fiddling with a random pen on the table.

"Then say yes, Miss Swift. What's stopping you?"

The very question cranked open a Pandora's box of insecurities. All she had to do was slam it closed. Bernadette stilled her hand on top of the pen she'd been fidgeting with. "Yes."

Mr. Bass slapped the table again. "Hot dog, here we go. I was worried you'd turn me down. Had me going there for a minute."

She pinched the pen, feeling like the writing instrument grounded her somehow. "Why?"

He shrugged. "Because we wanted you to have it so much. And because you've been put through the wringer here. Wouldn't be surprised if you decided to hedge your bets somewhere new."

"I have loved working at Lenox & Park since the beginning. I didn't want to leave." Bernadette glanced toward the glass wall that formed the barrier between the conference room and the corridor, expecting to see the raging bull stomping his foot and preparing to charge. "And Mr. Wall? He's really leaving?"

Mr. Bass nodded, his white bushy brows flattening, serious. "Oh yes, he had a string of complaints longer than Fifth Avenue. Complaints about his work ethic, employee interactions. You know, you weren't the first to complain about him to personnel. And you weren't the last. You inspired women whom he'd ill-treated to come forward. And when we found out how he was trying to claim the celebrity book copyedits as his own, we started to dig a bit more."

Bernadette nodded, sighing. "I feel bad for Patty."

"Mrs. Wall?" Bass cocked his head. If he was wondering how she knew Patty, he didn't voice the question.

Bernadette nodded. "She's such a sweetheart, dealing with him all these years, and now he's going to go home and torment her forever."

"I have a feeling Mrs. Wall will be just fine."

All Bernadette could imagine was Wall storming around the house, maybe even going so far as to tear her paintings from where they hung, destroying anything that was more successful than he was—which was basically everything. "How can you be sure, pardon my saying so?"

"I saw her carry a few paintings into Jane's gallery this morning. She came out empty-handed and with a big smile on her face." He leaned in, one elbow perched on the edge of the table. "Jane told me about what happened at book club. And though I do hate to gossip, so you didn't hear this from me, Jane also told me that Patty left her husband."

Bernadette couldn't help smiling, imagining Patty being surprised after years of her husband telling her that her art wasn't worthy that someone wanted to sell it. How freeing it must have been for her to discover there was interest after so many years of being held back. That she would no longer have to brace herself for his ire on a daily basis. That she could pursue her dreams in peace. "That's good news. My lips are sealed. Patty deserves happiness and her talent deserves to be showcased."

"I agree. And so does yours." Mr. Bass smiled and held out his hand for a shake. "Welcome back, Miss Swift—Chief."

For a split second, she wondered if Jane Bass had told her husband of the bet and encouraged him to bring Bernadette back. And she had mentioned it, clearly, but Bass had done more than bring her back. He'd changed her life and the trajectory of her career, and that was well before the book club had been a part of her life.

"Thank you so much, Mr. Bass." She took his hand and gave it a firm shake. "I am extremely happy to be back. And I won't let you down."

"I never thought you would. One more thing before you head to your new office. We'd like Frank to come back. As we understand it, he was agitated by Mr. Wall, and with that agitation removed, he was the best mail carrier we've had."

Emotion swelled in Bernadette's chest. This was quite possibly the best twenty-four hours of her life. Her brother was found alive, she was offered a promotion, and Frank could come to work with her every day. "Frank will be delighted."

Bernadette left the conference room and walked toward Graham's office, practically floating as she went. She hadn't even told him that she was coming in this morning, but by now, gossip had probably gone round the office.

Before she reached his door, he rushed out, a grin causing the dimple in his face to deepen.

"You're back," he said.

"I'm back." Gosh, it felt good to say that.

"Lunch in our usual spot?" Graham's face was so full of love, of excitement, that Bernadette wanted to kiss him right there in front of everyone.

It took quite a lot to restrain herself. In fact, she had to fold her fingers in front of her waist. "I could not think of a better place. Though it's getting chillier by the day. We may need to have a winter spot."

"Pizza?"

Her stomach growled at the thought of gooey cheese, delicious dough, the spice of marinara sauce. "Yes. Frank will love that."

"Ah, so he's invited back."

She nodded, biting her lip to keep the squeal of joy inside.

"See you at noon?"

"You betcha. Unless I can't help myself and end up at your office."

"You may do so only once a day," she teased.

"No guarantees."

Bernadette laughed and backed away, eventually forcing herself to turn around before she knocked into someone or her heel caught on something and sent her tumbling backward.

By the time she made it to the copyediting department, both Melanie and Sarah were rushing around inside Wall's former office, clearing it out. No more masculine paintings on the wall, the desk itself sparkled, and there was a nice floral scent.

"Is that Youth-Dew perfume?" Bernadette asked.

Melanie laughed. "Always have a bottle in my purse. It smelled like bullshit in here, and I thought you'd appreciate a more feminine and sweeter aroma in your office."

Bernadette sucked in an emotional breath. "You guys, I'm… I don't know what to say, I'm just so happy."

Her friends moved in and pulled her into a hug. "You did it," Melanie whispered.

"We're so proud of you. You're going to make this department really shine," Sarah said. "A woman's touch is exactly what it needed."

Bernadette moved around to the chair that Wall had sat in, only it wasn't his. It was her old chair. She smiled. "I won't have to sit where he sat."

"No way. We didn't want your gorgeous pink suit to be ruined by any leftover flatulence," Melanie said, sticking her finger into her mouth and gagging.

"And you know he did that often," Sarah added with a shudder that made her whole body tremble. "No way he didn't with all that wind coming out of his ass."

Bernadette laughed so hard she snorted. "I love you ladies."

"We love you too."

There was a knock at the door, and the three bozos stood on the other side. Greene's face was expressionless, Evans looked at her with respect, and Marshall looked a little like a kid who'd been told no ice cream after dinner.

Bernadette stood from her chair and waved them in. Melanie and Sarah ducked out. Her three male colleagues moved to stand in front of her desk. Each one likely wondering why he hadn't been chosen for the position over her. But at least none of them looked angry. That was a huge bonus.

"We wanted to offer our congratulations," Evans said. His tone didn't hold even a hint of sarcasm, but the way Marshall was pouting, she was pretty sure the *we* didn't include him.

Bernadette was surprised Evans had come to say anything at all. From what they'd put her through over the years, she'd half expected them to either insult her or put in their resignations.

"You earned it," Greene said. His smile was tight, but his words sounded sincere. "The chief should be a Grammarian."

Marshall was the only one who hadn't said anything, and he'd been the worst of the offenders.

She stared at him a moment, waiting, considered asking if her big juicy balls looked any bigger, and then decided it wasn't worth it, though she would have laughed like hell later.

"I appreciate your congratulations," she said. "And I hope you continue to work as hard for me as you did for my predecessor." She decided she didn't want to speak his name another day in her life. And that meant giving Frank a new shredding command.

Wall was gone, and with him all of his nasty vitriol.

Good riddance.

"We will." This was Marshall speaking, and it surprised her. Some of the petulance was gone from his face, but there was an edge to his tone. He nodded as if confirming his spoken words, or maybe trying to convince himself. Bernadette wasn't entirely convinced. Marshall had really seemed to dislike her presence. And it remained to be seen if he'd work as a team rather than for himself.

"Good. There's a lot of talent in that office, and we all deserve the recognition. Will you please let everyone know I'd like us to meet in the conference room in thirty minutes? I'm excited to get us moving in the right direction," she said.

The three bozos left the office, and she sat back down, taking in a deep breath, letting it out slowly. She'd been planning for a moment like this since she got her acceptance to Barnard College. And now it was time to implement her plans.

Bernadette pulled out a pad of paper, and one of her lucky pens, and started to make a list.

Chapter Thirty-One

THE FIRST TIME THAT BERNADETTE realized she was a leader was at her family farm. She'd been playing with Amaranth, who was really more like a dog, when the other pigs in the pen noticed. They'd lined up for the game of toss, too, and soon enough she had a line of pigs sitting in a row waiting expectantly for her next move.

Ben of course had called her a world-class weirdo. She'd called him an ignoramus, to which he'd tattled and told their parents she'd called him an anus.

Standing at the head of the conference table, the copyediting staff seated in two neat rows on either side and staring at her expectantly, reminded her of that moment on the farm, however inappropriate it might have been to think of pigs lined up the same way she did copy editors.

With a grand smile, she sat down, not wanting to lord over the group the way Wall had. She was going to run this department differently. With teamwork—which had two original meanings that both kind of worked. The yoking together of beasts to plow the field, and relating to baseball players.

Melanie sat at the edge of the room taking notes. Evans looked oddly eager. Greene was expressionless, and Marshall looked like he wanted to throw up.

"Good morning."

A chorus of good mornings answered, followed by a dozen pairs of blinking and expectant eyes focused on her. She picked up her pen where it lay on her notes, holding on to it as if that gesture might ground her in this moment.

"I'm sure by now you're all aware I'm the new chief of our department, and I wanted to take a moment for us to come together and make a game plan."

She ignored the few heads that looked at her oddly for that suggestion. There are usually three types of people in the business world: those who want to enact change and growth, those who think things should remain the same, and the dinosaurs who wish things were the way they used to be.

Bernadette was of the first frame of mind, and while she knew at least half the department formed the others, she was hoping at least for some support from the rest. Melanie, sitting on the side and taking notes, nodded at her in encouragement.

"I believe that a department functions best when all hands are on deck and invested."

"Are you suggesting we're not invested in this department?" Marshall asked, his body stiffening in his chair, giving the impression that he might just bolt up and send the chair flying through the window.

"Not at all." This was the moment of truth. She could back

down from the reality of how the department was run under Wall, or she could be forthright about it. Backing down was only going to set the precedent for how people expected her to behave going forward. Men like Marshall would feel they could bully her into not expressing what she thought was best for the department that she'd been entrusted with. That didn't sit right with her. "What I'm suggesting is that there might have been preferential treatment given, certain behaviors ignored, and that some worked a little harder than others."

Marshall glowered, the knuckles of his fingers turning white where he pressed them into the table. Bernadette wasn't going to let him intimidate her though. Beside him, Evans and Greene nodded. Not unusual for them lately. Marshall was clearly going to be the one she had to work on. And if he wasn't amenable to her leadership, then she would have to suggest he move on. There was a reason one rotten apple in a barrel had the ability to spoil the entire drum.

"Is there something you wanted to add, Marshall?" Bernadette watched him, keeping her expression plain, not showing any emotion, and most especially not showing herself being intimidated.

Marshall looked like he was literally chewing on his thoughts, his jaw muscles clenching and unclenching. This was clearly a mental wrestling match for him. He had to decide if he wanted to be a team player or hit the road. "No, Chief," he finally murmured, and though she couldn't visibly let out the breath she was holding, Bernadette exhaled in a long, slow sigh of relief.

He might have capitulated now, but there was sure to be more bluster when it came to Marshall.

"Well, do let me know if you change your mind," she said,

then addressed the rest of the room. "I'm going to set up an assignment board. Each copy editor will be assigned one book at a time, and it will be given based on the board."

Bob, at the end of the table, sat up a little taller. Next to Bernadette, he'd been assigned the most manuscripts to copyedit, and the three bozos the least. Wall had never had a system. Over the few years that she'd worked under him, Bernadette had tried to figure out what it was, even keeping notes on his assigning tactics. But none of it had ever made sense. There was no pattern, no order. It had been pure chaos and favoritism.

"When you've completed a manuscript, you'll be assigned another. Everyone will have the same amount of work."

"But what if we take a day off?" Marshall interjected. There was an edge to his voice that hinted that depending on her answer, his reaction may be unpleasant. Considering he'd been used to getting days off whenever he wanted, she'd been expecting this.

Again, this was a moment for her to be clear about her expectations. The boys' club had no place in a serious and efficient department. "If it is for a vacation or a sick day, then you've nothing to worry about. But if it's because you spent too much time at the Writer's Block the night before, your absence will not be excused, and you will be expected to turn in your manuscript on time."

Marshall tapped his fingers on the table. "How much time?"

"Each timeline will depend on the manuscript. Two to four weeks is standard in our industry. More complicated manuscripts will take longer. A children's book may only be a day or two. For quite some time, our timelines have been crunched tighter and tighter. And I believe this is due to delegation issues and time management issues. We have enough copy editors in our department—minus one, of course—to get everything done in a timely and efficient manner."

There was some grumbling around the table, but only by a few. Most of the copy editors were sitting a little taller, their expressions eager. It was eye-opening for Bernadette to realize she wasn't the only one who'd been completely overwhelmed. Leadership had an effect not only on workplace ethics but on morality as well. And Bernadette was determined to turn this department around.

"I think by shifting our priorities and assignment scheduling, we'll produce better finished products." She looked at Marshall. "And I'm not suggesting that any one person didn't do their best. I think we all did the best we could, given the circumstances and environment we were used to."

Marshall nodded, the little knot in his throat bobbing in agreement. A little weight, like she'd been carrying around shoulder pads made of iron, slid off down Bernadette's arms. Maybe winning over Marshall wouldn't be as difficult as she imagined.

"I took the liberty of compiling a list of current projects, and if I've missed one, please speak up." Bernadette went down the list, noting after each manuscript listed which copy editor had been assigned. "As you can see there is a bit of discrepancy as far as equal distribution is concerned. Bob has five manuscripts assigned to him, and Evans has only two."

Bernadette considered not mentioning that she had by far more than most, with eight, prior to her being fired by Wall. But then decided against it. They needed to know. "Prior to being dismissed by my predecessor, I had eight manuscripts assigned to me at once."

The room gasped, sucking all the air inside, before exhaling once more.

"I don't offer that information to elicit pity," she said, "but merely to point out that there have been a lot of inconsistencies in the department and with the equality of our assignments."

As she went down the line, something surprised her. Copy editors were offering to take the load off those who had more. Even Marshall asked the copy editor beside him if he could take one.

Bernadette's throat tightened with emotion that was both relief and satisfaction. She pressed her hands onto her knees to keep the copy editors from seeing how the emotion made her fingers tremble slightly. Part of her had expected utter chaos when she mentioned a change in the way things were going to run. People don't like change, don't like compromise, and no one likes adding work to their plate, especially if they'd been riding easy.

This congeniality was a pleasant, if unexpected, surprise.

Graham walked past the conference room, his smile warm and encouraging. He gave her a small thumbs-up that she hoped no one had noticed. She wanted to run out the door and tell him how well it was going, but her first day on the job probably wasn't a good time to abandon ship and brag to her boyfriend. Besides there was still a little part of her that worried the others would think she'd only gotten the promotion because of Graham, even if that was so far away from the truth as to be contradictory.

Bernadette returned her attention to the table. "If you have any questions about our new organization chart or the assignment board, please don't hesitate to come to me. Also, if you need time off, I'm not a monster. I believe people should have time off. And speaking of that…" This was not what she should be doing, having just gotten the job, but she believed in transparency. "This is a bit personal, but I feel the need to share so you all understand. My brother was stationed in Vietnam. His plane crashed, and he's recovering overseas."

There were a few gasps, and she felt warm to know that they sympathized with her.

"He's going to make a full recovery. But, when he does return to the States, I will be headed to Maryland to see him. I just wanted you all to know I wasn't jumping ship as soon as we set sail."

"Of course not, completely understandable." Evans was being much more cooperative than she ever would have expected.

"Thank you."

"We're so glad he's all right. You must have been worried sick," Bob said.

"I was, and thank you. I really appreciate that. Now, enough about me. Let's really show the executive board just how well we all work together."

Chapter Thirty-Two

OVER THE NEXT WEEK, BERNADETTE experienced a series of ups and downs, which was to be expected, but mostly ups. Of course, the pranks she'd been waiting for didn't happen, thank goodness.

Melanie had found a whiteboard and set it up just outside her office along the wall that had once housed some hideous artwork that Wall had hung—ironically not painted by his wife, who was a true artist. The assignments on the board, as it turned out despite some skepticism, worked very well. And so far this week, Marshall hadn't needed a day off.

With Bernadette being promoted to chief, that left an opening for a senior copy editor, which would leave an opening for a new copy editor.

Bob seemed like the appropriate senior copy editor candidate, so that was easily sorted. But for a new copy editor, she wanted to hire a female to start to balance things out in the department. Marshall was the most likely to balk, but she really didn't care.

And she was still holding out hope, as it seemed each day he grew a little less tense.

As for a new female copy editor, Bernadette decided to pay it forward, or perhaps it was backward, by following in Mr. Bass's footsteps and contacting Barnard. They were in the fall semester, so perhaps asking after their recent graduating class would prove constructive.

In her office, Bernadette picked up the phone and dialed her alma mater. She was quickly transferred to the English Department and just as quickly given the names of three shining recent graduates, though the department head was pretty sure they'd all been offered positions already.

Not willing to give up, Bernadette made the calls. One line rang and rang until the operator came on and asked if she'd like to continue the call. Bernadette declined and dialed the next number for Eleanor Baker, a young Black woman who'd graduated the year after Bernadette.

"Baker residence." The voice on the other end sounded like a young, tired woman. The kind of exhaustion Bernadette had only felt when Frank was a puppy.

"Hello, I'm trying to reach Eleanor Baker." Was it a sign that her first name was the same as a woman Bernadette greatly admired?

There was a long-suffering sigh. "Speaking."

Bernadette wasn't about to let the Eleanor Baker's fatalistic tone reverse her decision to make the call. Everyone had days like she imagined this young woman must have had. "Wonderful. My name is Bernadette Swift. I'm the chief copy editor at Lenox & Park. I received your name from the English Department at Barnard."

"Oh." There was immediate interest, her tone picking up spark. "So lovely of you to call, Mrs. Swift. I've heard great things about Lenox & Park. What can I do for you?"

Bernadette liked how direct she was, and how quickly she seemed to bounce from resigned to optimistic. Someone who could bounce back was exactly what she needed for the department. It had been hard enough for her, and whoever filled her old shoes would need to be able to roll with the attitude waves of their male-dominated industry. At least, Miss Baker, if she was hired, wouldn't have to worry about Bernadette harassing her.

"Just Miss, not Mrs.," Bernadette said. "I was calling to see if you'd be interested in interviewing for an open position we have in the copyediting department."

"Oh…" There was silence on the other end of the line. "Yes," she breathed out, almost the same way Bernadette did when a recipe came out really well, or a contestant on a game show she was watching won. "When?"

"Are you in the New York area, Miss Baker?"

"I can be."

"I was hoping to get together this afternoon."

Again silence. Long enough that Bernadette thought the line had gone dead.

"Miss Baker?"

"Yes," Miss Baker said softly, though the excitement that had been in her voice a moment before had vanished with the wind. "I am so grateful for the opportunity, but I'm in Philadelphia. I would need to check the trains for this afternoon, and I'm not entirely certain I would get there on time."

"How about tomorrow morning then?" Bernadette was easily

able to shift her schedule, and if the only reason for the lack of hope in Eleanor's voice was that she was afraid she wouldn't be able to make it to an interview, then why allow her another moment of distress?

"I can make that."

"Perfect. Have you been employed since graduating?"

"Yes, but not in the way I suspect you'd hope." Again, the downtrodden tone.

"How's that?"

"I was offered a position at the *Villager*, but I had to decline as my parents preferred I remain at home. I've been hired as a nanny by my mother's employer."

Eleanor's story was not an unusual one, mirroring much of Bernadette's own past. How easily she too could have gotten stuck at home rather than working in the literary world as she'd always dreamed. "I understand. I have one question for you."

"Yes?" A subtle trace of courage was all Eleanor needed to see this through.

"Are you willing to accept the position, if offered, and move to New York? I understand before you felt you didn't have a choice. Has that changed? Are you ready to pursue your own dreams?"

This time there was no hesitation in her answer. "Absolutely."

"Good. Then I'll see you tomorrow, say noon? We can conduct the interview over lunch."

"Thank you so much. I hadn't thought this would..." Eleanor Baker's voice caught, and Bernadette's heart squeezed. It was easy to see that Eleanor regretted having turned down her dreams before. This second chance was one she wasn't going to miss.

"I'm looking forward to meeting you, Miss Baker, and seeing what another Barnard graduate can do with a red pencil."

"Thank you, Miss Swift. I won't let you down."

Bernadette hung up and dialed the third number on the list, only to be told that the other student had accepted a position at the *Washington Post* in DC.

She couldn't help but smile. It seemed like Eleanor Baker was going to be her only Barnard candidate, and she really hoped that it was going to work out.

Bernadette stood up and walked to the window, taking in the view of the city, the traffic on the street, the swiftly turning colors of the trees in the park. How many times had she stared out this very window wishing she were anywhere but in this office? And now it was going to be her view for the foreseeable future. She smiled down at the pedestrians on the sidewalks and the hot dog and coffee stands, thinking about how a simple change of title had transformed so much, including this view.

A light knuckle wrap on her door had Bernadette turning. Graham stood in her doorway, leaning casually against the frame as if he belonged right there. Every time she saw him, a flutter in her stomach made her swallow.

"I've been wanting to come by all morning but thought I'd keep it professional until lunch." The dimple in his cheek dipped.

"Oh my, it's that time already." She glanced at the clock to see it was only a few minutes before noon.

Then she eyed the blinds on the glass window that looked out over the department. If only she had the guts to close them and the door, and press her mouth to Graham's like she wanted to.

"How has it been going?" he asked.

"Spectacular. The meeting went well." Bernadette kept her voice low, well aware that nearly everyone in the copyediting department would be trying to hear, and also knowing she couldn't close the door for fear of what they'd whisper if she did. "Everyone seems on board, with the exception of Marshall, but I think even he's going to come around. I promoted Bob, and I've got an interview tomorrow with a fresh Barnard graduate."

"Sounds like you've got all your ducks lined up in a row."

Bernadette laughed. "Funny you should say that. I was just thinking this morning how they reminded me of pigs."

"Amaranth?"

She gasped. "I'm glad you remember, or else I'd seem like a total donkey."

Graham grinned. "Somehow I can picture a young Bernadette Swift bossing around the swine on her farm."

"You'd be correct. To be fair, they seemed to appreciate my leadership."

"And did they all have matching hair bows?"

"Only the few females that would let me. The males I gave smart blue bow ties."

Graham chuckled. "Well, shall we head to lunch before I kiss you in front of everyone?"

"That depends." She cocked a shoulder, her hand on her hip. "Are you going to kiss me in the elevator?"

"If it's empty, I planned on it." Graham's eyes roved over her face, her mouth, and that flutter returned.

"Perfect."

They left the department, which was mostly emptying out now for lunch. Melanie was gone from her desk, but the elevator was packed. Graham stood a few inches from her, his pinkie finger brushing against hers down by their sides where no one could see.

"Pizza?" she asked, not having been prepared for lunch today.

"I was thinking something a little more celebratory. Since Frank won't be in until tomorrow, I thought we'd save the pizza for him."

"Oh, and what's that?"

"I'll show you."

He hailed a cab and gave an address. A moment later, they were pulling up outside the Ritz by Central Park. Bernadette had never been to the Ritz. She'd walked past it of course, and seen it in plenty of movie pictures, but inside was another glitzy story. The Ritz lobby smelled like plumeria and wealth.

"Oh, this is fancy," she whispered.

"I think today calls for it." He led her toward the restaurant, where he gave his name for the reservation.

She glanced down at her clothes, grateful she'd dressed in her favorite pink suit and polka-dot shirt. They were escorted to a table, the restaurant filled with socialites, a few famous actors, singers, and some businesspeople too. It was splendiferous and made Bernadette feel exceptionally special.

After the maître d' had pulled out her chair, given her a menu, placed her napkin on her lap, and then left, she reached across the table to hold Graham's hand. "Thank you, Graham. I would never spoil myself like this."

"I know. But you deserve it. Congratulations."

"Thank you."

They dined on shrimp cocktail, salads, and steak, and when

they were done, her stomach was so full, she felt she might burst from her skirt.

"Maybe we should walk back," she suggested. "It's only a mile."

"Good idea." They headed down Fifth Avenue at a leisure pace, talking about publishing, her promotion, and the plans she had for the department.

"I'm amazed you weren't promoted before now," Graham said. "You're a natural leader."

"There was a Wall blocking me," she said with a giggle.

"Well, good thing that Wall has been taken down," he added, and though they were both playing with words, they were each entirely serious.

"Today it's all new and shiny, and everyone is being just as polished and motivated. But I worry what the coming days will be like. Marshall, Evans, and Greene aren't used to pulling their weight. But with Bob on the same level as they are, I don't think he'll let them get away with their usual shenanigans, and I know I won't."

"You can cross that literary bridge when you get there. Maybe they will surprise you."

"I just hope if we are going to get there, we get there soon, so we can cross over it and move on."

"I give it a week."

"You think?"

"This is going to be the hardest week they've worked in years—and that's saying a lot, given how much work he piled on you. Absolutely."

Bernadette threaded her fingers in his, enjoying the warmth of his palm on hers in the cool air. "Thank you for all of your support, Graham. I couldn't have done it without you."

Graham stopped walking, causing a few people behind them to grumble as they walked around them. The look on his face was a mix of disbelief and dismay. "That's not true."

She cocked her head, narrowing her eyes. "How so?"

"You did all of this on your own."

"But you and Mr. Bass—"

Graham shook his head. "We supported you, yes, but we didn't do your job. You did that. It's your work ethic, your talent, your personality. It is Queen B who earned the promotion. Don't discount yourself by thinking it was anything or anyone else. It was all you."

"Thank you." She leaned in then, kissing him and not caring about the catcalls on the street.

"You're welcome," he murmured against her lips. "Own it, woman."

She laughed, leaning her head against his shoulder. "Can I at least give you credit for being a great person to talk to?"

"I'll take credit for that, but it's not my only talent." He winked and wiggled his brows.

"Oh, I see… We're fishing," she teased. "Come over tonight and prove it?"

"It would be my pleasure."

"And mine."

Bernadette breezed into Lenox & Park the next morning with Frank by her heels. They made their way to the mail department, where Mark and the rest of his crew were waiting with Frank's special vest.

"Welcome back, Frank." Mark beamed, and the rest of the

mail team clapped and cheered while he buckled on the vest. "We missed you down here, pal."

Frank barked and lifted up on his hind legs, pressing his massive paws to Mark's shoulders and giving him a huge lick on the cheek.

"He missed you too." Bernadette laughed.

Mark gave him a generous hug, scrubbing his hands down Frank's back and then telling him to get down so he could put on the vest.

Bernadette knelt beside Frank and gave him a kiss on his head and a good ear scratch. "He's got a new shredding word we've been working on." She stood and whispered it to Mark, "Jabberwock."

"Never heard of it."

She grinned. "Most people wouldn't be walking around saying it, and I thought that would be important this go-round."

"Agree. Where's it from?"

"It's a monster from a poem in *Through the Looking-Glass* by Lewis Carroll." The word was good for her too, since when she'd been little, she'd been pretty sure there was a Jabberwock under her bed, just ready to reach out and grab her.

"Ah, that makes sense, and it's perfect. Mind if I give it a whirl?" Mark asked.

"Of course not."

Mark grabbed a piece of paper from the to-be-shredded pile and placed it on the floor in front of Frank.

"Jabberwock."

Frank snatched the paper and went to town, pieces of paper flying around like confetti.

"Excellent," Mark nodded, a massive grin on his face. "That's not a word likely to get him into any trouble."

"Now try the other word."

Mark looked skeptical.

"Go on, try it," she encouraged.

"Wall."

Frank sat, looking up at him expectantly.

"He wants a treat," she explained.

Mark chuckled. "So that's how you got him to do it."

Bernadette beamed with pride and gave Frank a pat on the head. "Frank is a very motivated worker."

"That he is." Mark pulled a treat from his pocket and tossed it at Frank, who leaped up to snatch it from the air with expert ease.

With a sigh, Bernadette nodded. "I'll let the two of you get to work. I really appreciate your being willing to take him back. I'm so glad you didn't hold my predecessor's opinion as a value of Frank's personality."

"Thanks for bringing him back, Miss Swift. We were sorely disappointed when we had to let him go."

"He's really a good boy."

"Everyone makes mistakes, right?"

"And most of us get more than second chances," she pointed out, thinking not only of herself but even Marshall upstairs.

"True story. See you at lunch?"

"Actually, it will be Graham taking Frank to lunch today. I have an interview to conduct."

"Well, then we'll see Graham at lunch."

"Good luck today." Bernadette waved goodbye to the team and gave Frank one last rub on the head. "Be good, boy."

Frank barked, and the look in his eyes almost appeared to say, *Be a good girl.*

Chapter Thirty-Three

FRANK

THE LAST TIME WE HEADED to the farm, Bernadette's father picked us up in his red truck in the middle of the big city. I sat in the bed of the truck, basking in the sunshine—or *apricating*, as my girl says—with my tongue flapping the entire ride. It was stupendous.

Bernadette and her father had been singing to the radio, and she kept pointing at me, her lip curled and chanting, "You ain't nothing but a hound dog."

But this time, we're not in the pickup. And it isn't her father driving but Graham. He called this vehicle a Chevy and said he borrowed it from a friend on his rugby team. The blue of the paint matches my girl's dress. They've been singing a song about hitting the road and calling each other Jack.

I'm in the back seat, head out the window, and still have my tongue hanging out. What can I say? The air just tastes good that way.

They lean close as Graham drives, Bernadette's head on his shoulder. Cozy, like pack animals. I nudge between the two of them, wanting equal attention. Bernadette laughs and rubs my head, and I bark to let her know I'm happy.

All feels right in the world.

My girl is happy.

Graham is my new best friend.

I get to go to work with the two of them each morning, delivering mail, and at the end of the day, Mail Room Mark gives me a stack of paper to shred. It's a win-win situation. I've got a lot of jobs. First and most importantly is to be the bestest friend Bernadette ever had, and I think I've accomplished that one very well. The next job I have is to look after Mrs. Morris and to continue to provide Mr. Crumbs with treats—even though I had vowed never to help him again. I'm a forgiver.

Then there's my mission to protect the neighborhood— haven't had a mugging or missing child reported in months. And now I'm also a mail dog, which I quite enjoy. Squirrel catcher, I'm still getting the hang of, and prairie digger, just feels like I'm digging holes to nowhere. I'm thinking I might have better luck on the farm.

But today isn't about most of those jobs; this is a day to celebrate. A day to share with my girl, and her boy—well, both her boys. Me and Graham. I give him a lick on his cheek, chuckling on the inside when he discreetly wipes off my slobber. The answer is yes, I did make it extra slobbery on purpose. It's a game we play. I lick, he wipes.

We're driving to the farm, like I said, but we're going for a couple of really good reasons.

One is Graham has asked to meet my girl's family.

And the other one is even better—Ben is back. I can't wait to show him how well my mission has gone.

I heard his voice myself on the telephone when he called, and the tears that Bernadette shed weren't sad ones but happy ones that had me running around in a fit of the FRAPs. *Ben Ben Ben Ben Ben...*

She didn't even care when I crashed into the table and dumped coq au vin all over the floor, or as we dogs like to call it, chicken dinner. That was delicious.

Down the highway we careen, pulling over for us all to sniff out a spot about halfway through. I'm a little confused when Graham doesn't lift his leg. I may have to teach him how to do it later.

We hop back into the car and ease back out onto the road. Bernadette and Graham sing to the radio tune "You're the Devil in Disguise" by some guy they call Elvis, and I howl along.

And then I can smell it. Grass and corn and wheat and farm animals. All mixed up in air fresher than the city. I howl out the window, letting the town know I'm back.

"You tell them, boy," Bernadette says, and so I howl again.

We turn onto a long and winding drive, and Bernadette asks Graham to stop.

"He likes to run the rest of the way," she says, and I'm glad she remembered because if not I would have just jumped out the window.

Graham brakes, and my girl opens the door. "See you down there, boy. Go get 'em."

And I obey. Chasing rabbits and birds and field mice and

anything else that wiggles as I run through the field toward the vast farmhouse.

I beat the car while I'm barreling up the wooden steps with their familiar paint chips and creaks. The door bursts open and Bernadette's mom comes out first, followed by her dad, and Ben wobbling on long wooden sticks. I bark, howl, wag my tail, and lick and lick and lick until they are all covered in me.

"You got bigger," Ben says, giving me a massive squeeze, and I hold him up, letting him use my body as a crutch.

Mission complete, Sergeant. Bernadette is secure.

"Good boy, Frank." Ben grins down at me with such pride that I can't help but howl in return.

A moment later, the car pulls up. Graham and Bernadette exit, and there's a series of *ahhh*s and *ohhh*s as they shut the car doors.

Ben smiles, but his body stiffens a little as he eyes Graham. I wonder if he's going to sniff him the way I do other dogs in the park.

"What do you think of him?" Ben asks me, raising his brows and looking at me very seriously. I sense his worry, and I want to assure him.

I bark and wag, running toward Bernadette and then Graham, and running back to the porch, letting them all know that I approve. She's my girl, and he's my boy.

There really is nothing better than being with your people, having a reason to be there, a purpose, a full belly, and plenty of belly rubs to go around.

Chapter Thirty-Four

THERE'S SOMETHING ABOUT COMING HOME after being away for so long that sort of makes everything inside Bernadette sigh a little bit. The familiarity of the trees, the nick in the banister from a vigorous game of forbidden indoor catch, the scent of her mother's home cooking, or the wood oil massaged into the floors.

Bernadette breathed it all in, soaking it up with her eyes, but what felt the best was seeing her brother live and in person. He hobbled out on crutches in a pair of worn jeans and a faded Orioles baseball team T-shirt, letting the one crutch drop as he pulled her in for a hearty hug.

When they found him, when they got to talk to him over the telephone, it was all surreal, but being able to touch him, to actually wrap her arms around him… That was when Bernadette was able to finally believe that he was back. And it felt like the way he clung just as hard that he too could hardly believe he was finally home.

"You ignoramus," she whispered into his ear.

"Stop talking about my anus," he whispered back. "Shouldn't the copy chief have a better vocab?"

Bernadette laughed, the joke having lasted a decade now.

Ben finally loosened the hug but still held her at arm's length. For a split second his expression was full of brotherly love, and then he turned macho, dropped his hands. "Introduce me to your man, in case I need to challenge him to a wrestling match."

"You'd win. Be nice." She rolled her eyes.

"I don't know." Ben raised a brow as he assessed Graham, who was talking with their father. "He seems like the quiet-strength kinda guy."

Bernadette grinned. "He's a great guy."

With her brother's arm slung over her shoulder, she turned to Graham, who glanced her way with that lazy grin of his, the dimple deep, the way he did at the office when he was talking with someone and she happened to pass by.

"Graham, this is Ben. Ben, this is Graham."

Graham stuck out his hand, shaking Ben's in what looked like a firm grip, the two of them sizing each other up. And somehow Ben managed to keep his arm around her shoulder. She didn't know if it was because he wanted to show Graham he was willing to hold on to her or because he needed it for balance.

For a minute, she held her breath, unsure of how exactly this would go. In high school whenever she'd brought a boy around, Ben had always challenged him to some sort of contest set up for the guy to lose, and then he'd embarrass him, and the poor sucker would rush off in a tiff, and she'd run up to her room to sulk.

This time, however, was very different.

"Nice to meet you," Ben said, seeming to understand just how important this moment was.

"I've heard a lot about you," Graham said. "Glad you're back safe."

Bernadette now expected Ben to retort with, *Sorry I can't say the same*, but instead he said, "Likewise, man. When this leg gets better, maybe I'll join you for a rugby match. Can I get you a beer?"

"Yeah, beer sounds good. And you're welcome anytime."

Ben lifted his arm from Bernadette's shoulders and transferred it to Graham's, though she noticed he gave him a little bit of a roughhousing shake, which Graham laughed at, being the good sport that he was. Her brother hobbled his way back inside toward the kitchen, their dad following, leaving Bernadette on the porch with her mom, Frank, and her astonishment.

She raised a brow at her mom, who had a similar shocked expression, and said, "Wow, that's different."

Bernadette chewed on her lip, staring through the door as if a battle might erupt from inside at any moment.

"Should we be nervous?"

Frank barked, standing beside her, leaning in the way she loved. She rested her hand on his ribs, giving him a little stroke.

"Frank seems to think no," Bernadette guessed.

Frank wagged his tail and looked longingly at the fields behind him.

"You can go explore, boy," she said with a laugh. "I will not hold you back here." To her mom, she said, "The city is a little more restrictive, though we try to get in some good runs at Central Park."

Frank barked and leaped off the porch, skipping the four steps all together, and then he took off at a run, looking like he wanted to snatch the clouds out of the sky with his teeth.

Bernadette's mom linked her arm through hers. "He seems like a really nice man." She nodded toward the house.

"I really like him. Maybe even love him." Bernadette sighed, her heart giving her ribs a kick.

Her mom's smile was as bright as the sun embroidered on her apron. "You've not brought a boyfriend home since high school."

Bernadette shrugged, trying to take some of the seriousness out of this particular visit. "None have seemed worthy enough."

"Well, I'm glad that Graham seems to have passed the test. All the tests." She chuckled as they crossed over the threshold.

The house smelled like roasted chicken and fresh baked rolls, even a hint of apple pie. Bernadette's stomach immediately started to growl and her mouth to water. There was nothing so good as Mom's home cooking, except maybe Julia Child's if she were to come for a visit.

"I want to show you something, Bernie."

"I want to see it." She was glad for the distraction.

Her mother let go of her arm and hurried into the den, a small fire in the hearth giving off just a faint wood-burning smell. It was mid-October, the leaves were already turned, and soon a chill would blanket the farm, followed by waves of snow. Winter on the farm was different from winter in the city for so many reasons. First of all, she didn't have a fireplace, and second of all, walking on the slushy, icy sidewalks was a heck of a lot more dangerous than walking on snow-covered fields.

Her mother went over to the walnut secretary desk, turning a key in the door and pulling down the desktop to reveal the hutch behind. She pulled a magazine out of one of the slots and flipped it open to a marked spot, swiping her hand lovingly down the page. She thrust it toward Bernadette.

"Look." Her mother beamed as she held out the magazine as though it were a prized possession.

Bernadette took the magazine, reading the title of the article aloud: "Fashion for Farm Wives."

Beside the heading was a picture of her mother, smiling in the way she did that looked like she might hold a secret. Pride burst in Bernadette's chest.

"Mom! You did it!"

Her mother laughed and clapped, pride written all over her features. "Thank you for encouraging me, Bernie. I don't know that I would have taken the leap without your suggestion."

"I'm so glad you did. This is amazing." Of all the things she'd thought to see, it wasn't this. Her mother hadn't uttered a word about writing it, let alone submitting it, and definitely not about getting it published.

"Thank you. I wanted to surprise you. It just came out last week."

"This is seriously so incredible, Mom. I want to hear every-thing." Bernadette sat down on the sofa, her mother next to her, and read through the article, which suggested ways to spruce up aprons and offered ideas for special embroidery. There were even pictures of her mother's designs, which she'd modeled herself.

"Just because our hands are covered in muck by sunrise doesn't mean we can't look amazing milking cows and collecting eggs."

"I love that line," Bernadette laughed, pointing at it.

"The editor said the piece was so popular they want more.

Apparently, the day it came out, the phones were off the hook asking if it was going to be a regular series."

"That is incredible. Congratulations. What does Dad say?"

Her mother's smile widened. "He's proud of me. Bought up every copy at the store and then sent them to all our friends and even his farm contacts across the nation."

"I'm so glad that he's supporting you."

"He is very proud of me." Her mother glanced toward the kitchen where the men's boisterous voices could be heard. "I didn't realize how proud he would be. It's even gotten him doing dishes, can you imagine?"

"It's a miracle," Bernadette laughed. "Have you started to write your next column?"

"I have." Her mother rubbed her hands together with excitement. "It's due next week and will be published next month. With winter coming up I thought I'd focus on cold-weather gear. You know how I love my hats and gloves."

"I do." Bernadette hugged her mom. "I'm so proud of you. This is really so amazing. Do you have an extra copy I can take home with me?"

"Of course I do." Her mother hopped up and went back to the secretary desk, pulling out another copy that she handed to Bernadette. Then she came back to the couch and sat down next to her, looking her right in the eyes. "I'm proud of you, too, honey. And as much as I was telling you to come home, I know you're thriving in New York. Named chief? Incredible."

"Thanks, Mom. It's not been easy, but not incredibly difficult either." She told her mother about Marshall, and how each day he got better and had even brought her a coffee during one of their meetings. Of course, she hadn't sipped it until it was cold, afraid he'd dumped salt in it. Alas, no salt.

"And it appears you were able to find a man there after all." Mom winked.

Bernadette chuckled, beyond ecstatic that her mother wasn't begging her to come home and that it seemed she might finally have gotten her blessing. "Amazing that they have those there, huh?"

"And"—her mother wagged her finger—"he's surprisingly… normal."

That took Bernadette by surprise, of all things she expected her mother to say. "What did you think men in New York were like?"

"Actors, thieves." She shrugged. "Any type of man that would take advantage of my daughter."

"Nice." Bernadette laughed. "I promise I'm safe with Graham."

"I trust you, sweetheart." Her mother's expression was warm, reminding Bernadette what it felt like to get hugged after having fallen off her bicycle. "And your new position. Just incredible."

"I'm still pinching myself."

"You're on your way. Next stop, CEO."

Bernadette grinned. "I sure hope so." Then her stomach rumbled, reminding her that their lunch had been meager. "Any chance that chicken is ready? I'm starved."

"Soon. Come help me chop vegetables for the salad."

But by the time they reached the kitchen, Graham and Ben were already chopping the vegetables that her father was washing. Bernadette glanced at her mom, unable to hide her surprise.

Her mom just smiled and leaned against the doorframe

looking pleased with herself. "I took your advice on that, too," she said. "Turns out he's not just handy with dishes but with cooking as well."

Bernadette was pretty sure she'd never seen her father wash a vegetable a day in her life, and here he was instructing two other men how to make a salad.

She pinched her arm.

"Why are you doing that?" her mom asked, playfully swatting at Bernadette's fingers.

"Just making sure this is real life."

Her mom laughed so hard the men turned around.

"Don't tease us, Ma. We just wanted to help take a load off," Ben said.

Their father grinned. "Don't look so shocked, Bernie. A man can help his wife, and he should."

She smiled. "I'm not shocked, just...happy."

The table in the dining room was already set. And while her mother put the roasted chicken on the table for her father to carve, Graham made a vinaigrette for the salad à la Julia Child, and her brother mashed the potatoes, Bernadette stepped out onto the porch to call for Frank.

A blur of white-and-black fur whizzed through the field, and she had a sudden urge to run with him. To expend all the energy filling her, the happiness that made her think she might burst. Was that how dogs felt when they got the FRAPs? Bursting with energy that needed a release?

"Frank," she called, hopping down the stairs toward the grass. "Dinner!"

The whizzing blur of movement headed in her direction.

Frank barreling down on the house, his tongue flapping, long legs loping. She sat down on the front stoop to catch him, knowing if she remained standing, he'd knock her over, and the bruise from the landing would make the ride back to New York uncomfortable to say the least.

He crashed into her, almost like he needed her to stop his forward momentum, and she caught him, slobbery kisses and all. His fur was cool from running outside, but his breath was hot.

"What did you find out there?"

He looked back toward the field, barking as if to tell her just exactly what he'd seen.

"You'll have to show me later. Mom's made chicken."

His ears perked up at that.

"And potatoes."

Frank climbed over her onto the porch and into the house. Bernadette followed, laughing, amazed at just how much Frank seemed to understand when she spoke.

Her mother already had a bowl for him ready in the corner of the dining room. They didn't go so far as to give him a place at the table, which Bernadette wouldn't have minded, but they didn't banish him to another room to eat alone either.

Bernadette took her place beside Graham, Ben across from them, and her parents at the two ends of the table. They held hands and said grace, her mother getting teary eyed as she thanked heaven for Ben being safe and home.

At some point during the meal, Frank snuck under the table, lying at her feet, his head resting at an awkward angle on her shin as he waited patiently for anyone to drop just the tiniest morsel his way.

She didn't disappoint, giving him a hunk of carrot from her salad and a chunk of meat.

"So, Graham, you're an editor?" her father said, and Bernadette felt like groaning. She'd sort of hoped with them bonding over making salad that this sort of conversation had already been had. But apparently the third degree hadn't been on the menu for meal prep.

Please don't let him mention intentions with his daughter…

Graham wiped his mouth, setting down his fork and knife, and preparing to answer any and all questions, it seemed. "I am, at the same publishing house as Bernadette."

"And as a chief, is my daughter your boss?" Her father rubbed his hands.

Graham grinned. "Indirectly."

"How do you like the job?"

"I love it. Been there since I graduated. Worked my way up."

"Sounds like you two have a lot in common."

"We do," Bernadette said, holding Graham's hand under the table.

"And not just books," Graham said. "Bernadette's opened my eyes to food that doesn't come from a stand."

"A stand?" her mother asked.

"Hot dogs mostly." Graham chuckled.

Ben grinned. "I love a good hot dog."

"Same, though my wife doesn't often let me have them." Bernadette's father patted his stomach, which was mostly flat. "Only at baseball games."

"Bernadette mentioned you were a fan. I am too," Graham said.

"That right?" Her father narrowed his gaze and pointed at Graham. "But I bet you like those dang Yankees."

Graham chuckled and said unapologetically, "I do."

"Hate to toss in a wrench here, but I've become a fan of the West Point team," Ben said. "Go, Army."

"Another traitor! What about you, Bernie?" Her father's face was expectant.

Well, she certainly wasn't going to get in the middle of which baseball team was better. "I've decided I might become a football fan."

Her father gave an exaggerated groan, his head falling back, hand over his heart.

"I'm swearing off sports," her mother added, putting her hands up in surrender. "You know what I think would be fun? A bake-off contest. A bunch of contestants get together and bake all day for a prize."

"Can I be on your team?" Bernadette asked.

"Of course."

"Maybe suggest that in your next article." Bernadette wiggled her brows. "Fashion for Farm Wives, Bake-Off Edition."

"Oh, I like the sound of that."

The rest of dinner went by in friendly and teasing banter. Bernadette loved how Graham fit right into her family, just like the way he'd fit right into her life once she'd opened up enough to let him in.

After dinner, while her dad insisted on doing the dishes and Ben wanted to help, Bernadette asked Graham to take a walk outside with Frank.

"Have you ever seen stars like this?" she asked, staring up at the blanket of sparkling gold on a black backdrop.

"Only at sea—when I wasn't throwing up."

She giggled. "It's incredible. Out here the stars are in the sky, and in the city, the stars are all around us. See that star formation right there?" She pointed toward the sky, drawing her finger across the stars. "That's the Big Dipper. And down here, that's the Little Dipper."

"New York City is so full of its own lights, it's hard to make out the constellations in the sky. Funny how worlds can be different only a few hours apart." Graham put his arm over her shoulders, and she leaned her head against him while they stared up at the endless possibilities of the universe.

"I'm always amazed by it," she murmured.

"You know what amazes me?"

She glanced up at him, teasing. "My mom's chicken?"

He laughed, flashing his smile her way. "You, Bernadette Swift." And he tipped her chin up, kissing her until Frank interrupted, nudging his body between the two of them. "Somebody's jealous."

"Just a little bit, I think." She gave Frank's head a pat. "Go find a stick, boy. Bring me a stick."

Frank barked and ran off in search of a stick for her to toss for him, his body rustling through the tall grass.

"He's a damn good dog." Graham spoke with a sound of wonder in his voice, like a kid discovering something really groovy, which made her smile.

"He really is. My best friend, really." When her parents had first dropped him off in the city, his floppy long legs had popped up on her waist so he could sniff her better.

"And what am I?" he whispered.

"My best man."

Graham chuckled. "You're my best lady."

Frank returned with a stick as long as Bernadette's body, his head tilting a little to the side as he tried to balance it. "I guess I'll practice spear throwing," she said, laughing. Bernadette picked up the stick and launched it about five feet. "Wow, I'm terrible at this."

Frank loped the few feet and brought it back.

"See if you can throw it farther."

Graham laughed and picked up the stick, tossing it maybe twenty feet. "How did our ancestors survive? The buffalo would have to be right in front of me and already half-dead for me to hit the mark."

Bernadette chuckled as they took turns throwing the spear until Frank got bored and ran off after something scrambling through the field.

"I hope that's not a skunk," Bernadette groaned. "When I was growing up, one of our dogs had it out with a skunk and came through the house. Smelled awful for weeks. No matter how hard my mom scrubbed, that scent was everywhere."

"Perks of living in the city. No skunks."

"Ha, yes, we just have rats that eat pizza. Though to be fair, we've got plenty of rats out on farms too."

"What do you like better?" Graham asked.

"Rats or skunks?"

"The city or the farm?"

"The city." She didn't hesitate. "The farm is nice every once in a while, but I knew the whole time I was growing up that I wasn't meant for this world. I need the bright lights, the entertainment, the endless restaurants. I like a faster pace. I don't mind sitting out on my fire escape and staring at the city. I don't mind the rush of traffic. All of it invigorates me. And the publishing world, my world?" She shook her head. "I couldn't get that here." Bernadette wrapped her arms around his neck. "And you, Mr. Reynolds, I couldn't have you."

Graham's arms went around her waist. "I don't know, Miss Swift. I've got it bad. I'm pretty sure I'd follow you to the end of the earth."

She tilted up on her tiptoes and pressed her lips to his. "The end?" she whispered.

"Wherever the end is."

"You'd make the best company."

Frank howled from somewhere in the field, and they paused their kiss long enough to figure out where he was and if he was hurt. Frank barreled toward them as if to remind them that he too was good company.

"Well, the second-best company."

Graham chuckled. "I'd never come between you and Frank."

"He won't let you. As you can see."

"I admire that." Graham bent and picked up the massive stick, tossing it more than twenty feet this time. "Getting the hang of it."

Bernadette laughed. "Thank you for coming out here with me."

"It's a beautiful night."

"I mean to Maryland, to the farm. To meet my family."

"I wouldn't have missed it." He leaned down and brushed his lips on hers.

"I have a confession to make," Bernadette said. "I think I love you."

Graham's smile flashed wide in the moonlight. "I think I love you too."

A sharp whistle came from the porch of the farmhouse. "Hey, Reynolds, no pawing my sister. Time for pie!"

Bernadette groaned and Graham laughed. "Spoken like a true brother."

"I used to wish he'd just leave me alone, but not hearing from him for weeks and thinking the worst, as annoying as his teasing is, I'll take it over and over again just to know he's alive."

"It's a damned miracle." Graham whistled for Frank and then threaded his fingers in hers, leading her back toward the house.

"I always thought Ben had nine lives, like a cat. He's fallen out of trees, jumped off the porch roof, stood on the top of a moving tractor—gone to war. The man is a maniac. And yet he lives."

"I heard that," Ben called. "And I'm not a house cat. I prefer panther. Sounds cooler."

Bernadette laughed. "You're purrrfect."

Ben groaned. "Make her stop!"

Frank came running, not willing to miss out on any little bit of Mom's apple pie. He made it to the porch before Bernadette did, bounding up the steps with his large body, and waited not so patiently for them to hurry up, needing to make sure she was safe in the house.

"Good boy, Frank," she said, patting him on the head and ushering him inside.

She took one last look at the night sky, her mind comparing and contrasting once more. But she knew, she'd made the right choice.

Bernadette Swift was made for the city, made to lead, and ready to take on the world one book and one broken-down wall at a time.

Epilogue

VOGUE *MAGAZINE*

July 1998

POWERHOUSES IN PUBLISHING
by Leigh Reynolds

Four powerful women walk into the restaurant. Anna Wintour. Eleanor Gould Packard. Penelope E. Grynd. Bernadette Swift. I watch as waiters pause. Heads turn. The hostess leads them toward me, and my hands tremble a little bit, leaving tiny black scratches from my pen on the notepad where I was writing questions for this interview.

These are the names of female powerhouses in publishing not only today, but for the past several decades. Women who have become the first of their kind. Women who burned their candles at both ends, working tirelessly to not only earn a place in the industry but also take their place on the pedestals of history.

They are my idols and legends on the pages of magazines and books. The heroes of nearly every college student earning a degree in English with the intent of working in media and publishing. There's not a copy editor, editor, or writer out there who hasn't heard their names. And they are the reason I am writing this article.

Anna Wintour was named editor in chief of *Vogue* in 1988. She got her start in her career working in the UK for *Oz* magazine and then *Harper's & Queen* and by 1975 had moved to New York City as a junior fashion editor for *Harper's Bazaar*. From there she worked for several publications and even interviewed at *Vogue*, though at the time she told editor Grace Mirabella, who was interviewing her, that she wanted her job and was subsequently not hired. A few years later, however, she did in fact replace Mirabella at the magazine.

Penelope E. Grynd was named the first female CEO of publishing at Lion House in 1987. After graduating from Barnard, she applied at Doubleday as an editorial assistant and was instead hired as a secretary. A short time later, she was hired as an editor for William Morrow and then Simon & Schuster. By 1976 she was named editor in chief at Lion and continued to rise in the ranks until today.

Eleanor Gould Packard is the legendary Grammarian at the *New Yorker* who inspired a lot of words in generations of women and men. After writing to an editor at the *New Yorker* about a job, and pointing out two misuses of words she'd found in the magazine, she was offered a position. She's worked for the magazine for over fifty years. In addition to copyediting thousands of articles and stories in the magazine, she also helped to revise E. B. White's *The Elements of Style*.

Bernadette Swift was named the second female CEO in publishing at Lenox & Park in 1990. After realizing that her boss was only going to hold her back until she either quit or was fired, she decided to turn the publishing industry on its head by showing that women deserved a place in the workforce and were more than capable of rising to all challenges placed before them.

As a magazine columnist with aspirations of one day becoming Anna Wintour myself, I also had the privilege of growing up with Bernadette Swift as a mother and Penelope E. Grynd and Eleanor Gould Packard as mentors and frequent household guests. And though I was brought up in this world of literary enchantment, I had to work no less hard than they did in order to type these words today.

Women in publishing have been working tirelessly for centuries to make their names known and in some cases have had to use a male pseudonym to be seen as legitimate. When I think of powerhouses in the writing industry, writers like Mary Wollstonecraft, Jane Austen, Maya Angelou, and Harper Lee come to mind.

Dynamos in publishing, in addition to those I mentioned previously, are Elizabeth Timothy, Mary Katherine Goddard, Josephine St. Pierre Ruffin, Louise Seaman Bechtel, Phyllis E. Grann.

I had a chance to interview Wintour, Grynd, Packard, and Swift on a Tuesday afternoon in a restaurant that wasn't so busy I couldn't hear every word. But busy enough that those present could sense the power they had in front of them. The air in a room full of influential women is vibrant, shining, and electric. They've known each other for years, leaned on each other, and developed not only friendships but professional respect.

When these four women walk into a room, people stop speaking.

There is something in the set of their shoulders. The no-nonsense expressions, accompanied by confident stances. The command of language. They are intelligent, friendly, and discerning. They were patient, forthright, and humble.

Grynd will tell you to never stop reading. To read to your children. To share books with friends and family. Wintour believes in learning from mistakes, moving forward, and making connections with your audience. Packard insists on making things right and not being afraid to voice that. Swift will tell you to go after what you want, that it never hurts to ask the question *Why not me?*

The women commiserated on the 1960s Equal Pay Act, the lack of maternity leave, being overlooked for promotions, and worst still, being told by their male counterparts that they didn't belong. When confronted with any one of the dozens of obstacles in their way, they could have packed up their red pencils and tossed their typewriters out the window. But they didn't. Instead, they buckled down. They fought, made demands,

and showed the world that women belong in this space too. That equality in publishing is necessary and, dare I say it, that this has the chance to become a female-dominated industry?

When asked what advice they'd give women with aspirations in the publishing industry, there was one resounding opinion: *Knock down walls.*

Don't stop at the glass ceiling; don't stop until it's open air on all four sides.

They are proof that their advice changes lives, as they themselves have changed history. I am proof positive that this advice works, since I've had their shoulders to stand on since the moment I discovered I was meant to be a writer. Good mentors never tear you down. They hold your hand and tug you through the portal of dreams.

For every time these women heard no, I hope thousands of women in my generation hear yes.

READING GROUP GUIDE

1. Did you ever study the dictionary as a child or peruse words for fun? Did you have a favorite word?

2. Have you ever encountered a situation at work where you wish you'd been able to say something differently or advocate for yourself or someone else? What held you back?

3. If you were invited to a "Confessions of Office Buffoonery and Occupational Malapropos," who would you want to go with you, and what is something you'd want to share?

4. When Bernadette is stressed, she finds comfort in the inspirational quotes she's written down in her journal as well as the Julia Child recipes she makes. What do you do to relax when you're feeling overwhelmed?

5. A wave of feminism crossed the United States in the 1960s with

the production of the birth control pill (though not readily available to everyone), the Equal Pay Act, Title VII of the Civil Rights Act, and the founding of the National Organization of Women. These were all layers added to generations of women activists' actions and helped move us forward into the 1970s, which produced even more autonomy for women. It is amazing to think that was only sixty years ago. What do you think has changed, and what has stayed the same?

6. Do you have a favorite novel that you've bought in multiple editions?

7. Have you ever encountered a situation at work where a jealous coworker was sabotaging you? What did you do? What advice would you give your younger self if you could?

8. Frank is Bernadette's spirit animal. If you had a spirit animal, what would it be?

A CONVERSATION
WITH THE AUTHOR

This book is so fun and yet thought-provoking! What was your inspiration for the project?

I've always been fascinated by women's stories, and there are several women in our recent history who have made a name for themselves in publishing: Eleanor Packard Gould, the *New Yorker*'s Grammarian; Phyllis E. Grann, the first female CEO of a publishing house; Anna Wintour, the editor in chief of *Vogue* Magazine—the list goes on. I knew I wanted to share the story of a female pioneer in the publishing field, and the 1960s seemed like the perfect time to do it, especially given that the Equal Pay Act had just been signed. Bernadette Swift is a combination of the many women in publishing who worked hard to make a name for themselves and to promote other women in the publishing industry, which before then had been dominated by men.

Additional inspiration for the book was when a few summers ago, I walked into a bar and met Frank. THE Frank. A Harlequin

Great Dane who was a regular at this particular bar in Columbus, Ohio. He went from person to person, table to table, greeting the patrons like he owned the place. It's no secret I love dogs, and Frank was no exception. The moment we met, I turned to my husband and oldest daughter and said, "That dog needs to go in a book." I just wasn't sure which book.

A month or so later when I was listening to Taylor Swift's song "The Man" while driving around the country on a book tour, Bernadette's story unfolded in my mind. As the miles passed, Bernadette and her best boy, Frank, took root in my mind. During that drive, I had an event in NYC and I made a point to visit the library, and I just knew Bernadette needed to be in that library somehow—hence her clandestine book club.

What does your writing process look like? Is there anything you do to get creative inspiration?

I love to write in the mornings. I usually write Monday through Friday, unless I didn't finish my goal for the week; then I will work on a Saturday morning. I write for a couple of hours each day, and I'm fortunate to be a fast typer. I do a lot of prewriting with plotting and thinking about scenes in my head, so when I sit down, it all spills out on the page. Prior to starting a book, I will also do several months of research on the characters, the setting, and the era that I'm writing in. First drafts are messy for me. The revisions and subsequent drafts are when the magic happens. I will listen to period music from the era to get into the mood for writing and will sometimes look at pictures or videos from the time period to get it settled in my mind.

This book takes place in New York City in the '60s. What was it like to write in this historical period? Was there research involved?

I loved writing about the '60s in NYC! I had a lot of fun looking at pictures, reading articles, and researching which restaurants were popular—including the pizza place where Graham and Bernadette go on a date. I listened to popular music of the '60s and watched videos and documentaries. The music was particularly fun, because I was the nerd in high school (in the '90s) who listened to the oldies station on the way there, so it brought back great memories! I read newspaper and magazine articles as well. I really love to immerse myself in the time period. I did spend way too long looking for the name of the coffee maker in the office. I'm talking DAYS. But I'm glad I did because it's those little details about the time period that set the tone.

Bernadette Swift is a strong female protagonist. What do you hope readers take away from her story?

I love Bernadette so much. She has been my favorite character to date that I've written. This book started off as a passion project, something I was writing for fun, and then snowballed into this amazing book about women's rights, women's importance in the workplace, women opening up and talking about things that they've never shared before, the importance of female friendships, and building a community. I hope that readers find inspiration in Bernadette's story, that if they want something, they will speak up for themselves. That if they are being treated unfairly or unjustly, they feel empowered to stand up. That if they see someone else being mistreated, they can offer to help, even if it's just to be a sounding board. What I really want is for women to form a community and to be able to rely on that community. I want women talking, sharing their stories, and supporting one another.

In the book, Bernadette, a woman standing up for her rights in a male-dominated workplace, joins a secret book club and empowers the other women in attendance to take on the gatekeepers surrounding them. In our everyday lives, why do you think book clubs are so important?

I love book clubs! They are important not only because they keep us reading, and reading creates empathy as well as an escape, but also because of the shared bond readers can have in a story. How they can relate to a character and a character's situation. How they can talk about a similar situation and what they might have done in that situation. Sharing what they learned or took away from a book and the discussions books can spark help us grow as people. Reading and book clubs create a bonding experience we might not otherwise have. Readers and book people are some of the coolest people on the planet!

ACKNOWLEDGMENTS

Writing a book may seem like a solitary endeavor, but the truth is, there are so many people who knowingly and unknowingly are involved, and I'd be remiss if I didn't express my gratitude. I am a very lucky author to have the best agent in the world—Kevan Lyon—who listened to me discuss the concept of this book while I was on a road trip, and I'm so grateful for her enthusiasm and support. I am grateful to Frank's person, who brought him to Bodega in Columbus, Ohio, on that fateful day we met—whoever you are, you have the coolest dog!

Thank you so much to my husband, daughters, and parents for listening to me talk nonstop about the book and run various scenes by you and for reading early pages. I love you all so much!

My gratitude to my dear friends and critique partners, Madeline Martin, Sophie Perinot, and Heather Webb. My sprinting partner, Vik Francis, who pounded the keys with me as we added pages to our respective manuscripts.

I am so grateful to my editor, Shana Drehs, and the wonderful, hardworking people at Sourcebooks who have helped bring this book to you, the reader. I am so lucky to have readers who make it possible for me to share my stories far and wide.

Thank you to my brilliant Lyonesses for their sisterhood and Tall Poppies for their enthusiastic support of this book.

ABOUT THE AUTHOR

Eliza Knight is an award-winning *USA Today* and international bestselling author. Eliza is an avid history buff, and her love of history began as a young girl when she traipsed the halls of Versailles. She also writes women's contemporary fiction under the pseudonym Michelle Brandon. She is a member of the Historical Novel Society, Novelists, Inc., Women's Fiction Writing Association, Tall Poppy Writers; the creator of the popular historical blog, History Undressed; and host on the *History, Books and Wine* podcast. Her books have been translated into multiple languages, and most recently, her title *A Day of Fire* has been optioned for television. Knight lives on the Suncoast with her husband, three daughters, two dogs, and a turtle.